TAMING THE
Elements

THE ELWIN ESCARI CHRONICLES
Volume I

D1414243

DAVID EKRUT

For Jeremy K. Hardin, whose creative genius is a force yet to move through this world. Our two-man writer's workshop has been almost as invaluable to this book as his friendship has been to my life.

And for my wife, Jennifer Holliday-Ekrut, whose patience for my passions are more than anyone deserves. She has given her love and support through every "final" draft of this book without ever questioning my pursuit of the craft that is writing.

Arinth

The Blood Isle

Lost Sea

Nortic Ocean

Long Bay

Wyvern Tail Sea

Ardara
Graydon
Clifden
Carlow
Inland
Omnha
Kinsdale
Short Bay

Loking
Wieland

Isles of Nemwar

Norscelt

Isles of Maarda

Red Gulf

Wicklow

Denbar

The Bogs Plains

Dragon's Peaks

Grandbury

Alcoa City

Kings River

Natsdale

Ruins of Abadan

Wildwood

Alcoa

Chinwood

Shallow Shores

Sh Sh

Bemridge G

Menwar

Warwick

Trinneat

Napri

Ashdon

Trammel

Tharville
Brentworn

Benbrook

Tranquil Sea

Frenten

Cursed Mtn

Island Nations

Florence

Dalton

Abadd Ree

Adderton

Dracon Se

Northport
Goldspire

Witherton

Rockport

Paradise

Justice

Eastport

Justice

Dargaghm

Tendleton

Dragon Isle

The Fr

Ardara

Wyvern
Tail Sea

Graydon

Clifden

Lok

Carlow

Inland

Short
Bay

Isles
of Maards

Outland

Kinsdale

Wicklow

Red
Gulf

The
Bogs Plai

Grandbury

Alcoa
City

M

Pe

Sheridan

Coventr

Wildwood

A

Wars

Menwar

Trammel

Warwick

Thar
Br

Trimaray

Napri

Tranquil Se

Ashdon

Island
Nations

Florence

Goldspire
Mountains

Northport

Goldspire

Ari

Witherton

Justice

Rockport

Faraday Bryne

Benedict Area

Eastport

Paradine

Justice

Dargaithan

Tendleton

Orkin
Sea

Wieland
Isles of
Nemwar

Mionon

rscelt

Nortic
River
Sindri

Denbar

Kinsett

Eoiasis

Dephar
River

Dronsdale

Burton

on's Peaks

King's
River North

Kalicodon

Kings
River
Valespar

Karsdale

Delcoa

ry

Wiltshire
gs
well

Iremine

Ruins of
Abadaria

The Troad

Churwood

Turney Fay

Shallow
Shores

oa

Disputon

Shallow
Shores
Gulf

Meioic

Weatherford

Benridge

Peioic

The
Tangus River

Benbrook

Kailaea

ood
renton

Curst Mountains

The
Bleeding
Pass

Okana
Bay

Dalton

Abaddon's
Reef

dderton

Dracon Sea

The
Dead Lands

ath

Dragon
Isle

Prologue

The rest of the castle of Alcoa had yet to stir as a man walked down the steps into the library. Natural light had just begun to shine through the opaque glass of the domed ceiling to touch the corners of the expansive room. The entrance gave way to a central passageway. Tall shelves lined the walls and formed wide aisles. Polished with lacquer and clear of objects, long tables of redwood led down the center to the southern wall.

The man passed countless, leather-bound tomes that filled each shelf on the rows and along the walls. He walked to the farthest edge of the library, until the musky smell of old leather became the strongest odor. Most of the books in this wing had no markings to name them.

One of these forgotten texts would soon change the world.

Bain Solsec reached the rolling ladder, moved it into place, and took each step to the very top. Standing with his knees against the highest rung, he reached for a book on the upper shelf. He could just touch the cracked, leather binding with his forefinger. Stretching on his toes, he pulled the tome from the shelf and wiped thin dust from the cover. If there had ever been any painting to mark the book, the script had long since faded.

How long had it sat there? How many times had the castle librarian ran the feathers of his duster across the tome without giving it a second glance?

Cradling the old book close to his body, Bain climbed down the ladder and walked back to the center aisle. He placed the book on the polished table in front of a chair and looked at it in disbelief. The pages had yellowed from age, just like his dream. It had been a long time since he had dreamed, so he had known the dream to be special. The man in blue silks had shown him where to find the tome. He had said that finding it would lead to greatness.

Bain had always known he would one day find the greatness he deserved. He had always known he was different than the others. His black hair and dark eyes had always set him apart from his peers in Alcoa. He got his appearance from his father, who was from Norscelt to the far north. His mother had been born to the Alcoan royal line. Had he gotten her blond hair and sky-colored eyes, he would have looked like every other Alcoan.

Though his mother had been sister to the king, Bain would not sit upon the throne. Thirod, his cousin and childhood companion would be the next to rule all of Alcoa. Being cousin to the heir had placed him in the shadow of an inferior man, a man without vision. The Awakening would come, and the world would not be ready.

"Without me," his words echoed through the empty rows, "the dragonkin will rise and rule us all."

He sat down and looked at the book. Even as a boy he had loved to read. His mother and father had always been busy with the courts, so his older brother had taught him to read and write. How many books had he read in this library over the years? A hundred? A thousand? More than most men would even see in a single lifetime.

Mostly, he read the histories. There were many volumes on the Shadow Wars and all the wars that followed. As long as there were men, there would always be war. And to win a war, a man needed power. There was only one power greater than taming the Elements. That power was knowledge.

During the Shadow Wars, many nations had fallen, and new nations had risen. After the Shadow Wars had ended, the chroniclers of the great library of Tanier were nowhere to be found. But new chroniclers had emerged to make records of the events. All had wanted to forget the atrocities, and none had wanted to relive them. But, he who did not learn from the past was destined to repeat it. So, copies of the histories had been scribed and spread to every land.

Prologue

Heroes from the wars had become revered, while their villains had been despised. Tales had been crafted and told to children as bedtime stories. For generations, feats of battles had been shared around campfires and taverns. One name above all had been remembered.

Abaddon, the Seeker of Souls.

In the years following the Shadow Wars, the castle of Abaddon had been abandoned. None had wanted to live where the undead had walked. Though the location had been recorded, over three thousand years had passed, so the whereabouts of the castle eventually fell to apathy.

Only one book remembered the castle of Abaddon. He looked down at the faded cover. This was the last book from the library of Tanier before its disappearance during the Shadow Wars. The tome that would start it all.

"My legacy begins now."

Bain eased the cover open, but despite his efforts to take care, he felt the leather on the binding crack further. His fingers trembled as he held the book open. The first page named the tome, *The Book of Erudition*. He turned each page with a gentle hand, as he read every word with great care.

The Book of Erudition
Preface

During the time to be remembered in the world called Arinth as the First Age, the Shadow Wars brought about a new age. The Second Age began with the severance of the Elemental power called Spirit. Later to be remembered as the Age of Truth, rest assured that history once called this age by a different name. But I digress.

Details of the birth of the Element of Death, recorded here, are the first accounts of these events. Witnessed by the Chronicler of the Mortal Realms and transcribed through my hand, written in these pages, the Book of Erudition.

~Asalla, Transcendent and Scribe of the Forgotten Age

Chapter 1
Spirit Divided

Abaddon, called the Seeker of Souls in the current age, had risen to life. So powerful were his gifts in the Element of Spirit, it was once claimed that he was the son of the Lifebringer in the flesh.

It was once believed that the Lifebringer gave Abaddon a mortal's breath to give people a light in a world of warring and darkness. The Son of Life, he was then called. Abaddon's powers of healing, through the Elemental power of Spirit were beyond any other mortal. Abaddon brought light to the war stricken lands. He was the first to bring those fallen back to life, a detail forgotten to history, and healed the wounds of nations.

This, as all now know, was not to last.

Thirst for power and the ambitious desire to rule over one another led humans to war and suffering. Because of this, not all of the nations would receive the Son of Life peacefully.

He was gifted in all four Elements. Though many were gifted in this manner, Abaddon's powers were unparalleled in his time. Alcoa, then a fledgling city-nation, made Abaddon its High Counselor. King Thiroian Alcoa the First was an ambitious man. Having taken much of his power by force, Thiroian was determined to drive the city-nations around him to submission under the justification of peace.

The desert nation to Alcoa's east, called Maar, was comprised of wandering tribes. The desert lands of Maar were harsh and unforgiving. The tribes were divided and always at war with one another in territorial feuds. The most powerful tribe was, of course, the Tribe of Maar.

Thiroian declared a Holy Crusade against Maar and the rest of what he deemed the Untamed East. He set to conquer all nations who did not accept his offer of peace as subsidiary nations, and he called his High Counselor to lead the charge. By this time, Abaddon had taken a wife, Katina, and had a son, whose name will not be recorded here to protect the innocent lineage of Abaddon. Though Abaddon did not desire to go to war, he had sworn his fealty to the king. Thus, he was honor bound to do his duty. Abaddon conquered Maar in a few short months. King Alcoa sent his second born son, Kalicodon, to rule the region, renaming the nation of Maar after his favored child.

The Tribes of Maar, most particularly the Witch King Maar, was humiliated by the defeat. Being forced to swear allegiance to a foreign king left a bitter taste in his mouth.

Abaddon returned to his love, having forgotten the war and the Witch King by the time he crossed the threshold of his home. King Alcoa, pleased with the victory, rewarded his High Counselor with dominion over the Isles of Simbi, across the Tranquil Sea to the West. Abaddon moved his wife and child to this nation and ruled with benevolence as the Lord of Simbi.

Soon after, the Untamed East rose against Kalicodon, killing the king's second born. Infuriated, Alcoa called Abaddon to conquer these lands once more.

Abaddon answered his king's summons, once again, performing his duty. He marched against his king's enemies, but the Untamed East did not fall with ease. Another elementalist, named Menlar, had an artifact of power, giving him the strength to rival Abaddon.

The war waged for years. Each battle between Menlar and Abaddon ended in one fleeing from the other. Many men and women of all races were left to bury their dead.

Menlar conspired with the Witch King Maar to attack Abaddon's home.

While Abaddon was occupied in the east, Maar seized the opportunity to seek revenge on Abaddon. Using the Stones of Seeking, Maar traveled across the Tranquil Sea to the Isle of Simbi. The Witch King had a minor talent in the Element of Fire. During the cover of night, he stole into the palace while Abaddon's family slept, and he murdered Katina. Maar charred her corpse with Fire beyond the powers of healing. Maar dispersed her ashes on the northern winds and fled with the child to the Bloodlands, now called the Blood Isle.

When news of the treachery reached Abaddon in the Untamed East, he returned home.

The walls were painted with her blood. Without her body, Abaddon had no vessel to return his love back to Life. Not even his powers were great enough.

Rage consumed Abaddon and twisted his soul. He sought out the Witch King, but Maar could not be found. Abaddon had not known that his child still lived. Had he known, the world would not have suffered the fate that was to follow. Abaddon would have stopped at nothing to find his child. But fate had a different story to tell.

Abaddon turned his venom on the Untamed East. No longer caring whether he lived or died, he flung himself at Menlar. Many men died that day, but Abaddon defeated Menlar.

After his victory, Abaddon did not return from the Untamed East, blaming Alcoa's ambition for the death of his wife and child. Many of his men, elementalists and soldiers alike, stayed with their leader. They would become the first of his Undead Horde.

Abaddon spent years trying to find a way to bring Katina back from the dead. It was in this search he found that the Elemental Power, called Spirit, had two halves to its power. On one side, the Elemental power of Spirit could give Life; on the other, it could manipulate Death. He experimented on his companions and soldiers with this newfound power, trying to find a way to restore her. From the souls of his friends, he designed the first of the skeletal warriors, vampires, and spirit wraiths. The Death knights and soulless ones would come later.

Ruled by hatred and consumed by vengeance, Abaddon sought out the surviving Tribes of Maar. Under Alcoa's rule, the tribes had constructed civilizations. Abaddon visited these cities and annihilated all the living, adding their dead to his Undead Legions. The touch of the Undead Legion was infectious. The taint of the Death Element was so powerful that it could raise those fallen to a state somewhere between life and death.

Word had spread of Abaddon's treachery. Terrified of Abaddon, Alcoa appealed to any elementalist with power to rise against his former High Counselor. Thirteen of the most powerful answered his call, and the Sacred Order was born.

All the while, Abaddon's power grew. He conquered all in his path, growing his army off those fallen in battle. His Undead Legions scoured the lands. It seemed that Abaddon had become too powerful to be stopped. Many had given up hope, and all had seemed to be lost. People of all lands gave up fighting, seeking places to hide.

At the urging of the Transcendent Asalla, King Alcoa sought out the dragonkin for aid. The power of one dragon was great enough to rival many elementalists. However when a dragonkin slept, his slumber would last a millennium. Rarely did more than a handful of dragonkin wake at one time. When they did rise against the mortal cities, the battles lasted for generations.

Again, I digress. The Dragon Wars have been well documented in a separate volume.

An ancient dragon by the name of Althimorphianus slumbered in the Dragon's Peaks, the mountains to the northeast of Alcoa. Using the Words of Power, Thiroian Alcoa Awakened the mighty beast. The oldest and most powerful of the ancient race called the others of his kind to join him. As one, the dragonkin rose.

Althimorphianus agreed to lead the dragonkin into battle against the undead and save the mortal races. But then, the dragonkin would rule over all. Thiroian knew that if this were to befall the lands, his people would become like cattle to the dragonkin.

Alcoa had little choice. If he had not accepted the offer, his people would have been destroyed by Abaddon and his undead. Alcoa accepted the offer of the dragon.

The dragonkin took flight and battled against Abaddon and his Undead Legion. Taming the Elements, the rest of the dragonkin scattered the undead army, while Althimorphianus fought Abaddon.

The power of the ancient dragon was too great for even Abaddon to overcome.

When Abaddon realized he could not defeat Althimorphianus, he fled to the halls of his castle for protection, where their final battle took place. Before Althimorphianus could destroy him, Abaddon entered the shadow realm in the flesh, giving up his Spirit in the Spending.

This final act allows an elementalist to burn his essence and releases the last of his power in the form of his will.

Abaddon's Spending weakened all of the dragonkin. The dragons and dracons flew back to their lairs and fell into the Great Slumber. Althimorphianus, the greatest amongst them, resisted the longest. Eventually, he too succumbed to the Slumber at the cite of battle's end. As foreseen and recorded in the prophecies, The Awakening will come when the blood of his blood bid them rise.

The Spending had not destroyed Abaddon's soul. Remnants of Abaddon remained in the shadow realm, leaving his taint there. Somehow, he had become a Transcendent.

The Shadow Wars began with the birth of the new age and the rise of the Element of Death. Abaddon was given a new name, The Seeker of Souls.

Chapter 2
Castle of the Dragon

Abaddon's castle was constructed by the Elements, east of where Alcoa now stands ...

Chapter 1

IT BEGINS

Every heroic tale has but a hint of Truth, hidden by the ages. With the passing of time, the defeated is always the Villain, as the victor is ever the Hero. Their story is told and retold with each generation losing Truth with each telling.

Hero and Villain inexorably obstruct the other's path by acting in his own nature—a nature that is formed by a life rarely revealed in full. Tales of their actions may survive the test of time. But feats of strength are weighed and measured as good or evil by an unbalanced scale.

Thus, stories are made by partial observers.

The Villain arises in the land of plenty, bringing hardship and pain. The Hero is wrought by the struggle to defeat the Villain's malevolence. As well, the Villain's malice reaches its paramount in desperation to destroy the opposition, the Hero. Nations and castles rise and fall, as kings and queens are drawn to the cause of his or her own choosing.

The great cycle is told and retold by the victors without kindness to the Villain, the catalyst for this great tale. Yet it is a rare epoch, indeed, when a Hero is born without a grand Villain in the making. Thus begins the tale. Perhaps, Truth may be revealed by impartial observers.

Betrayal.

Taming the Elements

The word stuck in his thoughts as the man sat upon the rocky beach. The tide lapped at the shore several paces in front of him, sparkling in the noonday sun.

Behind him loomed the Curst Mountains with their brown and grey jagged rocks jutting into the sky between lush evergreens. One could stand upon the shore, staring at the massive stones and never see the mountainside for what it truly was.

After centuries of lying empty, he had been the one to find Abaddon's castle. Thick spires wrought from the mountain's rock stretched toward the sky in natural formations. Its grand halls had been formed by taming the Elements called Earth and Fire in an age far removed from most memories.

The reef spanned miles up the shore, giving further protection to his castle. A ship could be within a mile of the shore and see nothing more than a mountain. And the reef kept ships from coming within five miles of the shore. Only those well versed in the location of the castle would dare traverse Abaddon's Reef, making this an ideal respite for a king not wanting to be found.

Now, he alone held the secrets of its power. It was his destiny to hold the world in his hands. He alone could remake the world as it should be.

Bain closed his eyes.

He could feel the crash of the powerful tides against the shoreline. The Elemental power of Water made war with the Elemental power of Earth. There was a beautiful peace in this struggle. A battle as old as time and life raged right before him. These powers balanced one another.

Bain looked back out at the waters. The tides would push closer to him, winning the present battle only to lose the next. The sounds of the tide breaking the shore should have soothed him. That was why he had come here.

But it couldn't. Not this day. He had known upon seizing power that betrayal would be inevitable.

"Seizing power always starts with betrayal," he told the empty beach. "Mine and others yet to come."

The beach may have been empty, but he was never alone. Bain was well aware that He could hear him. That He was always listening, even if He remained silent. Bain looked down at the pendant resting on the crest of his leather breastplate. The armor had been touched with the powers of creation, created by taming the Elements. The pendant and his crest were one in the same.

The symbol was that of a black-gloved hand clutching a red dragon with the palm facing upward. Its long, sinewy head protruded between the hand's middle and forefingers. The dragon's head rested upon the tops of the fingers, eyes closed as if sleeping. The dragon's long, spiked tail wrapped around the small finger, like a snake around a tree.

Without touching the pendant, he could *feel* the power within. Powers that were his to command.

"Soon. So very soon, it will begin."

Bain stood and felt the cool breeze bounce across the surface of the ocean and touch his face. It too held power. The power of Air was the first he had known. He could *feel* it with his soul, his essence. Relaxing his thoughts as he had done a thousand times before, he opened his essence and allowed the power of Air to enter him.

The salt in the wind became more crisp, and he could sense every ripple in the breeze around him.

Bain *tamed* the power in his essence and manifested his desire. His body rose into the sky like a bird with no wings. Wind rushed by, roaring in his ears as he ascended. He turned north and west toward the capital city of Alcoa.

This time he would be the tide. Soon, the world would know Bain of Solsec.

Athina tried to ignore her racing heart as she glanced around her chambers one last time. The stone walls seemed darker in the dim light. She only had the lanterns on the southern wall lit, giving enough light to see her canopied bed at the center of the room.

The northern side of the room had an open doorway with darkness beyond. Drawers to clothing chests laid open; otherwise, her room was tidy. She had been forced to maintain pretenses until he had gone. Tapestries depicting battles from the Shadow Wars hung on every wall. Her bookshelf on the western end of the room had every tome in place. Her wooden writing desk on the opposite wall had ink and quill upon the upper-right corner and a blank parchment, ready for scribing.

Everything had its place. But she no longer did. Summer solstice, a month from now, would mark seven years she had lived in this dank castle.

She took a deep breath.

"I have no choice," she said aloud, knowing her resolve sounded weak.

She turned back to the bed. Its canopy was a bright turquoise. Thadia, her chamber maid, had acquired it for her because it was her favorite color. She would miss Thadia.

Athina took a deep breath and said with more force this time, "I have no choice."

Travel supplies littered the top of her feathered mattress. She looked over her stock once more. Other than the pale, grey dress she wore now, she had one extra cream-colored dress split for riding and a green gown. The three tiny shirts and two swaddling cloths would have to be enough. She had a bulls-eye lantern with a tenday's worth of oil, flint and steel, and a small bedroll.

The tenday's supply of trail rations and a single waterskin would get her through the mountains. She had no room for a travel tent, and she doubted she could sacrifice the energy to carry it at any rate. The journey would be long.

Lastly, she had her coin purse. She had filled it only with her heaviest coins of Alcoan mint, platinum and gold and a few precious gems. The rubies and sapphires would all go to pay for her passage through the Stones of Seeking. The handful of remaining coins and diamonds would charter further passage, not leaving much for food or shelter.

She took a deep breath. "This will have to do."

Taking her knapsack, she began to fit the materials into it.

The door to her massive chambers banged open, and she jumped from the sudden noise. A woman in a blue gown with flowing hair the color of the sun entered and closed the door behind her with the same force that had opened it.

Athina held her breath and glanced to the darkened doorway at the northern wall. No sound.

"Lana," she gave her twin sister a scowl, "are you trying to wake Elwin?"

Lana stood in front of the door for a moment, her smooth features and beautiful face blemished by a scowl of her own. Even in the dim lighting, Athina could see her sister's blue eyes narrow in anger.

Lana's long strides brought her across the room with a dancer's grace. She stopped an arm's length away and stared at Athina with wide eyes. "You mean to go through with this then?"

It was more of an accusation than a question.

Athina felt her heart racing. No one was supposed to know. "How did you find out?"

"Thadia saw you setting aside the knapsack. When she asked me if I would need one too, I knew. How can you do this?"

"What would you have me do?"

"I would have you stay and let your son have the glory that he was born to."

"I cannot."

Lana's voice was tight. "We will be a part of history. Do you not see that?"

She closed her eyes. "I will not sacrifice another son for Bain's selfish ambitions. Donavin is only six, and already, he is becoming something I do not recognize as my son. And I can do nothing to stop it. I will *not* see the same happen to Elwin."

"You cannot oppose Bain. No one can!" Lana snapped. "What would you do?"

She closed her eyes for a moment. Would her last conversation with her sister end in a fight?

"I am leaving, Lana," Athina said, proud of the resolve in her voice.

Lana's mouth opened to speak, and then it closed.

Silence.

The harshness in Lana's voice stabbed like a dagger. "You would be a rabbit running from a dragon. Do not be so daft."

"I thought of all people, you would understand."

Lana took a step toward her. "I understand. I do. But what you speak of will get you killed, or worse."

"I know the risks," Athina said, "but I must go. I have already made some arrangements."

Lana's jaw poised open. Athina knew she had hurt her sister. She had mentioned leaving to Lana, but had made it sound more like in idea, rather than something she would actually do. She had told Lana nothing of what she had planned. The first fight over the idea of Athina's leaving was mostly a shouting match that had not ended well.

"You kept this from me." Anger and pain resounded in Lana's voice.

"I planned on telling you today, but I did not want it to be like this."

"Where will you go that Bain cannot find?"

Should she tell her? No. It would be better if she didn't know. Not unless …

"You could come with me," Athina offered. "Together we will be able to hide from him, even in the shadow realm. I have seen to that."

"Eventually he would find us," her voice cracked. "Do you really want to be hunted? And I do not even want to think about what he would do to you. You should just do as Bain commands. Even this conversation is treason."

"Treason? After all that Bain has done … forced us to do? You would call my son's salvation treason?"

"Bain will rule the world. He will remember those who stood at his side."

"At what cost?" Athina said. "Bain is losing his soul. Can you not see he is not the same man I married?"

"He is not yet Death bound."

"Perhaps not." Athina shook her head. "Maybe not yet. But his thirst for power grows every day. He has gone to begin a war with his childhood *friend* and cousin. A man he has stood beside for over two decades."

"Thirod Alcoa is weak." Lana turned from her. "Bain will restore Elemental power to the world. The Guardians of Life have overreached for far too long. It is just a matter of time before the Awakening. Each generation produces fewer elementalists, fewer able to tame the elements than those generations before us. What will happen when the dragonkin rise with no one to stand against them?"

"If Bain embraces Death, will any of that matter? Someone as powerful as Bain raising undead could very well destroy the lives of all."

Lana was silent for a time. Her sister turned to face her. "I cannot change your mind?"

Athina gave a slight shake of her head. There was another long silence. She fought to look at her sister with as cold of a stare as she was receiving. Lana had always been more willful, but her sister would not have the stronger will this time.

What I do is for Elwin, she told herself. *He will have a chance at a normal life. As normal of a life as one with his gifts will allow.*

Lana's voice gave her a start. "What do you want me to do?"

Athina took a deep breath. "You will help me?"

"It goes against all that I believe in," Lana said in a terse voice. "But yes. I will help you."

Tears filled Athina's vision. "Thank you. Preparations have already been made. I already have the help of Elwin's uncle. But just knowing I have your support means so much to me."

"Bain's brother is going to help you?"

Athina nodded to her sister.

"No matter the preparations, you will need my help to flee the castle. Zeth overheard our last conversation and warned Bain that you might try to leave. Zeth has been charged with keeping you confined to the castle."

A piece of hope died in Athina's heart. What could she do? If she could not leave, all would be lost. And now Bain knew that she wanted to leave?

Before Athina could form a question, Lana spoke. "Do not fear, Athina. I will distract him. You will have plenty of time to flee."

"What will you do?"

Lana gave her a reassuring smile. "You will have to trust me."

"I wish you would come with us."

Lana took a resigned breath. "Someone must stay to endure Bain's wrath."

❧

Jhona Solsec paced along the antechamber to his quarters. Ten good paces across gave the perfect length for pacing. He eyed his humble pack on the chair by the outer door once more and considered rechecking his supplies, but he quickly dismissed the idea. It was good. What he did not bring, nature would provide.

He walked over to the tall painting at the end of the chamber.

The portrait was one of his few possessions from before. He still imagined himself as the strong figure in the painting that looked back at him. The man. No. The *boy* in the picture had short brown hair without the grey strands that now graced Jhona's head. The sharp grey-blue eyes were now surrounded by wrinkles, and each day more of the blue faded. He knew all too well, the lean, wiry strength of the boy in the portrait waned. Almost to his fiftieth name day, he was beyond his prime now. Though his powers in the Elements grew stronger, his body would continue to fail him. This was the way of nature. On the other hand, his younger brother was still short of his twenty-fifth year and peaking in his physical prime.

Though Jhona had trained his younger brother, Bain was stronger in the Elements than he. Stronger than any he had trained. If it came to a fight between the two though …

The eyes in the portrait seemed to become accusatory, as if to say, "What are you doing, old fool?"

"When your little brother has lost his mind," he reasoned with the portrait, "you do what you must."

"He has not given his soul to the Seeker," his younger self would have reasoned. "There is still a chance for him."

Jhona had been quicker to hope in the days of his youth.

He took a deep breath. "But are you sure he hasn't bound his soul to the Seeker? He has refused your counsel for several tendays. And he is, right this instant, on his way to begin a war with family. A friend, who would more than likely share his power if Bain were to just ask it of him. A boy, who you trained alongside Bain. Thirod and Bain were mere children when your paint had dried. Much has changed. Much will never be as it was once upon a time."

Hope was for the young, he decided. The wisdom of age brought careful planning.

A soft knock came from the outer door to his chambers. Without pause, the door opened and emitted a small hooded figure, then closed as quickly as it had opened. Athina's blond hair protruded from the opening of a brown riding cloak, which hid her face. She had a small knapsack on her back and a woven basket in her arms.

Jhona's heart warmed as he looked into the basket. The baby boy was wrapped in blue blankets and swaddled tightly beneath. His bright, blue eyes drank in his surroundings with a quiet contemplation. Jhona felt a moment of pride surge within him. For being a month old, his nephew was more aware than he should have been. When Elwin's eyes touched Jhona's, the baby smiled. The sun had never shown so brightly or the moon glittered so magnificently. Jhona felt his heart melt in a way that made taming the Elements seem insignificant.

Peering at the innocent babe, all of Jhona's resolve became firm. He would do as he must. Donavin was proof that Elwin could not be left to the devices of his father. There was no doubt that Bain intended to use his sons as weapons.

"The time has come," she said. "We must act swiftly while Lana distracts Zeth."

"He knows?" Jhona had thought he alone had known. He grabbed his pack and slung it onto his back.

Athina nodded.

"Aye," Jhona said, moving to the door. "We must be swift."

He opened the door and peered into the long hallway.

Across the hall another wooden door mirrored his own. Twenty paces or so on either side, more doors faced one another. So many of the rooms of the castle were empty of inhabitants. In fact, he was the only one living in this wing of the castle. Still, the quiet emptiness unnerved him.

He could hear the torches flickering on the walls. No other sounds. Left or right would lead them toward an exit. Left would take them past fewer people.

"Ready?" he whispered.

Athina nodded.

Jhona stepped into the hallway and turned left. Athina stayed close behind him, both arms wrapped around the basket.

Halfway to the next set of doors, he felt it. Jhona was Life bound. The battle for human souls between the Lifebringer and the Seeker was an ancient tale. A person could choose to be soulbound to either Life or Death, good or evil, by power of the Element called Spirit. Once the choice was made, it was final. Legends have been told of heroes who gave their souls to Death and overcame their sins, but Jhona had never seen or heard of any evidence of the possibility.

Jhona had been young when he bound his soul to the Lifebringer. Above all, he served Life. It was for this reason alone he knew the evil in the shadows at the end of the hall.

A vile stench knocked against his soul. His stomach churned as if he would be ill. He had heard that a Life bound could sense a person bound to Death, but he had never felt it before now. There was no mistaking the feeling.

He opened his essence and felt the power of Earth around him. The castle had been made with the Elements of Earth and Fire. He could feel the power in the floor beneath his feet extending into the walls around him. Taming Earth into his essence was second nature to him. Small lines of dust rose and conjoined with him as he pulled as much Earth into his essence as he could hold.

"Athina," he whispered. "Go the other way. You must run. Do not take the pendant off."

"But Jhona—"

"Do not argue," he cut in. Then he spoke more softly, so that other ears could not hear. "I will buy you what time I can. Follow my instructions, just as we discussed. You must flee now."

"Thank you." Her voice was a tearful whisper.

Jhona turned from her and stood ready. He could feel her feet pounding on the floor away from him. "The Lifebringer cradle you in his hands," he whispered back.

A man stepped from the shadows ahead of him. He had pale skin and long black hair tied in a warrior's tail. His cold eyes had an unnatural, dark shimmer as if light itself fled away from him.

"Zeth." Jhona made the name sound as if an accusation.

Zeth smirked. "You can feel the power flowing through my veins."

"I can feel the taint of the Death Element flowing through you." Jhona felt as if he had run through open refuse and slept in it, just being near the man. "How could you?"

"How could I what?" Zeth asked. "Take power that was freely offered? How could I not?"

"Free?" Jhona shook his head. "You gave up your soul, bound it to Abaddon, the embodiment of Death. Once you die, you are his. The shelter of Life has no place for you now."

"You old fool," Zeth spat. "The Awakening is coming. Soon. Abaddon will wake the dragonkin and call those bound to him into rule. I will never die now."

Zeth began to stalk forward. His flesh *morphed* with each step. Light fled from his skin as it dissipated into shadow. His eyes dissolved into a hollow nothingness as his face became like shadow, and he grew to an impossible height. Zeth's limbs elongated as he reached out toward Jhona.

For a moment Jhona was too stunned to move. But as the malformed limbs stretched for him, Jhona jumped backwards.

Taming the power of Earth, he formed the image of great swords in his mind and aimed them at Zeth's shadowy form. The floor, walls, and ceiling became massive blades, sharper than the best made steel, and lunged toward Zeth. The misshapen form dodged most of the blows, but one sword cut into an arm.

Zeth shrieked as wisps of dark smoke escaped from the wound. The sound was both shrill and deep, as if several minions of the abyss had been released into the halls. Zeth's dark foot became a blur too fast for Jhona to follow and struck his chest.

Jhona felt air surge around him for a brief moment before pain struck everywhere at once. He struggled to regain his breath and reorient himself, but his vision wouldn't focus. There was a metallic taste in his mouth, and he felt cold stone against his back. The torches above him would not stay still. It took him a moment to realize his side rested against a wall. His head dizzied at his motion, but he forced himself to a sitting position. The spinning subsided when he rested his head against the cold stone.

More than a dozen paces down the hall, Zeth's form approached with a casual ease. He flinched upon realizing how far he had been kicked with a single blow. Zeth had knocked Jhona the expanse of the corridor and into the adjoining wall.

This was the Death Element, its power an abomination to Life. How could Jhona fight this? No. He must fight. For Elwin and Athina. She only needed to escape. He would buy her whatever time he could. Jhona pushed himself to his feet and walked a few shaky steps toward Zeth.

Pulling more Earth into his essence, he crafted a dozen swords at every possible angle. Zeth dodged by jumping backwards. The walls began to shake with effort to hold the ceiling. Pulling the stone from the walls to form the swords had begun to compromise the structure's integrity.

"Fool," came Zeth's malformed voice. "You will kill us both."

Jhona smiled at Zeth.

Destroying evil so that an innocent could live would be a worthy death. He focused on the ceiling and began to tame all of his power. Forming the image of a hand in his mind, he prepared to flatten them both in the hallway.

The floor beneath him, the walls, and the ceiling began to shake in protest. The ancient power that had formed the castle resisted collapse. Without warning, a sharp pain struck the back of his head and his unspent power was ripped from his essence. He could feel the flow of Air surrounding him in strands that felt like iron ropes. No matter how he flexed against his unseen bonds, they wouldn't budge. Reaching for the power in his essence, he realized that it was blocked as if by a physical wall.

He could still see Zeth, several paces in front of him, but the source of the manifested Air was somewhere behind him. The darkened form began to materialize back into flesh as Zeth made his way through the sword strewn hallway.

Zeth's smirk returned. "What took you so long?"

A woman with golden hair materialized out of the air. "I have been here for long enough, waiting behind my veil for just the right time."

The woman, near identical to Athina, stood before him.

"Lana," Jhona breathed. "I should have known when Zeth appeared so quickly that you were working with him. But I never wanted to believe that you … It is not too late. You have not bound yourself to Abaddon. I cannot feel the taint on you."

"Nothing is ever as it seems, old man," Lana said. He felt a surge of power from her, then abruptly he could move. He flexed his essence against hers to no avail. She had him.

"Sit," she said as if commanding a hound.

Jhona wanted to defy her, but his legs seemed too weary to hold his weight for much longer. He leaned against the wall and lowered himself to the ground. When concentrating, Jhona could feel her hold on his essence with his mind's eye, but he could sooner reach the moon than touch his power.

Taken … he thought. *How could I let myself be taken?*

She held him like an iron vise. How could he have been so foolish? He had not even thought to feel for an attack on his essence from behind. Zeth had been his primary focus. She was draining him. He could feel his essence emptying.

"Bain's soul is already lost." Jhona had not meant it to be a question, though she had answered as if it had been.

"Not yet," Lana smiled. "But when he learns of his wife's *and* brother's betrayal …"

She leaned in and began patting his head and caressing his hair.

He jerked his head away. "You are lying. It is why he has refused me these last few tendays. He knew that I would sense him."

Her laugh was full mirth. It made him think of Athina.

"No matter," she said. "You would have known soon enough."

"But you are not Athina. She was always the best of us all. I can understand how your envy of her would lead you to such a path. Why did I not see it before?" Jhona shook his head. Despite it all, he felt pity for her. "Do you think Bain will love you now? With Athina out of the way? You are a fool."

The power of Air surged into her swing, and her hand connected with his face before he could flinch away. Pain wracked his senses, and the hallway went dark.

When he opened his eyes, his ears rang and his vision was slow to focus. The stone floor felt cold on his side. Soldiers in black and red livery stood a few paces away speaking to Lana. He struggled to sit upright, and his back ached at the motion. Deep crimson spittle dropped to the floor from his lips.

Lana turned to regard him with a cool stare.

"Where is she?" Jhona asked.

She stalked toward him and looked down her nose at him. "I did not have enough time to get the guards and lesser savants in place to stop her, but no matter. By nightfall, we will track her in the shadow realm. There will be no escape. You have caused yourselves pain for nothing."

She made it. With the pendant, they would never find her. Jhona smiled at the thought.

Lana's mirth vanished, and she knelt to look directly into his eyes. "I warn you. Do not mock me again, old man."

Jhona took a deep breath and said, "I have to thank you."

She winced at his words, and he felt the laughter in his throat before he could stop himself. The motion made his jaw ache. He could not say why he laughed. Maybe it was the look of confusion on her face. Maybe it was that he had lost his freedom to two of his former pupils, his own brother's companions. Maybe he had a concussion from being thrown against the wall like a child's toy. He could not say. But now that it came, he could not be rid of it. Leaving from his gut, the laughter took over like a disease. His stomach ached and his back began to spasm from the motion of it, but he could not stop.

Her voice was like ice. "I warned you not to mock me."

His laugh turned into a cough, and spittle flew from his mouth and hit Lana's face. She stood and raised her arm as if to strike him, but Zeth grabbed her arm before she could swing.

"Do not be so hasty. If he dies, he cannot talk. Another blow to the head might destroy his wits. What are left of them." Zeth turned to Jhona. "Save yourself the pain, and tell us where she is going."

"Thank you," Jhona said once more to Athina. It was still an effort not to chuckle. A few escaped as he spoke. "When Athina first came to me, I couldn't believe my little brother would do the things she claimed. The plan to attack Alcoa, our cousin and his childhood friend, that he was looking for gifted children to build an army. And the possibility that he was losing his soul. I just couldn't believe it. So I have to thank you ... I know now that I choose well to help Athina. You will never find her."

He closed his eyes and let the coughing giggles take over. Turning his cheek, he leaned his face against the wall to feel the cold of stone on his skin. It took some of the sting away from where Lana had struck him.

"What are her plans?" Lana demanded.

He kept his eyes closed. Though the laughter finally subsided, he kept smiling. He could sleep if it was quiet for long enough.

"You will talk." He could feel the heat in her words. "By the Seeker you will talk."

He felt the sickening power of Death enter her. He was not sure how, but he had not felt the vileness on her until this moment. Power flowed off of her and began to cover his skin. He opened his eyes to see a black fog rolling over him. Darkness enveloped him.

Pain.

He felt as if his flesh melted and fire entered his lungs. It choked him and shook him. He heard a scream in the distance and his throat burned.

Moments stretched into an eternity. Then as abruptly as it began, the fog and pain vanished. It took him a few heartbeats to realize he was still screaming. He clenched his teeth and wiped at his arms to brush away the lingering pain. He expected to see his flesh melted away, but there was no trace or hint of damage to his skin. The air around him felt cooler than it had before the fog.

Lana loomed before him. "Tell me what you know."

He forced a smile onto his face, met her gaze, and laughed at her. This time his laugh was deliberate. It held no mirth, but it made her unleash her fury in truth. Maybe this time she would kill him. Either way, he counted this day a victory. Athina had escaped.

The darkness covered him once more.

〜

A lone figure stood atop the tallest balcony of the palace, looking down at the night-covered city of Alcoa. The terrace provided a vantage like none other in the known world.

Below the guarded rail, lights escaped broad windows in rows of shining arcs. As the eye moved away from the tall spires of the castle toward the noble's houses of the inner city, the arcs became dots of white against a black canvas. Moving beyond the gates into the outer city, the lights turned to congruous rows of lights that parted the darkness to reveal taverns, inns, and cobblestone stretching as far as the eye could see.

Alcoa, the capital city of the Alcoan nation, spanned over thirty miles across. This night, every inch of the city would be alive with people.

From the vantage high above the city, the citizens of Alcoa seemed little more than dark masses moving as one, but the sounds of merriment reached the balcony in echoes of loud music and raucous laughter. The same sounds had reached this balcony countless times before.

Two hundred twenty-seven rulers had stood upon its terrace, watching the city below. King Thirod Alcoa, the fourth of his name had ruled the greatest city for a decade to the day.

A tall man of regal posture, Thirod leaned against the balcony and watched his city in quiet anticipation. Any moment, the night would become alive with the Artificers' firework display. He had hired them to celebrate the evening.

As if on cue, every known color burst into the sky as the artificers released their fireworks with intricate explosions. Bright arcs and balls carved pictures into the night's black canvas. Next, a yellow crown as large as his castle exploded into existence. Alcoa recognized the tribute to his patronage, as would his subjects.

A sequence of explosions followed, displaying a variety of iconic images. A circle divided into equal quarters of red, brown, white, and blue held a yellow rose bud at its center. As old as his nation, this was the symbol of Alcoa and the Sacred Order.

The moment in which the last spark of the symbol faded, the next explosions settled in the form of two right hands clasping forearms. This was another tribute to Alcoa and the peace he brought to the lands. Upon gaining the throne, Alcoa had forged a treaty with his neighboring nations. Where his father had failed, Thirod the fourth had succeeded. He smiled at the thought.

Under the Treaty of the Sacred Order, the world now knew peace. Every nation had signed it, even if some of those signatures had been persuaded to the point of coercion. Ten years this day, all Life loving people had known a world free of war and pain.

As the clasping hands dissolved, a great sword cut into the sky. In place of the hilt, balancing scales jutted out on either side of the handle. This symbol came from the island nation of Justice across the Tranquil Sea. Despite the distance, the small nation had been Thirod's strongest supporter, pulling the rest of the Island Nations into the treaty.

Following Justice was the symbol of Kalicodon, a fist grasping a snake's head. This nation had been the most difficult to attain. The tribes of Kalicodon refused to abolish slavery. In truth, slavery was as much a part of Kalicodian society as elementalists were a part of Alcoa's. The tribes of Kalicodon made slaves of one another as one tribe conquered the other. In time, slaves could earn their freedom in the pits, where they made slaves fight one another in an arena for sport. Yes, it seemed barbaric. Thirod would never tolerate such acts within his own kingdom. But allowing an ally to keep customs and traditions was not the same as advocating slavery. His father could not see this truth.

Thirod shook his head. Several symbols had flashed in the sky, but lost in his thoughts, he had missed them. Cheers reached his ears from the streets below. His people had not missed the display, and that was what mattered. This festival was for them. They needed to feel the reminder of the peace he had given to them. Tonight at the height of summer, they celebrated peace and Life.

His people would sing, dance, and drink the Summer Solstice away in both the inner and outer city. He had chartered every inn and tavern to give free drinks to all for the celebration. The lowliest of his people would enjoy the vibrance of Life as much as the highest this night. They needed this, so he owed it to them as their benefactor.

This was his kingdom.

People of many nations had come to his city and his lands seeking many things. His was the most vast and powerful kingdom in the known world.

Alcoa took a deep breath and smiled. "This is my doing. Father, even you would be proud."

"Would he be proud?" A deep voice spoke from behind him.

Alcoa opened his essence to the Elemental power of Air. He spun into the room, preparing to tame a lightning hurl, but he stopped upon seeing his intruder.

"Bain?" Thirod whispered.

A ghost stood before him. Had he gone mad?

Bain wore black, leather armor with a dark cloak made of silk. The symbol upon the man's chest made Thirod gasp. A black fist clutched a red dragon. Such symbols were bad omens or scrawled on the doors of the condemned houses of plague victims. This was not the Solsec family crest, but he could not mistake his childhood friend. Bain rested a casual hand upon the hilt of a scimitar.

"Bain," Alcoa said. "I thought—"

"You thought I was dead," Bain said.

Thirod had sent Bain into an unwelcoming land in search for artifacts of power. All these years, he had thought his friend dead. Bain, his closest friend, was alive! Thirod released the power he held and felt the Air push back into the room.

With arms wide open, he approached Bain. "I had given up hope."

Bain took a step backward and raised a hand to halt Thirod's approach. "There are events, which we need to discuss."

"Yes," Alcoa said, gesturing toward the balcony, "perhaps we should sit."

"I prefer to stand for the moment." Bain's smile held no mirth.

Something didn't feel right. Then a thought occurred to Alcoa. "How did you get past the guards and my wards? Even in times of peace, they are always in place. I can still feel the Elemental wards in tact."

Bain smiled. "I have learned many things over the past seven years."

"Why have you only just come to me? And like this?" Alcoa said. "Where have you been?"

"I found something valuable on my last mission."

Found something? Bain had been alive all these years. Still searching. Why had he not sent word? He opened his mouth to voice his questions, but Bain continued before he could form the words.

"Something that we have sought our entire lives to find."

"You found an artifact of power," Thirod said, "something from before the Shadow Wars?"

"I have found that and more." Bain's dark eyes glittered in the light of the fireworks.

Could it be? Could he have found the Orb of Inra? Something like that would ensure the success of his kingdom for the rest of time. Not even the Awakening could be a match against such an artifact.

When it was clear Bain would say no more, Alcoa said, "All this time I have mourned you for dead. You must allow me to welcome you properly. Please let us sit."

Bain took a few steps further into the room and stared at Thirod for several moments. "I have found Abaddon's castle in a land unclaimed by any. The castle bears my crest, and I have come to declare those lands the nation of Bain."

"What?"

He had not drank that much wine, but his mouth felt dry and his tongue thick. Nothing seemed to make sense to him. What was he hearing? Bain and he were cousins. Of an age with one another, they had grown up as brothers. Bain and he had been trained together in the Elements by Jhona Solsec, Bain's brother.

Bain hadn't aged a day. The face before him looked the same as the day he had left. But who was this man? An image of a friend he had given up for dead, now declaring himself a nation?

"This is not the proper venue, my friend. We are celebrating p—"

"Celebrating what?" Bain did not raise his voice, but his tone was cold as iron. "Our kind are dying. All the while, you let these fools, the so-called Guardians of Life, snuff out the powers of the Elements. Fanatics, who would as soon destroy any gifted as save them, hunt our kind, and you let the vermin nest in your very castle. What is there to celebrate?"

Thirod's mouth worked, but nothing came from his lips. No thoughts seemed to hold. No one had spoken to him like this in years. Not since … No one had addressed King Alcoa in such an informal manner since the day Bain left. From any other person in his kingdom, Thirod Alcoa would have never allowed such blatant insolence.

"Bain," Alcoa said in a calm voice, "the Guardians of Life hunt down Death bound and those who violate the Laws of Power, and they ensure our survival. That is their purpose. Nothing more. Their sect is almost as old as my nation and the Sacred Order. As old as the Shadow Wars. I did not make these laws. I only uphold them, as my father did and his before him. You know this."

Bain snorted. "They are like a weed choking the life out of a fruitful garden. Any weed allowed to grow freely will topple even the greatest plant. Over the last two thousand years, they have made accusations and convictions in a single breath. The sentencing for any crime against the Laws of Power is execution. And now fewer gifted are in the world than ever before with the Awakening upon us."

"Nonsense," Alcoa said. "The Awakening cannot happen until there is born an elementalist that is true. That has not happened yet. You know the prophecy better than any."

"Athina gave me a child." Bain's smile sent chills down Alcoa's spine. "The child has a spark of power in him so great that he will rival any who have lived in the past three thousand years. He will be the one to fulfill the first prophecy. We both know that if Athina has a Seeing that it will come to pass."

The first prophecy? It couldn't be. Not yet.

He started to repeat his thoughts aloud, but instead he shook his head and said, "She is still alive as well?"

"Jhona, Lana, Zeth. Even Fasuri, Ferious, and Mordeci. All of your old generals have joined me."

Bain had to be lying, but there he stood. And he had seen none of the rest since before they set out on that Life-forsaken journey.

"Finally," Bain said. "You feel regret for sending me on that cursed mission. Did you really think we would fight the Vampire Legion in their own lands to search for trinkets?"

"You never fought them?"

"Of course not," Bain said. "I parlayed with them and barely escaped with my life. But I knew I could not return here. The night before I left, He came to me and showed me the way."

"He?"

"I knew I could not return." Bain's words floated somewhere in his mind, as if this was some bad dream. The fireworks still boomed in the background, mocking his earlier thoughts of peace.

"I was not bound to Him, but He guided me still."

"Enough," Thirod said. "Do you not see what is happening to you? The Seeker of Souls is more gifted in twisting words than the most renowned orator. He is tricking you into giving him your soul. I can feel the reverence in your voice even as you speak of him."

Bain stepped closer. He was just more than an arm's length away when he spoke. "Shouldn't we revere those with power?"

This could not be happening. His thoughts raced. He had to capture Bain and make him see reason. As long as his soul remained free, there would still be hope for him. Pushing thoughts from his mind, Thirod made his decision.

He opened his essence to Air with the intentions to use its power to hold Bain in place.

"I wouldn't do that," Bain said in a voice that gave Thirod pause. "I did not come to fight you today."

"Why then? To declare that you are no longer my subject? You are my friend. If you wish to declare yourself a nation, then I will fully endorse you. I will mark lands for you to—"

"I came to give you a choice," Bain said. "You can disband the Guardians of Life and swear your allegiance to me, and I will leave your nation to your rule."

Though Bain had not moved against him, Thirod flinched as if slapped.

Let *him* rule *his* nation?

And the Guardians of Life were more numerous than even his own army, and half of them were in his nation. He could not disband them without a civil war, even if he wanted to. Which he didn't.

Alcoa made his voice like steel. "Or?"

Bain leaned forward and said just louder than a whisper, "I will unleash my armies and my power and tear your nation down around you."

Thirod clenched his jaw closed. He had sent his friend and so many others to battle the vampires, who were rumored to have artifacts of power. They were to be the last great victory to bring the known world to a true peace. His actions had been a fool's arrogance. After Bain's disappearance, he had assumed the worst. For over seven years he had felt the pain of regret for nothing. And now, his childhood friend had come to betray him? That had been Bain's purpose all along. Anger took hold of Thirod.

Taming Air to hold Bain, he shouted, "Guards!"

As threads of Air formed around Bain to hold him, soft wisps of light merged with Bain and a lash of Air knocked the threads into pieces. Thirod continued shouting for the guards, sending more bindings of Air to hold Bain. Without a hint of concern on his face, Bain knocked each attack aside with his own thin lashes of Air.

Bain tamed flight while countering Thirod's attacks, his body lifting slowly into the air.

Pulling more Air into his essence, Alcoa willed his body to move to the expanse between Bain and the balcony. He felt sweat drip down his face from the exertion, but he did not let up on his attacks. "GUARDS!"

"You have made the wrong decision," Bain said calmly.

Bain smirked then became a blur of motion, moving faster than Thirod's eyes could track. A rush of wind forced Thirod to turn toward the balcony. Bain hovered just outside, above the terrace. Behind him, the fireworks illuminated the darkness.

Alcoa blinked several times to be sure it had actually happened. He had been sure he had felt a burst of Air, Earth, Fire, and Water released from Bain. Thirod wanted to reason out what had happened, but Bain didn't give him the chance.

"Verinda looks as lovely as ever," Bain said. His smirk deepened into a smile that did not touch his eyes. "Your oldest boy looks more like you though."

Thirod felt a lump in his throat that tasted like bile. Verinda had taken the boys to the wharf to watch the display of fireworks over the ocean.

"If you have harmed them ...," his voice shook.

Bain raised a hand in a placating motion. "Do not fear. I have not harmed them. If I were to kill them, who would remain to watch your fall? Even after, I may yet them live."

Thirod began to tame Air, forming a lightning hurl in his mind. Before the power could reach his grasp, a force hit his essence like an avalanche and ripped his power from his grasp. The flow of Air sustaining his flight vanished, and he fell the few feet to the floor. His feet hit before he had time to adjust to the fall, and his knee collapsed with a crunch. He gritted his teeth against the pain, so he would not cry out.

The pain in his knee throbbed, but that was not what held him on the floor looking up at Bain through wide eyes. Bain had taken his essence. Thirod had been filled with the power of Air and aware of Bain, and still the other man had handled him as he would a child new to his powers.

Thirod met Bain's eyes. The Frozen Plains had more compassion in its icy wasteland.

"Before I take your life," Bain said, "you will see your nation in ruins. Your allies will become mine. Verinda and your children will grovel at my feet and beg for mercy. I will break their wills to mine, then I will rebuild your kingdom in my image and destroy the plague in its midst. You will live in the dungeons beneath this castle, begging for death. Only then, will you die by my hands."

Alcoa blinked, and Bain was gone.

It took several moments before Thirod tested his essence. His power was his own once more. He sat for a moment, watching the colorful display without letting his eyes focus on any of the images.

How had Bain become so powerful? An artifact of power? What else?

Thirod looked down at his knee. Even covered in trousers, he could see it swollen twice its normal size.

"Guards." His voice was not as loud this time. "Where are my guards?"

Taming Air, he gingerly picked himself up to hover just above the floor. His leg dangled without use, but stabs of pain still traveled up his thigh at the motion as he moved toward the antechamber.

The white hallway was well lit by lamp light. Red pools spattered the walls and floors. Four men, wearing full chain and white cloaks had been strewn haphazardly. Lifeless eyes stared at him from every man. None of them had even drawn a sword.

He wasn't sure if it was fear or anger that made his hands shake. But he was already making war in his mind.

"This ends our peace. It begins."

As the sun cast its first rays over the town of Benedict, Poppe opened the shudders, and light spilled into the tavern area of his inn. He took a deep breath and exhaled the crisp, morning air of Summer Solstice. There was a hint of fresh daisies and summer blooms.

He could hear Faron's hammer already banging the iron at his smithy down the street. There would be others in the town making last minute preparations for the festival. Every family from the outer farms and villages would be on their way as well. Some would bring crops for sale, and others would bring families with coin.

Within the hour, the town square would be filled with tables and booths with a plethora of wares. Soon after that, people would fill his inn.

Poppe turned and walked through the dozen empty chairs and polished the already clean tables. Nothing could ever be too clean after all. At least not today of all days. After each table was polished to satisfaction, he adjusted his spectacles for more accurate scrutiny.

He could almost see the day's patrons, all sitting at the redwood tables enjoying his fine ales and beers. Jansen had brewed a new wheat beer with darkened hops. The brewer had accidentally burnt the hops, but somehow that added to the flavor of the brew. It had a filling, smooth flavor that his patrons were sure to enjoy.

"Today is a big day," he told the imagined patrons.

He scratched his balding head, pretending that one of his many imaginary patrons had asked him, *Why is today a big day?*

"Well, today," he gave a dramatic pause, "is the Summer Solstice Festival!"

After the cheers and applause died down in his mind, he explained to his invisible patrons, "It is just the most magnificent day of the year. I can remember the day my great-grandfather proposed the idea of hosting the festival here to my father. And now the tradition is mine to uphold."

Poppe looked across the inn to the small stage next to the cold fireplace. Within two hours' time this inn would be an audience awaiting his theatrics. Which tale would the children want to hear first? The bridge troll who had kidnapped the princess, or the wizard who had spelled the king into giving up his kingdom?

He took another deep breath. The smell of eggs and ham wafted into his nose.

"And Momme has already started breakfast."

Poppe ran the front of the house, but he left the kitchen in his wife's capable hands. She seemed to prefer it that way from his reckoning. He never fancied himself as much of a cook anyhow.

After unlocking the latch to the front door, he peeked out the window. The common-goods shop across the street belonged to his good friend Willem Madrowl. The Madrowl family were among his usual first patrons of the day.

Willem didn't appear to be about just yet. The Madrowls were usually early to rise, but Willem had preparations of his own to make before the festival.

Poppe did not charge Willem the regular price for breakfast. A man raising two boys on his own. That couldn't be easy. One being an infant at that.

He had not seen anyone approach the door. When it opened, his heart fluttered, and he took a step backward.

A woman entered carrying a small basket covered with a light blue blanket. It was not uncommon for townsfolk to bring pastries. But it was a bit early for the festival, and Poppe did not know her. A cousin of someone visiting from one of the other villages, perhaps?

Upon first glance, Poppe thought she might have been the fairest woman he had ever seen. Her long, blond hair was healthy and clean. More so, he noticed her blue eyes. Such light eyes were more common in Alcoa than Justice. But hers were a pale blue, rimmed with a deeper color. Over fifty years of receiving travelers, he had never seen their likeness.

The woman wore green silks with a cut not of Justice make. The low V-neckline exposed the top of her milky bosom. Her dark cloak was of a material that he could not determine. It seemed to deflect the light, which made it appear darker. Whatever the material, it was surely expensive.

She had fair skin and a lovely face with high, broad cheekbones and a pointed chin. She was not more than half past her twentieth year, or he was a red-nosed gnome. The nation of Alcoa was across the Tranquil Sea, a quarter year's journey by the fastest ship. A long way to travel for a small town festival far outside of the capital city.

Maybe she hadn't come for the festival at all. Relative of Faron maybe? The blacksmith had come from Alcoa. Maybe she had come for him.

Yellow lights filled the space between them, and he felt woozy for a moment.

He blinked and rubbed at his spectacles. They must have taken on a fog. Removing his spectacles, he used his rag to clean them, but he didn't look away. He couldn't seem to remove his eyes from the stranger's gaze. Her blue eyes seemed to glow for a moment. That wasn't right. Brown eyes. The light must of have glinted off her golden orbs, making them look blue.

His skin tingled and his thoughts became difficult to focus. He had been sure the woman had clean blond hair, but it looked faded and tangled now. He replaced his spectacles and realized upon closer inspection, her fine pale silks were reduced to rags, worn from travel. Hadn't her attire been fine the moment before? No. That made no sense.

Her eyes were both light and weary. The hardships of the stranger were laden in the edges of her weathered face, which she hid behind the cowl of a dark cloak.

Where are your manners? Poppe chastised himself. *Not the first time you've seen a traveler in your inn. You simpleton.*

He gave his best smile and greeted his new guest. "Hello, milady. Welcome to the Scented Rose. Would you care for some breakfast this fine morning?"

She took a hesitant step toward the table nearest the door, while shifting the basket from her left to her right hand.

Poppe adjusted his spectacles. He couldn't say why, but this woman made him nervous. She wasn't scowling, and she wasn't an opposing figure by any means. If she was cleaned up, she would have been pretty to look at. Maybe it was the concern in her eyes?

She eased into the seat of the wooden chair and placed the basket at her feet. Staring into the basket as if the mysteries of all time were hidden there, she stammered at almost a whisper, "I … um … don't have any money. I … I just need to sit here for a moment … if that is alright?"

Her voice was as worn as her gown and her words as tired as her eyes. He suppressed a frown. He would earn plenty of coin over the course of the day from the festival. One plate for a woman in need would not be missed.

He looked at the woman a moment longer before remembering to smile. "That will be just fine young lady. My name is Bruece of house Lanier. But, everyone calls me Poppe. Where uh ... Where do you hail from?"

The woman looked up from the basket. The tenderness of her gaze sent chills down Poppe's spine and warmed him at the same time. His muscles, tense only moments before, felt relaxed.

Why had he been wary? The thought seemed far away.

It was as if some sort of magic took hold of him, but he could not look away from her. He felt a strong desire to protect. Something. *Someone*. The feeling had always been there. He was a father and grandfather after all. But his need felt stronger. Urgent.

A foggy haze filled his vision, and his skin tingled with a cold warmth. The inn faded around him as if in a dream. He could still see her eyes, though that image faded, too.

Solid wooden planks were beneath his face.

Had he fallen asleep?

Poppe opened his eyes. His spectacles had fallen off his face, blurring his vision. But he would know the floor of his inn blindfolded. He sat up and shook his head. Feeling around, he found his spectacles on the floor next to him. He replaced them and looked around the room from a sitting position. The door to his inn was closed again, but the woman had gone. He couldn't recall her face, but he could almost remember her eyes.

Was she ever even there? Must have been a dream, but why had he fallen to sleep on the floor?

He stood, using the table next to him for support. He hadn't fallen because nothing hurt, but as he stood, his legs waned. He steadied himself on the nearest table and tried to shake off the groggy feeling. Best not to tell Momme about this. She always did worry over the smallest of things. She might make him sit out the festival. He tried to work up the excitement he had felt before for the upcoming festivities, but an odd feeling washed over him.

Poppe felt an overwhelming desire to protect something. No. Someone. He couldn't explain it, but he knew that someone needed him.

There was a basket near the door.

"There had been a woman, and she left her pastries." Poppe's voice sounded as if someone else had spoken. He tried to rub the grogginess from his face.

As he approached the basket, the blanket made a subtle shift. He blinked and shook his head. His eyes were playing tricks on him.

Poppe blinked again as the basket made a strange muffled whine. "What in the Lifebringer's name?"

He hesitated, but kneeling down he knew what he would find. Even still, after peeling back the blanket that had been concealing the little one, he couldn't believe it.

He knew the eyes from somewhere, crystal blue with dark rims. The babe stared up at him, fully alert, but he couldn't be more than a handful of months old. This child needed to be protected.

"But I am too old to raise another babe."

There was a rolled up parchment on top of his blankets. Poppe reached for the letter, still wondering when he would wake up from this dream. He read it all the way through before realizing he had been holding his breath. He exhaled slowly.

He put the note aside and looked into the baby's eyes, which were intent upon Poppe's face.

"Elwin," he said. "Your name is Elwin."

Dear Kind Stranger,

The road that I travel is a long one. One that is not fit for my beloved child to accompany me. There is a kindness in your Spirit telling me that you will give Elwin the love and compassion he needs. The shadows of my past and the sins that lurk there shall not follow him here. I will see to that. The only item I have of value is this pendant that he now wears. Please keep it near him. If you ever tell him of me, please tell him that I loved him too much to stay with him. Tell him that I died so that he could have Life. I thank you for your kindness; there isn't an abundance of it left in the world.

Signed,
A Weary Traveler

Chapter 2

THE HOUNDS UNLEASHED

"Betrayal." The word stuck in his mouth like a bad taste.

Bain walked across the shore, pacing beside the ocean. He made every attempt to calm his mind. Anger, though a well-founded emotion, would not find her. Of all the inevitable betrayals, this was the one that he had known would hurt. The knowledge did nothing to assuage the pain inside.

It was a hurt not physical. It was an illogical, useless feeling. It was a weakness. One that he could not afford if he was going to bring the world to his rule.

"And what of my brother?" he asked the wind. "Is it weakness that allows him to draw breath still?"

His death would deter any others of committing treason, yet he could not bring himself to end Jhona's life. And how should Zeth be punished? The man had a simple task. Athina should not have been allowed to leave, even if she had help in doing so.

But Zeth would be the best choice to hunt her down.

War is at hand, Bain thought, *and already my attention is being diverted by incompetence and treachery.*

Bain clenched his fist as anger bubbled above his calm but quickly forced his hand to relax when he felt the life force of someone approaching. He had learned that each life had a unique aurora. This life was young and radiant and full of a darker energy, and it belonged to his most loyal, trusted servant.

"I told you that I was not to be disturbed," Bain said.

"I am sorry, Father." His young voice was without emotion. His son knew the right words to say, even though he had not felt them.

He faced his son. Donavin favored Bain's pale skin and wore his long black hair in a warrior's braid. He even wore the same black leather armor that Bain possessed. But his son's eyes reminded him of Athina. Donavin wore a scimitar, a curved blade that broadened toward the tip, but it was forged to fit a smaller hand.

"Can I be the one to kill the traitor, Father? I would very much like to kill him."

"No, son," Bain said. "*If* he is to die, it will be by my hand alone."

"If? But father, he has betrayed us," Donavin's forehead scrunched, as if confused. "You said that treachery could not be tolerated within a mighty kingdom. Are we not a mighty kingdom?"

Already, his son knew how to twist words to achieve a desired outcome. Maybe Athina had been right. Maybe Bain had ruined Donavin. Time would decide.

"There are exceptions to every rule, my son. A good ruler knows when to take a life and when to allow it to continue. There are reasons to allow the one who trained you to live, other than the fact that he is your brother."

"But you are more powerful than him now. I do not see how his life is useful any longer."

"He is the most skilled teacher that I know," Bain said in a patient voice. "And I am training an army of elementalists to be my savants. If I banish him to live in solitude and give him time to see me rise to power, then perhaps I can sway him to join me in the end." He spoke more to himself than to his son.

He decided to turn the conversation. "Now, tell me. Why do I expect Ulthgrar, king of the goblins, to sign Alcoa's treatise of war against me?"

Donavin's eyes sparkled with his smile. "That is easy, Father. He will use the treaty as a tool for negotiating more power under *your* rule. It is similar to the tactics the Kalicodian Tribal Nation did in the War of the Ascension. During the war, the barbarian tribes of Kalicodon were united by the *saizor* of House Duthikar of the Horned Boar tribe.

"Even united under a single tribe, the barbarians were not powerful enough to oppose the Lizard King—I forget his name—or the king of Alcoa on his own. So the *saizor* pretended to ally with the Lizard King to gain more land for his tribesmen from Alcoa. In the end, he joined with the Alcoan nation to eradicate the Lizard tribes."

Bain smiled at his son. "Well done. The Lizard tribes were scattered, not eradicated. The Lizard King was Vardwick. That is what humans called him. The language of the Lizardkin is impossible for humans to speak. To my ear it sounds more like high pitched clicking and screeching."

"I know this Father." Donavin's voice had a petulant tone. "What are we going to do next?"

Bain smiled at his son. "You are going to fetch Zeth. There are things he and I need to discuss."

Donavin's eyes grew wide with excitement. "Are you going to kill him for his incompetence?"

"No son," Bain said. "Now, do as you are told."

His mouth twisted in a downward expression, and he kicked the sand. As he turned to go, his shoulders slumped. His son did not leave in as much of a hurry as when he had arrived. As Donavin walked up the shore toward the castle, Bain turned back to the ocean's tides. It was only moments until he felt his son's life force fade from his senses.

Zeth was one of Bain's most gifted disciples, a master in the Element of fire and earth. He also had a unique Dark Gift that would be useful for hunting any prey. And he had a growing power in the Death Element.

The Elemental power known as Death was half of the Element called Spirit, now divided between Life and Death. As each living being had both darkness and light, so too did the very fabric of Elemental power.

And people often tried to destroy that which they did not understand. The Guardians of Life were such men. Fear-mongering bigots, whose time of oppression would soon come to an end.

He felt Zeth's life force approaching. It was a beacon of cruelty and ambition. Such men were as useful of a tool as any other, if properly aimed.

Bain turned toward Zeth. Instead of armor, Zeth wore a robe of black cloth that had been touched by the Elements. Items wrought from Elemental power carried many gifts. Such a robe was referred to as hard cloth. It warded the wearer from nature's heat and cold alike, and it was very difficult to penetrate but provided little protection from blunt weapons.

Bain watched his hound approach. Zeth was of mixed lineage. His Alcoan mother had been raped by a Kalicodon barbarian during a raid. His pale skin and light eyes were his mother's, but his long black hair had likely come from his father.

Zeth had never met his father. The thought made Bain think of Elwin. Unlike Zeth, Elwin was not a bastard. However, if his son was not found, Elwin would never know his own place in the world. His purpose. Bain did not let the anger rise. Elwin would be found.

Fist to heart, Zeth saluted. "What would you command of me?"

Though his face gave no hint of emotion, Bain knew Zeth only played at being a faithful hound. Submission to anyone was in direct opposition to his nature. He was a predator, and he liked submitting to anyone as much as a fox would to a wolf. Bain imagined Zeth's temperament had come from his barbarian father.

"Rise. I have the most important of tasks for you."

Bain let silence hang in the air like a wyvern on the prowl. The beast was a descendant of the mightier dragon. Though smaller and weaker than its kin, its poisonous strike could fell any living creature, even the mighty dragon.

He waited until the discomfort of the silence made sweat bead on Zeth's forehead. Bain could only imagine what Zeth was thinking under his cold stare. After such a failure, he likely imagined a very grim fate for himself, indeed.

He articulated each word like a whip. "You. Will. Find. My. Son."

"Yes, my king." Zeth's voice shook. Bain was not sure if it was from fear, confusion, or excitement. Perhaps all three.

Bain took a step closer to Zeth. "There is nothing more important than this. If he is harmed in any way, you will be harmed doubly. If he is killed, you will beg for death before your days are finished. But death will not come. Only pain. You will not fail me again. If possible, bring Athina back to me alive as well. But more importantly, you will bring Elwin to me."

Bain pulled a small object from the folds of his cloak. "I am not disillusioned. I know that it will take some time, but you will find him. And when you do, you will use this on whomever aided in his concealment. I will make an example of those who stand against me."

Bain held the device out to Zeth atop his palm. An aura of power emanated from the metallic object. To the ungifted eye it was just a hollow box that appeared to have no way of opening. In truth, this was one of a handful of its kind left in the world. Once touched with the Death Element, it was capable of the most amazing of feats.

Zeth's eyes widened with exasperated euphoria. "A soulkey?"

Zeth attempted to mask his elation as he took the soulkey, but did as well as a street urchin would had a rich merchant given him a fortune. The exultation was clear in his voice. "I will not fail you my lord."

"No. You will not." He turned his back to Zeth. "Now, leave me."

Zeth bowed and saluted fist to heart, then turned on his heel. His life force disappeared with haste as Zeth made his way toward the castle.

Athina had gone west. There was no reason to discuss such details with Zeth. Everyone living in the castle, even the scullery maids, knew which way she had fled. Being gifted in the Elemental power of Air, she had flown, thus there were no tracks to follow. But many had seen her flying west.

The guards had not been given orders to restrict her to the castle. That was Zeth's task alone. Had he made such an order, word would have gotten back to Athina within an hour. And at the time, he had not been certain whether or not she could be swayed back to him.

She would be found.

Bain felt another spark of life near, bringing him from his reverie.

The life had an exuberance like none other. It held mirth and joy that overpowered ambition. He glanced in the direction of the life's source but could not see her. She was under a veil, then. A veil was created by the Element of Air. It would bend light in such a way to make a person unseen. A very useful talent.

Bain need not lay eyes upon his wife to know this was her life force that neared him. In a patch of thorns, she was a rose. Her forgiving grace was an enemy to logic. The mere thought of her walking up the beach clouded his thoughts with emotion. She was alone. She did not carry the small life in her arms. He forced his hands to remain unclenched and turned his back on the approaching form.

She stopped several paces behind him.

He peered to the ocean for a moment before asking, "Where is my son?"

"Safe." He could feel the smile in her voice.

The sound was infuriating, but he forced his emotions under control. He would not allow her to use emotions against him. Not this time. He would need reason to find his son. She had only been gone for two months, so he hadn't left the continent. It would have taken the better part of a year to reach the Island Nations or the Blood Isle and return. But where? He needed some clue.

"Surely you would not be fool enough to hide him with the Chai Tu Naruo? I have agents amongst the Children of Nature, as well as Alcoa."

"No, my heart, he is not amongst the Chai Tu Naruo. You will not find him."

He felt his jaw twitch and forced his muscles to relax. He turned to face her. Her long hair hung about her shoulders like he preferred it, and she wore a white dress that clung to her bosom but was loose around her legs. Her wide eyes looked into his, searching.

"Do not call me that," he said. "You have wounded me more deeply than any sword ever could."

She took a few steps toward him, and he raised a hand in warning.

Her smile did not fade, but she stopped walking. "Though I wish there could have been another way, you will ever be my heart, my love."

He knew that she meant every word, and he needed to know. "When did you stop believing in me?"

Her lips tightened and her eyes shown with pity. "When you decided there was no price too high for victory."

"I will remake the world," Bain said. "There will be more sacrifices to be made, and I will do what I must. I regret nothing."

"Do you remember why you began this?" she asked, gesturing to the castle. "I thought that it was to save the world from the Awakening. I thought we were saving gifted children from the Guardians of Life. But it was vengeance all along."

"This is more than vengeance." His voice was harsher than he had intended. He took a breath and forced away his emotions. "I will make a stronger world than Alcoa and his fool order. That world will not fear the Awakening. It will embrace it."

She shook her head. "How will a world in turmoil be better suited to face the dragonkin? How can you believe that a war will make the world stronger?"

He looked into her pleading eyes. She had given him that look many times. They would win him over no longer.

"What would you have me do? Let Alcoa snuff out the spark of power from those gifted?"

"Alcoa made a poor decision in sending us to battle the vampires, but we all survived. And he is not the Guardians of Life. The Guardians have overreached their place for far too long, but that is why we found those gifted and brought them here. To save them from being put to the Inquisition. Not to build an army to seek your vengeance."

"How can you not see what is so obvious?" he said. "Alcoa has the power to oppose them with the Sacred Order, yet he does nothing! The world will fall if there is not a change. And *I* will bring that change."

"At the cost of your soul?" she asked breathlessly.

"What does that even mean? Do you even know?" Despite the anger building in him, he forced a laugh. It sounded weak, even to his own ears. "You serve the Lifebringer, but where is he? I do not see him raising a hand for anyone. He has left this world to ruin, and you give *him* your soul without question. It is foolish to serve Life at the cost of living."

"I do not feel the taint on you, but ...," He could see the light of realization, shining in her eyes. "You are bound, aren't you?"

He had the lie prepared before her lips formed the question. Just enough truth to be believed.

"The night I returned here from Alcoa, I had learned of your betrayal. You turned my own brother against me. That night the Seeker of Souls came to me. He offered me power, and I accepted. It was foolish of me to have resisted him in the first place, after he had already given me so much without my loyalty. I no longer fear the Awakening any more than a snake fears its own bite."

He pulled the pendant from his neck. Amongst other things, it had the ability to mask the power of the Death Element. Away from his chest, the effects of its power faded, allowing her to sense that he was bound.

The pity returned to her eyes, and she stared at him in silence. Saying nothing, she gave a slight shake of her head. He had wanted her to feel pain. Blame herself. Instead she felt pity for *him*. She might as well have slapped him or spat in his face. Instead of pushing the anger away, he embraced it.

Bain opened his essence to Earth and Air, readying to tame its power to trap her. The power of the Elements flooded into him, but before he could act, she had already tamed power in a weave foreign to him. Spirit energy without form flowed from her, and he felt the fabric of reality tear between them.

A thin, rectangular sheet of light appeared in front of her. Its blinding brightness forced him to shield his eyes. Her image was there for only a moment, as if he looked upon her through the clearest of water, and then she and the light were gone.

Her voice echoed, even after the image of her face had vanished. "Goodbye, my love."

Like snuffing out a candle, her life force was no more. He stared in disbelief for many moments. Slowly, he realized what she had done.

"But that is impossible."

The shadow realm was where an elementalist drew his powers. To enter there in the flesh meant to give up one's life force here in the world that was. She burnt up her essence in one final act, a Spending. He couldn't know the intentions behind her Spending. He only knew one thing.

"She's ... gone."

Forgetting the anger he had felt only moments before, he sat on the shore. He was vaguely aware of the sun descending in the western sky.

This time she was gone. Truly gone.

The night was long, but he did not stir from the beach.

Chapter 3

ELWIN ESCARI

The sun continuously rises and sets, carrying with it the shadows of the ages. History that is known shines on us like truth given to all. But the unknown history of the ages is like the darkness on the edges of the setting sun. With the passing of time, its elusive nature lays to rest our sense of truth. As the sun brings a waking light upon the land in the morning, inevitably darkness too must fall across the land.

Time blows by for a youth like a single leaf in the wind fluttering about in the direction nature takes him. The seasons come and they go. As one leaf falls, another one rises. The Lady Nature gives rays of sunshine to her creatures as well as storms. Trees that flourish in the spring and summer lose their way to the fall and winter.

The cyclical nature of life turns its great cycle, and a child grows from a baby to a toddler. The unending winds of change blow, turning the leaf through fourteen years, until the toddler becomes a youth.

While history casts its shadow, morning has come again, and like all mornings the mysteries of the past come with it.

Elwin Escari's blond hair bounced about his shoulders, as he swung down from the lowest branch of the large, redwood tree. The short sleeve of his green tunic snagged as he dropped into the dirt road beside the tree. He stopped to inspect the tiny tear.

"Phew," he said to himself, "it's not that bad. Mother will probably never notice."

The anticipation of climbing that particular tree was the reason for wearing the brown trousers. Dirt was harder to see on brown. After they were wiped to his satisfaction, he checked the coin purse at his belt loop that his father had given him. None of the coins were missing. Satisfied that he was presentable, he walked up the dirt road in the direction of the town.

The sun hit its zenith by the time Elwin reached the first building at the edge of town. The summer's cool, northern breeze brought apple-scented candles to Elwin, and he breathed in deeply. He could see Danna placing the new candles in the window of her small shop. It, like the rest of the buildings in Benedict, had been constructed of the strong redwoods from the Carotid Forest to the north, which Elwin could see at the edge of the horizon.

Danna's dark hair was pulled back and tied up. A smudge of red wax had dried to each cheek, just below her eyes. Elwin noticed that her apron was covered in waxes of various colors, but her linen dress remained spotless. Danna smiled and waved as he passed.

He waved back and continued into town.

The rich smells from Warne's Apothecary on Elwin's right and pungent odors from Jansen's Brewery on his left provided a stark contrast to the sweet-scented candles just moments before.

Several more paces brought him to the cobblestones of the town square in front of his Poppe's inn. Many of the townspeople had set up some wares for travelers arriving early for the festival.

A burly man wearing a sleeveless tunic beneath a blacksmith's apron gave Elwin a toothy grin. His massive arms sorted the weapons and armor on the wooden table in front of him.

Elwin returned the man's grin. "Hi Faron."

Faron had a full head of silver hair, which he kept short. Blue eyes nestled against his strong nose reminded Elwin of a hawk. He and Faron were the only people in town that had blue eyes. Everyone else had blends of green, brown and black colored eyes. But, unlike Elwin, Faron wasn't from around here. He had grown up somewhere across the Tranquil Sea.

Faron's voice had a deep tone and the touch of an accent. "Your dad let you off that tight leash he's had you on, I see. Last I heard, Feffer had gotten you into some trouble for hiding stinkweed under the bar at the inn."

"It was all Feffer," Elwin said. "I just happened to be there. But, I am just going to Madrowl's Wares to get some leather strapping for the plow. Father says it'll go out any day. He had wanted to get the beans planted before the Summer Solstice Festival, but it's unlikely now."

Faron reached across the table and ruffled Elwin's hair. "I could cut that for you if you want."

Elwin backed away, eying the sharp weapon Faron reached for. "I'm okay Faron. Thanks."

"Best be on your way then lad." Faron winked at him.

"I'll see you at the festival tomorrow?" Elwin asked.

Faron nodded. "I wouldn't miss it."

Elwin turned from the table and crossed the street, waving to Jadron the furrier and Bryne the carpenter, who had tables and tents being set up for their wares as well.

Willem Madrowl's Wares sat across the street from his Poppe's inn to the left of town square. Its shape made Elwin think of a large, wooden box two stories high. The small awning over the door extended the side of the building.

A few paces brought Elwin to the base of the wooden stairs, and two big steps brought him to the top. A bell dinged above his head as he entered. There always seemed to be an ever-present layer of dust in the front room. He covered his mouth and coughed.

The front room consisted of a counter that rested in front of a double door, which Elwin hadn't ever seen stay open for long. Willem Madrowl stood behind the counter, scrawling on a leather-bound book. He closed the heavy tome as Elwin peeked at it.

Willem scratched his red-grey hair. "Oh. Hi there, Elwin. By yourself today, eh?"

"Yes sir, I have come to your shop today to purchase leather strapping, cut for a plow."

"Well okay, my fine sir," he said with a smile. "That will be twenty-seven copper pieces." He opened the leather book, dipped his quill in ink and began to scrawl on the next line.

Elwin tried not to be nosy but couldn't help himself. He watched Willem write down Elwin's purchase. When Willem finished he said, "You can read then can you?"

Elwin's cheeks flushed. "Oh sorry, I wasn't trying to. Yes my mother taught me to read and write. Reading is my favorite pastime."

"Other than ledgers," Willem said, "what do you like to read?"

Elwin smiled. "I have a book that I got last Festival that talks about the history of wizards. But they are called elementalists, not wizards. I just call them wizards because that's what my Poppe calls them in his stories. They can do the most amazing things. I am going to be one someday."

Elwin pulled his purse out and began to count out the copper, placing each piece on the counter.

"A el-a … wizard, eh? Well wouldn't that be something? I saw the king's wizard, Jasmine Lifesong, a few years back. She was really a looker." Willem rubbed his chin. "You've been a good influence on Feffer. He sounds just like you, always talking about grand adventures and such. He has the great aspirations to become an elite guard to the mighty King Justice, may the Lifebringer bless him always. He might just do it, if I could keep him from influencing you."

"… Twenty-six, twenty-seven. All there," Elwin said. "Feffer, yeah. He wants to be a member of the White Hand. I don't know why. Elementalists are better. Where is he?"

Willem's nostrils flared. "Aye. Well. He's been in a heap of trouble the past couple of days. I don't know what I am going to do with him. Aside from the stinkweed stunt, he stole another one of your Momme's peach pies. I've a good mind to keep him from the Summer Solstice Festival." He paused. "Let me get that strapping for ya."

Willem pulled a cord hanging by the doors and began writing on some paper in front of him. A few moments later Wilton Madrowl, Willem's oldest, came out the doors. His auburn hair encased high cheek bones and a square face. He stood a hand or so taller than Willem. The girls of the town always giggled when they talked to him. Elwin could never figure out why. He wasn't even funny.

Wilton took the scrawling without a word and returned to the warehouse through the double doors. Elwin leaned over to peek inside the doors while they were opened. It closed before he could get a good look, but he did manage to see large racks with clothes on wooden shelves at the far wall.

Several moments later Wilton returned and handed Elwin the strapping with a smirk. He ruffled Elwin's head before returning through the doors. Elwin smoothed his hair. Why did everyone do that? He wasn't a kid anymore.

"Well," Willem said, "you have a nice day now, Elwin."

Elwin replaced the almost empty purse back on his belt loop and turned to leave. "Thank you, kind sir."

"Aye, and thanks to you as well," Willem smiled. "Send my best to Drenen."

"I will." Elwin returned the smile and left.

As he reached the second step, a gush of cold splashed his head and traveled down his spine. His muscles froze and his heart pounded. Wiping water from his face, he looked up at the clear-blue sky. No one in the square seemed to take notice of his dilemma. A muffled giggle came from somewhere above him.

"Feffer!" Elwin accused.

Elwin backed down the steps, studying the roof line for several moments in an attempt to find his attacker. Another downpour came from above. Elwin dove to the side of the steps as if lava poured down from the heavens. He heard the splatter of water hit the steps behind him.

He stood up and ran toward the western side of the building. A bamboo ladder leaned against the backside of the building and extended just over the roof line.

A small part of his brain tried to warn him against revenge, but he ignored it. Feffer needed to pay.

Elwin ran to the ladder as fast as his feet could carry him and pulled it to the ground. It felt lighter than he thought it would be, but it felt awkward trying to run with it. But ran he did. Heart pounding, he moved around to the back of the building and across to the eastern side. He adjusted the ladder to just under the roof line and pressed the base of the ladder deep into the grass until it dug into the dirt. Throwing the strap over his shoulder to free his hands, he put his foot on the first step and grabbed hold of the sides.

Then, he looked up.

Elwin hesitated. That voice to turn around and walk away became louder. The height of the building seemed much higher with the ladder next to it. He pushed the voice away. Not more than half an arm's length, each wrung had a comfortable distance to the next step. He could do this.

Sucking in a deep breath he took the second step. Then a third. He kept climbing, *not* looking down. After making it to the top, he peered over the edge. Racks and boxes were beneath an awning at the other end, but there was no sign of Feffer.

He pulled himself over the ledge and onto the roof.

Without thinking, he turned around and looked down. The ground seemed to blur and stretch further away than he thought possible. He teetered on his toes as if the roof shook. Backing away from the edge, he fell onto his backside and turned to clutch the roof with both hands. He felt as if the roof rocked beneath him. He could feel his heart pounding in his chest as if trying to escape.

Elwin closed his eyes. The roof couldn't have been moving. He had read about Fistledon the Great, a master elementalist who could conjure fire and shake all of Arinth with his powers. This wasn't that. He had never been so high up before. He needed to be calm. There was no harm in being so high up.

No you japed-up fool! The voice in his head said. *It's the impact at the bottom that'll dash your fool brains to bits."*

"Stop it," he told the voice. "That isn't going to help."

He took several deep breaths, letting his heartbeat slow to a steady rhythm and opened his eyes. The roof no longer moved beneath him. Slow, as to not startle the roof into motion, he sat up. Behind him, he could see a couple of buckets at the front edge of the building. He began to consider his options, when he heard a scraping sound on the roof line behind him.

His breath caught in his chest. The ladder!

Scrambling forward on hands and knees, Elwin dove in an attempt to reach the end of the ladder. His hand grabbed hold of the ladder's edge, and he pulled. The jolt on the ladder came from a tug at the other end.

A stifled laugh from below cut off with the jarring halt of the ladder. Elwin clasped a firm hand on his end and heaved with all of his might, but the ladder still didn't give.

Once more, Elwin found himself looking down. Feffer seemed smaller at the other end. His red hair moved about as he struggled to gain a better hold on the ladder.

The ground blurred, and the roof began to rock again. Elwin almost loosed the ladder, but Feffer's mocking laugh made him tighten his grip. He would not let Feffer get the best of him. He pulled with all his strength and gained an inch, then two. Then a foot. Then two. And then the ladder stopped moving.

He pulled for several moments without gaining half an inch, when an idea occurred to him. Elwin dropped flat to the roof, using the edge of the building as leverage. He put all of his weight into the pull.

CRACK.

Elwin tumbled backward, holding the ladder.

He stood up clutching his fragment. It was not quite as tall as he was. Ruined. The ladder was ruined. He peered over the ledge. His opponent stood, nursing his rump and holding the other half of his ladder.

"Now how am I going to get down?" Elwin said.

"I don't know," Feffer shrugged and threw his larger half on the ground. "You shouldn't have broken the ladder." Feffer smiled and ran toward the front of the building.

"Hey!" Elwin called. "You can't leave me up here!"

Elwin looked at the broken ladder in his hand. "He did. He left me up here."

He picked up the strapping that he had dropped during the scuffle and walked toward the center of the roof. Then, he noticed a trapdoor at the roof's center, a pace away from the front awning. His heart skipped a beat as he ran to it. Grasping the handle, he gave it a tug.

It didn't budge.

"Locked. Curse it all to the abyss!" Elwin looked around on impulse to make sure no adult had heard him swear. Then he remembered he was stuck on a roof. Alone.

Looking around for options, he noticed a couple of empty buckets next to two buckets full of water. Not sure how that would help him, he peeked over the edge and could see Faron and the others at the town square.

Elwin opened his mouth to call for help but stopped when he noticed movement off to the west. Several soldiers armed with long poles with axes at their heads walked alongside a horse-drawn carriage. Each wore silver armor made of chained links and had a sword at their belts. Chain mail, Elwin had read it was called. Stitched into the center of their red tunics and their cloaks was the right hand of a palm, facing outward.

The White Hand! These were the king's men.

"That could only mean …"

What? What did it mean? Surely it wasn't the King. Who could it be?

"Wow, that's the White Hand of Justice, the King's elite Guard!" Feffer said.

The surprise so close to his ear made Elwin jump.

"Feffer!" Elwin accused. "You trapped me up here!"

Feffer pointed to the procession. "But aren't you glad I did?"

Elwin opened his mouth to argue, but decided it could wait. "Why do you think they are here?"

"I don't know. Let's go find out."

Elwin turned to follow Feffer back toward the opened trapdoor and tripped over a water pail. The bucket sloshed and tumbled with him, spilling its water down the stairs.

Below, he heard a muted curse.

Elwin and Feffer looked at one another. Feffer's wide eyes spoke volumes. Before Elwin could ask, Willem stomped up the steps and peered onto the roof. His half-soaked head poked over the lip, and his glower made Elwin back up a step.

With surprising calm, Willem said, "Feffer. Hanck. Madrowl. You go downstairs and hitch old Hilga to the wagon and wait for me there." Turning his attention back to Elwin. "As for you, I think we need to go have a long talk with your father, young man."

"But it was Feffer."

"That's enough out of you. Come with me."

Elwin sat on the porch swing next to Feffer, not much in the mood for swinging. Feffer, however, swung his end. Several times Elwin put his feet down in an attempt to stop it, but his heart wasn't much into another battle just now.

The sun hung just above the horizon in the western sky. He didn't even get to see why the White Hand had come.

Elwin gave Feffer his worst *"this-is-all-your-fault"* look and just to be sure Feffer understood the message, he added, "This is all your fault."

Feffer smiled, "What? You climbed onto the roof of your own free will, my friend."

"I am not your friend," Elwin crossed his arms in front of him. "Friends don't dump water on their friends."

"Says who?"

"Says me."

Feffer rolled his eyes. "How many friends do you have?"

Elwin opened his mouth to answer and closed it. Counting Momme and Poppe ..., "I have plenty, thank you."

Feffer jumped off the swing. "I know you don't mean it, Elwin."

"Hey, where are you going? They said to stay here and not move a muscle."

Elwin followed Feffer to the window's edge.

"Have you lost your wits?" Elwin whispered with astonishment.

Feffer shrugged. "We are already in trouble, so we might as well make the most of it."

Unbelievable. Feffer would get him killed. Ignoring his instincts, Elwin settled next to Feffer and peered through the window. Inside, Mr. Madrowl sat at the dining table in the kitchen.

Elwin's father stood next to the table. Drenen Escari was not overly large, but he was tall and strong from years in the fields. He had dark hair and eyes, much like Elwin's mother. Elwin had always wondered who he got his blond hair and blue eyes from. He had never met his grandma and grandpa on his father's side. But that was who his father said his looks came from. His grandma's mother had been from Alcoa.

His father frowned much as he would looking at rotten crops as he listened to Willem's version of the story. Willem stood and began to pace, using the strap to emphasize his points.

"And then the two rascals dumped water on my head. They were in cahoots I tell you."

"What?" Elwin whispered. "That isn't how it happened."

Feffer muffled a laugh into his hand.

Elwin hit Feffer's shoulder with the backside of his hand. "Shhhh."

"Would you like some warm tea to calm your nerves a bit?" Mother offered. Her hair was pulled back into a bun, so he could see the worry lines in her face. "The kettle is just finishing."

"Thank you Melra, I would," Willem nodded. "I have got to do something about that boy. The last few years, he's been harder to handle."

She handed him the tea.

He took it with a grateful smile. "Thank you."

"It's my pleasure."

"What am I to do? Every year he's getting more and more unruly." Willem turned and began to walk toward the window. "I'd half expect him to—"

Elwin lost the words as he scrambled back to the wooden swing. Feffer was not far behind him. He listened for footsteps inside the house but couldn't hear anything over the sound of the pounding in his chest. Several moments passed before Elwin dared to say a word.

"Do you think they saw us?" he whispered.

"Nah," Feffer said. "They would have come out here and

blistered our backsides by now. That was really close though. What do you think they are going to do with us?"

Before Elwin could reply the door opened. He closed his mouth and looked down.

They did see us, he thought. *The Lifebringer help us, we are goners for sure.*

"The Awakening is upon us," Feffer gulped under his breath to Elwin. Feffer's lips curled into a small smile. A smile! He was actually enjoying this.

Both of their fathers stood in the doorway. Elwin looked up at Drenen. His furrowed brow half covered his eyes, and Mr. Madrowl's nostrils flared with each deep breath.

Feffer covered his smile with his hand.

"I am extremely disappointed in you, Elwin," his father said. "What were you thinking?"

"But it wasn't—"

"I don't want to hear it," he said. "Now go to bed, so I can decide whether or not you can still go to the Summer Solstice Festival tomorrow."

Elwin's heart sank. "Yes, sir."

He squeezed past them and into the house, daring to hope that his mother would at least hear him out. He ran up to give her a hug.

She crossed her arms over her chest. "You heard your father."

Without a word, he turned to his right and went down the hall to his room. He stripped to his small clothes and climbed into bed. Surely, they would let him go to the Summer Solstice Festival. They were already making him go to bed without dinner.

"Feffer," he cursed.

Elwin turned about, trying to find a comfortable spot on his bed and failing. He settled onto his back and stared at the dark ceiling.

❧

Elwin opened his eyes and found himself standing in the common room of his home. His parents sat snuggled together on the lover's bench by the fireplace.

"I'm sorry," he said. "I don't know how I got here. I was just in my bed trying to sleep and now, here I am."

Neither of them moved from the small fire or acknowledged him. He blinked. They had never been this mad at him.

"It was all Feffer," Elwin said. "I promise."

Still no response.

He walked around to stand between his parents and the fireplace. The warmth behind him had an odd feel. The heat of it seemed to pull at him. He pushed the thought from his mind. His parents stared into one another's eyes, not seeming to notice him.

"Hello?" Elwin said waving his hand at them.

Drenen moved slowly toward his mother and touched his lips to hers in a gentle kiss.

"Gross!" Elwin said turning from them. He would have rather been anywhere but there.

When he opened his eyes, he found himself in the fields next to the farmhouse. The porch swing sat empty and moved with the breeze. The chill wind touched his arms and legs, sending ripples through his body. It seemed to fill him until he shook from the cold.

"I'm dreaming," he realized. How else could he have moved out here? He hadn't walked.

He turned around to look at the fields. A thin fog covered the rows of crops, but the high moon provided enough light to reveal the forest beyond the fields. Tall redwood trees stretched toward the sky. Elwin could make out a clearing in the trees, where he knew a lake to be. Many long days in the fields ended with a dip in the lake. It was the best part of working the fields in the summer.

In the time it took Elwin to blink, he found himself in the forest. Trees towered over him, and the fog became thicker around him. The gentle voice of a woman's singing echoed somewhere in the distance. He listened for a moment to the lady's wordless lullaby. It seemed to beckon him. West. It sounded as if it came from the west. That would take him back to the farm.

"Who's there?" he called.

A mist formed over the lake and crept toward him like a massive serpent. Elwin stepped back, and the advance of the fog slowed. It moved into a *formless cloud of a size with Elwin, then patterns began to emerge from the fog. It was a face.*

He blinked and rubbed at his eyes. When he opened his eyes again, a man stepped from the fog. He wore blue silks cut in a fashion Elwin had never seen. His dark hair was cut short, and his eyes seemed to be cloaked in shadow. Despite the charming smile on the man's face, a voice in his mind told Elwin to run. Behind him, the woman's singing became more urgent.

"Hello, Son of Bain," the man said in a pleasant voice. "Long have I awaited this meeting."

"Son of Bain?" he said. "My name is Elwin."

"Aye," he said. "You are the one called Elwin. Your bloodline sings to me."

Elwin blinked. The instinct to run sounded like gongs in his mind. But this was just a dream. Wasn't it?

"Who are you?" Elwin said, ignoring his fears.

"I am called by many names," the man said. "I was once called the Son of Life. My enemies have called me by more names than even I know. You may call me by the name given to me by my mother. Abudan"

"Abudan?" Elwin said. "That name sounds familiar."

"Enough about me," Abudan said. "Let us talk about you."

"What about me?"

"This forest for example," Abudan gestured around him. "Where is it?"

The shadow cleared around Abudan's face for a moment to reveal eyes of black fog, as if the pupil had consumed all of his eyes. Elwin flinched back from the man's gaze.

Abudan held up his hands as if calming a frightened calf. "I meant no alarm. I know you are in the Island Nations, but I cannot be sure as to where. You are shielded from me. It is her, I have no doubt. Can you hear her?"

"The singing?" Elwin asked. The urgency hadn't lessened, but he still couldn't make out any words.

"Yes," Abudan said, frowning. "I do not know how she touches my realm, but I am certain you are the root of it."

"This is the strangest dream I have ever had," Elwin said.

Abudan's laugh sent shivers down Elwin's spine. Again he wanted to flee, but he did not allow his fears to get the better of him. It was just a dream. It was. Whenever he wanted, he could just wake up.

"This is just a dream," Abudan said. "But it is also more. I am your destiny, Elwin of Solsec. You will be the one to Awaken us."

"Solsec?" Elwin said. "That is not my name. You have me mistaken for someone else."

"As I have said," Abudan said. "Whatever you are called, I would know blood that is mine. Now, where in the Island Nations do you reside?"

Something in Abudan's tone made Elwin wary. He took a step back, but didn't seem to move away from Abudan. So, he took another step, a much bigger step, and nothing seemed to happen.

"Shh," Abudan said and made a calming gesture. "I mean you no harm. Just the opposite. I would like to give you a Gift. You are destined for power, Son of Bain. The world can be yours, if you only accept what is yours by birthright."

Abudan took a step toward him, and Elwin stepped back on instinct. Despite Elwin's efforts to get away, Abudan still moved closer.

"There is nothing to fear," Abudan said. "In the end, you will accept my Gift. Save the lives of those around you and take it now."

"I am not who you think I am," Elwin said, backing away. "I'm a farmer. I don't have any birthright. The land isn't even ours."

Abudan's hand felt like ice on his shoulder. Pain moved through Elwin as the cold began to spread to his arm and chest.

"It can all end," Abudan said. "Just repeat this simple phrase. 'I accept your Gift, Abaddon. My soul is yours.' Then, power over Life will be yours."

"Abaddon!" Elwin gasped. "You are the Seeker of Souls. Not Abudan. You are the Bringer of Death."

"Such an ugly name, that," Abaddon said in a soothing tone. "My gift is warmth. Take my hand and speak the words. Without my warmth, you will surely perish."

The cold continued to spread. Even his thoughts began to become rigid.

"Wake," Elwin said. "I want to wake."

He focused his mind on the comfort of his bed and the warmth of his room.

"This isn't real," he heard himself say.

The cold vanished, and he could see himself sleeping in his bed. For a moment, he felt as if he was staring down at himself. Then, somehow, he and the body became one.

Chapter 4

SUMMER SOLSTICE

Elwin sat up, feeling strong hands around him. He kicked with all of his might but couldn't shake loose the grip of those strong hands.

"Elwin, open your eyes." It was his father's voice.

Even though the morning's light spilled into his window, his mother stood in the doorway holding a lantern. Strong arms rubbed warmth back into Elwin's limbs.

He looked up into his father's face and saw concern in Drenen's eyes. "Your skin is cold. The night was not so cold. Do you need another blanket at night?"

"It was so real," he said, trying not to loose the tears filling his eyes.

Drenen continued to rub warmth back into Elwin's arms. "It was just a dream, son. You are alright now."

Elwin buried his head into his father's chest. No. It had been real. Elwin didn't cry. Not exactly. When he closed his eyes, tears came out, but it didn't count as crying, because the tears wouldn't have fallen had he not closed his eyes. Several moments passed before his father spoke.

"You need to dress," Drenen said. "Get some clothes on and come to breakfast."

A strong smell of fresh-baked pastries and sweet cakes filled the air. His mother must have risen early to bake them. How could he have forgotten? The festival was today.

His father went over to his storage chest, pulled out fresh clothes, and threw them on the bed next to Elwin. He picked up the clothes. It was his newest trousers and best, green tunic. "Am I going to get to go to the Summer Solstice Festival today?"

His father's tone became neutral. "Change your clothes, and we will discuss it at the breakfast table."

He changed clothes and dug beneath his dirty clothes for his leather shoes. Elwin pulled them on as fast as possible. After lacing them up, he bounced out of the door and into the kitchen. His mother and father sat at the table. They had eggs and salted ham, but in his place was a bowl of porridge.

"Sit," his father told him.

Elwin sat in the redwood chair and stared at the porridge. His bad dream had distracted him from his current predicament. He had forgotten that he had been in trouble. Obviously, his parents had not.

"Look at me son."

Elwin looked at his father. Stern eyes studied Elwin in much the same way they would have looked over a lame horse.

"What you did yesterday was not excusable. I have a good mind to keep you from the festival today."

Elwin looked back into his porridge, and tears began to fill his vision again. Feffer. Why did he have to follow Feffer onto the roof?

"We aren't going to do that. But your mother and I have talked it over with Willem Madrowl, and we have decided that Feffer is going to come stay with us for a while. Starting tomorrow, you and Feffer are going to learn some discipline. Like I did when I was your age."

"So," Elwin said, "I am going to get to go to the festival today?"

Elwin's father nodded. "And then Feffer will come home with us tonight. But just so you know, your mother and I are not happy with you."

Elwin picked up his wooden spoon and picked at his porridge. Blah. It didn't even have any cinnamon or fruit. And none of it had even been his fault, not really. Well, maybe the ladder was.

"Finish up so we can load your mother's pastries and head into town for the festival."

Town! The White Hand! He had forgotten the festival *and* the caravan. That stupid dream. Elwin finished his porridge in a few bites and tried to swallow without tasting it.

❧

Wilton stood in the alley that separated his father's warehouse and Jadron's Furrier shop and watched the town square. This time of the morning the square was always void of inhabitants. But, soon there would be many maidens awaiting the tender touch of Wilton Madrowl. And he was not one to disappoint.

Several guards came out of the inn's front door. The soldiers were the real reason for him being outside at such an early hour. Soldiers had not visited in such numbers in his lifetime. Why were they here? He watched them from the cover of the buildings.

Five of them walked away from the inn toward the square. Four wore chain shirts, covered by a red tunic. At the tunic's center was the right hand of a palm, the symbol of the King of Justice's personal guard. The fifth man was the largest man Wilton had ever seen. He was even larger than Faron. He wore a white tunic with a red hand at its center.

His black-red hair wove into a warrior's braid, and he had a short peppered beard. He wore full plate that had the white hand crested on its right shoulder. A sword as tall as Wilton hung on the man's back. Narrower toward the hilt, the blade broadened slightly before coming to a point at the end. Wilton had never seen its like. Maybe Faron would know the sword's type.

As the group wandered toward him, he stepped back into the shadows of the building.

The larger man's voice was deep. "Better to make the announcement at the height of their festival. Let them enjoy one last moment of peace before they learn of the war."

War?

"Yes, my lord," one of the soldiers replied.

"Biron," the gruff man said. "In the meantime, I want you to get a head count of the town's eligible recruits."

"Yes, sir."

Wilton started edging backward, away from the men. Maybe he would miss this year's festival after all. He had no desire to go to any war. No maiden, not even Elwin's cousin Dasmere with her pretty, brown eyes and long, auburn locks would be worth being recruited for war.

Something crunched beneath his feet. Wilton froze. It felt like bamboo.

"Shh." The gruff man looked into the alley, right at Wilton.

Run or stay?

The man in full plate moved with surprising agility toward him. Again Wilton froze, and an iron grasp took him by the shoulder. "What are you doing here citizen?"

"I ... this is my father's shop. I was just ... I didn't hear anything."

The man's dark eyes studied him. "What is your name?"

Lie to him?

"I am," he paused. "I'm Wilton Madrowl."

"You, no doubt, have heard me tell my men that war is coming to our lands. You must not tell anyone of this. I will make the announcement to your townspeople before the festival comes to a close. I am Zaak Lifesong, Captain Commander of the White Hand. That is an order citizen."

Wilton gave him an awkward bow with his head. "Yes, my lord."

When the large man released his grip, Wilton massaged his sore shoulder.

"It has been some time since anyone has gotten the drop on me," the man pondered aloud. "What is your age?"

Again Wilton wondered whether or not he should lie, but at last he said, "I have seen seventeen namedays, my lord."

"That's one Biron."

"Aye sir, one."

᠙

Elwin jumped in surprise when he saw Feffer running to greet their wagon. Mr. Madrowl didn't hold him from the festival either. Elwin started to jump from the back of the wagon, but a strong grip on his left shoulder stopped him. He turned to see his father's *"no-nonsense"* stare.

"Son, you two stay out of trouble. Now, promise me."

"I promise."

"Take this." His father handed him a purse of small coins.

"Wow, thanks!" Elwin took it and attached it to his belt.

"Just remember your promise. You too, Feffer. You two be good today."

"Yes, Mr. Escari."

Elwin jumped out of the back of the wagon and ran toward the inn. "Let's see if they are still here."

"Wait!" Feffer called to him.

Elwin stopped. "Don't you want to see?"

Feffer shook his head. "The door to the inn is shut and being blocked by the White Hand. They tell me to 'scat,' like a stray dog every time I try to get past them."

"What? Why would they do that?" Elwin shook his head. "Well, this inn belongs to my Poppe. Let's see them try to keep me out of there."

Elwin marched toward the inn. The square was full of so many people, it made his march more of a jostled strut.

As he passed Faron's table, the man stopped him. "Whoa, Elwin. What's the hurry?"

"I can't stop now Faron, there is something I have to do."

Faron laughed. "On your way to the book merchant I guess?"

Elwin stopped. "Asalla is here?"

"You didn't know? I'm surprised you aren't bothering the old merchant now."

Elwin shook his head. "I am going to find out why the White Hand is here first."

"Yeah," Feffer piped in. "*We* are going to find out why they are here."

Faron laughed. "Well, good luck. Many people are gossiping as to the why of it, but I am not much for gossip. I just hope they take a look at my weapons here. I have always wanted to be a king's blacksmith."

"You don't want to know why they are here?" Elwin asked.

"I am sure we will know when they want us to know."

"Come on, Elwin." Feffer pulled on his shoulder.

"Bye, Faron."

"You two stay out of trouble."

Elwin followed Feffer to the front of the inn. A man stood in front of the door, and he held a giant pole with an odd-shaped blade at the tip. "I wonder what his weapon is?"

"It is a halberd," Feffer said.

"How do you know?"

"Well, I have only wanted to be a member of the White Hand my entire life."

"Oh, right."

Elwin put a foot on the first step, determined to make it past the guard. The man placed his halberd in front of the door. "Scat, child."

"See. Come on Elwin."

"But this is my Poppe's inn. You can't keep me out of here."

The guard raised both of his eyebrows. "I said *scat.*"

He opened his mouth to tell him that he would do no such thing, but that halberd looked sharp. Instead he said, "Let's go find Asalla."

"Why do we want to look at a bunch of books?"

"You don't like to read?"

Feffer shrugged. "If it's raining outside, sometimes. Or if it has a story about Faragand the Red."

"Who?"

"I thought you liked books," Feffer said with a hint of indignation. "Faragand is the greatest swordsman that ever lived. He was a slave in the ancient lands of Maar. He fought his way to freedom. I can't believe you haven't heard of him. "

Elwin shrugged. "I only read about important stuff, like elementalists."

"Pfft," Feffer retorted. "How many elementalists are as popular as Faragand? I don't know any famous ones."

"There are plenty," Elwin said. "Fistledon the Great for one."

"I've never heard of him," Feffer said.

"Well I've never heard of Fargrim," Elwin said.

"Fa-ra-gand," Feffer said.

"Whatever," Elwin rolled his eyes. "I've never heard of him either."

Feffer scowled at Elwin. He sighed turning away from Feffer and spotted the covered wagon toward the east of town in front of Faron's smithy. It rose above the other wagons, and it had a large book, worn from weather, painted on its side.

Pushing through the crowd, Elwin didn't turn to see if Feffer followed.

The first time Elwin remembered seeing Asalla, the old man's appearance had scared him. The skin around his face was tightened and his long grey hair consisted of a multitude of thin strands. Half a foot shorter than Elwin, Asalla was the shortest man Elwin knew. He had an almost purple tint to his grey eyes. There was something about the way Asalla looked at people. Elwin knew if he ever told a lie, Asalla would know right away. Though, he never would. Not to Asalla anyway.

The old man sat on the steps that came out of the back of his wagon. Elwin noticed Feffer wasn't beside him. He shrugged, guessing Feffer must have gotten lost in the crowd.

"Greetings, Elwin," Asalla said.

"Hail, Asalla. What great books do you have this year?"

His smile was just a thin tightening of the lips. "This year I have a very special book that I have saved especially for you."

"Just for me? What is it?"

Asalla reached behind him and pulled out an old leather-bound tome. It was a thick volume of papyrus, yellowed by age.

Elwin could feel his eyes widen involuntarily. "What is it?"

"This book tells a story of an ancient past. It tells how the world once was and may yet be again. You see, Elwin. The path of each man is like a leaf on the wind. Though the elemental powers of the natural world guide the leaf to the ground, there are an abundance of paths the leaf may follow to his final destination. There are those paths that shall destroy the leaf, then there are those that will give it a place of regrowth. "

"I see," Elwin said. "Maybe I don't see? Is this a book about elementalists?"

Asalla smiled. "It is my curious friend. In a way. Bound within is an ancient language that has been lost for generations. Elementalists of old used to speak this language with the utmost reverence."

"How much?"

"There is no charge for this one."

"Really?"

Asalla nodded. "Just be sure that you apply its wisdom and learn from the failures of those that came before you."

"Thanks, Asalla. I will."

"There you are," Elwin turned to see Feffer coming out of the crowd. "I didn't think I would ever find you. They opened the door to the inn. There is about to be an announcement."

Elwin turned to thank Asalla again, but the back of his wagon was closed up and the old man was nowhere to be seen.

Feffer pulled him in the opposite direction from the inn. "I know where we can get a better view."

Elwin followed. "Where are we going?"

Feffer didn't answer. He ran away from the crowd behind Jadron's Furrier shop and to the back of Madrowl's Wares. When he saw the new bamboo ladder, Feffer's intentions became clear.

"I don't know about this, Feffer."

"I do it all the time. Besides, how else are we going to see over the crowd?"

Feffer went up without so much as a backward glance.

Elwin was slow to follow with his book under his arm, but he made it to the top without looking down. He slid the book over the lip of the building, then climbed up. Feffer was already at the front of the building. Elwin grabbed his book and ran to where Feffer sat.

The crowd below amassed toward the front of the inn. All the commerce had paused. A giant-sized man with a giant-sized sword on his metal back stood at the front steps of the inn. Next to him stood a girl with auburn hair and golden, brown eyes, sparkling in the sun's light. Standing on the other side of the man was a woman, an image of the younger girl.

He had never even read of anyone more beautiful. Feffer was right, this was a great view. The large man with peppered hair raised his hand. As he did, the roar of the crowd quieted until the only sound was the wind chime that hung on the sign to the Scented Rose.

The man's gruff voice carried. "Citizens of Benedict, I regret to inform you that war has been declared against our peace loving nation—"

A light murmur from the crowd.

"—War has not yet come to our shores, but it will. For years now, we have lent aid to the Alcoan nation against the tyrant known as Bain Solsec—"

The name tickled a memory for Elwin, but he ignored it.

"—who has declared himself king in the Alcoan lands. It appears he has now set his sights on our shores as well. For the first time in our nation's history, we must actively recruit volunteers. Any healthy man aged fourteen and higher will be trained in service of the kingdom. We have counted a total of twenty-seven from this village that are of age.

"By the decree of King Justice, I hereby announce that those eligible, whose list of names include: Wilton Madrowl, Brinsett Matire, ..."

Feffer grabbed Elwin's shoulder, "Did you hear that? Wilton is going to get to fight in the war."

Feffer jumped up and ran back toward the ladder.

"... Barth Gensong ..."

Elwin stood up and followed him, carrying his book.

Feffer reached the ground by the time Elwin made it to the ladder. The world below spun when he looked over the edge. He had forgotten how high up he was.

Elwin sat on the roof and edged toward the ladder, feeling for the first step with his boot. Once firmly touching the ladder, he eased his weight onto the top rung. Then, he took another step. He made it down two more steps with his back facing the ladder, when the wind made the bamboo wobble. His heart began pumping faster and his breaths got shorter. The ground spun beneath him. He took several steadying breaths and tried to force his heartbeat to be calm.

He could feel the wind hit his face, but it felt odd to him. Different.

It was just a breeze, but somehow it felt like something more. He was aware of the wind around him. Not just the invisible touch on his skin. He could feel the wind bouncing on the roof. It didn't make sense, but he could touch the wind, somehow from within. It began to push against him, and he didn't know how to stop it. But it made him feel, alive.

The crisp summer air touched his tongue. It was like the sweet of honey, and the scent held the fragrance of a thousand roses. He could see light shimmering off of every shiny surface. Not sure how, he let it fill him. It rushed into him like a storm, and his body began to ache. Elwin turned his touch into a grasp. He was holding it. He was holding the wind. How was this even possible?

He pushed it out of his grasp, and he felt his foot leave the ladder. He began falling ... upward? The book dropped from his hand to the grass below. His heart pounded as if he had run for half a day. The ache within him grew, forcing him to push more of the wind away from him. And he fell faster but still upward. Below, he saw Feffer round the edge of the warehouse toward the street, looking the other way. Elwin called out to Feffer, but he didn't see him.

"The Lifebringer help me!"

The warehouse began to grow smaller. Arms flailing, he tried to stop falling into the sky.

Elwin stopped pushing the wind. When he held it all in, his body began to fall in the right direction. The wind rushed past him, and the ground was getting closer and closer.

"THE LIFEBRINGER HELP ME!"

As the ground grew nearer, he pushed more of the wind and began flying back upward. Slower this time. He released it slower. Several paces from the ground, he stopped pushing it out, but slower than before. His body eased to the ground with a thud.

Every muscle throbbed. He wasn't sure if it was from the impact or his grasp on the wind. He saw two of the warehouse, and the ground spun.

"I still have some of it! What do I do with it? What in the abyss is happening to me?"

He stood up, grasping his head. He ran around the building toward the town square, swaying as he ran. The man that had spoken and the woman that was with him stood next to Faron's table of swords.

Elwin looked around for anyone to help him. A thought occurred to him.

Asalla might know what to do.

But Elwin couldn't see the wagon. Sweat began to stream down his face, and holding the wind became painful. His body ached all over, and he felt weary to the point of bursting. He ran toward Faron on shaky legs but fell when he got there. Faron's table of weapons stopped his fall. His stomach was sick, and the ground still spun.

"Elwin, what is wrong with your eyes?"

"Faron … there is … *something* wrong with me!"

Elwin couldn't hold it in any longer. Sweat stung his eyes. It hurt too much. He couldn't hold on to it anymore.

Elwin grasped the table, attempting to keep the ground from spinning. Just as he felt he would lose consciousness, he *pushed* the wind from his grasp. Everything happened as if in a dream, like one where everything moved too slowly to be real.

Elwin felt the energy form a burst of wind in front of him. Faron's table flew into the air, sending weapon's flying toward a group of the White Hand. Most of the weapons hit at odd angles, producing pained grunts from the men they struck.

Panic.

The crowd scattered for cover, moving as if the promised war had already found its way to their village.

Elwin was out of breath, and he still felt shaky. Working in the fields had never made him this tired. His legs gave out, and he sat down cross-legged, watching everyone run away.

Faron helped him to his feet. "Are you alright, Elwin?"

"Do not touch him," the woman commanded.

"But there is something wrong with him."

She placed a grip on Elwin's arm and eased him back to the ground. "I know exactly what is wrong with him, and there is nothing the king's newest blacksmith can do about it."

Faron stepped back.

"Elwin is what he called you?"

Elwin nodded. "What is happening to me?"

"You are not in trouble. But I have a very important question for you, Elwin. It is important that you answer me truthfully. Do you understand?"

Elwin nodded again.

"Have you had any strange dreams lately? Within the last couple of days?"

"Last night. How? How did you know that?"

The metal-clad man came back and placed a hand on the woman's shoulder. Elwin hadn't realized he had left until then. His gruff voice was monotone. "Biron is dead. One of the swords struck a killing blow. Everyone else is unharmed."

"Someone is dead?" Elwin's voice broke. "I ... I killed someone?"

The woman closed her eyes and took a long deep breath. When she opened them, they were fixed on Elwin. "I am Jasmine Lifesong. Do you know what it means when someone is an elementalist?"

Tears made her face blur. He nodded to her.

"Listen to me. None of this is your fault. Many in your situation have been less fortunate than you. I have heard tale of an entire village destroyed by a child coming into her powers of fire. You could have killed many more people or even yourself. You cannot blame yourself for this. Alright?"

Elwin gave her a slight nod. *I killed someone? I can't believe I killed him.*

She put her finger under his chin and made him look her in the eyes with a gentle prod. "You know you cannot stay here with your family. You must come with me to the capital city of Justice, so we may register you with the Guardians of Life. I will bear witness on your behalf that this was a grievous accident. That should be enough to appease the Inquisition."

He wiped his tears. "The Inquisition? But I would never serve the Seeker. Why would they—"

"Do not worry." Her voice was stern but not loud. "There are proper protocols to follow. You are very rare. Each generation has less of us than the previous generation. We cannot be so hasty as to destroy innocent children. My testimony should be enough to clear you. So do not worry."

She looked at him, as if expecting an answer. Not sure how to respond, he nodded to her. Then something she had said occurred to him. "Do I really have to leave my family?"

"You have more power in you than I have seen in a long time. Unless there is someone here with enough power to train you, such as a parent or a close relative, you are a danger to those around you. Even now they fear you. People always fear what they do not understand."

She gestured behind him.

Elwin looked around. The square was empty except for the three of them. People looked at him from windows and alleyways. He could see them whispering and staring, all avoiding his gaze.

Even Faron had backed a healthy distance away and stood by the alley next to the inn, though his eyes looked more concerned than afraid. Mr. Madrowl stood with Elwin's parents and grandparents in front of the inn. His mother looked as if she would run to him, if not for Drenen and Willem holding her back.

Then he saw Feffer standing next to Wilton, his mouth opened in a wide grin. He looked to Elwin like a boy who had discovered his favorite toy had just grown a new tail or sprouted wings.

He looked away.

"Come, Elwin."

She offered him her hand. He took it, and she helped him to his feet.

"On the morrow," she said, "we will round up the new recruits for training and depart for Justice. But before you sleep tonight, we must have your first lesson. In the meantime, stay within my sight."

She turned from him and walked toward his parents by the front of the inn, not waiting for a response. He stayed on her heels.

She stopped in front of his father. "I do not sense Elemental power within any of you, but as you are the only people still in the open, I assume you are claiming him as your own?"

Poppe stepped forward, resignation in his voice, "I am Bruece of house Lanier. I am the one who found him. I am his Poppe. "

"Found me?" Elwin asked.

His grandfather avoided Elwin's gaze, and his father held his mother to his bosom, while she sobbed.

"You see Elwin. Elementalists' power is a gift passed through bloodlines. Even those with lesser power are detectable for the trained eye. Your parents do not have the gift. Did you not find it odd that you are the only child from this town with blond hair and blue eyes?"

His words felt hollow, but they rushed out of him. "I know the gift of the Elements is passed through bloodlines, but not all of those with the gift can sense their powers. My parents never learned how to use the Elements. I read about it in a book. I knew they couldn't sense their powers, but I always hoped I would. I look like my great grandma on my father's side. They have passed into the shelter of the Lifebringer's hand now. Tell her Father."

"Elwin," her voice was soft, "if your parents had the gift, I would be able to sense their ability. After training, you will be able to sense it, too. You are the only person in this village with the gift. Your grandfather found you. Remember?"

Elwin's bottom lip quivered, and he felt tears in his eyes. He refused to blink and let them fall. If he cried, then she would be right. There was nothing to cry about. There was an explanation for this.

"My guess is that you are Alcoan in lineage," Jasmine continued. "The nation is across the Tranquil Sea. They are who we assist in the war effort."

The gruff warrior cleared his throat and gave her a stony look.

Jasmine smiled at the man. "Perhaps you can see to settling the men. I have a few questions for Elwin's family."

She had not given the last word any more inflection than the others, but for some reason, it had a sting. Elwin shook his head. Jasmine had to be wrong. They *were* his parents, but what did Poppe mean, he had *found* him? Why did nothing make any sense?

"Can we go somewhere without so many eyes and ears?" Jasmine said looking to the shudders and alleys, where people watched.

"This way." Poppe walked around to the back of the inn. Elwin followed without looking around. He heard Mr. Madrowl's voice saying, "Feffer, get back here."

He looked over his shoulder to see Feffer grumbling, but he didn't follow. Elwin felt a pang of regret. It would have been nice to have Feffer with him for this. Whatever *this* was.

The back steps had a porch with an awning leading to the stables beside the inn. Several soldiers stood at the opening. Two younger men with dark hair and dark eyes studied Elwin with deep scowls.

He looked down to avoid their stares and felt himself being herded. When he looked up, he found himself in the private dining hall that Poppe reserved for outlander lords and ladies passing through. He had never been allowed to play in here. The large, redwood table was lacquered and kept clean with a golden candle-stand for a centerpiece. The far window had been framed with white molding that also bordered the room.

On the wall above the entryway hung a large broadsword, handed down through Poppe's family. Elwin had never seen it taken from the wall. The many shelves had books and trinkets from around the world. Most of the books talked about history and didn't have much to do with elementalists. But his grandfather had let him borrow them on occasion. That was the extent of his time spent in this room, short enough periods to pick out a book for reading.

"Have a seat, Elwin," Jasmine said.

Elwin looked away from the bookshelf and let his eyes focus on the room once more. He was the only one still standing. Jasmine had taken the seat at the table's head, while his parents and grandfather sat in the three chairs on the right side of the table, closest to the head.

Elwin pulled out the chair on the other side and sat next to Jasmine.

"Now," Jasmine said. "Where did you *find* Elwin?"

"Uh," Poppe began, "You see. There was a woman that came here. She had a worn face, and she was dressed in rags ..."

Elwin listened to his Poppe recite the tale. It almost sounded like one of his stories. Elwin kept waiting for him to bring in the part about the evil wizard or band of trolls that had to be dispatched to save the village. Maybe it was a dream. Maybe he would wake any moment.

"That's it," Poppe sighed. "She left a letter and a pendant."

"Do you have them near?" Jasmine asked.

Poppe stood and walked to the far shelf. At the top was a small lock box. He opened it and pulled out a silver amulet with a green-stoned pendant and a folded up parchment. After handing them to Jasmine, he retook his seat without a word or so much as a glance at Elwin.

Elwin watched Jasmine's face as she read the letter, but she did not reveal its contents. She gave her head a slight shake.

"What is it?" Elwin asked. "Is it true?"

"Who has seen this letter?" Jasmine asked.

"Just us," his father said. "We have raised Elwin as if he was our own. Most of the farms are far enough out that most of the community is unaware that anyone has had a new child until the festival. Elwin was young enough, we just kept the letter secret."

"From everyone." Elwin did not wipe the tears. "How could you not tell me?"

"We were waiting for the right time," his mother said. "I am so sorry."

"What is important now," Jasmine said, "is that I have found you. I can begin your training."

She offered the pendant to him. "Take this."

The light glittered off the green stone. He could *feel* it, somehow. Elwin was sure he could close his eyes and point to it from anywhere in the room.

"What is it?" he asked without touching it.

"It is perfectly safe, I assure you. It has a protective ward on it, made from the power of Spirit, Air, and Fire. There might even be a little Water and Earth as well. It was a gift from your birth mother."

Elwin took the pendant. "I have never seen a stone like this."

Jasmine gave him a reassuring smile. "It has the appearance of an emerald, though it is far more rare. There are several artifacts in this world that give power to its owner. Some have minor powers, but some can destroy this village. This one was wrought for a peaceful purpose. Someday you will be able to feel the powers that created such an item. Maybe, you will even learn to craft one. Though it will take some time studying it in further detail to know its exact purpose. Wear the pendant beneath your shirt. There are those who would try to steal it for the worth of the stone alone. But the chain is made of silver as well."

Elwin pulled the chain over his head. Immediately he felt calm wash over his body.

"What was that?"

"It was the power of the ward taking effect."

Elwin placed the stone beneath his shirt. "What did it do to me?"

"The effects were nearly undetectable, but I believe it is meant to hide you from scrying."

"Scrying?"

"There will be plenty of time for questions, later," Jasmine smiled. "I will have your grandfather prepare an extra bed in my room for you. There are many things we must discuss before you sleep, but for now I must prepare for tomorrow's departure."

When Jasmine stood, his family stood as well.

"So that's it then?" his mother said. "You are just going to take him? And we have no say in the matter?"

Elwin's father grabbed her hand, but he said nothing.

Jasmine's smile was soft. "I need not remind you of what happened today. That is but a fraction of the power that Elwin will some day master. But without training, he will surely die. The only question is, how many will die with him? Besides, his name is on the ledger for recruitment, anyway. At least now he is not likely to see fighting anytime soon, which is more than I can say for the other boys leaving on the morrow, all of an age with Elwin."

His mother began to cry, and his father cradled her in his arms.

His grandfather spoke as he moved toward the door. "I will prepare that extra bed."

Poppe left without looking back. The door stayed open and sounds from the common room spilled in. There were no distinguishable voices, but he could hear music and laughter. Someone played the dulcimer. He could also hear the flute and harp.

Maybe they would not treat him any differently.

Jasmine moved toward the doorway. "This way, Elwin. Remember to stay within sight."

Elwin followed Jasmine down the hallway into the common room.

Jandar, the furrier, sat at the closest table facing Elwin. Faron sat with at the same table but faced the other way. Jandar's head was thrown back in mid-laughter. Upon seeing Elwin, his laughter broke off into a choking sound, followed by silence. He leaned forward and began to eye his mug of ale. Faron partially turned to look at him and gave Elwin a nod and thin smile.

A wave of silence, starting at the entry hall and working toward the front door, rippled across the room. One instrument at a time, the music faded until the room sounded empty.

Narma Shoemaker sat at the next table with her three children. Her arm stretched out as if to protect them from a wild dog. Tramn the horse rancher, Bryne the carpenter, everyone avoided direct eye contact. Even Danna. He wondered if she would still invite him to smell her freshly made candles next time he walked past her shop. Elwin looked around for any friendly face. Momme was the only person in the room looking at him. Her smile was warm and inviting.

Jasmine leaned over and whispered in his ear, "Go to the bar and get something to eat. Everything will be fine. I promise. Go on. I will not be far."

He didn't look at Jasmine. He didn't look at anyone. Elwin just watched each step to make sure he didn't trip as he made his way to an empty barstool between Barth Gadseden, the thatcher, and another empty stool. Without a word, Barth stood with his head down and left the inn.

Elwin put his hands on the bar and stared forward. Momme placed a mug that smelled like apple cider in front of him.

"It will all be okay, Elwin," her voice a whisper. Though her eyes filled with tears, she still smiled at him. He looked down at his hands, avoiding her gaze.

"I will be right back with some lunch."

After several moments, he heard murmured whispers behind him, but he couldn't make out any words. He wasn't sure he wanted to know what they were saying.

The inn door crashed open.

"Elwin!" Feffer's voice broke the silence like a shattered window.

Elwin could hear several chairs sliding on the wooden floor behind him as people quickly stood to the ready.

"Feffer H. Madrowl," Elwin heard Willem say. At the same time, he heard many others curse beneath their breath.

Feffer jumped onto to stool next to Elwin, "*I* was *chosen* to go to the capital for training. I will be going with you to Justice."

"Everyone over fourteen namedays was *chosen*," Elwin said.

"Yeah. But," Feffer said, "didn't you hear me? We get to stay together. We can watch out for each other."

"Greeeaaat," Elwin exhaled. "Best Summer Solstice ever. "

"I know," Feffer said. "I was thinking the same thing. Except for the guy who died."

Elwin put his head in his hands and closed his eyes. When would this nightmare be over?

Chapter 5

A NEW PATH

Being alone in the large room felt strange. There were only four such rooms of this size in the whole inn, all located on the top floor. Growing up, Elwin had never been allowed in here, even though the rooms had rarely been used. He supposed the reason had something to do with the extra decorations. The room had a similar feel to Poppe's study. The ornate tapestry might as well have an inscription saying, *Off Limits*.

He could see the failing light fighting its way through the opaque curtains. He sat on a simple chair in the corner by a window on the outer wall. Even with its red-gold cushion and lacquered finish, it seemed the least expensive place to rest his bum. Built from the redwoods, the rest of the furniture had been cushioned by silk pillows.

Next to him, the cold fireplace nestled between the two windows. A short hallway beside him led to two servant's rooms, and the door opposite opened to the master room. Altogether the suite could have passed for a small farmhouse. It seemed too much by far for a single traveler.

The door opened from the outer hallway, pulling him from his thoughts.

Jasmine entered with the girl from the square. She was even more beautiful up close. The white dress formed around the curves of her body, and long curls the color of honey framed her perfect face.

She carried a silver candelabra, housing a single candle. The light danced off her golden eyes. Like pools of dark liquid, a man could drown in their depths. He couldn't imagine a more beauti—

"Elwin," Jasmine said, cutting off his thoughts. "This is my daughter, Zarah."

Elwin jumped off the chair to greet them.

"Hi," his voice cracked. His cheeks burned as he cleared his throat. "Ahem. Hi."

Her smile was genuine and inviting, but her voice was formal. "Hello, Elwin."

"Zarah is going to join us for your lesson," Jasmine said, "if that is alright."

Elwin did not want to risk his voice cracking again, so he nodded his agreement, hoping he did not look as eager as he felt.

"Good. Let us sit by the fireplace."

Jasmine sat in the single chair, leaving the lover's sofa for Zarah and him. Zarah placed the candelabra on the round, lacquered table in front of the sofa, then sat.

He sat next to her, staring straight ahead. He could still see her from the corner of his eye, and the scent of her filled him. She smelled of flowers and fruit with a touch of salt from the sweat of a day's ride.

"First," Jasmine said, "you must relax."

Elwin exhaled and leaned his back against the cushion. He tried to appear relaxed, but found it difficult to do so with his heart pounded. He had to force himself to breath in and out. Every part of him wanted to turn and gape at Zarah, but he forced his eyes to watch Jasmine.

"Until we return to the castle, I will not know all of your gifts, but I do know that you are blessed with at least Air. Judging by the power that I sensed from you earlier, I would imagine that you have more ability than that, or will with time. I have the Elements of Air and Water, as does my daughter. And we are both Life bound, so we have the power of Life, through Spirit, as well."

Elwin took the opportunity to look at Zarah again. The light still danced around her dark eyes. She caught Elwin's gaze and gave him another smile. Elwin's heart melted, and his skin crawled away. He looked back to Jasmine, trying to keep his breathing calm.

"Your gifts do not always manifest at the same time. Usually, if you are to have more than one, the strongest will be the first one to show. And that will be the one we will focus on for now.

"Your essence is like a cup waiting to be filled with power, but as you drink from the cup, it gets smaller. As you exercise your powers, the size of your essence will grow. Like all people, your soul—or essence—resides in the shadow realm, which travels with you, parallel to the physical realm."

She smiled. "I see you have a question."

"I do," Elwin said. "What is the shadow realm?"

"The shadow realm, sometimes called the realm of Spirits, parallels this realm," she gestured to the room, "the physical realm, our world, all of Arinth. The dream you had last night was not a dream. When your physical body slept, your soul awakened in the shadow realm. All souls reside there, but only elementalists whose souls are awakened are aware of it.

"This is where you replenish your power. When you entered it last night, you gained the first of your Elemental power. When you call upon the Elements, they come from your essence in the shadow realm and are channeled through your body in the physical realm. We call this process *taming the Elements*. This is how you were able to do what you did today."

"I still don't understand. I will have to go to the shadow realm again? And how did I tame anything?"

She nodded. "You will enter the shadow realm each night when you sleep. You must be careful not to let your mind wander in the shadow realm. This is of the utmost importance. You must learn to master your thoughts. There is a danger in the shadow realm. Abaddon, the Seeker of Souls, has dominion there."

Elwin flinched at the name but remained silent. If Jasmine noticed, she did not let it show. She continued unabated.

"It is in the shadow realm that an elementalist can surrender his soul to the Seeker for the Element of Death. While in the shadow realm, your body is your sanctuary. As long as you remain near your sanctuary, Abaddon has no power over you. Those who surrender to him are the Death bound. If you wander too far, you give the Seeker the opportunity to tempt you with his *Dark Gifts*. Until you know what signs to look for and how to escape him, you should just watch over your sleeping body."

The gift. Life preserve him! That had been the Seeker in truth and not just a dream!

"In return for one's soul, Abaddon gives the Death bound a unique power. Great is the temptation to accept his gifts, but there is no greater price than one's soul. The Lifebringer imparts his followers with the gifts of Life, as well."

"I have Visions," Zarah interjected with a smugness in her voice. "It is my gift."

"What does that mean?" Elwin asked, trying to keep the trembling from his voice.

"It means Zarah needs to keep quiet and let me teach you," Jasmine said.

Zarah's cheeks reddened. "Sorry, Mother." Her voice sounded more petulant than chastised.

"Unlike most of us," Jasmine said, "Zarah has no control over her gift. But, in moments of need, the Lifebringer will allow her a glimpse of the future. I see you have a question. Ask it."

Elwin did have a question, but he didn't want to think about Abaddon. Or the gift *he* had spoken of.

"How do I become Life bound?" Elwin asked instead. "Will that keep the Seeker from finding me?"

"If you are bound to Life, he will have no power over your soul," Jasmine said. "But even so, he is still dangerous to all. And, I am afraid it is not possible until you can sense the power of Spirit. This happens at different times for every elementalist. I know some whom have not sensed Spirit until very late in life. I know others, like Zarah, who sensed Spirit before even coming to her other powers. When it happens, there will be no mistaking it."

Elwin didn't like her answer. If he couldn't be Life bound, how could he stay safe?

"I have read about the four Elements: Air, Earth, Fire, and Water," Elwin said. "But the books don't talk much about Spirit other than to say it has been split into Life and Death. How can I find it?"

"If I knew a way to guide you to sense Spirit," Jasmine said in a patient voice, "it would be the first lesson we would have. It is there for all. Even now, I can sense the tether from your Spirit to your body. It has always baffled me that it is so difficult to find, since together these are the sum of your existence. Our true forms are our essence, and this body is an anchor to the physical realm. The tether is somewhere in between and is difficult to see. One day, you will become aware of it, and that awareness will never leave you. When that day comes, you can be bound."

"Maybe that's why my books never speak of it," Elwin said, feeling annoyed and not bothering to hide it. "It doesn't seem to do anything beyond confuse people."

Jasmine gave a smile so brief, Elwin second guessed whether or not it had been there. When Jasmine spoke, her voice held no amusement.

"Even without becoming bound, Spirit has more use than you can know. Spirit allows the Elements to be tethered or attached to objects. The process of tethering is an advanced practice. I have been training Zarah for almost six years, and only now am I teaching her to tether."

"So," Elwin said, "our Spirits have tethers and the Elements have tethers?"

"No," Jasmine said in a patient voice. "We can use Spirit to transfer a piece of our tether to connect the Elements to an object or person," Jasmine said. "For example, the ever-torches lining the streets or ever-candles in nobles' homes are such. These are made with Fire and Spirit. Spirit is used to tether Fire to the candle or torch."

"Wait," Elwin said. "You said the tether is what keeps our souls attached to our bodies. If we take some of it and tie it something else, won't that hurt?"

She nodded as if in a gesture of approval. "Yes and no. If performed properly, though taxing, it does not cause pain. A tether regenerates upon sleeping as does our used essence. However, if over-extended, even the most skilled in Spirit can sever the tethering between his essence in the shadow realm and his body. If this happens, the body dies."

Her grim face made him shudder. Every part of being an elementalist seemed dangerous. Why had he ever wanted to become one?

"Maybe it is good that I can't even sense it," he said.

"Other than not being able to become Life bound," she said, "I agree. Much would become simpler if you were bound, but I would prefer no novice sense her own tether." Her eyes did not look at Zarah, but Zarah's eyes narrowed as if she had.

"So," Elwin said as the question formed in his mind, "is there a difference between taming Spirit and tethering?"

Jasmine smiled. "Questions are good. It means you are eager to learn, but you need to learn how to tame Air and release before any of this knowledge will be of use to you."

Elwin flushed. He had asked a lot of questions, but he had wanted to become an elementalist since he had first read of them. Now that he had one in front of him, he found every answer brought about a new question.

"But to answer your question," Jasmine continued, "tethering any Element is permanent, while taming Spirit is not. The talents vary depending upon whether or not you are bound. According to the Edicts of Fariomarus the Life binder, binding one's soul to Life or Death tethers you to good or evil, the Lifebringer or Abaddon. Choosing to bind to either does limit your capabilities in a way, by narrowing one's focus. This is why many elementalists remain neutral. Spirit alone can be used to alter the mood of a person. We will get to all of this in time."

Elwin opened his mouth to ask another question, then closed it. She had said no more questions. But, he wanted to understand his dream. Or whatever it was. If it meant being safer from the Seeker, he wanted to be Life bound as soon as possible. But if he couldn't be bound to Life, didn't that mean he couldn't be bound to Death?

"Alright," Jasmine said. "You look ready to burst. One more question before your lesson."

Elwin blurted his question out. "If I can't be bound, what does the Seeker want with me?"

"Ah," Jasmine said, "that is a very good question. There are many theories as to the why of it. Most are of a consensus that his seeking souls has something to do with the Awakening. No one really knows. However, one thing is certain. To be bound to Death, all one need do is seek out Abaddon in the shadow realm. Perhaps he has the power to show one his tether. We cannot be sure. But there is a very important lesson in this." Jasmine gave him a serious look. "It is easier to cause Death than to create Life."

Elwin shuddered. To think, he had already seen the Seeker. What if he had taken the *gift*? He would have been Death bound before even knowing he was an elementalist.

"You seem upset," Jasmine raised an eyebrow. "What is it?"

"I think I saw him," Elwin admitted. "He had shadows for eyes. He said things that don't make sense. I thought it was just a dream."

Jasmine blinked. "You actually saw him on your first visit to the shadow realm? What did he say?"

"He spoke like he knew me," Elwin said. "Solsec. He had called me Elwin of Solsec."

Then, Elwin remembered where he had heard the name. Bain of Solsec had been the tyrant the man had spoken of earlier. He felt sick. He swallowed an acid taste and forced the rest out.

"He called me Son of Bain and said I was of his bloodline. He wanted me to take his gift and give him my soul. He touched me. It was cold. I can't believe it wasn't a dream. He said he had been waiting for me for a long time, and that I would Awaken them."

"Mother," Zarah said, "does that mean he—"

"It means nothing," Jasmine said. "Abaddon is the father of all falsehoods. Elwin, have you spoken of this *dream* and what Abaddon said to you? Your parents? Feffer? Anyone?" The intensity in her voice scared him.

Elwin shook his head. "I didn't even know it was more than a dream until now. I didn't say anything to anyone. I probably would have talked to Feffer about it, but I didn't get a chance."

Jasmine took in a deep breath and exhaled slowly. "Do not tell him or anyone else, and in the meantime, do not leave sight of your body while in the shadow realm."

"What do you mean?" Elwin said, "I don't even know how I dreamed myself into the shadow realm to begin with. How do I *stay close to my body*? What does all of this mean? Why did he call me son of Bain?"

"Calm down," she said in a firm voice. "It will be alright, Elwin. Praise the Lifebringer that I found you the day your powers manifested. He works in mysterious ways. I will show you what you need to know when we sleep. The Seeker would deceive you in any way he thought would gain your soul. Push it from your mind.

"But now, I must begin your first lesson. I must show you how to fill your essence with power and hold it. Once you can do this, you will not be a harm to those around you. Your essence cannot yet hold much safely. With time and training, your power will grow, but for now you must only pull in a small amount. Now, tell me what happened today in the square. Start from the beginning."

The sudden change of topics left him with mixed feelings. He didn't want to think about any part of what had happened, but he wanted to understand. He took a deep breath and tried to remember.

"Well," Elwin said slowly to gather his thoughts. "I was on top of the Madrowl's shop. It is the building across the street overlooking the square. The man started talking about war, then he said Wilton's name. That's when Feffer ran off. I followed him to the ladder, but it was so high up, I got dizzy. That is when I felt a breeze. But I didn't feel it with my body. I felt it with my mind. Before I realized it, the wind had *filled* me. I know it sounds like madness to say aloud, but that is what happened. When I pushed against it, I fell upward. I held it in again, and began to fall toward the ground."

Elwin felt a chill go up his spine. "I thought I was going to die."

"You flew," Zarah said. "Your first time and you flew." He couldn't tell if her voice sounded full of awe or jealously. He turned to see her looking at him. When he met her eyes, his heart began beating faster.

"This is no small feat," Jasmine said. Elwin took the excuse to look away from Zarah. His heart was still pounding.

"Neither is what you did in the square. We call that a wind thrust. You pulled in more than you could handle at one time. When you could no longer hold the power, it came out in a burst. Just as one must train his muscles to lift heavy objects, you must train your essence to handle more power. Think of it like lifting a heavy boulder. Maybe you have the strength to pull it over your head, but you cannot hold it there for long. In time, if you lift the same boulder enough times, your muscles will be able to hold it there. If you attempt to lift a boulder too heavy, then you could permanently damage a muscle."

He gave her an annoyed look. She always seemed to speak in riddles.

She sighed. "In other words, it is alright to pull in some power of Air to hold, but never fill your essence unless you have a specific purpose in mind. Now, we have to find the right size boulder for you to lift. Does that make sense to you?"

No, he decided after a minute. It didn't make sense, but he didn't want to sound dim-witted in front of Zarah. So he shrugged and said. "I think so."

"Now, close your eyes and relax your mind," Jasmine said. "Be aware of the Air around you. It is a part of you and you of it. It is alive in your mind."

Elwin did as instructed. With his eyes closed he could *feel* the Air around him. Starting with his hands, the cool Air flowed down his arms and pulsed with a vibrant energy. It covered his body and touched every corner of the room. He could feel it surrounding Zarah and Jasmine.

"I can see by your face that you can feel it. But I want you to pay attention. You will feel the power enter myself and Zarah," Jasmine said. "Slowly, Zarah. There, Elwin, do you feel that?"

He did. It was as if the pulse flowed into where they sat. He said as much aloud.

"Good," she said. "Very slowly, I want you to open up your essence."

"Okay," Elwin said. "How?"

"You must allow it to flow into you, like you did earlier, when you 'touched' it."

Elwin focused on the pulse. It was like his own heartbeat. He was a part of the pulse. Slowly, he *reached* for it with his mind. His body began to pulse in rhythm with the energy, and it began to fill him. Slowly at first, then it came at him like a flood.

He could feel the vibrations from Jasmine's voice, but he could not make out her words. He could sense the ripples of heat from the candles flowing into the Air. The moisture in the Air between each strand, each breath. Each sound was a ripple of power, from which he could draw. But he didn't know how to turn it off. It kept coming and he didn't know how to make it go the other way. It felt as if he was in a rapid river of Air and could hear nothing over the roar of the flows around him.

Then there was pain. From head to toe, he ached. He opened his eyes. Both Jasmine and Zarah were on their feet. Their voices sounded odd, as if coming from a well.

"Do something Mother!"

"Link with me."

Elwin felt the flow of Zarah's power join with her mother's. It was like pouring two half-filled mugs into a larger decanter. Then he felt *something* seize hold of his flow of power and *rip* it from his grasp.

Pain wracked his body. Every inch felt as if he was on fire. He rolled off the sofa, grasping his head. The next instant the pain was gone, and he felt his body being lifted by an invisible hand. It eased him back onto the sofa. Neither Zarah nor Jasmine had moved.

She had lifted him with Air? He wasn't sure how he knew, but the power that lifted him had come from Jasmine.

He sagged into the sofa. "What happened?"

He could still feel the power, but it was seeping from them, all three of them. The Air stirred around him as Jasmine emptied his essence. His muscles felt weary. Elwin wanted to close his eyes again.

Zarah plopped down next to him, sweat beginning on her brow. Her wide eyes glowered at him.

"I said slowly." Jasmine's jaw was tight, and her breathing sounded as if she had been running.

"I'm sorry," Elwin said. "I tried to, but it just all happened so quickly."

"It is alright." Jasmine sat down. "We are linked now, which means I have control of your essence. You will still be aware of everything I do, but you will have no control."

"Why did you not do this in the beginning?" Elwin asked.

"A person must already have power in one's essence to initiate a linking. That was to be our next course of action had you been listening to me."

"Oh," Elwin said. "But we are linked now?"

"Yes," Jasmine said. "Of a sort. What I did to you is called taking. This process has the same outcome, but it requires me to battle your will. Fortunately for us, you do not know how to guard against this sort of attack. Had you fought me, even a little, I might have failed in taking your essence."

She was silent for a moment, watching Elwin. Her eyes did not hold any compassion.

"I understand." He looked away. "I could have hurt someone."

"You must focus at all times," Jasmine said. "At least in the beginning. Someday, it will be the same as breathing. And flying through the air will be the same as walking or running."

"You are so powerful," Zarah said with awe in her voice. "What you held in your essence by yourself ... it was so much. I was afr—"

"Yes," Jasmine said. "Like I said before, Elwin has more potential than I have seen in some time."

"Mother." Zarah stood up. "Are you not worried about what Abad—"

"Young lady," Jasmine said. "I am trying to give Elwin instruction. If you cannot guard your tongue, perhaps you should retire for the evening?"

Zarah sat back down and crossed her arms beneath her bosom. Elwin blinked as she cast him a look suggesting that he was to blame for her chastisement.

"Wise decision. Now, where were we?" Jasmine said. "Ah yes. Now that we are linked, I am going to use our combined essence to tame the power of Air. I want you to pay attention to every detail.

First, you will notice that I have drained our essence to an amount I can handle without much thought. I can—"

"I noticed how you released some of it back into our surroundings without hurting anyone."

"Very good. Now do not interrupt."

Elwin felt his cheeks heat up. "Oh. Sorry."

"The first task you will do on your own is exactly that. You will simply fill your essence and empty it. Before you are entrusted with this, you must observe me. Like I was saying before I was interrupted, I can handle the amount we are holding for long periods. However, if I pull in half again as much as I am holding, I will begin to have trouble just holding it. But I can always release the power harmlessly back into the air. Just as if you were to lift a large rock over your head, you can then ease it back down or drop it."

"Now, watch closely …"

Elwin didn't remember falling asleep, but he knew Jasmine had worked with him well into the night. He just remembered being exhausted one moment and standing next to his own body the next. To say it felt strange to look down upon himself was to say a dragon was a big lizard, but he had no words for the feeling.

He could see the slow rise and fall of his own chest. Both his sleeping form and the bed seemed smaller than he remembered. The room felt cramped to him here. Looking up, he could touch the ceiling. Elwin chided himself for wasting time.

Jasmine had said to meet in the common room. He brought the image of Poppe's stage to his mind and imagined himself to be there. A moment later, he was there. Elwin jumped when he saw the two translucent forms standing next to the bar. One of the shapes stood a foot taller than the other, but neither stretched much beyond the top of the bar. After a moment, the details of both began to stand out to him, and he recognized the two figures.

Zarah stared at him with a look of surprise and Jasmine blinked several times as her eyes followed up the length of his body, craning her neck to see his face. When her eyes met his, Jasmine said in a voice of icy calm. "How did you arrive here? Did you do it intentionally?"

"Yes," Elwin said. Why were they acting so odd?"I did the same thing last night when I went to the forest. And again when I returned to my bed."

"That is very good. It takes most of us many tries to be able to transport to other places with a thought. At least to do so intentionally is very good. You can only travel in this manner to places in which you are extremely familiar. With time you may be able to transport to people. But it is very difficult.

"Now, you will find that time does not pass the same while we are in the shadow realm as it does during the day. Time seems to move much more swiftly, so we must make efficient use of our time. Do you understand?"

Elwin nodded.

"Good," she smiled. "First, you must know how to defend yourself here. Otherwise, you can be taken as I did to you earlier. You must learn to have two minds; one on your physical body and the other on your essence here."

"Two minds?" Elwin said. "How am I supposed to do that?"

She gave him a reassuring smile. "It will come more easily than you think. When you walk, you are aware of your feet; even though, you are not focused on them. If you stub a toe or trip, your mind responds to the change and reacts. You will need to do so with your essence as well. If an elementalist takes you unaware, she can control your essence. The taking happens here in the shadow realm.

"Imagine a ship atop the water. An anchor on the ocean floor holds a boat in place, but the ship on the ocean's surface is free to move. As I have said before, our body is like the anchor to which our essence is tethered. Like the boat, our essence is free to move here, even as our bodies move in the physical realm. Understand?"

"Yes," Elwin said by reflex. Then he shook his head."Um. No. What does this have to do with taking?"

"That is the right question," she smiled. "Right now, your conscious mind is here. However, when your essence joins with your body, your consciousness joins with your body. But, your essence does not reside inside your body. It is tethered to your body and follows you."

"Ah," Elwin said, understanding. "Like the boat and the anchor thing."

"Yes," she said. "In the shadow realm our essence can roam very far."

Her eyes narrowed seriously. *"Again, I cannot stress the dangers of this enough. Until I tell you otherwise, you do not go farther from your body than you are right now. Understand?"* The word carried weight like a command rather than a question.

Elwin nodded with as much vigor as he could muster. Until he became Life bound, he wouldn't move far from his body. Even then, he may not.

Her smile returned. *"When you are awake, you still control your essence, but it does not stray far from your body. In time, you will learn to see with it in a way. Eventually, you will learn to send your essence out and see what the wind can see. This is called Riding the Wind. The other Elements provide other gifts. We will get to those in time. Once you can Ride the Wind, you will be considered a master in Air."*

Elwin frowned. Boats and tethers? His books hadn't spoken of any of this, and she didn't make much sense. How was he supposed to do any of this? He didn't even know how to hold onto the power without hurting anyone. When was she going to show him that? Maybe he could just learn how not to hurt people and come back to the farm.

"Elwin?" Jasmine said. *"Do you have a question?"*

"I don't even know what to ask," Elwin said, not bothering to hide his annoyance. *"Are we still talking about taking? How do I protect myself? How do I keep from hurting other people?"*

"Patience," she said in a calm voice. *"A baby needs to be aware of his hand before he can learn how to use his fingers. He needs to understand how to move his feet before he can walk."*

Elwin snapped his jaw closed and tried not to look sulky at the subtle rebuke. A baby. Hmmph.

"Now," Jasmine continued. *"Your essence will need to be conditioned. When an elementalist attempts to take your essence, his essence grapples yours. For this reason, we will need to train you in hand-to-hand combat. Though many of the skills learned upon training your body will help you here, the converse is not necessarily true. Here you will gain the knowledge of hand-to-hand combat, but you must train your body to feel the motions in order to make proper use of the knowledge in the physical realm. Does this make sense?"*

Elwin nodded. *"I need to learn how to fight with my hands."*

Jasmine sighed. *"That is the short of it. Yes. Our nights spent here will serve two purposes. First, we will teach you how to fill your essence with Air and release the Air back into the environment. Next, we will condition your essence for combat. Are you ready?"*

Finally. "Yes."

"Very good. Now, you must learn to control your breathing. This exercise will help you with control. Your essence draws the power, but it is your body that feels the flow of Air. Even though your soul roams here, you are still tethered to your body. Even if you cannot feel the strings that make it so, focus and you can feel your body."

Elwin listened as Jasmine guided him through the process. He could feel his body in the room above. He could point to where he laid sleeping as if there were no walls. His chest was still rising and falling in a slow, steady rhythm. He could feel the warmth of the day waning by the sun's absence.

"Now," Jasmine said, "in a moment I want you to allow the power of Air to enter you. Then you will release it without use. But first watch me. Zarah, on my cue."

Elwin could feel the Air enter Jasmine, then Zarah. But he could also see the effects. A white glow swirled around them and conjoined with their forms. After a moment, they became less opaque, and both began to glow softly. They held onto the power for several moments. As they released their hold on Air, they became translucent again.

"Your turn," Jasmine said. "Did you see how it was done?"

"I felt it," Elwin said. "I think I can do it."

He took a deep breath, and he focused on his body as Jasmine had instructed him. He opened up to Air by touching the flow around him. More softly this time. Like opening a sealed door, the Air wanted to flow into him. But instead of opening the door wide, he cracked it, and the power came in at a trickle.

To stop the trickle, he stopped focusing on the flow. Unlike before, there was no ache this time. He felt as if he could run for miles. Looking around, the corners of the room became more crisp. His arm was more solid, but it did not appear to be glowing like Zarah and Jasmine had been. But, he looked up to see Zarah and Jasmine both squinting.

"Not too much, Elwin," Jasmine said.

"This is a good amount, I think," Elwin said. "I could probably hold this all day."

"You do not feel strained at all?" Zarah said.

"No," Elwin said.

Jasmine gave Zarah a look of rebuke and said, "Okay. I want you to attempt to release it. Do not under any circumstances push it. Do you know what I mean when I say push it?"

Elwin nodded. "I think that is what I did to the table."

"Yes. Exactly. Now, releasing Air is similar to what you did to absorb it, but instead you turn the flow outward."

Elwin felt the power inside him and allowed it to flow out of him. It was faster than when it came in, like letting go of a leaf.

"Very good, Elwin," Jasmine said. "We have time for you to practice this task a few more times before first light."

"Already? But I just fell asleep."

"I told you, time seems to move faster here," Jasmine said. "And it was already late when we retired for the evening. Now, are you ready?"

Elwin nodded.

"Very well. I want you to focus on your breathing. You can feel your body above ..."

Chapter 6

THE JOURNEY

Sunlight spilled into the open window. The morning breeze of summer tickled the opaque drapes as it entered the small bedroom. The wind was cool. A nice contrast to what the day held.

Though, marching in the summer's heat was the least of Wilton's concerns. He was being ordered to march. Then he would be ordered to kill.

Kill or be killed.

Wilton pushed those thoughts from his mind, and he stared at his leather backpack resting on his bed.

He packed three sets of clothes and his life's savings into his backpack. His father had given him the pack and a good portion of his money, and he had done the same for Feffer. Wilton breathed in a slow, steady breath and exhaled just as slowly.

I can't believe the little snit is actually glad to be going, he thought. No. The word was joyful. Too young and naïve to understand what it meant to be a soldier. Feffer thought it all a big game.

"We could die."

The thought of death stuck in his mind. It was said that in the end, a soul would return to the Lifebringer. He would then be judged by his deeds in life. Then, he would either be sheltered for eternity in the Lifebringer's Hand or be cast into the abyss to spend eternity in darkness.

"I know I am a good person, but ..."

Wilton looked at his pack again and debated, yet again, whether or not he should defect. He could make his way north through the Carotid Forest to Goldspire. From there, he could make his way to North Port and book passage to Alcoa. He could get a job in a merchant's shop or on an outer farm.

But the rumors Wilton had heard did not make Alcoa a great prospect either. The war had not made it all the way to Alcoa City, but the southern lands were being overrun. Rumor said Kalicodon had been attacked as well. The Isles of Maards had yet to be touched, but from what he had heard, even they would join the war. The Blood Isle was not likely see the war, but it was the thumping Blood Isle. Cannibals and worse were said to live there. Was anywhere safe?

Now that war had come to the Island Nations and to Justice, it seemed he could not escape it.

"If I must fight in a war," Wilton said, "it might as well be here in defense of my home."

His door banged open without so much as a tap.

"Who are you talking to?" Feffer said, as he bounced into the room.

Wilton stared at his younger brother. He was almost of height with him and nearly three years his junior. He couldn't say why, but that grated him.

"What do you want, Feffer?"

"I am already packed. We are supposed to leave soon." Feffer's voice held an annoying amount of enthusiasm.

"Father will be left to tend the shop by himself. All of this work, for a single aging man. How will he get on without our help? "

"I hadn't thought of that."

Wilton suppressed a smile when Feffer's eyes widened with surprise. That would take a little pep out of his step, at least.

"Boys," his father's voice called from below. "Come down here, it is almost time."

Feffer walked out the door ahead of him. Wilton followed his younger brother to the railing of the loft, which went around the entirety of the large storehouse. The bedrooms and his father's office were located all on one side, jutting over the goods below. His father sold everything from weapons to grain, even some exotic herbs. Wilton had been raised learning the best trade routes in the nation. If he left Justice, that knowledge wouldn't help him.

Feffer ran ahead of Wilton, skipping most of the steps on the way to the ground floor. Wilton took each step with deliberate precision.

He stood next to his brother and faced his father.

Tears rimmed Willem's eyes. His voice cracked slightly on the first word. "Boys, I know you will make me proud. I am proud of you already. Neither of you needs to come back to me a war hero for me to feel proud. Just come back to me."

He pulled them both for an embrace.

"Now," he said as he pulled away. "I have something I want you boys to have."

His father pulled two purses off his belt. Wilton hadn't noticed there were two, until that moment. He threw one to each of them.

"But Father," Wilton said. "You have already given us coin."

"Everything is more expensive in the capital," he said.

Feffer's grin was childish. "Thanks Da!"

"Thank you, Father," Wilton said.

His father ruffled Feffer's hair. "Now, you go outside. I want to say something to your brother."

Feffer's grin faded, and he shrugged as if it didn't matter that he was being excluded from the conversation. As per usual, he oversold the gesture. "I want to find Elwin anyway."

After Feffer was gone, his father was silent for a moment.

"Wilton, I want you to promise me something."

Wilton wished he hadn't hesitated. But he had. "Anything father."

"I want you to keep a close eye on your brother and help him stay out of trouble. The people here may have a strong tolerance for Feffer's antics, but the city is another matter. Some of his pranks will be considered crimes there. Promise me that you will keep him out of the stocks."

"I will do what I can, Father," he said, not quite feeling the words.

"Thank you, son," he said, hugging him.

He pulled Wilton to arm's length and looked him in the eyes. His father had dark green eyes. Those same eyes had scolded him as a child. He had seen that calculated stare work an unfavorable trade to his father's advantage.

"I don't care what you have to do. Make a deal with the abyss if you have to, but keep you and your brother safe. Do you hear me? You two come back alive. I am counting on you."

"I will Father. I promise." Maybe it was the desperation in his father's voice. But this time, he meant it.

Elwin stood in the square. The remnants of the evenings festivities were everywhere. Apple cores from candied apples had been left littered about. Fresh mud made a circular pattern where the cake walk had taken place. Depressions from tables that had displayed wares were fresh in the ground.

But the people had gone.

He wondered if his presence had anything to do with that. People should be lining the streets to say farewell to the men and boys going to war. But no one had come.

He looked up at the inn. He had grown up playing in the square with his cousins.

Elwin shook his head. "Not *my* cousins."

"What was that?" Feffer said.

Elwin jumped. "Don't sneak up on people."

"What are you doing out here?" Feffer's voice held an excited curiosity.

"Jasmine told me to wait in the square while she paid for the accommodations."

"The acco- what?"

"The rooms she rented and food they ate," Elwin said. "Don't you read at all?"

"I have already told you that I read," Feffer said. "I just ignore the big words."

Elwin sighed.

"Is it safe for you to be out here by yourself?" Feffer asked.

"Jasmine is holding my essence."

"She what?"

"It's safe."

"Alright," Feffer shrugged. "Where is everyone?"

"I am sure they are avoiding … the square right now."

"No. I mean, where are all of the soldiers. We are all supposed to report to the square."

"I don't know, Feffer. I haven't seen anyone. I guess you are the first one."

Feffer grinned.

The door to the inn opened and his parents stepped out. His grandparents followed them. He avoided their gaze as they approached.

He flinched when his mother reached to hug him, but he let her take him into her embrace. Closing his eyes, he held on to her. He felt his father's strong arms wrap around the two of them.

"No matter what happens," he heard his father's voice say, "we will always love you."

He held on to them until he heard Jasmine speak, "It's nearly time."

His father, then his mother, released him.

Without looking at them, he said, "I love you, too."

He hugged his grandparents one at a time. His Poppe smiled. "Now, *you'll* come back with stories to tell *me*."

Elwin gave him a smile that he did not feel.

Then he turned from the inn and his family and walked away from the only home he had ever known. He could not help but wonder if he would ever see any of them again.

Feffer sat next to the evening's campfire and rubbed his bare feet. Traveling to the capital had been nothing like he had hoped. To begin with, he had to march with everyone else, while Elwin road in the carriage with the pretty ladies. He had to walk for hours without stopping, while Elwin got to ride in luxury. He hadn't even seen his friend since that first day.

Next, Wilton hadn't spoken more than a dozen words to him. And none of the other guys wanted to say much either. So it was just walking. Five days of walking and five more besides. If he slowed down at all, Lord Lifesong would ride up on his horse and yell curses at him, calling him rude names. Someone should wash the commander's mouth out with lye.

And worst of all, they wouldn't let him carry a sword. Wasn't that the whole reason they wanted him? When he had asked about one, Lord Lifesong had laughed at him and told him he would have to teach him how to carry it without stabbing himself in the foot first.

Then, everyone else laughed at him.

A white cloaked soldier walking toward him made Feffer look up. "Stew's ready."

"Ugh," Feffer replied.

Maybe *that* was worst of all. This was his fifth night of mutton stew. Their cook had obviously never heard of spices. Would it hurt to use a little salt or peppercorn? Barley or sage?

He slipped his boots back on and laced them, taking his time. Next, he would have to stand.

"How are you holding up?" It was Wilton's voice.

Feffer looked up to see his brother standing on the other side of the fire. The light danced off his face, and he stood with a casual ease. Feffer doubted that marching for five days had been as difficult for Wilton. He had always been better at things that were hard work.

Feffer felt his bottom lip quiver. He bit it so that he wouldn't cry.

"Hop up, Feffer." He walked over to him and offered a hand. "You need to eat. Tomorrow is going to be another long day."

Feffer took his brother's hand. "Have you seen Elwin?"

Wilton shook his head. "They are still keeping him away from the soldiers. Biron, the man Elwin killed, was well liked. It is going to take some time before Elwin is accepted, if he ever is. Can you believe it?" Wilton shook his head as if he couldn't.

"But that wasn't Elwin's fault!" Feffer protested.

"They don't see it that way. But it doesn't matter right now. Let's get some dinner."

Feffer began to argue, but Wilton cut him off by walking away. He had to run a couple of steps to catch up. Each step sent a jolt of pain up his leg.

Wilton slowed down once they reached the chow line. It was already quite long. Feffer was pretty sure that he and Wilton would be the last two served. That meant there would be little mutton in their mutton stew, which meant his dinner would consist of mutton flavored water.

Feffer sighed.

It was safe to say that being a soldier was nothing like the stories. But if they had talked about this part, he was pretty sure there would be much fewer soldiers.

Feffer sighed again.

⁓

"We are here." Zarah's voice broke Elwin's concentration.

He had been attempting to feel for the movements of his essence in the shadow realm, so he could find Jasmine's. From her perspective, he imagined himself to look like a halfwit bumbling around, his eyes closed and reaching for her with clumsy lunges. More accurately, he probably looked like a baby trying to open and close his hand, but he didn't care much for that analogy.

He stared at Zarah for a moment before her words made sense in his mind.

"What? We are?" he said, yawning. It seemed like he had to be half asleep to even feel the slightest movements of his essence.

"See for yourself." Despite the exhaustion in her movements, her voice bounced with excitement. She pulled aside the curtain and leaned back so he could see.

Dusk began to obscure the view, but enough light settled on the buildings that Elwin could still read the script marking shops on signs by the roadside. Several buildings hung close to the side of the cobblestones with closed shutters. Flames danced atop tall poles spaced every dozen paces.

Elwin jumped back to his seat when he felt a sudden surge of heat burst into life near him. It took him a moment to realize the heat had not touched his body. He had sensed the flames with his essence.

"What was that?"

"The firestarters," Zarah said.

"I …," Elwin licked his lips. "I felt it."

On the bench across from him, Jasmine sat a little straighter and studied his face. "You felt the Fire being tamed?"

Elwin nodded. "It felt like heat."

"Interesting," Jasmine said. "Usually, it takes time and training to feel other Elements being tamed. Feeling it without trying could mean you have the ability to tame Fire as well."

"That does not make sense," Zarah said. "He should not be—"

"We will need to test you," Jasmine said in a no-nonsense tone. Zarah narrowed her eyes in a look of chagrin but remained silent as her mother continued, which spoke to her level of exhaustion.

Ten days and nights of lectures from Jasmine had worn on Zarah as much as Elwin. She seemed to know as much about most of the topics they discussed as Jasmine. But most of the times Zarah tried to share her thoughts on the matter, Jasmine rebuked her.

Jasmine continued as if not seeing Zarah's glare. "It is rare that a person who tames Air can also tame Fire. Usually, those who first manifest Air can tame Water and vice versa. Those who first find Fire can later tame Earth. Even more rare are those who can tame three Elements. There have been none since before the Shadow Wars of anyone taming all four."

"How can I know?" Elwin asked.

"Before you sleep tonight," Jasmine said, "I will have you tested. The test is simple, but I could not perform it without my artifact."

Outside the wagon, he felt another burst of Fire. He peaked out the window on his own side to watch it being done. A man in dark clothes walked along the cobblestones not even slowing a step at each post. As he walked by each lamp, tiny embers glowing a soft red coalesced near the man and vanished. Now that he could see it,

Elwin felt the heat grow to a fine point and burst, as the top of each pole came alive with flames.

"Wow," Elwin breathed. "Do they do this every night?"

"We may not be Alcoa," Zarah said, "but we still have a few elementalists with minor gifts who stay here. There are not enough firestarters to form a guild exactly, but we have enough."

"Guilds?" Elwin said. "Like with the blacksmiths? Faron had belonged to a guild in Alcoa. I heard him complaining about their outrageous dues to my Poppe once."

Zarah raised her eyebrows and looked at Jasmine as if expecting her mother to answer.

Jasmine gave Zarah the briefest of nods and said, "You may answer this one." Though her tone said, "You may try to answer this one."

Zarah raised her chin and said in a confident voice, "They share some similarities. Blacksmiths belong to trade guilds. Each trade guild has different notoriety based on several factors. A guild master is usually a grandmaster. To be considered a part of one, a member must prove himself worthy to be a part of the guild. After being accepted as a member, a blacksmith can trade his wares with the sigil of the guild. The higher the esteem of the guild, the more a blacksmith can inflate his prices. However …"

Elwin found her voice beginning to lull him. He tried to focus on her words, but he had listened to lectures and trained by day in the wagon and by night in the shadow realm. He felt like his mind had performed a thousand press-ups and had run a hundred miles.

Before he could stop himself, he blurted, "What does this have to do with the elementalists who stay?" He wanted to take his words back the instant they were out.

Zarah flinched, then glared as if he had slapped her.

Even though she had likely heard much, if not all of it before, she had sat through every lecture. The very moment she had permission to take part in the discussion, he had ruined it. He *was* a half-wit. What was he thinking?

Her mouth worked for a moment as if to reply, but Jasmine spoke first. Zarah's glare seemed to deepen with Jasmine's every word.

"For every imaginable trade, there is a guild in Alcoa. I do not speak simply of blacksmiths and stone masons. In Alcoa, there are professions based on Elemental talents. Being part of an Elemental guild is highly profitable. But this is not the only reason young elementalists journey to Alcoa. The Elemental guilds answer to the Sacred Order.

"This group of elementalists have been charged with protecting the lands from those who would use the Elements for ill. Since the King of Alcoa leads the order, many elementalists sojourn to the city in hopes of finding acclaim by joining the order." Jasmine waved her hand in a gesture of annoyance. "Silly notion. After all, members of the Sacred Order are anonymous and do not need to be in Alcoa to be a member."

"Wait," Elwin said. "But don't the Guardians of Life protect people? Why is there any need for a Sacred Order?"

For a moment, Jasmine made a face as if she had tasted a lemon, but her voice remained the instructional tone he had grown accustomed to over their journey. "The Guardians were founded in Alcoa to protect citizens from elementalists, while the Sacred Order is a group of elementalists who work together to guide elementalists in Alcoa to benefit all. The Guardians will employ healers, but they do not generally welcome any not bound to Life and without a focus in healing to join their ranks. After all, they need healers in their temples."

Elwin's voice came out as a tired sigh. "But you just said the Sacred Order protects people. What do the guilds have to do with that?"

"Every Elemental guild must swear fealty to the king and the Sacred Order to operate in Alcoa. They train elementalists much in the way I will train you. Entering into an apprenticeship with a specific guild will choose your focus. For example," she said gesturing toward the light poles. "Firestarters in Alcoa belong to the Blazing Fist and are charged with lighting the fire poles, but this is not their only role. They are also trained in forms of combat to aid in defense of the city."

Elwin tried to make sense of her words, then realized he couldn't recall the original topic. Hadn't he asked about the Guardians of Life? He took a deep breath to sigh, but it came out as a long yawn.

Zarah's laugh didn't seem to hold much mirth.

"What?" he demanded amidst his yawn.

"Your nose scrunches in the cutest of ways when you are confused." Zarah's tone had no inflection, so he couldn't be sure if she mocked or complimented him.

His cheeks burned, and he found himself covering his nose. Zarah placed a hand on his arm and her soft laugh became a genuine giggle. Had she not been mocking him, he might have considered the sound of her laughing the most delightful sound to ever touch his ears. But no. She was mocking him. He was sure of it now.

"Zarah," Jasmine said in a sharp voice. "Your behavior is not appropriate."

Zarah placed her hands in her lap and made an obvious effort not to smile but failed to keep the mirth from her eyes. Elwin turned away from her and pulled back the curtain on his side of the carriage to avoid her gaze. Thoughts of Zarah fled from him and his breath caught as he really began to look at the city. How had he not seen it before?

Fire from the poles gave a clear view of stone buildings rising from the side of the cobblestone road. Small alleys separated most of the buildings, while some had been built one right atop the other. A few of the buildings had a small fence to bar passage to the doors of the buildings from the road. The shortest structure stretched taller than even his Poppe's inn, and he couldn't see the tallest without sticking his head out the window and craning his neck upward, which he almost did but stopped himself. Zarah already thought him a country bumpkin. He didn't want to give her more evidence to support that theory. Even if it was true.

"It's so big," he said.

He could see Zarah's smile in his periphery and closed his mouth. So much for not making a fool of himself, gaping like a simpleton.

"Maybe on the morrow I can show you around," Zarah said in a casual, almost bored tone. "It would be a shame if you got lost and never found your way back to the castle." Her look suggested that without her help, this would happen.

"No," Jasmine said. "It will be some time before I will want him leaving the confines of the castle."

"The castle?" Elwin said.

As if summoned, the coach made a turn and Elwin saw a castle come into his view. He felt his jaw loosen but did not attempt to hide his awe. The castles described in his books could never compare with the monument before him. Beyond a tall wall made of grey stone, round towers reached into the sky and disappeared into the growing darkness.

When the carriage rolled to a stop, Elwin found himself unable to move. The driver, a man named Javus, opened the door and offered Zarah his hand, then Jasmine. Javus only nodded to him as Elwin climbed out after them.

His legs stiffened as he took a few steps into the stone courtyard. The vast space seemed even larger by the emptiness. Two boys, both a handful of years younger than him, hurried to the horses and began to care for them. Deft hands worked at harnesses and bridles.

Then a thought occurred to him.

"Where did all the soldiers go?"

"Hmm?" Jasmine said. "Oh. They have gone to the barracks. It is near the docks district."

"They don't stay in the castle?"

"New recruits?" Zarah said laughing. "In the castle? Bhalindra's vein would hemorrhage."

"Bhalindra?" Elwin said scowling. It had been an honest question. Why wouldn't soldiers stay in the castle? Every story he had ever read had soldiers in the castle.

"She is the mistress of maids," Zarah said, still smiling. "She gets upset over the slightest mess. And you can always tell when she is angry because the vein in her temple bulges. And soldiers are messy with their marching in the mud and dirt and all."

"Zarah," Jasmine said. "That is quite enough. Escort Elwin to the lecture hall."

"The lecture hall?" Zarah said. "But it is late. And we have been traveling for a tenday. I always get the evening off when we get back. I do not see why I need to be treated like a novice when Elwin is the one—"

"It *is* late," Jasmine said in a terse voice, "so do not argue. I need to grab the tuning sextant to test Elwin. Now, off with you."

Zarah's lips pouted, but she didn't argue further. "This way," she said to Elwin as she stormed off.

Elwin had to run a few steps to catch her.

As they approached a side entrance to the castle, Elwin looked up. Light escaped from balconies and windows on almost every level as far as the eye could see. A guard opened the door for Zarah as she neared. She stopped to face the man.

"Hargin," she said, raising her chin into the air, "even though he looks like a simple farmer, this is Elwin of house Escari. He is under the tutelage of my mother and is to be confined to the castle grounds until you are told otherwise."

"Aye, milady."

She walked past the guard without a backward glance. Elwin couldn't say why his cheeks heated at Zarah's words or why he avoided the guard's cold stare. There was no shame in the way he looked. He *was* a farmer.

He had to hurry down the dim hallway to keep pace with Zarah, but he made it a point to remain several feet behind her. Maybe he should apologize? But it wasn't as if he had meant to interrupt her earlier. She was talking around the point and putting him to sleep. And *he* hadn't asked her to escort him to the lecture hall. Apologizing wouldn't do any good if he had nothing to be sorry about.

All of the doors they passed were closed, and most of the sconces were cold, making it difficult to see the details of the paintings or tapestries lining the grey walls. Not that he had much time to take in any of the scenes.

Zarah raced around several corners and up several sets of stairs without ever turning to look in Elwin's direction. He had a good mind to stop following her just to see if she noticed. But if he got lost, he would never find his way. And the other guards might wonder why a farmer roamed about the castle.

He would have to find a way to make things right between them.

Once more, he considered apologizing and rejected it. Zarah had a smug way of making him feel as if a half-wit was smart by comparison to him. If he apologized, she might hold it against him.

Were all girls this ... bah! He didn't have the word.

Wilton seemed to know how to get on with girls. If he ever got a chance to mingle with the soldiers again, he would have to ask about Zarah. The way Wilton made his cousin, Dasmere, and the rest of the girls of the town giggle, surely he would know how to handle this situation. Not that he wanted Zarah to giggle. Well, maybe he did.

Elwin hadn't known Zarah had stopped until he ran into her. His feet tangled in hers, and he bulled over her, sending them both to the ground. He landed roughly atop her and laid stunned.

"Get off, you ... you!" She pushed him aside and scrambled away.

He staggered to his feet, offering her his hand. "I'm so sor—"

She batted his hand away and stood on her own. "Are you simple or just a clumsy oaf?"

"I ...," Elwin began. "You stopped, and I ..."

"So it's my fault you tackled me?" Her voice was incredulous.

"No," he said quickly. "That's not what I meant!"

"Hmmph." She opened the door and stepped much wider than necessary and said, "After you. I insist."

Holding one arm with the other, he walked into the room feeling the fool. From his periphery, he could see her glowering at him as he passed her.

The room was dark, so he took two steps into the room and stopped.

"Don't break anything while I turn on the lantern." Her voice dripped with venom.

She took an obvious effort to step wide of him, pressing flat against the wall to move around. She reached up toward a lantern by the door and clicked a lever. A light flared into being inside a glass case. Elwin felt heat much like he had with the firestarters outside.

"An ever-candle," Elwin said.

"Yes," she said smugly. "Do you not have one on your farm?"

"Zarah," Jasmine's voice said from the hallway.

Zarah jumped as if goosed and turned toward the door. They both turned to see Jasmine standing in the doorway.

"Your attitude is unbecoming, young lady," Jasmine said. "Do you need a penance to remind you how to behave?"

"No," she said in a voice that sounded only slightly petulant.

"Apologize to Elwin. Now."

Elwin met her gaze and flinched. The heat in her eyes could have roasted him where he stood and razed half the castle besides. Yet her voice sounded as sincere and heartfelt as any apology he had ever given.

"I am so sorry, Elwin. I am weary from travel and not accustomed to … I am sorry. Will you ever forgive me?"

"Of course," he said. "I am sorry, too. I should have been watching where I was walking."

She gave him a tight smile. "It is quite alright."

"Very good," Jasmine said. "Now both of you have a seat."

Elwin turned around. The light from the single ever-candle filled the whole of the small room. Across from the door, Elwin could see moonlight enter from a small window near the ceiling. In front of him and to the right, four small tables with wooden chairs beneath them faced the western wall, where a slate tablet as long as the wall hung behind a larger desk. The back of the room had a large wooden contraption. The top had a round face with hands pointing to numbers. Beneath the face, a large pendulum made of gold swung back and forth.

"If you would please?" Zarah said in a tight voice. "I am trying to reach my seat."

Elwin walked to the desk closest to the window, but stopped when Zarah cleared her throat. Her raised eyebrow and hands on hips told him that he had done something wrong. He gritted his teeth and took a deep breath.

Before he could ask what he'd done this time, she spoke in a tight voice. "That is my seat."

"Zarah," Jasmine cautioned.

She gave him a polite smile that did not touch her eyes. "But, you can sit there today."

He pulled out the chair, plopped into the seat, and faced the front of the room. From the corner of his eye, he could see Zarah do much the same. Only, instead of plopping, her movements were graceful, and instead of leaning on the table, she placed her hands in her lap and sat straight-backed. Trying to appear nonchalant, Elwin sat up straighter.

Jasmine sighed and placed a metallic object on the front table. Rounded on the bottom, two long metal spokes protruded from the base.

"This is called a tuning sextant," Jasmine said. "By placing the Elements onto the tines, we can determine which of them will tune to you."

She grabbed the sextant and brought it over to place on the table in front of him. Up close, he could see symbols etched into the metal. He had seen a few of them written into the margins in some of the books he had read. But he never knew what they meant.

"What do these symbols mean?"

"Ah," Jasmine said. "These are eloiglyphs, the language of elementalists. This is how we converse with one another. Eloi, in the ancient tongue means Elements and glyph means etchings. These glyphs provide instructions for recreating the sextant. In time, you will learn each of these. Alright. Now, we need to find your gifts. Try to relax."

He looked at the apparatus again. The metal pieces protruding from the base came to fine points. Leaning back from the device, he said, "What am I supposed to do?"

"Nothing," Jasmine said as she dug in a pouch at her belt. "You just need to be close to the device so that it is close to your essence."

She pulled a flint and steel out, along with a wax candle. "Hold this candle Zarah."

Zarah frowned, but complied without complaint. Jasmine struck the flint and steel until the wick caught. Taking the candle from Zarah, she held the candle up to the fine points of the sextant. She made a small motion with her wrist and the flame's tip slid onto the ends of the two spokes. Tiny wisps of smoke rose from the wick and the smell of sulphur filled the air.

"Step away Zarah," Jasmine said as she moved back herself.

Zarah rose from her desk, watching the flame with an intense stare. By her curious expression, Elwin guessed she hadn't seen this either. But that didn't make sense. Why had Jasmine not tested Zarah? Or, surely Jasmine had trained others.

She moved to stand next to Jasmine but didn't take her eyes from the device.

"Zarah and I are not gifted with fire," Jasmine said. "But, we do not want to confuse the sextant with attempting to tune with either of our essences."

Elwin watched the small flame, wondering how it burned without any fuel source. Before he could voice the question, he felt the source. He could feel heat stir from around the sextant and move into the metal. In the same moment, the sextant began to rock on the table. At first, the motion was gentle, but after a few seconds, it rocked so violently it looked as if it would fall over.

Jasmine moved as if to grab the sextant, but as she did the flame vanished in a puff of smoke. Her hand froze a few inches from the device and blinked in disbelief. After a moment, it stopped rocking.

"That has never happened," Jasmine said.

"What does it mean?" Zarah asked. She peaked over Jasmine's shoulder at Elwin. Her eyes weighed him in the same fashion his father appraised a prize horse.

"It means Elwin will be very powerful with fire," Jasmine said. Her gaze had a similar feel as Zarah's. Elwin frowned.

"Step back," Jasmine said to Zarah. The seriousness in her tone made Zarah jump, and she moved away from the table. The look Jasmine gave Elwin reminded him of the look Momme had given him after finding the stinkweed Feffer hid beneath the bar in the inn. His mouth became dry like it had then.

She pulled a flask from her pouch and opened it. Elwin licked his dry lips as Jasmine poured a single drop of water on the tip of the sextant and stepped back to stand next to Zarah. They both stared at him, unblinking.

He shifted in his seat, trying to make himself relax, but his lips felt as if he had not drank in days. He moved his tongue around in his mouth, trying to generate moisture without success. The drop of water in front of him seemed like all the water in the world. He could feel the curves of the droplet. As he focused on the drop of water, his mouth seemed to feel less dry.

Again, the sextant began to rock violently. After a moment, the water became like vapors and the sextant stilled.

"Three," Zarah said. "Abaddon had said—"

Jasmine shot Zarah a look so tense, it silenced her. Elwin's mouth began to feel dry again. What about Abaddon? He had been about to ask, but not wanting that gaze turned on him, he thought better of it.

Jasmine walked up to the desk and pulled a polished stone from her pouch. Her hand gave a slight tremor as she placed the stone atop the sextant. Her eyes touched Elwin's for the briefest of moments, and the intensity in her gaze made him want to lean farther back in his chair. But he dared not move a muscle. Jasmine backed away from the desk without taking her eyes from the sextant.

Elwin could feel his heart beating. He wanted to look away from the stone, but he couldn't take his gaze from the fine polish. It looked like any rock he could find on his farm but smoothed into a sphere. There was something more to the stone, like an ancient song. He felt more than heard reverberations in the piece of earth.

Once more, the sextant began to move back and forth. Slow at first, the stone swung back and forth with the rocking of the base, then it sped to the same intensity as both times before. The resonance of the stone increased to a whine in his mind. When it seemed the sound could go no higher, the rock crumbled to dust that rose into the air and vanished with tiny flashes as if falling into some invisible fire.

When the sextant became still once more, he looked up to Zarah and Jasmine. He had expected some sort of explanation. Despite the weariness he felt, he almost welcomed another lecture. Instead, both women looked at Elwin as if a viper had appeared in their midst.

The wideness of Zarah's eyes could have been awe, fear, or complete surprise. The twisting of her mouth moved without words.

Under her gaze, Elwin felt his face flush with heat to such a degree that sweat began to bead on his forehead. What had happened? He would tame all four Elements. What was the big deal?

Elwin glanced to Jasmine for support. Her face had paled, and she stared with an unreadable expression. Jasmine said taming four was rare, but why was she looking at him like he had grown horns and threatened to devour her firstborn? What had he done?

He glanced back and forth between them, waiting on either of them to say something. Anything.

The silence stretched on until he broke it in a shaky voice. "What is wrong?"

Zarah jumped as if woken from a dream. "All four," she said just above a whisper. "He is … all four."

Jasmine stood up straighter, regaining some of her normal composure. But her words seemed distant, as if she did not believe her own words. "Some day you will tame all four Elements. As I have said, none have tamed all four Elements since before the Shadow Wars. I knew you were strong, but I had no idea …"

As her voice trailed off, Jasmine shook her head as if shaking off a spider. "None of this matters now. Right now we—"

"But Mother," Zarah said indignantly. "The prophecies!"

"Prophecies?" Elwin said. "What is going on? Did I do something wrong?"

"No Elwin," Jasmine said in a firm voice. "You have done nothing wrong."

Zarah opened her mouth to protest, but Jasmine spoke over her with an ere of finality. "Zarah speaks out of turn. We do not need to concern ourselves with the prophecies." The words were spoken with a touch of reverence. Her voice hardened as she continued. "At least not right now. All I know for certain is that you need to be trained. This will be our focus."

"Born as one there will be two wielding the Elements true," Zarah said in a poetic voice. "Who is the second?" If her confident voice didn't suggest it, the gaze she gave Elwin spoke in no uncertain terms who she thought the first was.

"That is quite enough!" Jasmine said, raising her voice for the first time Elwin could recall. Then, a touch softer, she said, "To bed with you. Both of you."

Zarah narrowed her eyes at Jasmine and made a petulant sound of protest as she stalked toward the door.

"Zarah, child," Jasmine said.

Zarah stopped at the door and turned to look at her mother. She crossed her arms beneath her breasts and glared.

"Escort Elwin to the guest chambers in our wing." Then, she turned to Elwin and said, "As soon as you enter the shadow realm, meet in this lecture hall. Do not tarry. Now that I have confidence in your ability to release, we need to begin your hand-to-hand training. There is much you still need to know."

Elwin rose from the desk and stood on shaky legs.

Prophecies and four Elements? Tethering and hand-to-hand combat? Elementalists saved people in the stories. They didn't kill people by accident. Why didn't any of his books warn him about this? He had a few words to say to Asalla next time he saw the book merchant. *If* he ever saw the book merchant.

"I am sorry." Jasmine gave him a thin smile. "I have worked you hard this last tenday. I assure you, I only do as I must. I will give you and Zarah both some time off soon. I promise."

"I ...," Elwin began but closed his mouth.

I don't belong here, he wanted to say. *Zarah was right. I'm just a simple farmer. I should be resting, so I can rise early to help feed the chickens and milk the goats. Who will help Father with the plow?*

"What is it?" she asked.

He shook his head. "What if I can't fall asleep right away?"

"You can," she said reassuringly. "Just remember the trick I showed you. You've been doing very well."

What if I don't want to fall asleep ever again? What if I don't want to be part of some prophecy? What if I just want to go back to the farm near the forest of redwoods?

Instead of voicing his thoughts, he nodded.

"This way," Zarah said in a softer voice than she had used before. But her eyes studied him with pursed lips as if trying to solve a puzzle.

"I'm ready," he said.

Spots of color appeared on her cheeks. "Right. This way."

She turned from the room and moved through the darkened corridors. She walked much slower than she had before, keeping pace with him instead of making him keep up with her.

After leading him down several winding corridors and up a few flights of stairs she said, "I am sorry, Elwin. Truly. I misspoke before."

He started to thank her, but stopped when he felt the tears in his eyes for fear his voice would crack. Elwin nodded in hopes that it would suffice for acceptance of her apology. He rubbed at his eyes as if wiping away sleep, but the tears didn't seem to want to stop.

He gritted his teeth. This was no time to cry. He had wanted to be an elementalist. Well, now he would be. There was no sense in asking the Lifebringer for something and being upset when he gave it to you.

"Zarah?" he said once he had regained control of his tears.

"Yes?"

"Will you tell me about the prophecy?"

For several corridors, the only sound was their boots on the stone floors.

"Zarah?"

"I am sorry, Elwin," Zarah said in a voice of resignation. "I will let Mother tell you."

"But what does it have to do with me?" Elwin asked. "Does it mean I am really Bain's son?"

"I do not know," she said in a tight voice. "Look. Mother is right. You need to be trained. What does anything else matter? We do not really know anything about the prophecies anyway. No one can agree on what they mean. Maybe taming four Elements does not mean anything." The last sounded as if she spoke more to herself than to Elwin.

"If it doesn't mean anything," Elwin said. "Why don't you just tell me?" He was quite pleased with his own retort. It made him miss Feffer. His friend would have been proud of Elwin's infallible response.

"Nice try," Zarah said. "But I'm not going to tell you. Mother will tell you when she's ready."

Well, maybe not so infallible then. Elwin had taken a few steps before realizing she had stopped.

"This is you," she said, opening a door.

They had stopped in a wide hallway that came to an end with large, glass doors. It stretched out to a round terrace with lacquered furniture. Beyond, he could see the lights of the lamp poles and houses in the distance.

"That one is me." Zarah pointed to the room at the end on the right. "After entering the shadow realm, I will join you in the hallway."

"She said to meet in that room," Elwin said. "Won't it be too far from our bodies? We must have walked ten miles to get here."

Zarah laughed and hit him on the arm with the back of her hand. "Do not be silly. We went up more than we moved away from the lecture hall. Besides, as we grow in our powers, our Sanctuary grows as well. Presently, I can travel more than a mile from my body. You can probably travel half that." Her chin rose as she made the last proclamation.

"Oh," Elwin said.

"Aright," she said. "Off to bed. I do not want another lecture for being late."

Without further discourse, she left him by the door and entered her room without a backward glance.

Now that he was alone, the dim corridor seemed even darker. He could feel a draft in the hallway. The desire to draw Air into his essence was always there. It beckoned him, but he ignored it. He knew how to not draw it in now, which seemed almost as important as being able to release it, once held. He could almost hear Jasmine's voice lecturing him through the process.

His eyes lulled, and he almost fell over. He shook his head. How long had been standing in the hallway alone?

Elwin took a deep breath and stepped into the dark room. He left the door open for the light of the hallway as he fumbled at the ever-candle just inside the door. The fire inside the glass burst into life as he clicked the lever on the side. Focusing on the flame, he could feel heat shift from the surroundings to fuel the fire. It gave him a chill as he sensed the draft created as the heat around him vanished into the ever-candle.

"Hmm," he said as he looked at the candle, feeling a spike of curiosity.

Somehow the heat and flow of Air were related. He would have to ask Jasmine about it.

He closed the door and took a look around. The ever-candle lit the entirety of the antechamber as long and wide as the porch on his farmhouse. Pillowed chairs made of redwood were on either side, and a rack with pegs for cloaks hung on the wall by the doorway leading to the inner chamber.

The door to the inside had been propped open. Elwin walked into the room and lit another ever-candle. His breath caught as his eyes drank in his surroundings.

A room larger than the common room of the Scented Rose Inn opened to a balcony across from him. Double glass doors opened up to the city. Every few seconds the lights in the windows of the houses below began to darken.

To the right, several rich furnishings surrounded a fireplace with a bookshelf to either side. And on each shelf rested books. Hundreds of books. A part of him wanted to run over and begin to look over the bindings. A different and much larger part of him wanted to curl up on the throw rug by the cold fireplace and fall asleep. His eyes continued searching out a bed. Surely this monstrosity had a bed to sleep in.

Another door to the left was open. The light from the ever-candle stretched far enough inside for him to see a canopied bed on the far wall. He walked into the bedroom and clicked on another ever-candle just inside.

His farmhouse could have fit in the space. To his left, a doorway opened to the privy, where he could see a massive bathtub. Just inside and across from the bath was a high-seated mompot similar to the one at his Poppe's inn. A redwood cabinet cornered the wall beside the privy and stretched almost to the bed. To his right, another set of glass doors opened onto the balcony. The breeze flowed into the room flirting with the drapes around the canopy.

Once more he realized he stood in the doorway, staring like a small-town farmboy. He shook himself off and looked at the bed. He felt a smile spread across his lips.

He ran the half-dozen paces to the bed and dove toward the mattress. The curtains parted as he bounced on feathers and rolled several paces. Paces!

"Five families could sleep on this thing," he laughed. "Wait until Feffer sees all of this!"

He climbed beneath the blanket and hugged the soft pillows. Several moments passed of him lying there in stunned silence before he remembered why he was there at all, which reminded him that Jasmine and Zarah would be waiting for him.

His mind briefly considered climbing out from beneath the comfort of the blankets to douse the ever-candles. Before he could even fully reject the thought, his eyes lulled shut.

Chapter 7

A NEW LIFE

Feffer tongued the tasteless porridge. It was the same gook that he had eaten on the road for breakfast. He wanted to ask for some fruit to put in it, but he knew better than doing anything to stand out. They seemed to look for excuses to make him run or do press-ups. He chewed each bite until it was small enough to swallow and washed it down with a drink of water.

Wilton sat on the bench next to him. He didn't seem to mind the meal. In fact, nothing seemed to phase his older brother. One day he would have to ask him how he did it. At least Feffer knew why Wilton had not been excited about becoming a member of the White Hand. Somehow, his brother had known.

This was what it meant to be a soldier.

Looking around the room, he felt like cattle jammed into a barn. Two windows, each on opposing walls, gave little light into the room. Not that Feffer saw any friendly faces. All the boys from Benedict avoided him. They acted like he would get them into trouble. He was done with making trouble. That had been the old Feffer. He was going to be a soldier now. He'd show them.

Someone walked by and bumped him none too gently, making him drop his spoonful of porridge. He wanted to bark a curse at the boy, but he had already shoved down the line. Not that he could blame the guy with so little room to move about.

The chow room had filled to the breaking point with people from all over Justice. Those who hadn't arrived early enough stood by the walls, shoveling white slop into their mouths with wooden spoons. Conditions weren't much better in the barracks. No one had an individual room. Everyone had been herded into a large room with hundreds of bunks and assigned a bed. If he could even call it that. Each bunk had a thin mattress that did little to cushion the wood beneath. Worst of all, Feffer had to share chests for his belongings with his bunk mates.

Feffer had shoved his purse at the bottom of his pack, but he didn't feel comfortable leaving it unattended. He did though. Marching with the pack for a tenday was painful enough. He did not want to run or do press-ups with any extra weight. And that was what they meant when they said "training" would begin after breakfast. Running and press-ups didn't seem much like training. When were they going to give him a sword?

The first morning of being a soldier. Thus far, it was nothing like he had expected. They had arrived late the night before and had been escorted straight to the barracks for sleep. Then, he got woken up in the night to do press-ups. And, he had to do more press-ups for being slow to rise that morning. Pfft. Morning. If it could be called that. The sun hadn't even come up yet.

Now, he was eating porridge, and every piece of him still felt sore for marching a tenday.

A loud bang resounded from behind him, causing him to drop his spoonful of porridge a second time. This time it fell onto his lap.

"Curse it all!"

The sound of wood hitting stone silenced the movement in the chow hall. Feffer turned his head toward the man in white garb, who walked through the open doorway. Feffer didn't think he would ever feel the same about the White Hand again. They all appeared to be bullies by his accounts. Just big thick-headed bullies with swords.

The man staring at them was almost as large as Lord Lifesong. He had dark hair and a beard that was split at the chin by a scar. Most of the soldiers he had seen wore the red tunic with a white hand. This man, like Lord Lifesong, wore a white tunic with a red hand at the center. He hadn't needed to ask what it meant. This man would order him to do something he didn't want to do.

"Alright, worms. Eat up and get to the yard."

Feffer swallowed his last few bites in a couple of large gulps. He stood and wiped the bite that had gotten away off his shirt and onto the floor. Then he followed the others toward the door.

The boys in front of him placed their bowls in the wooden bin opposite the door on their way into the hallway. Feffer dropped his in behind Wilton and continued to follow.

The long hall led past the barracks to a large door, which opened to an expansive yard area surrounded by a tall fence. Rows of wooden practice weapons rested on racks alongside the wooden fence posts. Several devices sat unmoving in the yard. Feffer could only guess as to their purpose. One stood out amongst the rest. Rows of large, vertical walls stretched into the air with minimal hand and footholds. Between the walls, troughs were filled with muddy water.

He noticed that several of the other recruits had gathered into lines, facing the barracks. Wilton nudged him toward the back of the line. "Remember what Father said. We don't need to be heroes. The less notice we draw the better. Just do as you are told."

Feffer followed his brother to the back row.

"Alright," the man said. "Those of you in squads already know your drills. The rest of you, press-ups. Now."

Feffer watched several of the others leave the lines and form groups. Some of the groups began to run toward one of the devices, while others sprinted toward weapon racks.

"Get down, Feffer," Wilton whispered, loudly, about a moment too late.

Feffer hadn't noticed the white clad man's approach, until a fist hit his midsection. He dropped to the ground, trying to find his breath.

"When I tell you to do press-ups, the only thing that should stop you is a severed limb. Do you have a severed limb, worm?"

A sarcastic remark made its way to his lips, but he found himself unable to speak without breath. Had the words come out, the man would have heard Feffer say, "Worms don't have arms, you thumping bastard." Instead, it came out like wordless grunts.

"I asked you a question." Feffer felt a heavy boot push on his back. "What's your name, worm?"

When his breath returned, Feffer forced his full name through his teeth.

"Well, Feffer Hanck Madrowl, are you a trouble maker?"

He glanced over at Wilton, who was still doing press-ups. His brother glanced at him, eyes squinted with anger. He could almost hear his brother's voice say, *I told you not to get noticed.*

"No, sir. I don't make troubles." His breath came easier than it had.

"I don't see you doing any press-ups. I told you to do press-ups."

The boot was still on his backside. He gritted his teeth and did his first press-up. The boot held a steady pressure on his back.

"You are all pathetic. Not one of you knows how to do a press-up. On the next press-up, hold at the top. And you hold until I tell you to drop down."

Feffer did another one with the man's foot on his back and held it.

"That's one. Everyone has done one press-up. You are finished doing press-ups when I count to ten. When I say down. You drop to the ground, come back up and hold. If anyone fails to complete this task, we start over."

"Down."

Feffer did another press-up with the man's boot pressing on his back. His arms shook and tried to rebel against his mind's requests.

"Two."

"I am Sir Gibbins. You will address me as Sir Gibbins."

"Down ... Three."

Feffer wasn't sure, but it felt like *Sir* Gibbins was pressing harder with each press-up.

"Down ... That's four."

The pressure increased, until he saw Gibbin's other foot leave the ground. Feffer's arms shook for a few seconds before he collapsed into the dirt. The impact forced the air from his lungs.

"I didn't say down, Feffer. Because of you, we get to start over. Let that be a lesson to you, worms. An army is only as strong as his weakest soldier. You will continue to eat dirt until you are strong enough to do anything else."

Weakest soldier? Thumping son of a dragon stood on his back. Gibbins stepped off of Feffer's back and began to walk through the ranks.

"Down ... One."

Feffer clenched his teeth and forced his arms to do another press-up. He had never heard of anyone being killed while training to be a soldier. He found himself wondering if he would be the first.

Morning light spilled in from the balcony, causing Elwin to squint as he opened his eyes. He grabbed a pillow and held it over his face.

He wanted to scream into it, but restrained himself. Jasmine had not answered any of his questions. Worse, Elwin hadn't even really begun to learn hand-to-hand combat. He had spent his entire night in the shadow realm stumbling around and crouching in odd stances, trying *to be like water*. It was all so ridiculous.

He threw the pillow and rolled out of the bed. That was when he realized someone had peeled back the canopies of the bed and tied them to the posts. He jumped when he saw a man standing in the doorway. Short and plump, the man wore a liveried coat of white and red. His bald head seemed to reflect the light as if polished.

"Good morning, young sir," he said with a slight accent, foreign to Elwin. "I trust you slept well?"

"Who," his voice cracked. "Ahem. Who are you?"

"My name is Harkin of Trenivar," he said. "If it would please you, call me Harkin."

"Harkin," Elwin said. "Right. Why are you here?"

Harkin's eyes widened and his voice might have explained that water was wet. "I have been assigned by His Grace to see to your needs, young sir. If it would please you, the Lady Zarah has requested your audience. She waits for you in the corridor."

"Ah," Elwin said. "Of course. I was supposed to meet her to see the seamstress. Apparently, my clothes are not good enough for the castle."

"Indeed," Harkin said.

Elwin scowled at him, which was difficult to maintain while brushing out the wrinkles. Bah. It was useless. He shouldn't have slept in his clothes.

Jasmine hadn't let him go by the farm to get his belongings, but she had said she would send for them. In the meantime, they would have the palace seamstress fit him with clothes.

All he really wanted was his books.

"Asalla," Elwin realized.

"Young sir?"

"I left the book he gave me in the grass behind Madrowl's store in Benedict," Elwin said. "I can't believe I forgot it."

"If it pleases my young sir, I will send an inquiry on his young sir's behalf to someone in Benedict."

He nodded. The first rain would ruin it, and Asalla had said that it was a special book. Maybe he could get a letter to Drenen or Poppe before it rained. He walked over to the balcony to look at the cloudless sky. His balcony faced north and east, providing a nice view of the city of Justice.

Near the northern wall, a wide lake separated large homes on the west from smaller homes on the east side. The western structures had all been made of stone with slate roofs, and most were surrounded by tall gates. The smaller buildings on the east had also been crafted from stones but had little if any space between them. The coloring and styles of their stones differed as if they had been conjoined at different times.

Narrow cobblestone roads split the buildings on the east side of the lake, while wider roads provided room for horse-drawn carriages on the west. But the roads leading to both the north and east gates stretched the widest.

Beyond the gates, Elwin could see the countryside for a league or more. Many of the buildings outside the stone walls were larger than the ones inside with more distance apart and were built with redwood or stones of various colors.

Below him, people already began to fill the streets. From his vantage point, the people moving in and out of shops and buildings seemed like the wooden soldiers he played with as a child.

"Ahem," Harkin said, "if it would please my young sir? Lady Zarah?"

"Oh," Elwin jumped. "Sorry Harkin. And please, just call me Elwin."

"As my young sir commands," Harkin said. "This way please."

Harkin turned and walked toward the outer door.

Zarah waited for him in the hall. Her long hair hung loose about her shoulders. She had on an emerald dress that draped around her shoulders and exposed all of her neckline and the top part of her bosom.

Elwin swallowed. He had never seen a dress so ... No one in his town wore anything that ...

"Good morning, Elwin."

Zarah's voice made his eyes snap up to her face. Her red lips smiled in a way that made him feel warm and cold at the same time.

"Oh. Uh. Go—," his voice cracked. "Good morning."

Her smile deepened as her eyes studied his. "Mother wants me to show you about the castle. We cannot have you getting lost now can we?"

"Hmm?" He forced his eyes to remain on her face. It took an effort not to glance down at her ... dress. "No. I guess not."

"The first place we are going is the seamstress. We need to get you out of those farm clothes."

"Out of my clothes?" Elwin's voice cracked again. He began to imagine himself naked and standing in front of Zarah. His eyes flickered to her bosom again, and he quickly looked away. Despite the breeze from the balcony, he felt sweat appearing on his forehead.

"Right," she said with a smile. "Those clothes will not do for anyone living in the castle. We need to get you new ones."

Right. New clothes. She hadn't meant ... Elwin felt his cheeks flush again. Of course she hadn't meant for him to take off his clothes. It seemed to be getting warmer in the hallway by the moment. He looked down at his brown trousers and green shirt more to avoid looking at her than to study his attire.

But, he couldn't help but feel a tinge of irritation at her casual dismissal of his best clothes. He had only worn both shirt and trousers a few times. Even wrinkled, he would look dressed up enough for the temple on Lifeday in Benedict. He had been about to tell her as much, but she spoke first.

"Shall we then?" She turned and offered him her elbow.

Scowling, Elwin looped his arm through hers, and she led him down the long corridor.

Her skin was like silk, soft and smooth. She had the sweet smell of flowers. Or, maybe it was honey. He hated the way being near to her always made his heart beat faster. He glanced at her from the corner of his eye but immediately looked away, feeling abashed. Being taller, he could see much more of her bosom than was decent at this angle. His hands began to feel like heated clams.

He made a point of studying the tapestries to avoid his eyes wandering to places they shouldn't go.

Most of the embroidered textiles depicted various battle scenes, but a few had images of strange animals. One animal was grey with a long, white horn. Another picture had a massive animal of a grey-brown color with a long nose above large white tusks coming out the sides of its mouth.

"Those are called monotooths, and the others are elephants," Zarah said. "They are found in the Kalicodon nation. It is east of Alcoa, across the Tranquil Sea."

"Oh," Elwin said, still not looking directly at her.

Half an hour passed, and she continued to lead him around corridors. Aside from the tapestries, not much else seemed to change. Most of the doors were propped open with plain wooden chairs or tables outside.

"We are here," she announced, coming to an abrupt stop. He felt a moment of regret when she released his arm. Focusing, he could sense the warmth of her arm fade into the Air around him. When she spoke, his eyes snapped to her face. She gave him a wry smile.

"It will be an hour or so of fitting. I will be back in time to take you to breakfast. If I am not, can you make it back to your quarters?"

Elwin thought about it for a moment. He had not been paying attention to their path at all. And the castle was huge. "I don't think so."

Zarah shook her head and rolled her eyes lazily. She probably thought Elwin was the biggest country bumpkin.

"If I am not back before you are finished, you will have to wait for me. Well, go on, then." She nudged him for the door. "Mahindria is waiting for you."

He turned from her and walked through the doorway. Not sure why, the sounds of her retreating footsteps made him feel exposed. As her footsteps grew more distant, the fresh smell of honey faded. With Zarah's absence, the feeling of exposure became something more. There was no word for it. Bah. What was wrong with him?

Elwin forced Zarah from his mind and glanced around the large room.

To his right a large open window provided an abundance of light. Various fabrics hung on racks in rows to either side of him, and more fabrics were folded and stacked in corners. A wooden table twice the length of his mother's table back home rested at the center of the room. Next to it stood a portly woman with dark hair pulled into a bun.

"Well get yourself in here," an accented voice said. "I haven't all day to get the size of you."

He hurried over to her. Without further discourse, she began to position him and hold a slender wooden tape for measuring up to him. He flinched. The tape had the same look of the one his father used to measure wood for cutting.

She nudged him with a surprising amount of strength. Then, she herded him around the table to a wooden stool and all but lifted him onto it. The large woman brought several fabrics over and held them against his chest. Several of the fabrics went back to racks or corners, while a few made it onto the table.

This went on for some time.

Elwin tried to stay rigid or bent as she directed him. But nothing he did made her happy with him. She would express her displeasure by a tap, none too gently, with her measuring stick to the area she thought needed adjustment. If he slouched too often, she would tap his backside. If he leaned too long on one leg, she would tap his lazy leg. Sometimes she would preempt her strike with a warning of, "Up now," or, "You slow me down."

But even when he scrambled to heed her warning, she would still strike him. After a few times, he learned bracing for the blow was better than trying to avoid the venomous bite of Mahindra's stick. He decided that he would go to great lengths to avoid "fitting" in the future.

Without preamble, she struck his backside and said, "Off with you now. I will have an outfit or two for you by the end of the day."

She pointed the stick at his face, almost hitting his nose. "And you best not let me see you in rags again."

"Rags?" He looked down. "These are my Lifeday best."

"Off with you, I say!" She waved the stick at him once more. Had he not ducked, she would have struck his cheek.

Elwin ran from the room, watching over his shoulder to ensure she hadn't chased him with the stick. She didn't give chase, but he did not slow.

Zarah waited for him in the hallway. She had a hand covering her mouth, but he could see the smile in her eyes.

"You could have warned me," he said accusingly.

Replacing her smile with the perfect visage of innocence, she shrugged. "Whatever do you mean?"

He wanted to storm off, but he didn't know which way to go. She didn't hide her smile from him this time. He stomped off in the direction they had come.

"That is the wrong way," she called after him.

He stopped and turned around. "You did that on purpose."

"Maybe." She offered him her arm, again. "Hungry?"

"Sure." He looped his arm in hers. Once more the warmth of her skin sent shivers up his arm and down his spine.

He tried not think on the feel of her skin as she led him down several corridors. Instead he focused on the path to the seamstress. All the hallways looked about the same, but he kept up with the turns. Not that he wanted to make it back to Mahindra's. But it would be good to know how to avoid that corridor.

After the last turn, the end of the hallway opened up to a large room with a stone table the size of a small field at its center. The table stretched longer than the Scented Rose was wide. By Elwin's best guess, over a hundred people could fit in the lacquered chairs surrounding the table. Though, at the moment, less than half the seats held people. Of those, Elwin only recognized Lord Lifesong and Jasmine sitting across from one another next to the table's head.

The chair at the table's head held a silvery hue and stood an arm's length higher than the rest of the chairs. Elwin wasn't sure what it could be made of, but he was certain its price would fetch ten farms, complete with livestock. An aging man sat in the chair. He had a muscular frame that was distinguishable beneath his red robes. Upon his head rested a silver crown. The golden gilding made the symbol of a sword with balanced scales replacing the hilt.

The king! He was in the presence of the king. Should he bow? No. No one even acknowledged Elwin and Zarah as they stood in the entryway. If he bowed at this distance, he would look the fool for sure. He glanced to Zarah to be certain.

Her eyes were wide as she pulled on his arm. She had only stopped because he had. He felt his cheeks color and let her lead him toward the table. Elwin glanced to the head of the table. No one had seemed to notice them. Elwin tried to look at the others around the head of the table without staring.

To Jasmine's right sat a thin, tan-skinned man. He wore no shirt, and Elwin could see twin blades, jutting up from his waist. They were curved and had short hilts.

Across from that man was a short man, stout in build. His torso made a redwood's trunk look thin. He had long red locks of hair, which wound into his thick beard. His thick nose was as wide as Elwin's hand. Elwin almost stopped again, but caught himself just short of gaping like a yokel.

"A dwarf," Elwin said much louder than he had intended.

Zarah's elbow jabbed his ribs hard enough to knock the air from his lungs. "Yes. Now, please do not embarrass me. Mother has charged me with teaching you proper etiquette."

"No one heard me," Elwin said glowering at her and resisting the urge to massage his ribs.

"This time," she whispered. "Mind your tongue."

He gritted his teeth and let her guide him to the foot of the table. No one else sat near this end. After releasing his arm, she grabbed the sides of her dress and squatted. Belatedly, Elwin realized that it was a curtsey. The noble women in his books did that.

Zarah raised her voice, "Thank you, Elwin Escari. You are quite the gentleman."

She pulled out her seat and sat with a graceful ease.

He felt his cheeks burning and sat across from her, attempting not to look at anyone.

"Why are we sitting so far from everyone else?" he whispered.

Her voice was just above a whisper. "We sit in order of importance. As we are not members of the council or head of a noble family, we sit toward the foot. If there were more noble children here, we would sit further up the table, since my family is next in line for the throne."

She looked up. Two men dressed in white leggings and tunic with red trim walked toward them. The first man placed a covered plate in front of each of them. The second placed a goblet with an amber drink beside the plates. She continued after they moved away.

"If the king dies having no heir, my father is next in succession as Captain Commander of the White Hand. So that places me at a higher ranking than the children of other families. Since you are here as my guest, you would sit with me."

"Oh," Elwin said. "There seems to be a lot of things I don't know."

"That is why Mother wants me to teach you. At least she trusts me enough to teach you how to behave."

"I know how to behave," Elwin said. "And I can already pull in Air and release it back into my surroundings. And there is that whole I can tame all four Elements thing."

Zarah's eyes widened and turned into a scowl. "Shhh. We aren't supposed to speak on that yet. Remember? There are a lot of superstitious people that will see you as … uh … a bad omen."

"Bad omen?" Elwin said. "How come I have never heard about this prophecy?"

She gave him a wry smile. "Because you grew up on a farm. People in civilization know of the prophecies because the priests preach about it every Lifeday in the temples."

"Every Lifeday?" Elwin asked. "How can this prophecy be so important that people talk about it at the end of every tenday?"

"The beginning," Zarah said matter-of-factly.

"What?"

"Lifeday starts the tenday," Zarah said. "Evesday ends the tenday. Evesday is the day that comes before. The eve of Life announces an ending. Then the cycle begins anew on Lifeday, and we begin each tenday in reverence of the Lifebringer."

"Well," Elwin said feeling a bit agitated, "on the uncivilized farm, at the end of the tenday we rest. It is the only day of the tenday we don't spend in the fields. Some people go to the temple, sure, but most people just rest. What does it matter which day is first anyway?"

"It matters," Zarah said. "Anyway. Where was I? Ah. Right. The noble families."

Elwin blinked. They hadn't been talking about the families. He had asked about the prophecies. Zarah continued without giving him a chance to object.

"There are several lords and ladies that help King Justice rule the realm," she said. "The power of each house is in the order of succession. Though, the western lords sometimes forget that we are one kingdom. Lord Paradine is regent in the lands west of the River Serene, but he answers to the king of Justice, as does my family."

Elwin stared at her for a moment. Her smile made her eyes brighten in the morning light. He sighed. Perhaps he would just have to go to the temple to learn about the prophecies. Better for now just to play along.

"So," Elwin said at last, "if the lords and ladies live in other places, why is the table so large?"

Her voice seemed to explain that one should not eat dirt. "There are frequent balls and tournaments held for nobility. The table must be large enough to house all of the noble families and their children for the duration of the events."

"Oh," Elwin said. Then after a moment, he said, "I guess you have many friends and suitors?"

Zarah's eyes widened and her cheeks turned a light crimson. Elwin could not help but feel a moment of complete satisfaction at her reaction. She took a drink from the goblet in front of her. After replacing the cup, her face had regained its cool composure.

"Ours is one of the few noble families gifted with the powers of the Elements. The gifted lords and ladies seldom leave their estates to attend the events held by other nobles. I have been to several balls with lordlings of noble families, but I make those who are not gifted uncomfortable. It is the same with the maidens. Sure, they will speak politely with me, but they have never treated me like one of them. Mother says it is because they are jealous of my power."

"But you don't think so?" Elwin said.

"No," she said in a resigned voice. "I think they fear me. They know someday I will fly and tame lightning. No man wishes to be wed to a woman who has such power. Few women care to befriend a woman whose power they can never rival."

"But," Elwin said, "your father does not tame the Elements, but your parents seem to match."

"Yes," Zarah said. "But he was born to the first noble family. And he has touched weapons and the training to combat the Elements."

"Touched?" Elwin said. "Like my pendant. So it was a weapon made by tethering the Elements?"

"Yes," she smiled. "Only, touched weapons are forged to combat elementalists."

"That doesn't make sense," Elwin said. "Why would elementalists make weapons to be used against them?"

"There are several reasons," she said. "First, there are elementalists who would use their power for evil. We need a way for the ungifted to combat the Death Element. Touched weapons serve this purpose. Also, we cannot always protect ourselves. Even elementalists have vulnerabilities. If we overexert our essence with taming, we can lose consciousness or worse. Having a trained swordsman to protect us against the power of the Elements can mean the difference between life and death.

"Anyway," Zarah said. "We should eat. Mother will expect us shortly."

"Oh," Elwin said. "I forgot."

He removed the cover and examined the contents on the plate. It looked like eggs, but it had other things stuffed into it. Some sort of meat and fruit or vegetables, maybe. He took a small bite. More flavors than he could place filled his senses. One of the spices made his eyes water, but another spice had a sweet flavor as well. He wasn't sure that he liked it. But he kept eating it, taking small bites.

Zarah muffled a giggle with her hand. "Do you not like it?"

"I am not sure," Elwin said honestly. "It's different."

He took a drink. "Mmm. This tastes like apples. Almost like cooled cider."

"That is because it is appled juice. Like cider, it comes from apples, but sugarcane is added with water."

"I definitely like this."

When she smiled at him, he found himself wondering how soft her lips would feel. Her eyes consumed his. When the silence stretched on and neither spoke, he became uncomfortable under her gaze.

"I wonder how Feffer is getting on," he said to break the silence.

Zarah grimaced. "I have seen the way Sir Gibbins trains the novice soldiers. I imagine that he is not having a pleasant time."

"Oh," Elwin said. "I wonder when I will get to see him."

"Not for some time," she said. "Mother was clear that you are not to go near the soldiers. Some of them are still … Well, it would be better if you would not go near them for a while. Perhaps you should write a letter to Feffer."

Of course. The soldiers wouldn't want to see Elwin. He had killed one of theirs. Elwin wasn't so sure he wanted to see them either.

Perhaps a letter would be better. Zarah was probably exaggerating about the training anyway. Feffer had always enjoyed playing at being a solider. Elwin would bet his favorite book against a copper, Feffer loved the idea of becoming a soldier enough to go through anything. He probably still thought it all a game. At least Feffer would never change.

Elwin smiled.

Chapter 8

UNEXPECTED

Feffer balanced on the tall, wooden post with his left leg straight out behind him and both arms stretched out in front of him. He was atop the fourth post in a row of twelve. The rest of his squad stood atop the others. It had taken a tenday for Gibbins to separate the new recruits into squads, and Feffer hadn't been grouped with Wilton or anyone else from his town. He only saw the others in passing, but he hadn't seen his brother since they had been split up. That had been what? More than a month? With all the training, keeping up with the passing of days had become too much of a chore.

Wilton was chosen by Lord Zaak Lifesong, along with several others to train with more experienced soldiers. It didn't bother Feffer though. Wilton always talked to Feffer like he would mess up. He'd show him.

Besides, he liked most of the others in his group. Everyone except Gurndol.

"Switch!" Sir Gibbins yelled.

Feffer jumped into the air as high as his one leg would take him and maneuvered his legs in the opposite position, landing on his right foot.

"Six."

This was one of Feffer's favorite exercises. Wait. What was he thinking? Favorite exercise? Well, he could at least admit to himself that the different routines could be a little fun. At least the ones he was the best at. Which was most of them. In fact, no one in his squad could keep up with him. Well, no one except Gurndol.

"Switch!"

Again, he jumped into the air and performed the maneuver.

"Seven."

Each new squad had a member of the White Hand overseeing their training. Gibbins chose which group that he trained, and he had made it clear that he chose the group needing the largest amount of special attention.

Feffer heard a thud behind him. He knew who had fallen, before Gibbins yelled the name.

"Fandar, you worthless worm! Ten press-ups, now!"

Fandar came from a village far west of Justice, too small to even make it on the map. Feffer spared a glance back at the large boy on the ground. Taller by a foot than even Feffer and wider than any other recruit, Fandar's sandy hair shook as he struggled through his press-ups.

On a pedestal in front of him, Feffer heard a derisive snort. He glanced to see Gurndol's scowl directed at Fandar. Almost as tall as Feffer, Gurndol balanced on his own pedestal with the same lithe grace Feffer himself possessed. Almost. Gurndol's rear leg swayed with the wind to help maintain balance, while Feffer could keep poised without moving.

When Gurndol's eyes met his, Gurndol's scowl deepened. Feffer gave him a smug smile.

Gurndol was from Justice proper. Feffer had heard that he was from a noble family, seventh in line to succession. Even though Gibbins hadn't named a squad leader, Gurndol already tried to assume the role. And every time anyone made them start over, Gurndol punished him with a prank. They were never friendly pranks. More often than not, the recipient of the malicious deed was Fandar.

The larger boy had a difficult time even doing the ten press-ups. Feffer wanted to do something to help, but there was nothing he could do for him.

"Everyone else gets to start over," Gibbins announced.

Even though they had all known the command was coming, the other boys joined Gurndol in staring daggers into Fandar, who slunk back to his pedestal and began to scramble up. Gurndol rolled his eyes and shared a look with the others.

Feffer gritted his teeth. He decided that he very much disliked bullies. His pranks had always been for a laugh, but they were harmless. He would put stink weed under a bed or dump water on someone in the middle of summer. Maybe steal a pie or two. He would never fill a pillow sack with soapstone, hold someone in his bunk, and hit him til he cried.

"Switch!"

"One."

Fandar had bruises all over his mid-section. The worst part was, Gurndol convinced the other squad members to hold Fandar down. The others went along with it because they didn't want to be singled out. Except maybe Marlin. If not so high and mighty as Gurndol, Marlin was also nobly born, and he seemed to enjoy the pranks. But, without Gurndol's influence, Feffer doubted Marlin would have been so bad.

Gurndol was the problem. Noble prat. When Feffer tried to stop them from hitting Fandar with the soapstone, Gurndol threatened to do the same to *him*.

I'd like to see him try.

"What was that, worm?"

Feffer realized that he had spoken aloud when Sir Gibbins was eye to eye with him.

"Did you address me?"

"No, Sir Gibbins."

"Everyone go get five laps. You can thank Feffer here for speaking out of turn. Then, we get to finish our post stands."

Feffer hopped from the post and took the lead. One lap consisted of running the length of the fence and back on the far side. Each lap was about a mile. Thanks to the slip of *his* tongue they would have to run five miles. That was far worse than extra post stands. He would have to grow eyes in the back of his head for the next several days. Maybe his slip would get Fandar off the hook this time.

Gurndol caught up to him. "Always running your mouth, *farmboy*. It's going to get you hurt one of these days."

He had tried to explain to the thick-headed prat that his Da was a merchant not a farmer, but Gurndol didn't seem to care. Feffer thought about tripping him but didn't want to even consider the consequences of fighting during a punishment.

I may not be able to sleep well over the next several days, he thought, *but by the Lifebringer, I will win this race.*

As Feffer sped up, he heard heavy footsteps pick up the pace behind him.

Elwin sat in the wooden chair, leaning on the writing table in front of him. Zarah sat at the desk to his right with her back straight and her hands in her lap. She looked straight ahead, her expression attentive.

In front of him, Jasmine's voice made a sea of words. He found his mind more intent on the melody in her tone than the meaning of her speech. Preferring to give history lessons, Jasmine still hadn't spoken of the prophecies.

He knew some of the other things she spoke of were important. For instance, the more common tamings were called talents. Each talent had a specific name, which was useful in combat situations. But why did he need to know where the name *lightning hurl* originated? Wouldn't it have been far more useful to learn how to make a veil than to know who first discovered it?

Many tamings had no names. Each elementalist learned his own little tricks with taming that others did not know. No one bothered to name these, or sometimes there were many names for the same taming.

Elwin resisted the urge to look at the contraption in the back of the room. Zarah had called the thing a water clock. Each hour it would chime the number of hours that had passed in the day.

Elwin wanted to see the inside to figure out how it worked. When he had mentioned the idea to Zarah, she had told him it was worth a thousand gold crowns. He decided that it would be better not to touch it. Ever. Still, it was a fascinating device.

Elwin had learned to tell time by watching the sun and by reading a sun dial. The clock had been constructed by a dwarven artificer, named Pwintus Tarficer, and had hands that told the hour and minute of the day. It even tracked a tenday. In the center, a plaque of silver rotated inside a square that named each day.

Two more days until Lifeday, the only day of the tenday he wouldn't have to attend lecture. He was promised the morning to himself, but then he would begin to learn swordplay with Zaak and Zarah. Thus far, every day had consisted of a morning of attempting to sense Zarah's or Jasmine's essence with his own, followed by an afternoon of lecture. Playing with a sword would be a nice break from sitting in the hard chair. The seat might as well have been constructed from stone instead of wood.

Mahindra had been true to her word by delivering his two new outfits, and in the days that followed, one or two new sets came each evening for an entire tenday. He couldn't imagine ever needing that many sets of clothing. But he had to admit, his new trousers were softer than the cotton he was accustomed to wearing, which made the summer heat more bearable. But it did little to cushion his bum from the hard seat. Even his boots were softer, though he could still walk on the stone hallways in them without hurting his feet. Both his trousers and his tunic were a deep blue. He had never owned anything like them.

"Elwin," Jasmine said. "Are you listening?"

Elwin sat straighter in his seat and nodded, hoping that she didn't ask him to repeat what she had been saying.

"It is very important that you understand the things that I am telling you. Your life will likely depend on them some day." She cleared her voice. "As I was saying, there are weapons that exist to deflect the power of the Elements. Others are made to absorb our powers to be used at a later time. These weapons, like your pendant are touched, and they are made by elementalists and used to hunt down those that are Death bound. This is the primary task of the Guardians of Life."

From the corner of his eye, he noticed a thin smile on Zarah's lips at the mention of the touched weapons. Elwin did not interrupt Jasmine to tell her that Zarah had already explained touched weapons to him. Jasmine did not slow down to give him the chance anyway.

"These weapons are difficult to make, and they should only be given to those who can be trusted. But several have fallen into nefarious hands. So we must always be aware, because there are those out there who fear you so greatly that they hunt you.

"The Guardians of Life is an order that was founded to preserve elementalists. We entrust them with governing our actions. The laws that they put forth are for our protection. So the people that do not share our powers do not need fear us.

"The laws are not many, and all violations are given a trial. But he who is proven to have *willfully* broken the law is given a speedy execution. No one will force you to become Life bound, but the Element of Death is forbidden. Those proven to be bound to Death by trial are in violation of the law. Murder by way of the Elements is also forbidden. Using the Elements to compel others to perform actions that lead to the death of others is also a crime."

She paused. "Are you listening, Elwin?"

Elwin nodded. "So, I really will have a trial?"

Jasmine nodded. "As I said before, it should mostly be a formality. Since I was there to witness the accident, and I am Life bound, you will likely be exonerated. Though, the incident will be filed away, and you will likely be watched. It has not been verified, but there has been rumored to exist a faction within the Guardians, called the warders. One will likely be assigned to you, if such a faction exists.

"Which reminds me, theft by way of the Elements is not strictly forbidden by the Guardians, but one would be wise not to make it a habit. These crimes typically fall to local magistrates, but several suspected Elemental thieves have disappeared. It is likely that this task is given to the warders as well. Any questions?"

"When will this trial be?" Elwin asked.

"I will appear before them this afternoon on your behalf. Hypothetically, which you need to understand for educational purposes, if the inquisitors consider me an unreliable witness, which is not likely, they would seek you out for execution."

Elwin stood up. "Seek me out execution?"

"I said there is nothing to worry over. If you would like, you can witness the proceedings? Now that you know about the trial, it might be a good lesson for you. I did not suggest it sooner, because I did not want to worry you. But you asked, and I do not make a habit out of lying to my pupils."

He looked to Zarah, who gave him a tight-lipped smile.

"Should I go too, Mother?"

"Yes," she said. "I think this will be educational for all."

Elwin sagged back into his chair. His mind registered Jasmine's voice, but he didn't hear her words until she said his name. By her tone, she had spoken his name more than once.

Once his gaze touched hers, she said. "It appears my instincts were right. It is obvious there will be little more instruction until after the trial. Very well, then. Zarah, I will trust you to escort Elwin to the Temple of Life by the sixteenth hour. You two are dismissed."

After Jasmine left the room, Elwin sat for a minute, trying to sort his thoughts. One word stuck out in his mind the most. Execution. Execution? It had been an accident. Still someone had died.

Zarah leaned over toward him and placed her hand on his. "It will be alright, Elwin. Mother will take care of everything."

The touch of her hand gave him comfort. When he looked at it, she pulled her hand away. Her cheeks reddened. "My apologies," Zarah said. "I overstepped myself."

"No," Elwin said. "I ... um ... thank you." He moved his hand half toward hers on the table.

She smiled and touched her fingers atop his. "You are going to be alright, Elwin. You have a kindness in you. The Guardians will surely see that."

His eyes lingered on hers for several moments. He could feel her heart pulse through the tips of her fingertips on his hand. It seemed as though their hearts beat as one.

"Besides," she said with a wry smile, "they will know a poor country bumpkin who is in over his head when they see one. They could sooner sacrifice a baby lamb."

He pulled his hand away from hers and narrowed his eyes. "Is that supposed to make me feel better?"

She shrugged, never losing her smile. Elwin sighed.

"Mother is not worried," she said. "So you should not be either. You will be fine."

"I killed a man, Zarah."

Her wry smile faded into a thin grimace and any sign of amusement left her eyes. "It was an accident. It was tragic, but it was not your fault."

"Did he have a family?"

There was a moment of silence. When she answered, her voice was soft. "I heard Father tell Mother that Biron was from a farm with a large family."

Elwin wasn't sure why, but that made it worse.

"Are you sure you want to go to the trial?"

He met her gaze. Her smile held more concern than he deserved, but looking into her eyes made him feel like he could have done anything. Finally, he nodded.

"I need to be there. I need to see Biron's family and tell them I'm sorry."

"We should go, then. The trial will begin within the hour."

An hour. Elwin took a deep breath. Within the hour, he would face the inquisitor. No one from his hometown had ever been taken to trial, so he only knew what he had heard in stories. He had thought only those unfortunate few who pledged their souls to the Seeker faced such a trial.

Had he stayed in Benedict, would his friends and neighbors have turned against him? After Biron's death, they had looked at him as if a stranger or some dangerous creature. Their downcast eyes and accusing stares lingered in his mind. Would they have scrawled a dragon on the door of his father's farm in accusation of his lost soul?

A sudden fear gripped him. What if the inquisitor found him guilty? Word would reach Benedict. What would happen to his parents? His grandparents?

He looked to Zarah for strength. Her face appeared a mask of calm composure as she stood next to him with quiet patience.

His legs trembled slightly as he rose to join her.

༄

"This stance," Sir Gibbins yelled, "is water form."

Feffer stood in line with his squad watching Sir Gibbins. His feet held a wide base, and he held a practice sword in both hands. Feffer wanted to take his own wooden sword and imitate the stance, but he made his limbs remain still.

"Water bends around the rock," Gibbins said. "When it freezes, water then breaks the rock apart from within. You must learn to be like water. Now watch."

Moving the sword from rest, Gibbins pivoted to the side and made a slight sweeping motion with his sword. He held the pose for the blink of an eye, then moved back to the original pose.

"This is called sweeping tide one," Gibbins said. "It will deflect a lunge. We will talk more on lunges and other attacks later. Now, I want each of you to attempt to parry my lunge. I will demonstrate the maneuver a few more times. Watch carefully."

Again, Gibbins performed the maneuver and returned the sword to water form. Then, he repeated the action several more times. Feffer found himself holding the sword in imitation of Sir Gibbins and performing the maneuver along with him. Sir Gibbins' glower could have wilted roses in spring. Feffer dropped the sword's point so quickly, he almost stabbed the ground.

"Oh," Gibbins said with a cold smile. "We have a fast learner, do we? Feffer has volunteered to go first."

As Gibbins approached, Feffer raised his practice sword into the water form. Something inside Feffer seemed to wake up. The sword in his hand and the bend in his legs felt right. Without moving into any stance, Gibbins lunged forward. As he had done before, Feffer moved the sword in sweeping tide one.

When Feffer struck Gibbins' sword and pivoted, the larger man's sword pushed to the side with comfortable ease. Feffer felt his jaw slackened, so he forced his mouth closed. The shocked expression on Gibbins' face suggested he shared Feffer's feeling of surprise.

Feffer recovered from the lunge a moment later and moved the sword and his feet back to water form as Gibbins had.

Gibbins blinked a few times and said, "That wasn't … terrible." Gibbins' face hardened and he shifted back into water form.

"Again."

Gibbins stared at Feffer for several moments without so much as blinking. No part of the other man moved or twitched. Feffer imitated him, fixing his eyes on the other man's sword. Sweat began to roll down his back. At last, Feffer blinked. Before his eyes came fully open, something inside told Feffer to move through the sweeping form, and he obeyed without thinking. His practice sword struck his teacher's weapon and pushed it aside as before.

No shock showed on Gibbins' face this time. He nodded to Feffer in a gesture he had never seen from the man. Not quite sure what it meant, Feffer returned the nod.

"At ease soldier," Gibbins said.

Feffer dropped the sword from water form. Then he smiled. Gibbins had called him soldier. His commander's scowl returned, and Feffer quickly smoothed the smile from his face. Curse him for a fool. Soldiers didn't smile like idiots.

"Alright. The rest of you worms get ready."

One by one Gibbins lunged at them. Each boy took a few bruises before getting the maneuver somewhat correct. Every one of them looked sloppy. Except Gurndol. He pushed the sword aside with the same ease Feffer had. Then it became Fandar's turn.

After ten attempts, Gibbins stopped trying to instruct Fandar and announced, "I guess this worm needs to see me bruise the rest of you a few more times before he gets it. Gurndol. Water form. Now."

This time, Gibbins stood without moving and waited for Gurndol to blink before striking. The first lunge struck Gurndol in the midsection. Gurndol grunted and stepped backward.

"Broaden your stance," Gibbins said. "Anticipate the attack."

When Gibbins turned his attention to one of their other squad mates, Gurndol gave Feffer a look that could have baked bread.

Feffer glared back. None of it had been his fault.

It had been several days since the incident on the poles, but no prank had been directed at Feffer or Fandar. And Feffer had continued to cause them extra work, trying to take the blame from Fandar. By the glint in Gurndol's eyes, Feffer would have wagered an ox cart of gold to a copper pence that Gurndol would do something soon.

"Feffer," Gibbins said. "Water form. Now."

Almost without thinking, Feffer moved into the stance and parried the coming blow. As if the sword had grown a mind of its own, Feffer found his body countering with a lunge. Shock filled the other man's eyes as Gibbins blocked Feffer's blade with a downward strike.

The larger man moved his feet backward and slashed down at Feffer's face. Feffer jumped back and repositioned his feet into water form. Gibbins lunged again just as Feffer's feet settled. Mimicking Gibbins' block, Feffer struck down at the lunging blade and countered with the downward strike he had seen from his teacher.

Gibbins parried with a different form, then countered with a new strike, which narrowly missed Feffer's skull. He felt both of the new moves imprint onto his mind. Gibbins gave Feffer an opening to repeat the attack, and Feffer took it. Gibbins blocked with an upward parry and gave yet another counter attack. Without pausing, Gibbins gave Feffer an opening for the new attack.

Back and forth they went. Feffer attacking and blocking in imitation of his teacher. After going through twelve attacks and twelve blocks, Gibbins moved even faster without giving any new maneuvers. He cycled through the same attacks several times, then without warning, he began to do the attacks in a random order.

Feffer's arms moved through the motions of each maneuver, keeping his center in the water form. Each block seemed to give Feffer more of an advantage, but every counter Feffer made was batted aside with ease. Without warning, Gibbins' attacks increased in intensity, until all Feffer could do was block. Gibbins' blade began to move too swiftly to follow, so Feffer had watched his shoulders and continued blocking. After several moments, Feffer's arms began to burn and the sword became heavy.

Sweat stung his left eye, then WHACK! WHACK! The loud sound of cracking wood filled his senses.

Feffer smelled fruit pies baking. Maybe Momme had placed them in the window to cool. He could sneak up and take one without her ever noticing. It seemed like forever since he had eaten anything sweet. Because he ... wait. That wasn't right.

The lights above him began to move and take shape, and he heard voices.

"In all my years of training new recruits, I've never seen anything like it. He mimicked every new maneuver with near-perfect precision." It sounded like Gibbins. Was he dreaming?

The lights and shadows still moved, but his eyes wouldn't focus on them. His skull throbbed with pain. Another voice spoke in an agitated tone.

"I don't care if he is Faragand the Red come back to life," the other man said. "You don't split a new recruit's head the first time he has a sword in his hands."

At last the two men came into focus. The other man was Lord Zaak Lifesong himself. Neither seemed to notice Feffer. He decided to lie there for a moment to figure out why he was flat on his back. Hadn't he been looking for pie a moment before?

"I tell you sire," Gibbins said in a defensive tone. "He could be the best I've ever seen. I've trained thousands. His first day, and he's mastered water form!"

"Are you sure your head wasn't the one that was split?" Lord Lifesong asked skeptically.

"The Seeker take me if it isn't true," Gibbins said, "but if we can condition his body to keep up with his mind, the boy will be the greatest swordsman we've ever seen."

Feffer could see Lord Lifesong's face clearly. He had an annoyed expression, and his tone would have made Feffer recoil had it been directed at him. "The boy won't even be able to hold a sword if his brains are leaking out of a cracked skull."

Then, the memories of his training session came into his mind. He could recall every detail of the fight. The Lifebringer save him.

He had *fought* Sir Gibbins. Had he lost his wits?

Gibbins cast his eyes downward. "Aye sire. Of course. I ... Every weapons trainer can only dream for such a student. I might have gotten a bit carried away."

Who were they talking about?

"We will speak on this further," Lord Lifesong said. "It appears he has awakened."

"There he is," Gibbins said, kneeling beside Feffer. "Can you sit?"

Feffer tried. Pain shot through his midsection and his vision reeled. He closed his eyes and said, "No." The word sounded odd in his ears.

"I think I cracked his ribs," Gibbins said.

Lord Lifesong knelt beside him as well. Both men stared at him with probing eyes.

"What is your name, soldier?"

His mouth was dry, but he forced the words out. "Feffer Hanck Madrowl."

Gibbins spoke next. "Where in the abyss are you from?"

"I'm from Benedict." The words came easier this time. "To the east."

"Have you had any previous training?" Gibbin's asked.

"No."

"Open your eyes wide," Lord Lifesong said.

When Feffer obeyed, a large thumb pealed back his eyelid. Lord Lifesong's dark eye peered at him for several moments.

"Dragons take me," Gibbins cursed. "Looks like I'm going to have take him to the temple for healing."

Feffer blinked as much from the curse as from the idea of healing. Swearing by dragons was a bad omen, but the idea of having another person use the Elements on him didn't seem much better.

Lord Lifesong looked at Gibbins with an emotionless mask. His words held little inflection. "Yes. That would be wise."

Feffer closed his eyes again.

Chapter 9

ESCAPING THE INQUISITION

Feffer awoke in a bed.

The thick cushions beneath him suggested he was somewhere other than his bunk. Light came in from windows all around the room. Outside, he heard the sounds of someone shouting, but he couldn't make out the words. The inflection of the voice had the sound of a city crier. He had heard a few throughout the city upon their arrival.

He sat up to get a better look at his surroundings. The large room had several rows of beds covered in white sheets. As far as Feffer could tell, he was the only occupant.

"He wakes," a woman's voice said from beside him.

Feffer jumped, almost falling off the bed. He turned to see a woman not more than a handful of years his senior sitting in a chair at his bedside and smiling at him. Even beneath her simple white robe with yellow trim, he could make out the round shapes of ample breasts. On her shoulder was a teardrop falling on a yellow flower. Her round eyes seemed too big for her narrow face, and her nose came to a sharp point. He found his eyes drifting back down to her breasts.

"Uh," Feffer said. "Where am I?"

"This is the Temple of Life," she said. "By His powers of Life, you have been healed."

"Healed?" Feffer said not bothering to hide his confusion. "Why did I need to be healed?"

She laughed as if he had said some great joke. Her bosom bounced in a pleasant fashion, and he found himself grinning at them. Uh. Her.

"Oh," she said. "Well. Your skull was cracked by a practice sword. Do you remember being brought here or any of the events before or after your incident?"

Feffer frowned, making himself look up at her face. Incident. What incident? He remembered training in the yard with water form. Then, he had learned the sweeping tide one.

"Gibbins," Feffer said. "I was in the yard and … Wait. He cracked my skull?"

"And three of your ribs," she said with a smile. "They are healed now. What else do you remember?"

He reached up to touch his skull and found cloth wrapped around his head. "What's this? If I've been healed, why do I need a bandage?"

"It soaked up the blood," she said. "We will move you to the bath and have you cleaned up after you have had some stew. Now, what can you remember?"

Feffer closed his eyes and tried to think. He could feel the moves he had learned working through his mind. A large part of him itched to grab a sword and go through all of the maneuvers. The match with Gibbins was fresh in his mind, all the way up until the sound of cracking wood. No. Not wood. That had been the sound of his skull being cracked. Everything after that was a blank. He told her as much.

"This is a very common symptom," she said, her smile never wavering. "You will need to eat to get your strength up. Here." She placed a wooden bowl in his hands. "Take this."

It contained a brown broth with chunks of something in it.

"What is it?"

"It's a stew of sorts," she said. "Eat it all."

He grabbed the spoon and tasted it. The texture did not have the consistency of meat, and it all tasted like … salt and sage? Still, it wasn't any worse than the porridge and stew in the mess hall. He ate it in large bites, trying to get it into his belly as quickly as possible.

"Very good," she said in a patronizing tone. "I will have more brought to you shortly."

She stood as if to go, and Feffer grabbed the sleeve of her robe. "What am I supposed to do?"

"You are to rest."

"For how long?"

"Until you are better."

Feffer gritted his teeth. "How long will that take?"

"Oh," she said in a reproachful voice. "Irritability is also a symptom. Rest will make you feel better."

The sounds from outside became louder as if a crowd had gathered. A second crier joined the first, and Feffer could just make out the words.

"A Death bound has been captured! Bear witness to the trial! Come see the trial of Elwin the Dark!"

Feffer dropped his spoon into the broth. He shook his head and strained to hear the crier. He repeated the phrase over and over.

"What in the abyss?" Feffer said.

For the first time, the woman's smile faded. "Mind your tongue. You are in the Temple of Life."

"Did he say Elwin?"

Her lips thinned into a frown and her voice sounded remorseful. "Yes. Some young boy murdered a soldier in some small town to the east. A pity one so young was corrupted by the power of Death."

"Dragons take you for a fool," Feffer said. "He isn't a thumping Death bound."

The woman's mouth dropped open, and she stared at Feffer as if he had grown a tail and breathed fire. Her jaw worked for several moments without producing any words. She crossed her arms beneath her ample breast, making some of her cleavage show at the nape of the neck. Feffer felt as if his eyes had become attached to her milky skin by some invisible string.

She quickly covered her breasts with both hands and spoke in a shrill voice. "Young man! You will mind your tongue, or I will take soapstone to it."

He felt a profound sense of disappointment at no longer being able to see her cleavage. The feeling became replaced by an intense anger.

"Where is this trial?" Feffer said, getting out of the bed. His legs wobbled beneath him, but he forced them to work with sheer will. And anger. "The Seeker take you all. Where is this thumping trial?"

⁓

Elwin stared at the Temple of Life, while standing to the side of the cobblestone road to avoid the flow of traffic. He hardly saw the people leading carts or walking with wicker baskets filled with goods. The temple seemed to loom over him.

Made of plain stones, the front of the building made a giant L. The shorter part of the L jutted toward the street, while the longer part running parallel to the road had several windows. A fenced garden rested in the crook of the building facing the street. Flowers of many colors surrounded tall redwood trees.

Behind the L, tall walls stretched into the sky as if trying to reach the sun. Several of the windows on the upper floors were stained with colors. The top most window looked like the tip of a candle flame, but the lower glass held an array of patterns that didn't seem to look like anything at first. But, when he looked at the building as a whole, the windows formed a red crescent with a golden circle inside it.

"We should go," Zarah said.

Elwin jumped at the sound of her voice. Though she had led him there, he had forgotten she was with him. He felt his cheeks burn and felt a nervous laugh escape his lips.

She smiled at him. "Are you ready?"

He nodded.

Though the double doors were propped open, two guards stood to either side of the entrance. Standing against the wall, each man struck the same rigid pose with a hand resting on the hilt of his sword, eying passersby down the length of his nose. Both men wore a tunic with the symbol of a golden circle resting between the tips of a red crescent moon.

When Zarah approached the door, they regarded her without blinking. She walked up the steps as if she had every right to the place, not even bothering to glance at the men standing at the entrance. The guards regarded her for the briefest of moments, before their eyes settled on him.

He attempted to mirror her confidence, but he couldn't stop himself from looking at their faces. Cold eyes seemed to pierce his thoughts. He quickened his steps, eager to cross the threshold of the temple to move beyond their gazes.

Once inside, Elwin stopped.

Light spilled into the expansive courtroom from the entryway, but no windows lined the walls to give light to the room. Bare walls surrounded several rows of wooden pews, split by a center aisle, facing a raised platform at the other end of the room. Sparse lanterns made the space between the rows of benches seem darker at the front, but provided enough light to see seven ornate chairs atop the platform. Beyond the chairs, a hollow doorway opened up to darkness.

Zarah grabbed his hand and pulled him toward the last row. "Let us sit."

"Are you sure we are in the right place?"

"Yes," she said. "We are half an hour early. Others will come."

He let her guide him to the middle of the pew and sat next to her. Half an hour. He wanted it to be over with, but at the same time …

He never wanted any of this.

Biron had brothers and sisters, a mother and father who would miss him. A man was dead because of his actions. It was an accident, sure, but did that excuse it?

The sound of boots came from behind him. He turned to see a woman with brown hair tied in a tail enter with a balding man. Their movements were rigid, as if each step landed on pikes. Several children of varying ages followed the first two. The one who stood out to Elwin was a pretty girl no more than a handful of years older than him. She carried a young child and glanced at Elwin and Zarah as she passed by.

Elwin flinched when her eyes settled on him. Her lips quivered as if she might cry at any moment, and her eyes appeared swollen as though she had already been crying for some time. One by one they walked to the front of the room and filled the first two rows and part of the third.

Biron's family, Elwin realized. It had to be.

Elwin could hear town criers start to yell in the streets. "Come see the trial of Elwin the Dark!"

"A Death bound has been captured! Bear witness to the trial!"

"See the Death witch crucified!"

Zarah leaned into him and gave his hand a gentle squeeze. "It will be alright," she whispered. "Nothing is going to happen to you, I promise. They just do not understand."

Elwin didn't look at her. He couldn't take his eyes off the family at the front of the room. Other people began to fill the empty seats. The criers continued shouting, and before long there was not an empty seat. People began to line the walls around the courtroom. Eventually, men bearing the same crest as the guards out front began to push their way through and stand at even intervals along the walls. Several would-be witnesses to the trial were displaced. Two more men stood by the doors and crossed halberds to prevent further entry.

Elwin could still hear a crowd at the front of the building. He couldn't hear individual curses, but he heard several words that conveyed their intent.

"Burn ..."

"... Witch ..."

"Behead ..."

No windows to escape through and a crowd blocked the exit.

Sweat tickled his forehead, and he found his mouth too dry to swallow, as if cornmeal had stuck in his throat. Breathing became labored, and his vision began to blur.

Zarah leaned over and whispered into his ear. "Shh ... you are going to be alright. They do not understand us. It is alright. It will be over before you know it."

He closed his eyes and felt tears roll down his cheeks. Taking several steadying breaths, he forced his thoughts to relax as he did when searching for his essence.

Elwin could feel the Air in the room connecting all of the people. He could feel it pulsing with life and power. He felt his heartbeat. There was peace in its rhythm. All the while, he heard Zarah's soothing voice whispering in his ear.

He continued taking slow steady breaths. Calm washed over him.

He opened his eyes. Elwin felt the man's gaze to his left. When he looked at him, the man narrowed his eyes and looked away.

Elwin heard metal slide across metal from behind him. The halberds had uncrossed, and the crowd at the doorway parted. Jasmine walked through them and marched down the center aisle. Her face was a portrait of calm serenity.

The crowd quieted somewhat with her passing, but Elwin heard several people whisper Jasmine's name. Many people avoided looking at her all together.

She stood several paces in front of the central chair.

Many people believed that an elementalist could control a person's mind through direct eye contact. Jasmine had spoken of using the Elements for compulsion, but she didn't tell him how it worked. Still, it didn't make sense. These people were afraid of her, yet her purpose was to protect them.

Waves of silence filled the room, and Elwin followed the crowd's gaze to the front of the court.

Two women in white robes emerged from the dark opening as one. Their robes bore the crest of a red crescent moon with a golden circle centered between its tips. Each woman had more than a touch of silver in her hair. They paused in the doorway and bowed their heads as one, then turned and walked away from one another, coming to a stop at the furthest two chairs from the center.

Next, two men in white robes stepped out together and bowed. Both men were of an age with the women and similar in height to one another. Each stepped to the opposite ends of the platform and stood next to either woman.

Another pair of men stepped from the opening. And though they moved in unison, their differing sizes did not give the same picture of symmetry the other pairs had presented. The larger of the two had naturally tanned skin and arms as thick as tree trunks. He had long, dark hair that had individual braids.

"He's from Kalicodon," Zarah whispered, "the nation northeast of Alcoa." Zarah gasped. "The other man is a dwarf."

Next to the large man, stood a stocky man with short cropped hair, half the height of the first. His broad nose reminded Elwin of the dwarf he had seen in the palace, but he had no beard. From what Zarah had said, a dwarf would rather sever a limb than even trim his beard.

The six turned in unison to face the opening. A moment later, a bald man holding a shepherd's crook stepped from the darkness and stood behind the center chair. His white robes had red embroidery, and the crest on his breast differed slightly from the others. An orange flame, like the tip of a candle, rested atop the crescent moon.

He raised the crook for a moment, then slammed the end into the floor. It felt like thunder rolling across the room. Two more times, he raised the crook, sending reverberations across the room.

An old voice articulated each word. "Let us all, under the Lifebringer, bear witness to the proceedings. We call forth His righteous truth to guide our hands over the fate of one Elwin Escari, who under the powers of the Elements, has prematurely ended the life of another, Biron Onderhill of Justice, by way of the Elements. We, the Guardians of Life, Searchers of Truth, will judge him under the Lifebringer's wisdom. Let the proceedings begin."

Three more times he pounded the floor with the shepherd's crook in slow succession. Then, as one, the seven members took their seats.

The man at the center cleared his throat. "Whom, if any, has come to serve as the defender of the accused?"

Jasmine's voice filled the room. "I, Jasmine Lifesong, High Counselor of the White Council, right hand to his majesty, King Brannon Justice the twenty-sixth, have come to defend the accused."

Several people gasped, and others began to whisper loudly.

"There must be a mistake."

"How could she defend a murderer?"

"Could he be innocent?"

The man with the crook pounded the end in rapid succession. The people quieted on the first strike of the crook, but he raised his voice as if they still whispered. "There will be order."

"Now," he said after a pause. "The defender will call the first witness."

"My thanks, your honor," Jasmine said. "I am the first witness."

"Please," he said, "continue."

"I have seen the actions that took place, leading to the death of Biron Onderhill. The accused, Elwin Escari, had just come into his power and absorbed the power of Air without willful knowledge. When he—"

"How do you know it was without his knowledge that he controlled the power of Air?" His voice held no venom, but something in his tone sent chills down Elwin's spine.

Jasmine gave a brief pause. "He had only first entered the shadow realm upon the previous evening. It was the next d—"

"Does this knowledge come solely from the word of the accused?"

"It does," Jasmine admitted. "However, I am certain of his words. He had no control over his taming and pulled in so much power that he almost consumed himself. He held in his flow as long as he could. And not having the knowledge to release or tame his powers, he thrust his power in a single burst. The flow caught a table of swords, which were thrown into the air. One of them accidentally struck Biron. He died instantly."

The man nodded. "If you were in such a proximity to have witnessed this, how were you unable to stop his flow?"

"I ...," Jasmine said, "I tried, but his flow was too great."

Elwin could see the widening of the man's eyes. There were several short whispers from the crowd around him, but Elwin could not make out any words.

The large man to the bald man's left leaned closer, covering his mouth with a hand. His face moved as if speaking and the bald man nodded.

"The extent of your power is well known," he said. "If one so young has power so great, is it possible that he has bound his soul to the Element of Death and is deceiving you?"

Jasmine shook her head. "No. It is not possible. If I believed this was possible, I would not have come to his defense. I am bound to Life, and I would sense any that was Death bound."

The man was silent for a time. Elwin could hear his heart pound with each moment of silence. The man did not move and did not speak. The other members on the platform did not move either. They all regarded her with unblinking eyes. The silence lingered.

Elwin wished he could see Jasmine's face. He imagined her a mask of perfect serenity, but seeing her eyes would have made him feel better.

When the man spoke, Elwin flinched at the break in the silence. "We have heard tale of a Death bound warring in the lands of Alcoa, who is able to conceal his *vileness*. We have yet to ascertain exactly how, but there is overwhelming evidence to suggest this truth. Perhaps, this child has done the same?"

"You would like me to speculate on rumors?" Jasmine asked. "Or would you prefer that I speak to the obvious innocence of the accused?"

The man made a sound with his tongue and teeth. "One would be rash to suggest innocence without due consideration. We, the high members of the council, must deliberate on the matter. Have you anything further to add?"

Jasmine took a deep breath. "For near two months, I have observed and instructed Elwin in controlling his powers. I can sense his essence, and it is pure. I believe that he will be a great force for good and Life. He just needs to be trained. And he has spoken of his desire to be bound to Life.

"I have seen and killed my fair share of the Death bound. I have experienced evil at its core. Evil does not show remorse for a death of any kind. Elwin shows clear remorse for the death of Biron. I would wager my life that he would have done so, even had the fault not been his. This was a tragic accident. Please, I beg of you, do not make this tragedy worse by condemning an innocent child."

The man showed no reaction, and neither did the other members.

After a moment, he said, "Are there any more witnesses to come forth on the accused's behalf?"

"I am the only witness available." Jasmine said.

A familiar voice shouted from outside the front doors, "I can bare thumping witness. Move aside. Let me pass."

"Feffer," Elwin said as he recognized the voice.

The people around Elwin jumped as if goosed and glared at him as if he really had pinched them.

"I said let me through."

Neither of the guards moved from the path. Elwin could see his friend on the other side of the doorway. He wore a white robe, open to his small clothes and had a blood-soaked bandage wrapped around his head.

Elwin stood up and made a half-step toward the door, but stopped when Zarah placed a hand on his arm. He could read the command in her wide eyes as if she had spoken the words aloud. Her gaze practically screamed for him to sit. The people around Elwin had similar shocked stares. Some moved away from him as if to announce they were not with him. Elwin sat so hard the wood creaked.

"Take your hand off me," Feffer screeched. "I was there. Let me through."

One of the outside guards had a hand on Feffer's arm. Feffer pulled and tugged to be free, but his legs wobbled as if struggling to keep him upright. The guard's face was unperturbed by Feffer's attempts to escape. Feffer balled a fist as if to swing at the guard.

"No Feffer," Elwin said beneath his breath. "What are you doing?"

The cracking of the crook drew attention back to the front of the court.

"Let him pass," the bald man said. "If he wishes to give testimony, we will hear it."

When the man released Feffer, he jerked his arm as if breaking free had been his own choice and said in a haughty voice. "Now, move aside."

The guard glared holes into Feffer's back as he strutted down the aisle. Well, he tried to strut, but Feffer's legs staggered every few steps as if the ground moved beneath him.

Jasmine had turned to face Feffer, and her eyes did not look pleased to see him.

Feffer nodded to her and said, "Milady."

Her jaw clenched shut, and she moved to the side so Feffer could stand before the court.

"What is your name?" the bald man asked.

"I am Feffer Hanck Madrowl of Benedict, initiate of the White Hand."

"You witnessed Biron's death?"

Feffer nodded. "I was there."

"Please. Tell the court about the events before and after the murder."

"There was no thum ... uh ... murder," Feffer's voice held a slight tremor. "I have known Elwin all my life. Every bad thing he's ever done, I had to talk him into. Uh ... what I mean to say is ... When we were young. Much, much younger, we used to play pranks on people. Mostly, I had to drag Elwin into each one. He was never even any good at it. And he always felt ba—"

"Not quite that far before the event, child." There was no mirth in the bald man's smile.

Elwin felt his jaw hanging open and forced it closed. Feffer was making a mess of everything. What was he thinking? He wasn't thinking. Judging by the crimson stains on the bandage, someone had addled his wits when they cracked Feffer's skull.

Feffer's head bobbed up and down and his words came out in a rush. "Well, it was the Summer Solstice Festival, and the Inn was closed up tight. Guards were everywhere, and we couldn't get in. Everybody was trying to figure out what it all meant, and since we couldn't get into the inn for some sweetcakes, Elwin and I climbed to the top of my Da's shop. It overlooks the square, so we had a better look.

"Soon after Lord Lifesong announced that we were at war and needed recruits. When he called my brother's name, we got excited and went to get off the roof to find him. When I turned around to see if Elwin was following me, he was gone. At first, I thought he was just slow. Then I saw him *flying*. Well... It looked more like flailing than flying. His arms went all crazy and his face went like this."

Feffer flailed his arms and shook his head side to side, screaming.

Elwin wanted to look away, but he couldn't force his eyes to even blink. He felt sweat begin to appear on his forehead.

"Anyway," Feffer continued, "by the time I got back around to Elwin, he ran the other direction. Toward the square. He ran straight up to Faron. He's our town blacksmith. Well. He was. Now he's the king's blacksmith. I guess we'll need a new blacksmith now. Or maybe old Gryne will open his forge back up. He retired soon after Faron moved in. Faron's from Alcoa."

The bald man's voice was curt. "What happened next?"

"Right," Feffer said. "Sorry. I took a bit of a blow to the head. I've been healed, but I don't quite feel tip-top."

The bald man opened his mouth as if to speak, but Feffer's words ran over him.

"Elwin ran up to Faron and started to scream for help. This white light was leaking from his eyes, and he was scared like I've never seen him. Honest to Life, he looked like he had been promised the beating of his life from a thousand giants. Then, with no warning at all, the table just flew into the sky and swords went everywhere. The end. Clearly, it was an accident. Because, if Elwin had known how to fly and shoot tables into the sky before then, *I* would have known about it."

"Interesting," the bald man said. His smile held no warmth. "I must ask. Are you Death bound?"

"What?" Feffer said with more than a touch of incredulity. "No. That's ridiculous."

"You say you are not, but you also have admitted to habitual theft," the man said. "We may need to hold you for further questioning."

"I am no thief," Feffer protested. "I swiped sweetcakes before dinner. It was all in good fun. That doesn't make me a thumping Death bound. How do we know *you're* not a Death bound?"

Everyone around Elwin, including Zarah, gasped in unison. A few people began to rise as if to move for Feffer. The crook came smashing down.

"Order. I will have Order."

"Your Highest Honor?" Jasmine said before the crowd quieted. "If I may?"

The man gave her a single nod, but his glare suggested his patience had gone.

"I will be succinct," she said giving Feffer a look sharp enough to sever hairs. For a wonder, Feffer remained silent as she spoke. "It is obvious Feffer has recently been healed. The act of healing taxes both the mind and the body. He should be in a bed. Judging from the amount of blood on his bandage, it is highly possible that he will wake tomorrow and not remember any of his actions here today. I do not believe it is prudent to hold him responsible for his words this day."

The man regarded her for a long moment. His eyes narrowed as he looked upon Feffer. His words held no room for argument. "If he cannot be held responsible for his words, then his testimony will be disregarded. Does the Lady Lifesong have anything further to add?"

"I do not."

He looked over the crowd, "Would any others care to offer testimony?" Without pause he stood and said, "It is done."

When the other council members stood, the bald man struck with the crook three times. "Let us enter an hour of prayer to ascertain the fate of the accused."

Without further preamble, they all exited in the same order they had arrived.

People started to talk at a loud whisper. All of the conversations were the same. Half of the people argued for his innocence and half for his guilt. Most of the arguments repeated what had been said already.

"Why would Jasmine stand to defend someone if he wasn't innocent?"

"She was obviously deceived."

"She would know good from evil ..."

Before a full minute had passed, the arguments became an indiscernible jumble of shouts.

Elwin glanced at the man next to him. Cold eyes regarded him as one might watch a fox outside a henhouse.

"Excuse me," he said to the man. "I need to get out."

Zarah pulled on his arm, "Where do you think you are going?"

"I need to get to Feffer."

"Mother will take care of him," Zarah pointed.

Jasmine escorted Feffer toward the door. Feffer's face twisted in protest, but Elwin could not make out the words. Then Feffer's gaze met Elwin's.

Feffer's eyes lit up, and he pointed. And though Elwin could not hear his friend's voice, he could see Feffer's mouth form the words, "Elwin. There's Elwin."

Several people followed Feffer's finger to Elwin. Jasmine jerked Feffer's arm down and all but pushed him the last several paces out of the courtroom.

But the damage had been done. The conversations became more muted as people began to point out Elwin's location. The man with the cold eyes sitting beside Elwin stood and moved toward the exit, but he didn't take his eyes from Elwin until he had cleared the doorway.

Elwin looked around, hoping to find a friendly face but found none. Most of the people avoided his gaze, but not all. The young woman who had carried the child looked right at him. Her lip still quivered, but the tears had left her eyes. She never blinked as her face twisted into a sneer. Elwin watched her for several moments, unable to make himself look away.

"What is it?" Zarah said in a soft voice.

He tore his eyes away from the girl and made as if to rise.

A hand on his knee made him freeze in place. He looked at the hand and followed the arm up to Zarah's face. She snatched it off his leg as if from a fire and her cheeks colored.

"I need to get out of here," he told her. "Everyone is looking at me."

"You cannot," she whispered. "They want you to be guilty. If you leave, they will think you are guilty."

"But I'm not," he said. "Why doesn't that matter to them?"

"Do you not see?" she asked. "They are afraid of what they do not have. This is precisely why we have the Guardians. Their laws make those ungifted feel safe. Look around. What do you see?"

He looked up. Several eyes darted away from him, but the girl still glared at him. She looked as if she had not blinked once. He could feel others staring at him from his periphery.

"They are angry," he said at last.

"Some," Zarah said. "Yes. Some are angry. But their anger is born from fear."

"And loss," he said.

She touched his hand. "It will all be made right. You will see."

Elwin glanced to the girl. She had finally turned her attentions back to the child in her arms. He took a deep breath.

"I hope you're right."

"Of course, I am right," she said nudging him with her arm. "I spoke."

He met her gaze. Her smile managed to be both playful and smug. Despite himself, he felt his lips returning her smile. After a moment her smile faded, but she held his gaze for several heartbeats.

"Practice your breathing," she said without looking away. "It will be good practice for you trying to move your essence in a crowd."

He nodded and closed his eyes, but the image of Zarah was slow to fade from his thoughts. Dragons take him if there was anyone more beautiful. But that wasn't why he did as she suggested. It *was* good practice. She could make a good suggestion every once in a while.

Pushing Zarah from his thoughts, he focused on his breathing. He felt for the power of Air around the room but did not open his essence to the flow. He felt ripples in the room as people shifted in their seats and whispered to one another. He tried to focus on individuals, but there were too many people moving at once.

Ignoring the people, he cleared his mind and felt for his essence. It was much like closing his eyes and thinking about his heartbeat. Even though he rarely paid attention to it, if he focused on the rhythm, he could feel the beats in his chest.

When he didn't try to move it, his essence seemed to stay near his head. Or at least, every time he found it, that's where it rested. He took deep breaths and didn't try to search for it so much as he tried to make his mind aware of his essence, like he would his hand or foot.

Just like that, he felt his essence hovering above his body. Each time seemed to be faster than the last.

Jasmine compared willing it to move to walking, but it felt more like crawling with a knapsack filled with boulders. He envisioned his essence like a mirror of his own body, like it looked in the shadow realm. Focusing on the limbs of his ethereal extension, he forced the arms and legs of his essence to move through the forms as Jasmine had instructed him.

It did not stir the air as it moved, but he could feel the power of Air pressing against his essence. The power sought to fill him like rain fills an empty cup. Only, it would not unless he allowed it to do so. Jasmine had tried to explain the physics of it to Elwin, but her explanation had sounded like gibberish. A person existed in space and time, but, like the shadow realm, his essence existed both inside and outside of space and time. Then, his essence acted like a conduit for taming the Elements. There had been more, but he couldn't remember it. It was all blather anyway. None of it helped him.

He realized his essence had stopped moving through the forms and hovered above his head once more.

"Curse it all," Elwin said under his breath.

"What is it?"

He opened his eyes. Each person his gaze settled on flinched and looked away as if he had threatened them with a stick.

Elwin sighed. "I can't focus. I started doing the forms, but I lost concentration."

"I saw," Zarah said.

"You saw?"

"Yes,"shesaid,"Iwaswatchingyoudotheforms.Abitslow,butoverall... not bad. Then you began to drool like a simpleton."

He gave her a flat look. "An essence can't drool."

"Maybe not," she said. "But if they could, yours would have been."

"How long until I can see like you?"

She shrugged. "No telling. Try a few more times. I'll squeeze your hand when they come back in."

Elwin closed his eyes and tried to make his essence go through the forms, but his thoughts roamed. First, he thought of Feffer and tried to imagine what under the Lifebringer had happened to his skull. Zarah had said training would be rough, but that had been a lot of blood. What, short of a giant's hammer, could be strong enough to split a skull so hard?

But, Feffer was healed now, so Elwin need not worry over his friend. Pushing Feffer from his thoughts, he found his essence drooling once more. Not drooling, curse Zarah. Resting. He found his essence resting. As soon as he began the forms anew, the image of Biron's family entered his mind. Most of all, he could not shake the image of the young woman. Elwin had never felt hatred for anyone, but he was certain he had seen its face. Was she Biron's sister? Biron was several years older. The woman could have been his wife. Was the child in her arms Biron's son?

When he felt his hand squeezed, it shattered his thoughts, and his eyes popped open.

The seven white robed figures were in place behind their chairs. Jasmine stood in the same spot as before right in front of the bald man. Elwin spared a glance to the woman holding the child. She did not look back, but for reasons Elwin couldn't explain, he wished she would.

Again the man in the center struck his crook on the platform. They remained standing, towering over the crowd.

"We have reached a decision of indecision" he said in drawn out tones. "Haste does not make for wise choices. Therefore, we will reconvene in one year's time. We do not doubt the belief *you* have in your words, Jasmine Lifesong. And we do not discount the faith that your king has placed in you. It is for this reason alone, we are willing to place the accused's actions in your care. From this moment, your fates will be as one. If a single innocent life is lost as a result of his *willful* actions, then this will be the same as if you have performed the act yourself.

"These will be our terms," he said. "Are you still willing to place your faith in this child?"

There was not a moment of hesitation and clear confidence in her voice. "By my life, I will care for this child. So long as I have breath, I ensure that he will return here in one year, so that you may see the validity of my words."

He struck the crook in rapid succession once more.

His eyes met Elwin's as he said, "If the accused, Elwin Escari, attempts to elude judgement, his actions will be taken as an admission of guilt. He will be found and executed without further proceedings. A date will be set after Summer's Solstice not more than one year's time from this day. Until this time, our proceedings are concluded."

They all exited once more.

Elwin heard sobs coming from the family at the front, and he noticed that several people were now looking in his direction, though no eyes seemed to land on him. Jasmine walked out the doors without even glancing in his direction. The other people began to stand and leave as well.

Elwin sat there. He wasn't sure how to feel. It wasn't over. He was still alive, but it wasn't over. Would they assign a warder to watch over him now? Would he become one of the number of elementalists that disappeared?

Finally, all of the other people had gone. Only the family remained, huddled together. He could see their backs quivering as if their sobs wanted to escape through their bodies.

"We should go," Zarah whispered to him.

Elwin stood. He wanted to go to the family and tell them how sorry he was, that it was an accident.

As if reading his thoughts, the young woman's eyes shot toward Elwin like an arrow released from a bow. He felt himself step backward and almost stumble over the pew. Bowing his head, Elwin turned and left the family to their grief.

Elwin sat in his chair in the lecture room, leaning on his desk. Zarah sat next to him and shared the silence. He wanted to be alone with his thoughts, but he felt better with her presence.

Jasmine walked through the open doorway, rubbing her forehead with the side of her forefinger. She sat in the empty chair next to him.

Her eyes held a soft look that he had not seen from her before. Her lips were tight and her hair slightly disheveled.

"I am sorry, Elwin," Jasmine said. "I was wrong in my assessment. I have never actually had to defend against the Inquisition. I ... I made a mistake. I should have brought forth more witnesses. I should have spoken with Biron's family and many other things that are too late now. We will return next year, and I will be more prepared. But in the meantime, you must train."

She leaned forward. "We need to prepare you for ... whatever may come. There are events occurring that will require every ounce of power that we can find. And yours will be valuable. You have a purpose. The Lifebringer brought you to me for a reason. Rest assured that I will not let your life be taken for vanities."

Of the many questions racing through his mind, the one that escaped his lips was, "Where's Feffer?"

"He is resting." A touch of surprise sounded in her voice.

"Can I see him?" He felt a mountain of hope rising in his chest.

She shook her head. "That is not a good idea. He will need to return to training as soon as possible. And so will you."

"What about the Inquisition?"

"Let me worry over that. In the meantime, we must return to your studies."

Her words felt like a weight settling onto him, and he found it hard to breath.

He had been stolen from a life to which he could not return. And he was not sure that he would even want to now. Knowing his family was not real made his entire life feel like a great falsehood. Would he forget that if he could? Would he want to live a lie?

His actions had taken a life.

A family had lost an irreplaceable treasure. A life, a force for good, was no more. Because of him. He could see the woman's grief. He could feel the family's pain. It was a part of him now.

The tears began to fall. He had no strength left to fight the agony within. He covered his shame with both hands. He couldn't hold it in any longer.

Elwin wept.

Chapter 10

A SOLDIER'S LIFE

Feffer elbowed the thin mattress beneath him, trying to smooth out the lumps. Perhaps he should have played the cripple for one more day. The mattress at the Temple of Life had been softer than anything he had ever slept on. Putting up with the surly healer for one more day would have been worth sleeping another night in the bed.

He had acted the perfect gentleman his entire stay, but the woman had behaved as if his very presence was an insult to her existence. Feffer couldn't remember much about the first day or so, but he couldn't have said anything too terrible.

Though, the healer had been blessed with a beautiful bosom. Perhaps he had commented on it? Of course. Curse him to the abyss, that must have been it. Maybe he should try to make it up to her. He could find some way to apologize without ogling her breasts. Otherwise, she might think his apology a mockery. And that would make matters worse.

He rolled onto his back and sighed. At least he had a top bunk. Each bed was stacked three high. Not that he had much of a view. The support beams above him stretched the full extent of the barracks and made layers up to the ceiling. At the top, the wooden supports came together to provide the perfect cubby to hide his belongings.

He had not been up there since before getting his skull cracked. That had been half a tenday. As much as he itched to climb up and check his coin purse, it would have to wait. The best times to get up and down without being seen were just before meals. It was rare that anyone skipped a meal, regardless of how tasteless and measly the food. He could wait until then. If someone had found his cache, there would be little he could do about it.

He looked to his left. The bunks were an arm's length apart, but his eyes had adjusted to the dark well enough to see the other figures sleeping on the bunks around him. Before his accident, Feffer had grown accustomed to looking for motion in the night. His squad slept in the four bunks closest to the east wall, and Gurndol had yet to make good on this threats.

Before getting his head cracked like an egg, Feffer had started making it a point to incur extra drills by making mistakes. At first, it had been to take the pressure off Fandar. The larger boy had the grace of a pregnant cow. In truth, he didn't like seeing pranks acted out on Fandar, but Feffer mostly wanted to agitate Gurndol. There would be no reason to think Gurndol would have forgotten such slights to his pride in Feffer's absence.

Tomorrow would be Feffer's first day back in action, so it seemed tonight would be a good night to catch him off guard. It's what Feffer would do if he was a pompous prat looking for undue vengeance.

Feffer crossed his arms behind his head and sighed. One more tenday until Sir Gibbins assigned a squad leader. It would likely be Gurndol. They tended to choose members of noble families as squad leaders. And while Feffer had been resting up, Gurndol had likely moved ahead in the ranks.

Three round slender strands landed across his upper chest, waist, and legs at the same time. He felt a heartbeat of confusion until his mind realized what held him. Rope. It pulled tight against his chest as if someone played tug-of-war from the other ends. A dark wad hit his midsection, knocking the breath from him. He had just enough time to tense as a second blow struck down. The throb was instant and he struggled to catch his breath.

It took him a moment to realize his arms had not been caught by the rope. Only a single rope held them at the pits of his arms. He wiggled his head and arms free of the top rope as another blow came down on his stomach. He grunted against the pain and grabbed the headboard. Pulling from the headboard and kicking with his legs, he was able to free his lower half.

He sat up and rolled the last rope down his legs. The pillow case filled with soapstone struck his foot, and Feffer muffled a curse.

A loud whisper came from below. "I think he got this rope loose, pull tighter on your ropes."

Feffer leapt off the top bunk in the direction of the whisper. His feet struck the top of someone's head, and he heard Gurndol cry out and crumple beneath him. Feffer caught the top bunks on either side to keep from falling with his target, then pulled back up to his bunk.

"What happened?" he heard one of the others whisper.

"Gurndol's not moving." That was Marlin's voice speaking well above a whisper. He had become Gurndol's number two. "Get back to your bunks."

Feet scrambled up wood as the boys got back into their beds. The creaking of wooden bunks echoed through the silence of the sleeping room.

The shadowy figures on the other beds began to move as well. Feffer laid back down and got under his thin blanket, despite the heat. He made his best attempt to appear to be in a sleeping state. One hundred beds, filled three high, shifted in the silence. It sounded as if a giant lumberjack was making his way through a forest of dried timber.

A voice from the other end called, "What was that?"

"Shut it."

"You worms get us drills and your dead."

"Shh. You idiots."

The moments were few before the outer door slammed open. As one, all the other boys returned to a sleeping position. Feffer squeezed his eyes shut and froze every muscle.

"What in the abyss is going on in here?" It was Gibbins' voice.

He heard several large men walking through the rows of bunks.

The torch light became more intense as the sounds of the heavy feet grew closer.

"Someone tell me what the commotion—What in the abyss?"

Feffer remained motionless, but the sun might as well have been out for the intensity of light around his bunk.

"What are you doing out of bed soldier?"

Feffer's heart was pounding, but he did not move.

"He's been knocked out cold," said Gibbins.

Sweat began to cover him. He wanted to peak over the side of the bunk to see if the torches had set his bunk afire.

Gibbins shouted, "What happened here?"

His bunk shook, as if struck, "By the grace of the Lifebringer, if someone doesn't speak up by the time I count—Feffer is that you at the top of this tier?"

He felt his bunk shake again under a blow. "Feffer *Hanck* Madrowl. I see that ginger-stain poking out the top of your bunk. Down. Now."

Curse it all, Feffer thought.

"Get down here, worm!"

Feffer swung down from the bunk, careful not to land on Gurndol. Feffer could see the other boy's unconscious face. He tried to feel some sympathy for him, but it was not an easy task.

Gibbins stood in his small clothes. He had several scars of various shapes and angles scratched into his torso and arms. His muscles were not overly large, but they were honed from use. He stood only a hand taller than Feffer, but that did nothing for Feffer's confidence. He felt a slight itch where Gibbins had cracked his skull open.

Feffer could taste Gibbins' breath. "Back less than an hour and already causing troubles? What happened here, Feffer?"

If Feffer gave up Gurndol and his other squad members, then he would never survive when Gurndol became squad leader. If he didn't give up Gurndol and the others, then he might not survive the night. He scratched the itch at his skull and met Gibbins' gaze ready to toss the other boy to the wolves, but he stopped as Gurndol began to rouse.

The other boy brought a hand to his head and groaned. His eyes squinted against the light for a moment. Gurndol's head came up first, then the rest of him. He opened his eyes the rest of the way, then froze when they settled on Gibbins and Feffer.

Gibbins spoke through his teeth. "I am going to ask this one last time … what happened here?"

"Uh …," Gurndol said. "Um …"

"He was walking in his sleep," Feffer blurted, "and he tripped and bumped his head."

Gibbins leaned within an inch of Feffer, staring into his soul for several moments. He did not flinch at the heat and stink of Gibbins' breath. Feffer had been scolded by many adults in his day and had learned the most important aspect to selling a ruse. Do not blink, do not look away, and do NOT swallow.

"Is that the right of it, Gurndol?"

With obvious confusion in his voice, Gurndol said, "Uh … I don't quite remember. I was in bed one moment and then waking up here the next. It must be as Feffer said. I have been known to walk about in my sleep."

Feffer didn't want to admit it, but once the confusion worked clear of his voice, Gurndol sounded sincere.

Gibbins stood straight and raised his voice for the room to hear. "Alright worms, it appears that we are giving you too much sleep. We need to work you hard enough that you don't have the energy to walk about in the night. Squad leaders, start your scheduled routines. The rest of you worms are with me."

"But," Gurndol said, "it is only an hour past sundown."

"Everyone do ten press-ups," Gibbins shouted. "You can thank Gurndol for speaking out of turn."

Gibbins walked between the rows of bunks as everyone dropped in position for press-ups. "Anyone else want to complain?" He paused. After no one offered complaint, Gibbons counted out the press-ups.

Though he had rested for near a tenday, Feffer's arms felt shaky with each press-up. He wanted to glare at Gurndol, but couldn't find the strength to look up from his press-ups.

"Alright then," Gibbons said after reaching ten, "meet in the yard in ten minutes. I expect everyone to run their routines until sundown on the morrow."

When the torchlight moved away from Feffer, he sat up. Gurndol sat next to him.

Feffer whispered, "How's your head?" It sounded more sympathetic than he had intended.

"I will be alright." He still sounded groggy. "I will not forget what you did for me tonight. You are a better man than I."

Feffer flinched as if slapped. Then he felt himself grin. He almost laughed. He had kicked Gurndol senseless, and he had actually thanked him. Feffer vowed to remember that tactic for future disagreements with the noble prat.

His smile faded when he stood on wobbly legs. Drills for a full day with no sleep would be rough. He might find himself back in the Temple long before the sky turned pink. His smile returned even deeper as he thought of the healer's bosom looming over him again.

The sunlight faded in the west as shouts of men echoed through the field as a single cacophonous voice. Rising above their cries came the sounds of wood cracking against wood in rapid succession. Stripped down to their leggings, a circle of men surrounded two combatants. The smaller of the two danced around wide swings and countered with quick strikes toward limbs, but the other man was nimble for his size and struck back with powerful swings.

After several minutes of quick exchanges, Wilton Madrowl struggled to keep a hold of his weapon. He moved through forms and evaded his opponent's skull-splitting swings, but he could feel his muscles wearing down.

To buy himself a reprieve, he feinted a lunge and jumped wide of the counter. He would only have seconds to gather himself, but in a duel, seconds were like minutes. Wilton studied his opponent.

The man's name was Horac of some minor house, but everyone called him Bender. Before the war and against his family's wishes, Bender had joined the city's watch with aspirations to move up the ranks. A large scar ran down the right side of Bender's face where a dagger had sliced his cheek. He had gotten the scar breaking up his first tavern brawl and had refused healing because he wanted the scar. The absence of the scar would not have improved the look of his thick face much, but having the scar made him look more intimidating.

The wooden sword looked small in his giant hand, but Bender's shaven head had sweat beading on it. So Wilton had at least worn him down as well.

Wilton squared up to Bender in rock form. Unlike water form, the stances of rock made an opponent match strength against strength. Against Bender, Wilton might as well have been a child challenging his father by matching muscle for muscle.

Bender took the bait. He attacked high in an overhead strike. The moment Bender's sword struck his Wilton, dropped the sword and pivoted around the larger man. A lack of resistance propelled Bender forward, making him overstep and stumble forward.

Wilton kicked the back of Bender's knee, causing him to fall forward and stumble past the dropped sword. Without hesitation, Wilton retrieved his fallen sword and pounced on Bender's back, touching his sword tip to the nape of his opponent's neck.

Bender said something into the dirt, but the cheers of their comrades muffled whatever he had said. Curses no doubt. Wilton got off the large man and offered him his hand.

Bender clasped Wilton's hand and stood. "Not bad for such a scrawny feller." His voice was deeper than any Wilton had heard.

Wilton laughed, "Good thing you're large enough to mount like a horse."

"I always knew you were too pretty to be a man, but you just forget any ideas of mounting me."

Laughter filled the field.

"Alright men," Zaak's voice cut a hole in the soldiers' circle, and he stepped through.

"Well done, Wilton. Everyone gets a furlough tonight. But be rested and ready tomorrow. Training in the trees."

The soldiers cheered as one. "The Seeker fear the mighty White

Hand. May the abyss rise to meet us, we will stay and fight. The Seeker fear the mighty White Hand …"

Wilton turned to follow, but Zaak grabbed his arm. "Not you soldier."

"Sir?"

"You have exceeded your training and have become the first amongst your peers in just a few short months. The Lifebringer has a greater calling for you than a simple soldier. You have a quickness in your step that others do not have. You will be trained as a thief-catcher."

"Thank you sir. But, permission to speak?"

"What's on your mind, son?"

"How is my brother faring?"

Zaak smiled. "He's like you, the first amongst his peers. He could be here beside you if not for his age. The king has instructed that all men under the age of sixteen years receive a full year's training before seeing battle. To be honest, I wish that year had come. We will need more thief-catchers before this year ends."

"What do thief-catchers have to do with war?" Wilton asked. Don't they prowl the streets for criminals?"

"In times of peace, thief-catchers keep our streets clean. But, in times of war, they are the difference between victory and defeat." Zaak clasped his shoulder. "You'll be trained for reconnaissance with a handful of others. Do you see the man behind you?"

Wilton looked over his shoulder. The field beside the castle was empty, save for the soldiers retreating to their furlough. "There is no one there, sir."

A vice took hold of Wilton's hair and bared his neck with a sharp yank of his hair. Cold metal touched the edge of his throat.

"Meet Tharu, Wilton Madrowl."

Wilton craned his head back, stretching his eyes as far as they could go without disturbing the blade. The grip released Wilton's hair, and he turned around. Tharu wore nothing more than a loin cloth and shoes crafted from animal skins. His tanned body was not large, but it was chiseled and honed. The man carried two short blades that curved back toward his elbows.

Wilton rubbed his neck, sure he would find blood. When he saw there was none he said, "Pleased to meet you, sir."

Tharu's emerald eyes sparkled like that of a hunting beast. "The winds of our Lady Nature have carried you to me, Wilton Madrowl. The time has come for your training to begin."

Wilton blinked. Training? What in the abyss did they call what he had been doing for the last few months?

Wilton suppressed a sigh. He knew the answer, but he had to ask. "I guess that means no furlough?"

Tharu showed Wilton his teeth in what might pass as the man's smile. It looked more like a wolf baring his teeth to another wolf. Well … a wolf pup.

"Come," Tharu said, then turned to walk west toward the forest by the river.

For a moment, Wilton watched him go. Not for the first time since being recruited, Wilton wished he had deserted. He couldn't now. It was too late. They knew his name. Besides, he needed to keep his promise to his father. If he deserted, there would be no one to look after Feffer.

A year. The kid still had another year until he saw any real fighting. Pray the Lifebringer made it so. First among his peers?

Wilton almost laughed. First to get to mess, first to find trouble, and first to get himself killed acting the fool. Feffer probably still saw training as a game. The kid couldn't see two steps in front of him, let alone what the training meant.

How could he keep his promise to his father with a brother like Feffer?

He would find a way. Being first amongst his peers felt like a good start. He ran to catch up to Tharu.

Chapter 11

MIND'S EYE

"Concentrate."

Zarah's voice shattered Elwin's focus.

He opened his eyes. Zarah sat cross-legged next to the fountain. Water flowed from a top tier to four lower tiers before coming to a rest in a small pool at the base. It was the largest of many fountains in the castle garden. The wide clearing around the fountain made it an ideal place to train with swords and the Elements. So he had been told.

Thus far, he had trained with neither. Though he had played with wooden sticks and tried to move his essence aplenty.

"I was trying to," he said through his teeth. "I can't do it if you're talking to me."

Her look held no sympathy for him. "You cannot do it because you will not stop thinking about the Inquisition."

"Of course I can't," Elwin said. "Did you see Biron's family?"

"You cannot dwell on things outside of your control," she said in a patronizing tone. "Right now, you need to train. "

"You keep saying that," Elwin wagged his finger in her face. She raised an eyebrow, but he ignored her disapproving stare. "But train for what? No one will tell me."

"You know I cannot speak on the prophecies."

"You can. You choose not to."

"Because she is obedient," Jasmine's voice said from behind him.

She strode through the rows of redwood trees. Her white dress was much more ornate than those he had grown accustomed to her wearing, which meant this one could have sold for enough coin to buy three or four farms instead of just one. An amber pendant hung from the end of silver links woven through Jasmine's hair and rested on her forehead. He forced his jaw to close before Jasmine reached the fountain.

Her gaze settled on Zarah. "How far has he gotten through the forms?"

"The third stanza."

Elwin studied his feet to avoid Jasmine's grimace.

She remained silent until he looked at her. He had expected her gaze to set him ablaze, so he flinched when his eyes met a look of compassion.

"You are important in a way you cannot imagine," she said. "Come. Let us walk."

Elwin bounced to his feet. "Important how?"

"First, let me explain why I hesitate to speak of the prophecies," Jasmine said as she turned to walk toward the hedges.

"Mother," Zarah said, "why are you wearing a Verande gown?"

Elwin felt an intense desire to push Zarah into the fountain. How long had he been waiting to hear about the prophecies? Three months since he had left home. Now that Jasmine was prepared to tell him the purpose for all of this, she asked about a *dress*? He had be debating on whether or not to act on his urges when Jasmine spoke.

"I had a meeting with an emissary from Alcoa," Jasmine said as if discussing her favorite tea.

Zarah nudged Elwin roughly as she stepped between Jasmine and him. "An emissary! What did he want?"

"That is not your concern. When I want you to know, I will tell you." Jasmine said. "Now, let us walk."

Jasmine turned toward a northern path. Elwin had to take a couple of quick steps to catch her. He did not turn to see if Zarah followed.

"The prophecies were born during the Shadow Wars." Jasmine

paused. "You remember what the Shadow Wars were?"

"Yes," Elwin said.

When she did not continue, he added quickly, "After Abaddon and the dragons disappeared, all of Arinth was left in turmoil. Death bound emerged and attempted to seize power in all nations and tried to turn souls to Abaddon. The wars that followed pushed the Death bound into hiding and were called the Shadow Wars because they were said to fight their battles from the shadows."

She sighed. "Close enough for our purposes, but you will need to reread the 'War of the Shadows' by Niccol Machiavel and write a report due before next Lifeday. Also, you should cross reference his first book, 'The Princeps.' It discusses the city-states during and after the wars and gives philosophical accounts of rule. I will expect excerpts quoted."

"I will," he said, trying to sound enthusiastic. "I promise."

The path forked and Jasmine took the right side, continuing as if she had never detoured the discussion with a new assignment. "After the Great Slumber, people feared the return of the dragonkin, but fear of Abaddon, the Seeker of Souls, was even greater. People became wary of all who accepted his Dark Gift. In time, that fear began to include all Elemental power. As mistrust grew, farmers and merchants became assassins of their neighbors. People fled cities to hide with the dwarves in their caves or sought seclusion in the mountains.

"The Guardians of Life arose from this conflict and began to alleviate the fears of the ungifted by bringing order and law to elementalists. The priests of Life began to remind the people of their purpose. Once more, they had a symbol to trust. And probably most important of all, disobedience of the law incurred swift and precise penalties."

Elwin felt a chill at the mention of the Guardians. To think, they had actually saved elementalists. He found it difficult to see them as anything other than the Inquisition. "But I know all of this," he said. "What does this have to do with the prophecies?"

"Everything," Jasmine said. "People feared the Elements, but without elementalists, we would be powerless against the dragonkin. The Shadow Wars killed many elementalists on both sides and ended many fears with the birth of the Guardians of Life. Becoming Death bound was outlawed, but the damage had been done. As you know, our power is passed through bloodlines, and over time, we began to grow weaker. We have seen fewer elementalists gifted in two Elements than in any other time. Taming three is as rare now as four was before the Shadow Wars."

The trees and bushes opened to a stretch of sand that surrounded a pond. Jasmine stopped at the edge of the pond and turned toward Elwin. Beneath the clear water, Elwin could see countless fish of multiple colors swimming in schools.

"This is where you come in," Jasmine said. She looked at him for several moments without speaking. Despite his best efforts to meet her gaze, he found himself fidgeting.

"You are he who is True." Zarah's voice beside him caused Elwin to jump. He had forgotten she was there until she spoke.

"What?" he said. "What does that even mean?"

"A true elementalist can tame all four Elements," Jasmine said. "Even before the Shadow Wars, such gifts were rare, but none have existed since the time of Abaddon. Until now."

Elwin tried to work moisture into his mouth, but swallowing didn't help. When he spoke, his voice came out a croak. "What does it mean?"

"Few can agree on all the implications," Jasmine said. "This is why I hesitate to tell you of the prophecies."

Elwin threw his hands in the air. "Then why did you ever mention it at all?"

"Because," Jasmine said in a serious tone. "There is one point upon which all scholars agree." Jasmine licked her lips and took a deep breath. "Once a true elementalist comes again, it will mean the Awakening is upon us."

Elwin stared at her for a moment. The Awakening? That was a children's tale. If a child misbehaved, the dragons would take him in the night. The Awakening was no more real than wyvern or gnomes. What creature could sleep for three thousand years and survive?

"The Awakening is real," Jasmine said as if reading his thoughts. "The dragonkin will rise. And you are at the crux of it all."

"No," Elwin said. "I don't believe it. How can I be at the *crux* of anything? I'm a farmer."

"You may have been raised a farmer, Elwin. But you are from an old and noble bloodline. Bain Solsec is your father. I have confirmed it with Thirod Alcoa, king of the nation of Alcoa. You are the Son of Bain."

Elwin backed away from her, shaking his head. "No, I don't believe it. How can you *confirm* it? He's never met me."

"It does not matter," Jasmine said. "He is aware of you and has trusted you into my care. What matters is that you are a true elementalist. The dragonkin will come during your lifetime. And you need to be ready."

"But what am I supposed to do? If the dragonkin are real, what does it have to do with me?"

"The prophecies are not clear. Most scholars believe that whether you act or not, the dragonkin will rise. If you Awaken them, then you will bring about a new order. If someone else Awakens them, then the world as we know it will end. And another will rise."

"Someone else?" Elwin said. "Who? Bain?"

"I do not know. There will be at least one other true elementalist. Maybe more."

"I don't understand. If there will be more ... more like me, how do you know I am the one that needs to wake them? It could be—"

"It is you," Jasmine said in a firm voice.

"But how do you *know*?"

"Because I know."

"How?" Elwin said, not attempting to hide his frustration. "How do you know?"

"Because I have faith in the Lifebringer."

Elwin stared at her at a loss for words. The Lifebringer? What kind of answer was that? He had faith too, but he couldn't see how faith made him the destroyer of all Arinth. He opened his mouth to say as much, but Jasmine spoke first.

"Because the alternative is not possible. I am not sure how many true elementalists there will be. Many assume there will be no more than two for the simple fact that even one seems improbable. The prophecy says there will be two, but it also says powers lost will become like new. Some believe this means there will be many like you. Perhaps we will rediscover the Words of Power. This is not known. However, it is widely believed that one such true elementalist *will* be bound to Death. If he Awakens them, we are lost. You are pure of heart, Elwin. I must believe that you are the one to bid them rise. You *must* be the one."

He looked away from her. Why had he asked? He didn't want to know about the prophecies anymore. Jasmine had to be wrong. This had nothing to do with Elwin.

"Who came up with these *prophecies* anyway?" Elwin asked.

"The prophecies were said to have come from the Librarian of Tanier. Legends say the Librarian could see all possible futures and wrote the prophecies to give Arinth hope for the future."

"Hope?" Elwin asked. "How could dragons rising give anyone hope? Where is this Library?"

"Sometime before or during the Shadow Wars the great Library of Tanier vanished. There are many theories as to what happened to it. The most prominent being—"

"Never mind," Elwin said. "I don't care. I'm not going to wake any dragons. Ever. If they are even real."

Her gaze hardened, and she crossed her arms beneath her bosom. "I understand that you are upset, but you will mind your tongue."

"Upset?" Elwin said. "I was *upset* that I lost my new book. I was *upset* that you wouldn't let me see Feffer after his injury. I'm *upset* that I've been training for two months, and I have still learned *nothing*. You just told me that I will bring about the *end* of the *world*. Upset? Upset?"

Elwin sat hard on the sand.

Zarah knelt beside him. "You have not been listening," she said. "The Awakening is not the end. It is the beginning."

"Enough," Jasmine said. "You need to train. Whether you choose to believe in the prophecies or not, you have already begun to fulfill them. The Lifebringer save me, you will be ready."

"Fulfill what?"

"Enough," Jasmine said with such force Elwin flinched. "When

I feel you are ready to hear more, I will tell you more. We need to open your mind's eye further. You have made remarkable progress in these few tendays. Even when your thoughts are distracted you can make it to the third stanza. Though you have much work to do, I feel you have gained enough control over your essence that I am comfortable moving on to the next step."

She turned to Zarah. "You will be included in this lesson as well. Sit next to Elwin."

Zarah settled her skirts into the sand next to Elwin without so much as glancing at him. What had he done to upset her? Nothing. He hadn't done anything. Elwin didn't write any thumping prophecy. Some librarian did that. And apparently, he hadn't done a very good job with it. After all, no one could agree on what the thumping thing said.

"Pay close attention," Jasmine said.

Elwin felt the Air stir the moment Jasmine opened her essence. Wisps of white light gathered around her and disappeared as the power fused with her.

"It is necessary to continue the flow through your essence even as you use the power. You must remain mindful of your essence. Remember, your essence will become exhausted as you tame the Elements. If your essence becomes exhausted while you are in flight, there may be no pond to break your fall. Now watch me."

As the breeze became stronger, more lights began to fuse with Jasmine's essence and vanish. A moment later, Jasmine's feet lifted a pace above the sand. The light began to leak from her eyes.

"Going up and down is the easy part," Jasmine said. "After you master this, I will show you how to go forward and backward. It is a matter of altering your will. The flow of Air is not what sustains flight. The flow of Air is essential, of course, but your consciousness is what guides the Elemental power. This is why you must master your mind's eye. Feel what I am doing through your essence. The vibrations from my flow of power can be felt by your essence much in the same way you can see me with your eyes. Focus."

Elwin did as told. But, in truth, he didn't have to focus. He could *feel* the pull of Air flowing around her body to lift her. Elwin thought he could replicate her actions in a similar way he could reproduce the fighting forms by watching Jasmine or Zarah go through the motions.

Jasmine reduced her flow and her feet eased back to the beach.

"Now," she said, "Who wants to tell me how it was done?"

Zarah opened her mouth to answer, but Elwin cut her off. "I don't know if I can *tell* you, but I think I can show you."

"Very well," Jasmine said. "Proceed."

"What?" Elwin said, not bothering to hide his shock. She had not let him do more than open his essence to Air and release the power. Having the permission granted so casually had taken him off guard.

"I said, I want you to show me. Go on."

Elwin stood up, a sudden feeling of excitement creeping onto his face. He smoothed the grin away with his hand. This was no time to look like a country bumpkin.

Then he took a deep breath and focused on the Air. Feeling the power all around him was much easier than trying to move his essence, and by now opening his essence to Air was a simple exercise. As it filled him, his heart beat faster. This was the part where he had always pushed it back into his surroundings. The palms of his hands began to sweat.

The breeze around him felt cooler. He could taste the spray of the water and smell the scent of bark from the trees. Forcing his breathing to slow, he willed the Air from his essence. Flows surrounded him slowly and became a part of him as if he had grown a new arm or leg. Or wings.

Before attempting to lift himself from the sand, he worked on maintaining the balance of Air going through his essence. He could feel his essence drain as the flow of Air surrounded him. But, he could balance the amount he tamed by leaving his essence partially open to the incoming flow.

"Here goes," he said.

He willed the flows surrounding him to rise. His feet lurched from the ground, and he found himself falling a dozen paces upward. Not again. No. He wouldn't allow himself to panic. He focused on the Air around him and in his essence and realized significantly less Air remained than when he had started a moment before.

His memories darted back to the day of the solstice festival, and it became clear to him. He remembered thinking he had *grabbed* the Air to lift him. And he had. He had pulled Air through his essence to fly, just like he did at the moment. To fall, all he had to do is not pull more Air into his essence. If he pulled too much, he would go up, but he need enough to sustain his flight.

Trying to judge how much had been required to go this high, Elwin opened his essence to what he gauged to be the right amount of Air and let it fill him while willing himself upward. His stomach lurched as his body jerked another dozen paces upward.

Halving the amount of Air, he repeated the process. This time he only went up a few paces. He continued this process a few more times until he didn't go up or fall. Air surged through him, sustaining his flight.

Then he looked around.

More than twenty paces below, he saw the pond. Red and yellow leaves mingling with the green, announcing the coming fall. He was higher than many of the trees, but the tallest redwoods still hovered above him. They were sparse enough that he could see the castle beyond the garden.

His already rapid heartbeat began to feel like thunder in his chest. Below him, Zarah was on her feet staring at him in stark disbelief. He couldn't believe it either. It felt amazing.

"I did it," he called to her. "I'm doing it!"

Jasmine nodded, the corners of her mouth turned upward in the briefest of smiles.

"Now," she called up to him. "Can you come back down?"

Elwin thought about it for a moment. "I think so."

Unlike going upward, he didn't have to will the flows to take him up. He simply had to lessen the amount of Air flowing through him. His body eased back toward the sand. When his feet touched, he sat down and released the remaining Air. Sweat touched his forehead, and he found his breath labored as if he had run a league. His heart still thundered in his chest.

"Very good," Jasmine said. "The fatigue you feel right now is normal. In time, you will become more efficient at taming the Air necessary to sustain your flight. The amount you used just now is far more than you will need with practice." She turned to Zarah. "Would you care to try?"

She nodded, but her face had paled.

"You can do it," Elwin said.

Zarah's scowl could have peeled flesh. "I know I can. I have been waiting for permission to do this for at least a year."

She rolled her shoulders and took a deep breath with a look of determination gleaming in her eyes. A moment later, a breeze stirred and Air fused with her essence. The flows surrounded her and for several moments, she didn't move. Elwin could feel the adjustment in her taming the moment it happened. Zarah's feet lifted from the beach with much more control than Elwin had demonstrated.

Her body rose no more than four paces above the pond and hovered in place like Elwin had. A smug smile crept onto her face as she looked down at Elwin. Then, she lowered herself back to the beach without a flourish.

Jasmine nodded in approval. "Very well done Zarah. Perhaps, I could have let you learn this sooner. But, if your father had his way, you would never learn to fly."

Zarah's smile faded at the mention of Zaak, and her chin rose a few notches. She crossed her arms beneath her breasts and puckered her lips in a sulky expression.

"In any event," Jasmine continued, "waiting has proven no harm. Now, I want you both to practice a few more times before Lord Lifesong meets you for sword training. Elwin, you first. This time, I want you to ease yourself from the shore. Careful now. Follow my instructions … "

Chapter 12

A DIRECTION

Bain sat up in his bed.

The words, "Seek him in the nation of islands," hung in the air like a dissipating fog.

The Father had not come to Bain's dreams in years. Not since he had shown him where to find the Book of Erudition. Bain would be a fool not to listen to the Father. The book had led Bain to the castle of Abaddon and to his position of power. And of course, there was the Father's other gifts. He would be nothing without those.

And now he had a direction.

Hours remained before first light, but near-on fifteen years had been long enough to wait. Bain dressed and shouted orders to Bertavan, his manservant, as he hurried toward his war chamber.

Taming Fire and Death, he untethered the wards around the double doors and entered and walked to the massive, stone table that stretched across the room. A miniature replica of the known world protruded from the top.

In several places on the board, wooden figurines in the shape of skeletons had been placed in areas of Bain's control. Hundreds of black-robed figurines rested on every major city in every nation. Each had a number carved into the back of the head, matching a corresponding name in the ledger lying open in front of him.

Even while he dominated southern Alcoa, his agents gathered

intelligence to conquer others. He had taken many of the cities south of the Tanges River and could finish them if he continued his current stratagem. Of course, those plans would have to wait.

His eyes settled on the group of islands to the west. Somewhere in the cluster of islands far south of the Blood Isle, called the Island Nations, someone held his son. After she had stolen Elwin away, Athina had returned such a short time later, so he had never considered a search so far west. Travel by sea would take a quarter to a third of a year to reach the islands. And, the islands were scattered and many. Searching them would have taken years. And likely still would.

Why had the Father not been more precise?

No. He would not question the Seeker's wisdom. The fault was his own. None of Bain's agents in Alcoa or elsewhere had found his son. All these years, Zeth had failed in his search for Elwin, because Bain had sent him north to scour Norscelt and Kalicodon. At last, Bain now had a direction to send his hound.

Bain looked back to the ledger. Who all would he send to conquer the islands? Some must stay behind. Losing ground to Alcoa was not an option. He simply needed to hold their advance.

Fasuri entered wearing only his small clothes and saluted. The man's bald head accentuated his gaunt face.

"My liege."

"Sit," Bain said. "You are from the Island Nations. Correct?"

"Aye," Fasuri said taking a seat. "I was born in Napri. It is amongst the smallest of the islands."

Bain nodded. The smallest island far to the west. Athina was wise.

"I am changing course for our savants, and I want you to lead them. Zeth's orders will supersede yours only in matters of finding my son. This is what I would have you do ..."

Chapter 13

REGRETS

A man follows his destiny like a leaf blown in the wind.

At times the wind is a soft breeze, carrying its passenger to some quiet place, where the gentle hand of nature caresses him as a mother does her child. There is peace in this haven, where the traveler is at one with his destiny.

A storm is most vicious when it finds one in his haven. This storm is like a living force, the Tempest, who ensnares her unwary prey. With all the fury her name implies, she thrashes and tears apart what is safe, unfettered by the damage caused. In her wake, she imparts to her lowly victim knowledge that strengthens and binds, destroys and rebuilds, brings love and harbors hatred. It is in this place where a man is made or unmade.

This is her gift. But in exchange, she takes something as precious as new life. Once taken, this treasure can never be returned or held again.

For he who gains the most in knowledge, loses the most in innocence.

Elwin closed the book and glanced at the setting sun. Spending his day studying the words of Machiavel had become one of his favorite pastimes, but his free day had almost come to an end.

He stood and stretched. The spire beneath his feet was the tallest of the castle. It was one of the few places he could go to feel at peace. No one ever bothered him up here. He stepped to the top of the parapet and watched the setting sun.

The pink rays stretched out over the city of Justice like a blanket of warmth. The sun was already too low to make out the details of the larger houses belonging to the nobles quarter of the upper city to the west, so he faced the commons to the east of town.

Shadows from the redwoods fell across the wide lake that separated the common's quarter from the noble's. Though it seemed natural to the eyes, the divide had been created by the Elements. When close to the lake, he could feel the power that kept the water from escaping.

He had learned much this last year, but as his trial approached, he could not feel success from his achievements.

Worse, war had come to the northern isles. Already, so many lives were being lost around him. Before, war had only been a word that he read in stories. The meaning had been lost in glorious tales of heroism and valor.

In real life, war meant that soldiers and friends would leave, and many would not return. It made him think of Feffer. He had not seen Feffer since the day of his trial. Communication at all took place over days, if not an entire tenday via letter. Furlough for soldiers was rare, and most of the time it appeared to be given with spontaneity. This allowed Feffer to leave word at the castle, but not enough time for Elwin to respond before the day of furlough ended.

And, every day was full for Elwin while he trained with Jasmine and Zarah. Between lecture and working on his talents, he had little time to send word to Feffer. His only free time was in the evenings after supper, most of which he spent up here. He enjoyed most of his studies. Except, once a tenday, he and Zarah were given training with wooden swords by Zaak Lifesong. Though Zarah took to it with a natural grace, Elwin found he did not much care for swords.

Swords had one purpose. Even though it had been an accident, he had already killed with a sword. However, Jasmine insisted that learning would save his life one day.

As the trial day grew closer, he found it difficult to focus on much else.

"If only I could go back," Elwin told the fleeting sun.

He had flown off the warehouse and then wind thrust the table. He knew that now, and he would have given anything to go back in time to stop it. Childish fancies.

But, maybe there was a way to slow time. He did not want to see Biron's family and open the old wound. Six days until Summer Solstice and a tenday beyond that, he would return to the trial. Not quite the full year they had promised, but it would be good to be done with it.

Jasmine had suggested for him to go back to his home town for the Summer Solstice Festival. No. She had ordered him to go.

Elwin had his trepidations about going back to Benedict, but he missed his mother and father. And he wanted to see Poppe and Momme as well. Even if they weren't his real family, he would always care for them. In their absence, he knew this to be true. And in a couple of tendays he may be executed.

He had wanted Zarah to go with him, but Jasmine would not allow it. Jasmine did not tell him the reason for his journey home, and he couldn't figure out what it could be. Today had been his first day off in a month, and it had only been given for him to ready for departure. Now he would receive a tenday or more off to travel home? It didn't fit.

"I wonder if she is testing me, somehow," Elwin said. "Giving me a chance to run?"

Maybe she wanted him to run. Elwin shook his head. Of all things, that made the least sense. He wanted to run. But he wouldn't. He would face the Inquisition with his head held high. He had been an infant with a knife. Elwin had flung the knife without knowledge of the danger he held. He would never stop mourning Biron's death, but he would not blame himself either. He would make the inquisitor see the truth in this.

Shaking his head, Elwin pushed the trial from his mind and turned his thoughts on home. What would they think of him now?

At least he didn't have to face them alone. Feffer would go with him. All of the soldiers in training were to be given a tenday furlough. The order came down from the king. Elwin had already coordinated their trip home with Feffer. In the morning, he would meet Feffer at the Kicking Breed near the east gate. It was a stable. Feffer had been receiving soldier's pay and had money that his father had given him. Now he claimed that he needed a horse.

Of course, he would have to meet Jasmine for training one more night, but all that stood between Elwin and seeing his friend was a single night's rest.

He made his mind empty and felt the Air around him. Upon first glance, the northern breeze seemed to caress the castle. The wind flowed around the castle's sides and spires, but this was the result of a resisting power laden in the castle's walls. Grey stones of the southern mountains had been used to form the castle.

Teams of men had carried unshaped stones down the River Serene to this location. Masons and artificers had dedicated their lives to the construction of this monumental palace. That was the power of Earth. Old and unyielding, stone must be shaped by a careful hand.

Feeling this strength, he understood the limitations of his own power of Air. The wind beat upon the stone in a frontal assault, but the earth resisted with an unrivaled strength. Elwin could feel the power of the age old blocks resisting the flow of Air around it and altering its natural course. It was as if an ancient battle was ensuing over the right to be in the space where the castle lived.

Jasmine had yet to work with Elwin on anything other than Air and Water, but when he returned, she would begin his training with Fire and Earth. Jasmine didn't want to train him in the other two before the trial. If the inquisitor learned he was a true elementalist, he might find a way to twist his gifts into something they were not. Jasmine hadn't said as much, but he couldn't see any other reason for the delay. He had much more to learn in Air and Water, but she did not want him to be weak in the other two Elements.

Someday, he would tame Spirit. First, he would have to sense his *tether*. He had come a long way with moving his essence around in the shadow realm, but he had yet to sense the power of Spirit through his tether. If he had, he would have become Life bound in that instant, then proving he wasn't Death bound would have become moot.

Elwin pulled a leather cord from his belt pouch and banded his hair back into a warrior's tail. He peered over the edge of the spire. The lingering rays of the sun had vanished, so he could not see the inner courtyard in the darkness below. But, he could see the small lights of lampposts making a large square around the garden at the courtyard's center, and he knew the path below by heart.

Hundreds of grey columns surrounded the garden and spanned upward for each level of the castle. Starting at the lowest level, several of the columns were etched to form the likeness of the kings that had ruled since the nation's beginning. The majority of the columns on the upper half were unformed, awaiting the kings of the future.

Elwin could not see their faces from this distance, but he knew their faces well. Each new king had similarities to the previous generations. He couldn't look upon them without wondering who his own face favored. Did he get his nose and eyes from his mother? Or from Bain? So many questions still to answer. *The letter* claimed that his mother had died so that he could live. Was the letter from his real mother? If so, then she would have been alive to deliver the letter. If not, then who was it that cared for him until he was passed off to his Poppe? Maybe he could find her.

He took a deep breath and suppressed the thought once more.

Leaping into the night air, he dove toward the square's center. He calmed his mind and touched the power of Air flowing around him and let it into his essence. The night air tasted crisper, and his skin tingled with the remaining day's warmth. It was like the nectar of life, flowing through his veins.

The ground was rushing toward him. No other experience could describe the exhilaration of free falling. His body felt weightless and light. The wind rushed in his ears and pressed against his body, slowing his acceleration.

Using the power from his essence, he tamed this force to slow his decent. Repositioning his body to be upright, he tamed more power and willed his body away from the courtyard. Flying high above the castle, he stopped taming flight and fell freely once more.

He had discovered that if he flew too high, it became difficult to breath. Diving back toward the castle, he spread his arms and legs out wide to aim his body toward the northeastern side of the castle.

As the balcony to his room came near, he tamed enough power of Air to slow his decent. His curtains rippled when he crossed the balcony into his room. He maneuvered his body to face upward and crossed his arms behind his head. Intertwining his legs at his ankles, he eased himself onto the bed. He released the remaining bit of power in his essence and felt the other breezes of air displaced by the flow.

He sighed.

Had he only known *this* skill, the first every elementalist learned, the year before …

He pushed the thought from his mind and prepared for another night of sleep. Another night training with Jasmine and Zarah in the shadow realm.

Feffer balanced atop the wooden beam, ignoring the cheers and jeers of his squad and fellow soldiers surrounding him below. He pushed the roar of the crowd down to the buzzing of a fly in his mind and focused on the man-sized pendulums before him. Each wooden blade left just enough room between them as they passed in front of and behind him to fit a rigid body.

Though all of the blades were blunt, the shape and width of each blade varied, alternating the timing of each swing. The slowest ones were the two behind him, and he had four more to go. Each one narrowed in size, but had enough force to knock him to the mud pit below.

Neither he nor his comrades had made it through this particular obstacle. Sir Gibbins had given the challenge, which offered a nice reward. If any of them could make it across, then all squads got an early furlough. There wasn't much light left to the day, but early furlough was early furlough. An hour or a minute of his own time had become as precious as his coin purse.

Any who wanted to attempt the gauntlet would get a single try. Feffer had seen several of his fellows fall before this point. One more step would take him as far as Gurndol had gone.

He closed his eyes and listened to the swooshing sound of the pendulums. Focusing on the one in front of him, he worked out the timing. He could feel the air become cooler as it sliced on either side.

Feffer took a deep breath and opened his eyes. He timed his step to take place the moment the blade crossed the beam. He had to judge the spacing as he moved.

The pendulums came back and just missed his front and back. His heart raced, as he teetered to keep his balance. He had less space between the swinging blades than the previous step, but he could just fit by balancing on one foot.

When he stopped swaying, he gave a long sigh of relief. The crowd's voice became a single cheer, and they started chanting his name.

His heart pounded to the point of bursting, but with arms out to either side, he could maintain his balance without much effort. This was fire form stance.

Three more to go.

He pushed the noise from his mind once more, and he watched the three remaining blades. The next step had been Gurndol's last. None had made it past this point. And Feffer realized why.

The swinging blades beyond this point left no room to stand. Few children could squeeze between the next two falling blades, let alone a grown man. He would have to take the last three without pause. But each blade fell one after the other in rapid succession. He closed his eyes and focus on the blades as he had before.

Swoosh, swoosh, swoosh.

They would reach the pinnacle in one direction.

Swoosh, swoosh, swoosh.

Then, they would reach the pinnacle on the other side. Over and over, the cycle repeated.

He forced his heart to slow down by taking steady breaths. Mindful of the swinging blade at his back, he crouched just enough to get a strong start.

Waiting for the first swoosh, he threw his other foot forward, jumping for the beam in front of the final blade. Airborne, he felt the air from the first blade brush against his back as he moved past the second blade. He passed the final blade and landed on the beam just as it made its decent.

He felt the force of the blade hit the heel of his back foot before he could pull it clear. Raising onto the ball of his foot, he used the force of the blow to spin around to face the swinging blades. Cool air brushed his face as he turned.

Using his spinning foot, he kicked the top side of the beam in an attempt to balance his body. But, his balance was too far forward. The mud pit loomed below. Rather than trying to regain his balance, he dropped. Turning in the air, he grabbed the side of the beam. He hung for a moment, stunned. Then, he swung his feet and heaved to pull his midsection up to the beam. He stepped atop the beam, stood, and thrust his fists into the air.

Three hundred or more soldiers cheered.

Feffer felt himself smiling, and then he spotted Wilton leaning against the fence on the far side of the training yard, next to the outer gate. He hadn't seen his brother in over six months. The last word Wilton had left for Feffer, a mission had taken him off-island. Something to do with the northern isles.

Even at this distance, his brother's face looked pale and his hair a mess. But, he nodded in approval as their eyes touched. Feffer smiled and waved to his brother.

Wilton looked away and began walking toward the open gate.

Feffer dropped from the high beam and rolled as his feet touched the ground. He came up in a run, moving toward the gate. The other soldiers patted him none too gently on the back as he passed by. Everyone still cheered his name, but he didn't slow.

Feffer ran out the gate but stopped for a thumping horse cart moving in his path. He couldn't see any sign of his brother until the cursed driver moved. Across the cobblestone road, Wilton stood at the opening of an alleyway. Both buildings were merchant stores, higher than they were wide.

He crossed the street, attempting not to jostle too many people. As he approached Wilton, Feffer almost stopped. He had never seen his brother worse for wear. Dark circles surrounded eyes reddened from lack of sleep or excessive drink.

"Are you alright?" Feffer said.

Wilton rubbed both eyes with one hand, "Yes. I just need a bit of rest. I will be fine."

"Did you just get back from your mission on the northern islands?"

Wilton winced as if slapped. There was a brief pause. Wilton didn't look away from him, but his eyes never actually met Feffer's.

"I arrived in time to see your conquest," Wilton said with strained enthusiasm. "Well done, Feffer."

"It was a cinch," Feffer forced a smile. What was wrong with his brother? "I could do it again and not get nipped this time."

"I am sure you could," Wilton nodded. "And you should."

"Elwin and I are going to go back home for the Summer Solstice Festival. Do you think you can join us?"

Wilton's eyes widened. "Elwin you say? When do you leave?"

"At first light," Feffer said. "I know Da would love to see you."

Wilton looked into Feffer's eyes for the first time. They lacked the luster they had the last time he saw his brother. He opened his mouth to ask about the northern isles again, but Wilton spoke first.

"I have done what I could to keep you safe, Feffer," Wilton said. "I am proud of you, and Father will be as well. You have a pure heart. I hope you always do. I want you to promise me that you will not try to be a hero in this war. If anyone asks you to be a thief-catcher, say no. Or take the training and disappear."

Wilton grabbed the back of Feffer's neck and brought their foreheads together. His voice was a tired whisper. "We are pawns in this life. Don't die for a king who doesn't even know your name. Promise me."

Feffer felt pain from the grip on his neck, but he returned his brother's embrace. He could not recall the last time his brother had shown him any affection. He said the only words that seemed to matter.

"I promise."

Wilton pulled away, avoiding Feffer's gaze. "I have something that I must do this evening, but I will meet with you and Elwin in the morning. I am looking forward to leaving this place."

"That will be ...," Feffer began. He started over, forcing enthusiasm into his words. "That will be great. It will be nice to see our home."

Wilton's lips tightened into a smile that did not touch his eyes and nodded.

"I must go. Do not try to follow me."

Feffer nodded. Try? He *would* follow him.

"Hey," Wilton pointed toward the gate. "Isn't that Gurndol, your squad leader?"

Feffer turned his head to see through the open gate. Gurndol watched them talk, but looked away upon being noticed.

"He probably just wants to meet yo—" Feffer began to say. But Wilton was no longer in the alley. He was simply gone. Feffer made a complete turn around and looked up to the roofline. The two buildings were close enough together to scale but too high to do so unnoticed in such a short period.

"That isn't possible," Feffer said. Then he thought about it for a moment and found irritation creeping into his thoughts. "Why in the abyss have they not taught *me* that trick?"

Feffer walked toward the open gateway still glancing behind to see some sign of Wilton. He wasn't sure if he was more irritated at being dismissed by his brother or that no one had taught *him* how to disappear into thin air.

"Yup," Feffer decided. "I am going to have to find out where he learned that trick."

Gurndol met him at the gate but looked toward the empty alley. "Was that Wilton?"

"It was."

"Did he tell you what happened?" Gurndol said.

"What do you mean?"

"Curse it all!" Gurndol said. "He did not tell you, then."

"For the love of Life," Feffer said. "Tell me about what?"

"Wilton's entire squad of thief-catchers was given over for dead," Gurndol said. "The word is that they were captured by something called dark savants. Or was it black savants? Some sort of savant.

Either way, they are all Death witches that use the Elements in battle. He was the sole survivor. Somehow, he escaped them in the night and stowed away on the enemy vessel that brought him to the coast of Justice. Rumor is, Wilton tracked them here."

"No," Feffer said. "Wilton said nothing of the sort. Don't go trusting idle gossip."

"I heard Sir Gibbins talking to Lord Lifesong about it. That Chai Tu Naruo named Tharu was there as well. They discussed while you traversed the gauntlet. Well done by the way."

"He didn't say anything." Feffer shook his head, skeptically.

Gurndol clasped his shoulder. "You know I wouldn't lie to you about your brother. I am not the boy I was a year before."

"I know," Feffer said. "I just ... I don't want to believe it. But he was acting off."

His friend nodded. "Let us get an ale to celebrate our early furlough. All the guys want to buy you a drink. You get to save your coin tonight."

"The abyss knows I could use a drink. Or ten." Feffer's heart was not in his smile. "I did save you a bit of running drills."

"You did," Gurndol started toward the barracks. "That is why the first round is on me."

"I better sort my pack before we hit the pub."

"Are you going on a trip, then?" Gurndol said.

"I'm going back home for the Solstice Festival," Feffer said. "Want to come?"

"My parents would have me locked in the stocks if I did not make an appearance at their Festival here. Besides, I wouldn't give up a few stolen kisses from a pretty face for a couple toothless farm girls."

Feffer laughed, "Better a toothless farm girl than a nose-stuck city girl. You'd be surprised what a farm girl will do in a darkened hayloft. And we actually touch each other when we dance."

"We touch hands," Gurndol said in defense. "Still, my parents would not allow it. Perhaps, next time."

"Alright," Feffer said. "Well, into the night then."

"Aye," Gurndol cheered, "into the night!"

Regrets

The night was darkest in the city of Justice for a man lurking through the Commons. Few lamp posts lit the streets, but none carried into the alleys. Unlike other parts of the city, no footpaths lined the sides of the cobblestone. Even the road itself was narrower in the Commons and less maintained than in the upper city of the Nobles' and Merchant's District.

The buildings were built atop one another in large blocks of various earthen stones. The slate tiles of most buildings needed major repairs. Between most blocks, the alleyways provided enough space for one person to squeeze through, but rubbish and rotting crates littered the widest paths. Some of the homes or shops had gardens, but few had fences to shelter plants. In the upper city, the footpaths, gardens, and alleyways would be gated, but here Wilton could for the most part walk uninhibited.

Despite the fact that the majority of thefts and murders occurred in this section of the city, this gave him a sense of freedom. For reasons he couldn't say, he felt safer here than amongst the other soldiers.

Perhaps, it was the integrity that these streets maintained. The boarded up and barred windows warned off intruders. No welcome wreaths hung on doors, but the shadows held no secrets here. Predators lurked in them. The darkness held an unspoken truth known by all living here.

Given the chance, I will devour you.

But few were those that would descend upon a man with raqii dath, the two curved blades on Wilton's belt. He gave the hilts a familiar stroke. Wilton hated them. But he also knew he would not part with them.

"I'll die wielding them." He could hear the challenge in his voice as the words echoed back to him.

Fool, he thought. *You don't need a fight this night.*

He strode passed the Ravenous Fray, a tavern known for its bawdy crowd. Light made dull from pipe smoke spilled from the windows and open door. A dozen men and half as many women made a circle around two men at their center. Sounds of wet slaps resounded over the cheers of the crowd. When he got his first good view of the fighters, Wilton shook his head.

The smoke had a sour smell, like burning ale. But, Wilton didn't need the odd smell to tell him the clouds surrounding the gathering hadn't come from a legal leaf like sweetweed. Only men japed-up on dragon tail or wyvern juice, dueled with rotten fish in place of swords. Though he gave the gathering a wide berth, Wilton studied the people as he walked by.

The women wore dresses cut to reveal enough bosom and leg to wonder why they bothered to wear anything at all. Most of the men wore tattered tunics, stained from wear. A few wore roped sandals and trousers, tight about the waist and ankles but baggy around the legs. Those men wore no shirts and had ink tattooed into their flesh. The tattoos varied from scripts in a foreign tongue on arms, chests, and backs to swords or beasts of other lands.

Sailors, Wilton guessed.

One of the dueling men had the tattoo of a black, serpentine creature with outstretched wings. Its long tail wrapped around the man's right arm, and the head rested on the left shoulder, blowing a spout of red-orange fire, down his arm.

A dragon.

Few decent men would have openly worn a dragon. No decent man would have permanently scribed a dragon into his flesh. Then again, no decent man would have smoked dragon tail or drunk wyvern juice.

Wilton almost laughed. As if he was an authority on decency. He may not wear a sign welcoming the Awakening to destroy the world, but he could no longer consider himself decent. He passed the japed-up brawl, watching the crowd from his periphery.

Upon seeing Wilton and his raqii dath, a couple of the men hid their pipes. One man emptied his pipe on the heel of his boot.

Wilton did not slow. He strode past them into the comfort of the dark alley next to the Ravenous Fray. His eyes took only a moment to readjust. The light from the tavern had been too deluded to damage his night vision.

He moved down the alley to the road, emerging onto a street with no lanterns that pitched him into utter darkness. On light feet, he ran in the center of the road, moving east. He entered another random alley, crossed to another road and turned north. He never stopped moving as he crossed dark roads and darker alleys, until he came to a road with a lamp.

Rather than moving up the road, he crossed the street to another alley.

Movement at the end of the path pulled his attention. A large man carrying a cudgel lumbered toward Wilton. At this distance, he couldn't determine if his size was due to muscle or portly girth. His overcloak made it impossible to determine. Either way, the width of the alley would be just large enough for Wilton to squeeze by the man. Whether fat or muscle padded his cloak, close quarters would allow the man to use his size to the advantage.

Glancing behind him, Wilton saw he had already halfway committed to the path. If this was an ambush, there would be someone blocking his retreat. The roof was too high to make efficient use of arrows, but not so high as to prevent dropping from rope into the alley. If it was not an ambush, then a retreat would place his sole attacker at his back.

Through him, then.

Wilton stopped walking and shifted the bulk of his weight to his rear leg, while placing his right hand across his chest. His left forearm rested on the hilt of his left blade. From this position, he could quickly draw both blades and assume any form.

The man still advanced.

"I do not wish to harm you," Wilton said, "but if you take another step, it will be your last."

The man stopped, but his head made a subtle shift toward the roofline.

Not alone, then.

Wilton's swords marked him as a thief-catcher. Not speaking the language of the Children of Nature, he wasn't sure what the words meant, but the blades were called raqii dath and were the style of the Chai Tu Naruo. When not at war, the twin blades of his profession would prowl these streets in search of known criminals. Any person who carried the blades had an understood reputation. Even the most foolish of criminals would bring larger numbers for an ambush.

Part of training as a thief-catcher had forced Wilton to prowl the streets before he left for the northern isles. He had likely made a few enemies during that short time, but being his first night back and the nature of his unofficial mission, he doubted anyone had planned this ambush for him.

Besides, he would have noticed any movement trailing him for an ambush.

He must have wandered into a known criminal's domain. Which meant if there was one man on the roof, there were half a dozen. Probably waiting for a victim, rather than planning for one.

"And tell your friends on the roof," Wilton said, "the same goes for them. Any man who moves against me will draw his last breath. Last warning, drop your weapon and move aside. I am not here to make examples, but I will do what I must."

The man stood watching the roofline. After a moment, he dropped his cudgel and stepped to the right side. It was a muscular form hidden by his overcoat. The loose fit made him appear less honed at a distance, but seeing him up close made his size clear. The man was a bruiser.

He did not make eye contact with Wilton, and he kept glancing at the roofline, likely waiting for a change in orders. Wilton stopped next to the man and thumbed the blade on the right side.

"Look at me," Wilton said.

It took obvious effort for him to look away from the roof, but his eyes were wide and alert as they regarded Wilton.

"You realize that had you attacked me, you would have been the first to die?"

The man gave him a flat gaze. His left hand was held out of Wilton's sight, behind the bruiser's leg. If the man gave the slightest movement with that shoulder, Wilton was ready to intercept any hidden dagger with his right blade. He would slice the man at his wrist with an upward blow and the edge of his blades would continue upward to the man's throat.

"I was raised in a small, farming community," Wilton said. "One summer, a wolf appeared from the forest nearby. It was killing sheep and cattle, and it had to be stopped. One of the farmers, a man named Drenen, devised a plan for catching the wolf. He used a rabbit for bait. In the end, they captured and killed the wolf."

Wilton leaned closer to the man and lowered his voice, "But, do you know what happened to the rabbit?"

The man shook his head. Wilton stared at the man for several seconds. He began to shift back and forth, and the bruiser didn't blink or look away. Sweat began to appear on the man's forehead.

Wilton spoke in a soft voice. "Before springing the trap, the wolf bit the rabbit's neck with such force that its neck snapped, nearly severing the head. I was young, but I learned a valuable lesson that day." Wilton glanced at the man's concealed hand and back to the bruiser's eyes. "The proper bait may catch a predator, but the bait is unlikely to survive. In the end the wolf went down, but how much do you think that mattered to the rabbit?"

Wilton thumbed the hilts of his raqii dath, pulling the bruiser's gaze to the blades. His eyes widened and the sound of metal clanked onto the cobblestones at the man's feet. A small dagger glinted in the moonlight. The bruiser held his hands up in a show of surrender and glanced to the roofline, giving a slight shake of his head.

Stepping up next to the man, Wilton said, "Perhaps you would be wise to change your profession."

He walked by, watching for movement in his periphery. The man stood rigid, keeping his hands out in front of him. As Wilton exited the alley, he heard heavy footsteps running in the opposite direction.

Wilton continued his course, moving north and east, but for several streets, most of his attention watched for signs of pursuit. When none came, he allowed himself to relax somewhat. As much as anyone should relax in the Commons at night.

Wilton felt a half-smile make its way to his lips.

The story he had told the man was true. His father had purchased the wolf skin from Drenen Escari. It was still in front of the hearth at his father's home. When they were young, he and Feffer would sit on the rug by the fire and listen to their father's stories.

The smile faded.

His fondest memories as a child had been sitting on the carcass of a predator. It seemed like there could be a lesson in all of this somewhere. As he reached the darkened building in the farthest corner of Justice, it came to him.

Sometimes it was better to be seen as a rabbit than a wolf, but whatever it took, don't be someone's bait.

Chapter 14

HAVEN

The light pounded against Feffer's eyes and face with each step of his horse. Every clank of the sword at his side felt like a hammer on an anvil inside his skull. What coin he had saved in drink the previous night, he had spent on the horse. His head had been too sore to barter a better deal with the thieving stableman. But the dapple mare was his.

He would have to give her a proper name.

Just not today …

Thinking, moving, or breathing was painful. But worst of all was the cursed light.

He squinted against the noonday sun. Wilton was just ten paces ahead of him, heading east toward Benedict. It took several days by horse, but it was better than walking it for a tenday. Feffer covered his eyes, leaving just a slit in his fingers. He looked up and around for Elwin and shivered when he thought about what his friend was doing.

But, Elwin was not in sight.

"I am sure he can see us," Wilton said.

His brother had stopped. Feffer only realized it because he had spoken. Had Wilton not said anything, he would have passed him.

Feffer pulled on the bridle to stop his mare and closed his eyes.

"Are you alright, Feffer?"

Feffer groaned, "I am never drinking again."

Wilton's laugh didn't seem quite so forced. "I have made that claim a time or two. Well, hop down. Let's break for lunch."

Feffer leaned forward on his mare and slid from the saddle, still hanging onto the pommel. That and the saddle bags had cost almost as much as the horse. He really did get robbed.

Wilton guided his horse to a small tree just off the road. Feffer followed him and tied his mare off next to Wilton's. His horse was mostly white with speckles of black around the ears, while Wilton's was mostly black with speckles of white on the nose.

"Here," Wilton offered him a waterskin. "This will make you feel better."

Feffer took the skin and eased down to the grass next to the road. He took several large gulps before noticing Elwin several dozen paces above him. He choked off a drink and stared at his friend. Elwin's head faced the ground and his eyes squinted with his hands held tightly to his sides. It took Feffer a moment to realize Elwin wasn't slowing down.

"What in the abyss?" Feffer said.

A rush of air gushed around Feffer as he rolled to the side. A pace above him, Elwin hovered in the air with a full-toothed smile painted on his face. Feffer felt a steady breeze as white embers of light appeared and disappeared around Elwin.

Feffer forced the awe from his face and threw the waterskin at him. "What in the abyss is wrong with you?"

Elwin caught the waterskin, laughing. "I was just having a bit of fun. Now we're even."

"For what?"

He eased to the ground as if by some invisible hand. The breeze and lights vanished when Elwin's feet were firmly planted on the ground. Feffer suppressed a shiver.

"If I remember correctly," Elwin said, "I owed you from dumping water on my head."

The excitement was passed, but Feffer's heart still raced. Each beat felt like a hammer branding the inside of his skull. He thought he might lose his stomach.

"That was a *year* ago," he said as he massaged his temples. "*And, I don't do that sort of thing anymore.*"

"Well then, I guess we are even for good."

"Eat up," Wilton said, then gave them both some dried bread.

Elwin and Wilton sat across from Feffer and began to munch on their lunch.

Feffer tongued the dried bread until he could swallow it. He closed his eyes and pretended the dried crumbs to be Mrs. Escari's famous pastries. Maybe she would have some already baking.

"Feffer," Wilton said, "do you still have the lock picks I gave you?"

Feffer opened his eyes. The sun was just as bright as it had been. He squinted at Wilton. "Hidden in my belt compartment," Feffer touched his belt, "like you suggested. I have been practicing as often as I can with the heavy lock you gave me, too. I think I could move on to shackles next."

"Good," Wilton said. "You never know when that skill will be useful. It might save your life some day."

Finally, the opening Feffer had been waiting for. He just wished that his brain didn't throb.

"Wilton," Feffer said. "Can I ask you something?"

Wilton looked at him with a flat stare. Some time passed before he said, "Ask."

"What happened to your squad?"

Elwin looked up from his half-eaten bread.

"They all died, Feffer. They were tortured and killed."

"What?" Elwin asked at the same time Feffer said, "So it is true, then."

"Were you … hurt?" Feffer asked. He had almost said *tortured*.

Wilton stood. "It is time to go."

His brother untied and mounted his mare, then spurred his horse to a gallop. Feffer mounted his own horse, but it took several minutes to catch up to his brother. The short gallop had not been kind to his splitting skull, but it didn't seem as important as it had.

Wilton did not even glance at him.

Curse it all, he wished he could take his question back. More so he wished there was something he could do or say to make things better. Tortured. His brother had been tortured. The rumors had all been true. Feffer couldn't help but wonder.

How had he escaped?

As Elwin passed above him, he felt a chill in the air. He pushed thoughts of torture and escape from his mind. Home. A few more days and he would be home.

"Haven." He patted his horse. "Because you are taking me home. Everything will be alright, as soon as we get home."

Air rushed around Elwin and through him as he flew high above Feffer and Wilton. Facing the ground allowed him to keep his eyes open, but the rush of air made him want to close them. Each time he blinked, his eyelids wanted to stick together and not open. But it was the wind. He could keep going. They were almost home.

Maybe he could close them for just a second. No. He had to keep them open, or he could veer off course and lose...

A moment panic struck him when he realized he couldn't see Feffer or Wilton. He slowed to a stop and scanned the trees. When the two horses emerged on the road from beneath the copse, Elwin sighed with relief.

As if they could hear him at this distance, he said between breaths, "Go ahead. I'll catch up."

He shook his head. Jasmine found a way to make him train without even being there. He could almost hear her voice the question when she saw him next.

Elwin raised the pitch of his voice. "Now, what did you learn about flying long distances?"

Well, at least he had an answer for this one.

Balancing the tide of Air flowing into his essence to sustain flight over short distance had become like walking or running in bursts. However, flying for over miles felt like working all day in a field or marching for hours on end. But, he had discovered, hovering didn't take much effort. It felt more like standing. Sure, after a day of running, standing took effort, but it felt like taking a rest after a run. Hovering felt just like that.

Once his heart slowed, Elwin tamed more Air and moved to catch Feffer and Wilton. Once they were below him, he slowed to match them.

"See," he said. "I told you I could catch up."

Being alone was another negative side of flying while they rode their horses. Talking as if they could hear him helped to alleviate some of the monotony. He could fly near them, but he preferred solitude to biting-gnats and blood-flies splattering against his face. Jasmine spoke of creating an Air shield, which would help with bugs and the rush of wind in his face. But Elwin had mostly been worked on flying and the wind thrust. And he had begun to work on a veil and the lightning hurl. Veils would bend the air in such a way to make him invisible. Perhaps, she would teach him the shield next.

In the meantime, he had to fly above the bugs. That meant being alone in his thoughts. Just a few days ago, he had wanted some time alone. But he couldn't read while flying, and he hadn't been able to talk to Feffer for almost a year. He was so exhausted by the evening meal, talk around the campfire didn't last very long.

And the mood felt tense.

Wilton had not said much since admitting to the loss of his squad. Talking about his own year in Justice and the trial seemed insignificant in comparison to torture. Feffer didn't seem to remember the trial, and Elwin wasn't ready to talk about the Awakening.

Elwin shivered. Probably from the chill in the air. The prophecies were just superstition. The Awakening had nothing to do with him.

He glanced around. Dark clouds moved in from the north, and even at this distance he could feel the energy in them. Perhaps, they would miss Benedict. Poppe would be disappointed if it rained on his festival.

A surge of excitement went through him. His Poppe had found him. Whoever his mother had been, she picked the best person he knew to look after him. Of all the people in Benedict, he couldn't have asked for a better grandpa.

The edge of the land flattened out on the horizon, and Elwin saw a log home made of redwood. Smoke rose from the chimney and spread out above the farm and farmhouse. The fields flourished with green leaves in neat rows. This was the first farm on the west side of Benedict.

Home.

Butterflies fluttered in his stomach and a chill ran up his spine. Behind those walls, his mother prepared the meal, while Father sat by the fire to read a book or tally his yield.

Elwin felt a renewed vigor.

He ceased his flow of Air and stretched into a dive, angling his body toward the moving horses. As he neared the ground, he jerked upward while taming Air to fly at a level with Feffer and Wilton.

He slowed as he reached them and said, "The farm is only a few miles, not more than a league. I'll meet you there."

"Finally," Feffer said. Then his eyes widened. "Do you think they are cooking?"

Elwin smiled. "I saw smoke in the chimney."

Opening his essence wide, Elwin let the Air flow through him, and his body lurched up and forward. He heard Feffer's shout of, "Wooohooo," as the land rushed by, and he felt bugs bounce off his head as he ascended. But he didn't care. He covered the last few miles to the farm in less than a minute.

He slowed to descend and landed in the field by the barn, leaning against it to catch his breath. His heart raced, and he wanted to sit. Refusing to give in to his weary legs, he marched toward the front porch.

As he approached the farm, he stopped. The farm was different.

His father had expanded the farmhouse. Gutters and new wooden tiles surrounded the entire house to help the home withstand the frequent summer storms, like he always said he would. Fresh timber extended from the older wood of the house several more paces toward the barn. He turned to look at the barn and gaped. It had doubled in size. Two extra plows rested in the fields alongside the old one, and the crops stretched farther than they ever had. Much more than one man could handle alone. There were too many cattle in the pen for Elwin to count.

He looked at the home again. Had he come to the right house?

Then he saw the porch swing. Worn and weathered, the names Elwin and Feffer had been carved into the side. He stared at the names for a moment. Feffer had chipped the knife while carving his name, and Father had switched them for using his good knife without permission. He hadn't been able to sit the next day without feeling the sting.

It should have been a bad memory. Who liked to be punished? But it made Elwin smile, and the lingering nervousness at seeing his parents again faded. This *was* his home.

He walked up to the door, debating whether or not to knock. People left home all the time. Did they knock when coming home? Or did they just walk right in?

As he raised a hand to open the door, a booming laugh from within stayed his hand. The voice was way too deep to have been his father. Then, he heard others talking and laughing.

What in the abyss? What if his parents no longer lived here? Was it possible that they sold the farm or gave the land back to Lord Arca?

Elwin crept up to the porch window and peeked in. The new part of the house extended the dining area to fit a much larger table. At least two dozen people he had never seen sat at a long table. Hands extending from dirt-stained sleeves reached for fresh bread at the table's center.

"Who is in my house?"

He had been about to turn and walk away, when he looked at the table's head, which was wide enough to seat two people. His mother and father sat side by side.

The smile on his mother's face lit the entire room, but dark circles hung beneath her eyes. He couldn't hear her words over the other conversations, but her laugh carried through the window.

Elwin went to the door and knocked. It felt like the right thing to do. The conversation and laughter died off, and he heard his mother say, "Well, who could that be at this hour?"

He found himself shifting his weight from foot to foot in anticipation. His heart started racing and his palms felt sweaty.

The door opened without hesitation. His mother's eyes widened, and she covered her mouth like she always had after being surprised.

"Hi, Mama," Elwin said, like he had when he was little.

She stared at him without speaking for several moments. Tears filled her eyes, and she pulled him into an embrace. He hadn't heard him leave the table, but he couldn't mistake his father's strong arms holding him.

Elwin felt the worries melt away, and he cried happy tears into his parents arms.

By the time Wilton tethered his horse next to Feffer's aside the Escari's house, only a hint of pink remained in the sky. Wilton had several experiences with Drenen, but they were mostly in passing. Whereas, Feffer had practically grown up with Elwin. So upon approaching the farm, Wilton let Feffer take the lead.

It would make everything easier in the long run.

The last time he had come to this farm, he had been a boy of ten. It had been the day his Da bought the wolf's pelt. He remembered it being smaller, but some of the wood on the house seemed fresh. The smooth seams between the old and new wood could have only come from the work of an expert carpenter. Wilton had always admired Drenen Escari. He was a man of many talents. A part of him regretted not getting to know the man better.

Maybe this farm would be spared from war.

Wilton shook his head against the thought. He knew that war *would* see these lands. It was inevitable.

Dangerous thoughts. With effort, he pushed them from his mind.

Following Feffer onto the porch, he recognized the porch swing but Feffer's name had been scratched into the side next to Elwin's. That hadn't been there before. The scrawls made his memory of the swing seem wrong somehow as if he invaded someone else's mind. Black fog seemed to swirl in his vision as he forced the memory into his thoughts.

He had sat on that swing while his Da bartered for the pelt. Drenen was at a major disadvantage in making that deal, since both parties had the knowledge that Melra Escari hadn't wanted the wolf's pelt in her house.

Father hadn't used the disadvantage against Drenen. In fact, he bought the pelt for far more than its worth. On the road back, Wilton asked his Da why he had given so much.

"It is never a loss to give too much to a friend in need. A man should give his life for those he loves, son. A life given over to vanities is a wasted life."

Wilton had not understood at the time, but now he did. Now, more than ever. The wolf had taken a good portion of the Escari's livelihood. So his father had made a sacrifice for his friend. That was another lesson.

Sacrifices must be made, he thought, *and when it really counts, the price is always high.*

"Are you coming?" Feffer said.

Wilton had the feeling Feffer had called his name a few times. Mrs. Escari stood in the doorway with an inviting smile.

"Please," Melra pointed to his blades. "You don't need those at the dinner table."

Wilton hesitated to leave his blades, but he unfastened his belt and left both blades beside the door next to Feffer's longsword.

To the right, a couple of sofas and chairs boxed in a large, stone hearth that had a sizable fire. Straight ahead twenty-two men sat at a dinner table. There were three empty chairs next to the table's head to the far left, where Drenen stood.

Meat, potatoes, and greens rested on a wooden plate in front of each empty chair, along with a wooden mug filled with cider. He licked his lips when he smelled the spices wafting from the cider.

Feffer took the seat next to Elwin, leaving him the third seat from the head. Wilton felt his hand shake as he pulled out the chair. He hadn't eaten a meal like this in some time. His heart began to beat faster as he sat. He tried to keep his breathing calm, but the man next to him smelled of dirt and sweat. The stench threw off his rhythm. He stared at the meat to avoid meeting anyone's gaze.

"Please," Melra said, "we can make introductions as we eat. I am sure you boys are famished. "

Glad for the excuse to remain looking down, Wilton began to cut into his meat and potato. Focusing on each action, he placed a bite in his mouth, chewed, and swallowed. He continued eating each bite with the hope that the routine action would calm his racing heart.

When Drenen introduced his name, Wilton made a polite smile without quite meeting anyone's gaze. The farmers around the table made small talk with Elwin and Feffer, but he continued to focus on his meal. After a few bites, his tongue began to taste the food. The meat was spiced to complement the cider.

Feeding so many would have been cheaper without the added expense. The cider was freshly made as well. Melra and Drenen were good people. They didn't deserve the coming war. He felt tears well in his eyes, and forced his thoughts back on his food.

But he didn't like having his back to the door. On its own volition, his hand went to his sword belt, and he was struck by a moment of panic at his missing sword. Glancing over his shoulder, he could see the raqii dath resting by the door. He wiped at the sweat on his brow with the sleeve of his forearm.

He jumped at the mention of his name.

"Wilton," Drenen said, "as I understand it, you are a thief-catcher. Willem is really proud of you. What is it like working for Lord Zaak Lifesong, himself?"

The pride in Drenen's voice was like a punch from a hand he shook and trusted.

Like with any assault, Wilton felt the instant rush of his heart and the tensing of his muscles. All the farmhands stared at him with wide eyes.

Did they know?

He tried to rest his left hand on the hilt of a sword that was not there. His heart started beating faster. Why were his weapons so far away? He remembered black fog swirling around him. Pain wracked his senses, and he could see dark eyes staring into him.

His mind began to calculate getting out of the room alive.

First, the wiry man with long hair across from him would need to fall. Wilton had seen a quickness in his step when he had returned from the privy that suggested training with a sword. Next, the smelly man to his immediate right would be dealt with. He seemed clumsy, but his size and proximity would be the second greatest threat. Drenen was no small man and would likely be the next to die.

A part of his mind cried out at the thought, and he realized his hand held the steak knife in a reverse-grip as he would his raqii dath when facing multiple opponents.

What are you doing? A voice said in his mind. *This is Drenen, your Da's best mate.*

The war did not need to see the inside of this home. At least not this night. He forced his hand to loose the knife. It took a moment for his fingers to respond to his will. The knife clanked off the wooden plate.

Wilton stood, knocking his chair backward.

"Excuse me," Wilton said, "I need to use the privy."

On the way out the door, he grabbed his belt and fastened his weapons. Perhaps staying the night at the Escari farm was not the best idea. He longed for the cover of darkness.

Untethering his horse, he leapt into the saddle and spurred his mare to a gallop.

"Home," he told her. "I have to see my home one more time."

Elwin sat next to Feffer on a cushioned sofa. After the others had cleared the table, his parents had extinguished the lanterns, which made the fire in the hearth the only source of light.

His mother placed a kettle atop the fire, then she joined his father on the sofa across from him and Feffer.

"Tea won't be long now," she smiled.

"You look tired, Mother," Elwin said.

"Elwin," she teased, "that is no way to speak to a woman. You will never attract the ladies if you insult them."

He shared a smile with his parents.

Feffer laughed. "I think Elwin only has eyes on *one* lady."

"Feffer," Elwin warned. He should have never told him about Zarah.

"Really," Father said. "Who is the lucky lady?"

"Well—"

"I told you not to say anything," Elwin said.

"No," Feffer said. "You told me not to say anything to *her*."

"I know what I said," Elwin told them. "I was there when I said it. You couldn't say anything to her, because new recruits aren't allowed in the castle. I said not to say *anything*."

"It's someone in the castle?" his mother smiled.

"Yup," Feffer said. "It's Zarah Lifesong."

Elwin could feel the heat of the fire in his face. He covered his eyes. "I will never trust you with another secret."

His father raised his eyebrows and whistled. "As in daughter to Lord Zaak Lifesong, second to the throne, until there is a proper heir?"

"That would be the one," Feffer said.

"She is *third* to the throne," Elwin said. "Jasmine is second, after Zaak. And I can't stand her. She's a prat." A beautiful prat. But a prat, nonetheless.

"Son," Father said, "you do stare into the stars."

"Can we talk about something else, please?"

The three of them laughed. Elwin's cheeks burned hot enough to boil the kettle, but he jumped when the kettle whistled.

His mother stood and prepared four wooden cups of tea, cooled with cow's milk. "We have honey, if anyone would like some?"

Only his father didn't.

His mother handed Elwin his cup, and he sipped it despite its heat. "This is better than what they give me in the castle."

"Oh come now," she said as she sat, "you expect me to believe that?"

"I promise," Elwin said. "They use sugarcane instead of honey. This *is* better."

"Well, thank you."

"Is that flour I smell?" Feffer asked.

Elwin's mother smiled. "It is. I will be rising early to bake my pastries for the festival. And I expect some help loading them."

"We will," Feffer said. His grin reminded Elwin of the boy he had grown up with.

"Father," Elwin said. "I've never seen you hire this many farm hands. Where did they come from?"

"The town has grown a bit, Elwin. People from the coasts fear being attacked, so many have moved inland. Several people of other nations are beginning to be displaced by the war, as well. People are working for food as much as coin. That is why we have so many here. I am making up jobs just to help people out."

"That's right," Mother said. "Most of the people are bringing trades that we didn't have before, but there are a few that bring competition as well. The prices for most things have gone down because of it. There is a new foresting crew to help with new construction. Old Gailin didn't have enough of a crew to do it on his own. There are even artificers that have come. Your Poppe has purchased a grand display of fireworks for the festival tomorrow."

"Zarah said they had fireworks every year in Justice," Elwin said.

He almost struck himself for bringing up Zarah's name. He let out a sigh of relief when the conversation continued without acknowledgement of the slip.

"How's my Da?" Feffer asked.

"He has never done better for himself," Father laughed. "Your Da could turn a profit by selling a farmer his own dirt."

Feffer's smile split his face, then his smile drooped into a frown.

"Feffer," Elwin said. "What is it?" He knew the answer before Feffer spoke his name.

"Wilton. I'm worried about him."

"Me too," Elwin said.

His mother and father exchanged a look of concern, but they didn't voice the unasked question. Feffer answered anyway. Hearing Feffer tell them about Wilton's torture and the death of his squad was not any easier the second time. It sounded like something out of a book, but it wasn't. Wilton had seen his companions die. By the end, Mother had tears in her eyes, and Father's face paled.

For several moments, the only sound came from the crackling fire.

"Where do you think he went?" Elwin asked to break the silence.

"Home."

"That is probably for the best," his mother said.

Father nodded. "Willem will take care of him."

The silence lingered for a bit more. Feffer looked up and said, "Elwin, what is it like living in the palace?"

"My rooms are too big, really."

Feffer rolled his eyes. "Rooms? Bah. If you want to trade, you can have my bunk in the barracks. It smells like old sweat and rotten small clothes."

"You make such a compelling argument, but I will keep my accommodations."

"Accommodations," Feffer said rolling his eyes. "Really. What's it like?"

"Honestly. It's exhausting. There is protocol for everything. I have multiple forks and spoons for every meal, and I can't wrinkle my clothes a hair, or I hear it from Harkin three times over."

"Harkin?" Feffer said.

"Ah," Elwin said. "He's … uh … He's my … uh … manservant."

"You have a manservant?" Feffer said, incredulity thick in his voice. "I eat slop and run drills all day. But you are exhausted with your *manservant*? Unbelievable!"

"I hardly ever see him," Elwin protested. "He mostly just lays my clothes out and keeps my quarters clean." Harkin   tried to dress him, but Elwin refused. He wasn't about to tell Feffer about that part.

"Oh," Feffer said dramatically. "He only keeps your *quarters* clean and lays out your fancy shirts. Does he fluff your pillow and make your bed? My mattress is so thin, the ground must be more soft."

"I work hard too." Elwin crossed his arms in front of his chest. "I train almost nonstop. And when I say nonstop. I mean. Non. Stop. After breakfast, I train with the Elements until lunch, then I get lectured to for *hours*. Before supper, I train with my mind's eye, where I try to will my soul to move about through fighting forms. Which, by the way, *is* as exhausting as it sounds. After the evening meal, I have one hour of free time before I have to meet Jasmine in the shadow realm for more training. That's right. I even train in my sleep. Then I wake up and my day starts over. Oh. Right. And every Lifeday, we train with swords."

"Okay," Feffer said. "Maybe you do work hard. But you have a *manservant*. If I spill my slop, I go hungry and have to do press-ups for making a mess. Your manservant probably apologizes to you for the mess you made." Feffer stuck his nose up in the air and made a mocking tone. "I am so sorry you spilled that. Please allow me to clean it up for you, sir."

"That's ridiculous," Elwin said. Then he smiled. "I don't eat in my quarters."

Feffer rolled his eyes again.

Elwin looked to his parents for support. They both had amused smiles.

"Would anyone like more tea?" Mother said while pouring water into her own cup.

Elwin and Feffer both held cups out for her to refill.

"Soldiering can't be all bad," Elwin said after taking a sip.

"Nah. You get used to running through the drills. I'm the best in my squad with the forms. I was the first to learn all of the stanzas of every form, and I get to spar in the advanced class. It's my favorite part."

"Wow," Elwin said. "You'll make the White Hand yet."

"I intend to." Feffer's face grew somber once more. Elwin didn't have to ask to know Feffer was thinking about Wilton.

"Well," Father said, "we have an early start, tomorrow. We should be off to bed."

"Finish your tea boys," his mother said. "The sleeproot will help you have a good night's rest."

"Sleep in a bed." Elwin stood, stretching and yawning, "I can't wait."

"Where do I sleep?" Feffer asked.

"If you recall," Father said, "Feffer, you were going to come stay with us last year. The night before you boys left, I began building bunk beds. After you were gone, it was a good project to keep me busy for a few days."

"See, " Feffer said, "the mischievous days of my youth weren't all bad."

"It wasn't all that long ago," Mother said. "Have you changed *that* much?"

"I have," Feffer said. "I swear."

"I don't know," Mother said. "You'll have to show me before I believe you."

"I will show you," Feffer said. "What would you like me to do?"

"Come help me with these dishes."

Feffer's smile slipped for a moment, but it returned in an instant. "I will. I am excited to help you."

Feffer walked ahead of Mother into the kitchen and began to sort plates.

"Good night, son," she hugged Elwin and went into the kitchen.

His father patted him on the back. "It gladdens my heart to have you home, son."

Elwin leaned in for a hug and watched his father go down the hall. He stood and took a deep breath. So much had changed, but this was still his home.

As he rounded the corner to his room, Elwin heard his mother ask Feffer to go outside to draw water from the well. He smiled. Feffer had talked himself into chores. That had to be a first.

Elwin stopped in the doorway of his room. It was just as he had left it. The books were all straightened and the bed was made. Nothing was out of sorts, except, atop his blanket was the book that Asalla had given him the year before. The one he had left in the grass.

"I found it in front of the inn before I got your letter," his father said from behind him. "It looked like something you might like."

"That is odd," Elwin said. "I wonder how it got there. I had left it behind the Madrowl's shop."

"One of the kids must have found it."

"I'm glad you got it before the rain did. The book merchant gave it to me before everything happened. He said that it was a rare find. If it is alright with you I would like to take it back with me when I go."

"Of course." Father sat on the bed next to him. "I wanted to wait for you to bring this up, but I have something I need to say to you."

"What is it?"

"Your mother and I realized long ago we couldn't have children.

When you came into our lives, we thanked the Lifebringer for giving us such a precious gift. You were so young, too young to be away from your mother. We had to hire a wet nurse until you were old enough to have goat's milk. Before we knew it, you started walking. You were quick to learn everything. We were so proud of you. And we still are."

His vision began to blur.

His father placed his strong arm around Elwin's shoulders. "What happened last year. It was an accident, Elwin. No one could have known that you had this power within you. What happened to that man was a tragedy. No one will argue that. But your mother and I love you, and we will always have a bed for you. I want you to know that."

"I do." He wiped the tears that started falling. "I love you, as well. And I will come back as often as I can."

His father hugged him for several moments.

"Deed is done." Feffer said as he bounced into the room. "I get top?"

"You can have the top," Elwin said, wiping his tears.

His father hugged him one more time and said, "Night boys," as he left the room.

"Good night, Father," Elwin said, as Feffer called, "Good night, Mr. Escari."

Feffer climbed into the top bunk. "I guess it would be easier for you to get up and down from here though, eh?"

"Yes," Elwin said, as he settled into the bottom bunk. "I guess it would."

"You have to tell me what it's like," Feffer said. "Flying. Even as I see it, I can't believe it."

Elwin took a deep breath. He could feel the Air connecting Feffer to him. The power was always there, waiting to fill him.

"There is nothing else like it, Feffer. Even touching the Elements makes you more alive. I feel connected to everything. Even now, I can feel you moving your hand through the Air, as if it were a bird."

Feffer stopped moving his hand and Elwin laughed.

Feffer peeked his head over the side of the bed. "How did you know that?"

"As your hand moves, it create ripples," Elwin said. "I don't know *how* exactly. I have to focus on the Air, then I can see it in a way. How do you see or hear? You just do."

"You see with your eyes," Feffer said as he lowered his hand to the bed, "and you hear with your ears. What do you *see Air* with?"

"My essence," Elwin said.

"*Oh*," Feffer said. "*That* explains everything."

"We should get some sleep," Elwin said.

"Night, Elwin."

"Good night, Feffer."

Elwin woke beside his bed.

He could see Feffer already asleep above him. Watching the slow rhythm of his friend's breathing, he wanted to make this moment last.

"We made it," he said. "Feffer, we're home. This Summer Solstice Festival will be much better than last year's."

He could hear the voice of his parents in the common room. He willed himself next to the fire. They sat on the same sofa as before, only they faced each other.

"He has grown so much," Father said. "I couldn't be more proud of him."

"I know," she said after a time, "but don't you wish he could stay here?"

"I do, but he is meant for greatness, above the life of a farmer."

"Do you regret your life as a farmer?" she asked.

"You know that I do not," Father said, "but I do not have Elwin's gifts."

She took a deep breath. They were quiet for a time, staring into one another's eyes.

He touched her face. "He will be alright. I have only met one other with a kinder heart."

Elwin felt as much as heard lightning roll through the clouds overhead. He returned to his room. It didn't feel right spying on them.

They loved him, and that was all that mattered to him.

Chapter 15

VISIONS AND BARGAINS

Zarah sat up in her bed, trying to catch her breath.

Her shift was wet with sweat. Her muscles ached and her head was sore. If she let herself, she could have laid back down to sleep. She had not entered the shadow realm in the night.

Instead she had been given dreams.

She could not go back to sleep. Zarah had to find her mother. The sun had not quite risen, so she would likely be in bed. Her mother shared quarters with her father in the next room over.

If it was much farther, Zarah was not sure she could make it without rest.

It took a lot of strength to push her blankets aside and roll out of bed. Her legs had nothing left to support her weight, and she fell to the cold marble.

She felt the power of Air flowing around her canopied bed and around the corners of her large room. Even if she had not heard the water splattering off her opened balcony, she could feel rain disturbing the Air as it fell. The fluid nature of Water intertwined around the flow of Air. Water nourished all living things, but Air brought the life-giving Water to the land.

She wanted to let the power fill her and fly to her mother's quarters, but her essence had been drained. Having Visions always drained her essence so that taming a drop of power would render her unconscious. Or worse, she could damage her essence permanently.

Taking several breaths, she focused on the task at hand. Zarah crawled to her vanity dresser next to the door. Wrapping her arms around the sides, she pulled with her arms and pushed with her legs to stand. Her stomach heaved, and she closed her eyes to stop the room from spinning.

The door felt like moving a boulder placed by a giant. She pulled with all her weight to get it open and almost fell as it swung inward. Ever-torches lit the hallway, but no guards or servants walked the corridor.

Using the wall as support, Zarah worked her way up the hallway. When she reached Father's door, she stopped to catch her breath, leaning against the door for support. Her first knock had not been as loud as she had hoped.

Balling her fist, she pounded with the last of her strength. Her legs gave out, as the door opened inward. She never made it to the floor.

Zarah felt strong arms lift her and carry her into the darkened room.

"Father," she said. "I must speak to Mother."

"Are you alright?"

"I had a Vision," she said. "I will be fine, but I must speak to Mother, now."

She did not need light to know that he had placed her on a cushioned chair next to the fireplace. Flint and steel sounded and the torch caught. Her father placed it into the fireplace along with kindling and a small log.

"Are you alright?" It was Mother's voice. "I was about to come see why you had not met me for your lesson."

With the light of the fire, Zarah could see her father had robed before answering the door, but Mother only wore her shift.

Zarah tried to sit up, but the room spun. Remaining slouched, she said, "I had a Vision. Elwin is in danger. We all are."

Mother sat on the ottoman, next to her. "What did you see?"

"I saw our city from above, as if I were flying. A fog too dark to be natural surrounded it. At the center of the fog, I saw Elwin in a cage. A man in dark silks stood next to it, holding the key. I could not see the man's face, but I *felt* his power. Feffer Madrowl was dressed in a loin cloth, like Tharu wears. He crept up to the cage wielding raqii dath and moved with the grace of a cat."

Zarah stopped to catch her breath. Her stomach still felt as if she might sick up, and she tasted bitterness at the back of her throat.

"Is there more?" Mother asked.

Zarah nodded. "Yes. But, I saw two things happen at once. They were both shadowy with solid pieces. In both of the Visions the most solid image was Elwin fighting against the cage. Feffer became transparent, as if a ghost. In one of the images, Feffer was opening the cage. In the other, he was dead at the feet of the man in silks.

"In the first image with Elwin free, he and Feffer fought the man in blue silks and drove him from the castle. In the second image when Feffer died, Elwin laid in his cage and wept himself to sleep. The man in silks laughed as the castle walls crumbled to dust. He said, 'You are mine at last *son of Bain*. At last, the world is mine.'

"The castle faded and a field of corpses began to rise, though they did not draw breath. Large winged creatures made of bones, like dragons without scales, covered the lands. People were made to swear allegiance to the Seeker.

"The field faded into mountains, where dragons rose from their rock cocoons. They were much more massive than any bard has every told. The dragons were divided by the color of their scales. Gold and green dragons hovered over Alcoa, like guardians, while the black and red dragons tried to destroy them. There were dragons of other colors, who went to other nations, and others still who scattered to odd corners of the world.

"Mother." Zarah swallowed. The next part was difficult to say. Her mother and father were listening to her every word.

"What is it Zarah?" her mother asked.

"The dragons were gifted in the Elements, and they could all do things from legend. Beneath their power, the world began to crumble. Mountains shifted, the lands quaked, and the seas rose. The Alcoan nation was fissured and the Island Nations were swallowed by the sea."

Her heart was beating faster, she realized. She swallowed the acid taste in her mouth and closed her eyes. "Then, I woke up."

Her parents remained quiet for a long time. Her heartbeat returned to normal by the time her mother finally spoke.

"Zaak, would you please inform the king that we have an urgent matter to discuss?"

Her father's jaw was tight. He gave her a single nod and exited, not stopping to dress. Mother did not speak until the door closed.

"I prayed this day would never come," Jasmine said, "but you must soon be ready for war. Including you and I, there are three elementalists in the city. We had to send most of ours in defense of the northern isles. Those who remain on the island are in the port cities, preparing for attack.

"I am afraid that some of the northern isles have fallen to the enemy. Bain has elementalists using the Death Element in battle. They call themselves black savants."

She took a deep breath. "The only reason we have this knowledge is due to a brave survivor, named Wilton Madrowl. He is one of the king's thief-catchers. According to his reports, these black savants are going from city to city, looking for someone they call the Son of Bain. He followed one of them to our city."

"Here?" Zarah wanted to stand up but knew her legs would not support her. "Why did you send Elwin away? And by himself? We should have gone with him."

"Mind your tone, young lady. Neither of us could easily leave the city without notice," she said. "We are both too well known. Elwin has been mostly restricted to the castle and is not well known outside its walls. I have spied on him in the shadow realm, and he is safe. No one has followed him. Sending him away was the best decision I could have made. *Especially* now."

"What about my Vision?"

Mother looked at her for several moments.

"Elwin being captured is tied to our city in ruins," she said, more to herself than Zarah. "It will take some time to puzzle out the rest. For now, he is safe in his hometown. He will not return until the day before his trial. That will give me the time to find this *black savant* in our city. Elwin's power is so great that even a novice could find him if he was to remain here. After the trial, I will send him with Tharu to the Chai Tu Naruo people or with Hulen to the dwarven city of Dargaitha."

"Mother," Zarah said. "The prophecies are real, and Elwin will begin it. He will cause the Awakening. And if he dies, our nation will fall." She could not push the images of dragons fissuring the lands from her mind. "The whole world will fall."

Mother took a deep breath. "I know child. I know."

The first streams of predawn light escaped the storm clouds in the east, giving the small village of Benedict a few pink rays. Wilton sat atop his father's store with his legs hanging over the ledge, not bothering to wipe the rain from his face. Drops of water thrummed off the roof and dampened the red wood, turning it to a deep crimson. Dark pools gathered at sags in the roof like puddles of blood.

Beneath him, the square was desolate.

Maybe less people would visit this year's festival. He knew it to be an empty hope. The rain would cause everyone to be inside the inn. Wooden walls provided flimsy protection, even if they were crafted of the thick redwoods from the Carotid forest.

It was not long ago when he remembered this height being the pinnacle of his life. He would come up here as a boy and watch people go by. He remembered being afraid of falling forward. The memories betrayed his current view. The ground was not so far away, ten paces. If he fell now, he knew how to roll into the fall to avoid injury.

If he jumped the right way, perhaps he could find his life's end. People would say he fell. No one would know what he had done.

He felt tears in his eyes. How many of his family and friends would die?

Wilton had already seen more death than he cared to see. Zaak had been a fool to send him and the others to that island. They were like untrained children against giants. No. Children would have stood a better chance against giants. It was madness to have thought they could have defeated the black savants in their own camp.

Garrin Haysworth of Paradine, a lordling to a major house, had been in command. Like the rest of the thief-catchers, Garrin was lean of stature. Wilton knew that Garrin's birthright wasn't the sole reason for his leadership. His dark eyes had a way of weighing a man as if Garrin could see his inner thoughts.

Even now, Wilton could not fault Garrin for his strategy. The lordling had made the best of an impossible charge. With his eyes closed, he could see that night as if he was still there.

The moon almost waxed full, providing ample light by which to see.

Their ship dropped anchor a mile from the shore. Captain Tidworth had been a smuggler of wyvern's tail before the war, but his ship had been torched by the savants. Seeking revenge, Tidworth confessed his crimes to the king's court, and the king took the smuggler into his service against Bain. Tidworth's unique skills took them unseen through the dark.

Not a single torch was lit. Tidworth sailed them by moonlight and memory.

From the deck of the ship, Wilton saw dying campfires, casting shadows on large tents. The encampment of Bain's army stretched across the sandy shores and onto the rocky plains beyond the beach.

If there were sentinels, none cried out. Garrin said there would likely be no watch on the sea by night. The underwater crags on the east side of the island made it difficult to traverse even by daylight, so Garrin counted on the foot patrols to be apathetic as well. In truth, the enemy had little need for a diligent watch. Being one of the smallest of the northern isles, Napri had been conquered first. If any of the citizens had survived the attack, there would not have been enough of them to have been a threat.

Garrin tapped him on his shoulder and pointed to the ropes hanging over the ships rails. A dozen moonlit faces bobbed in and out of the sea.

Wilton felt his heart flutter when he swung his legs over the rail.

His raqii dath bounced against his naked thighs as he eased himself down the rope. The rope rubbed against his bare chest, reminding him that he wore only a loincloth.

It had taken a few months to grow accustomed to the lean apparel. Now he hardly noticed.

Summer had just begun, but the water still had a chill. The waves were calm, but they still made him rise and fall. The feeling was quite different than the lucid lake of the Carotid where he had spent the summers of his youth. He tried not to think about the water's surface beneath him. The Lifebringer alone knew what creatures dwelled in the ocean's depths.

Wilton kicked his legs and moved his arms to stay afloat, while the others lowered to join those in the sea. No one spoke. He and his thief-catcher brothers had grown accustomed to silence. Dark and quiet were close allies to a thief-catcher. Even their commands were all given by hand signs.

Garrin was the last to join them. Once submerged, Garrin immediately began swimming toward the shore. Wilton followed Garrin's lead, as did the others.

They were fifty in number. Fifty thief-catchers against an unknown number of enemies. It felt like madness. They were to cut the black savants down in their sleep, then swim back to the ship without raising an alarm. In and out unnoticed. That was the plan.

Wilton moved his arms and legs, trying not to think beyond the moment at hand. Even an apathetic sentry would notice fifty grown men splashing in the sea. Quick careful kicks and slow steady arm strokes carried him closer to the shore. After a time, the waves stopped working against him and started working for him, carrying him closer with each wave.

When his feet struck sand he began to crawl forward and let the wave wash him onto the beach. When he was completely out of the water, he forced his breathing to slow.

After standing, he realized he was not the first on the beach. Garrin waited up the shore next to a large boulder. The shore was littered with large boulders and crags. Beyond that, the beach gave way to rocky plains.

He followed Garrin up the moonlit beach, his heart racing from the swim.

His legs froze when he realized men slept on the beach atop blanket rolls. They were scattered, but there were dozens of them, stretching up and down the beach.

Despite his training, Wilton felt fear seize him. He couldn't make his legs move. The light from the moon made him feel exposed. His heart seemed loud enough to wake the closest sleeping soldier. He was a large man with long, braided hair. He wore only his small clothes. A longsword and pack laid to his right side with a wooden buckler on his left.

Tharu had trained him to move in the darkness like a shadow. But in training, a misstep would mean longer days of working routines. A wrong step now meant capture or worse. If a single soldier were to rouse and see him, he and his brothers would be outnumbered ten to one.

Garrin signed them to move forward. The familiar signal freed his legs, and he moved on the balls of his feet across the sand, making no more noise than his brothers. Once he was in the crags, he felt some relief. Dark shadows hid them from all directions, but his heart still raced as if he had run the few dozen paces from the shore.

In front of him, the crags gave way to plains where hundreds of tents had been erected, each several paces apart. The tents would hold lords and black savants. They were the targets.

There was not a single sentry. The arrogance of Bain's savants had given them an advantage. For the first time, Wilton was hopeful for their success.

Garrin signed them into position around the fifty closest tents, then signaled them to pull their raqii dath. As silently as he had moved up the shore, Wilton unsheathed his blades in unison with his comrades and awaited the command.

Garrin held his hand straight up for several moments. Then his hand fell like an ax. Losing sight of his companions, Wilton entered his own tent with raqii dath in hand ready to spill the blood of the enemy.

The moonlight spilled into the tent through the open flap,

allowing Wilton to see clearly.

The tent made a small dome on the inside. A black robe hung on a peg opposite the entrance. In the middle of the tent, there was a straw cot with a small, wooden chest at the foot. A small figure slept upon the cot.

Wilton moved closer to the cot, getting a better look. The boy's face had the beginnings of stubble in patches on his chin and cheeks. Wilton would have wagered the boy had never shaved his budding stubble. He could not have been older than Feffer or Elwin.

The blades began to feel heavy in his hands. His heart pounded. Wilton had been trained for this moment. He had been trained to take lives, but he could not make his hand move to slit the sleeping boy's throat.

He is a child, Wilton thought. *How could a child be as dangerous as they say?*

In that moment, he had remembered Elwin's accident at the Summer Solstice. Elwin had not meant to kill Biron, but the man had still died.

How much more dangerous was a child trained to kill with such power?

A cry of alarm sounded in a distant tent, and the boy's eyes sprang open. The tint of his eyes made him look even more like Elwin, until an orange-red glow entered them.

Wilton's hesitation ended then. Before he was truly aware of his movements, Wilton stretched his blade across the boy's throat. A warm viscous substance sprayed across his hands and face, causing him to flinch.

The boy never had a chance to cry out. He gurgled and drowned on his own blood, and his fiery-red eyes extinguished into a cold blue.

Wilton staggered out of the tent, almost dropping his blades. His hands were red in the moon's light. Flames and lightning began to materialize behind him in the distance. Voices began to cry out in agony.

One loud cry of pain was cut short. It had been the voice of Jard of Laslow.

None of Wilton's training prepared him for what he felt in that moment. He couldn't move. His heart was still pounding, and his head had begun to spin.

He had a faint memory of hearing a boot scuff on rock just before a hard object slammed into the back of his head.

Wilton awoke in a deep trench with an ache in his head. Six of his companions were with him. Morning light spilled into the entrance above. The hole in the earth formed a perfect circle and spanned five paces across and five paces in depth. The walls of the trench were a smooth stone. He knew immediately, no spades had dug that trench. No shovel could cut into rock. They had made a prison with the Elements.

At the top of the trench stood a single black-robed figure. Another blond-haired boy. Cold eyes regarded him, and Wilton looked away.

He pushed himself from the hard floor. His raqii dath were beneath him. They had not considered him enough of a threat to even disarm him. Wilton leaned against the wall and studied his hands. Red-brown flecks stained the crevices of his fingernails. He wiped them on his loin cloth, but it wouldn't rub off without water.

He noticed his brothers watching him. Six. There were only six of them.

Garrin was there, along with Blanden Paysworth and Dacker Cobstan. Blanden was a squat-nosed man with patchy, dark hair and Dacker had a narrow face with high eyebrows. They were both from Goldspire.

Blane Dudswin of Bentonville and Wharrin Barfit of Westertin . were there. They hadn't known each other before joining the White Hand, but they could have been brothers. They had the same short auburn hair and dark eyes. Last was Briad Karsth of Kinset. He had eyes that reminded Wilton of Feffer.

Wilton groaned and opened his mouth to speak, but Garrin placed a hand over his mouth and pointed to the savant above.

Cold eyes still regarded him. He looked to Garrin. When his leader began to sign, a cold wind entered the trench. Wilton felt an invisible fist crash into his face and side, knocking him to the ground. Garrin had cried out and Wilton heard the other man crash into the wall.

Wilton's head spun, but he remained conscious.

The entire time he had been imprisoned, he had not made another sound, not until the invisible fist had pulled him from the cave. He was not ashamed to admit that he had screamed when the hand came for him.

Wilton shuddered and opened his eyes. What had come next was not something he wanted to remember while sober. Though it haunted his dreams, he would not let it haunt his waking thoughts.

Movement from the west road pulled at his eye.

Though he could not see the sun, enough light now leaked through the dark clouds to light up the square below. A man approached from the west. His walk had a casual grace. There was a silhouette surrounding his form where the rain did not touch him. It struck empty air and slid down the invisible shield. The man's dark hair flowed unbound about his shoulders. He wore black robes under an open cloak. Attached to his belt, just visible under the cloak, was a sword with serrated teeth on the side opposite the edge.

Wilton held his breath as the dark-clad man approached the Scented Rose Inn. The wooden steps creaked beneath the man's feet. As he opened the door, Zeth Lifesbane glanced up to where Wilton sat. Even through the rain and the distance, he could see the man's smile.

Wilton felt a chill travel down his spine.

He thumbed the hilts of his blades, knowing how useless they would be against the black savant. Not bothering to stand, he dropped from the roof, rolling as he hit the ground. His feet were running north and west, even before completing the roll.

Wilton Madrowl did not even glance over his shoulder. It was far too late for good-byes.

Rain droplets echoed off the wagon's roof. The scent of fresh baked pastries next to Elwin made his stomach growl. This was the latest he had ever arrived at a Summer Solstice Festival. It was already after the noonday meal, and he hadn't eaten lunch. He had been thinking about sneaking a pastry since they had first started loading them into the wagon. But his mother knew the exact amount.

Feffer sat across from him, making a game out of the leaking spots in the roof. He would hold his hand beneath a drop and move it out of the path of the falling drop at the last second.

Elwin looked to his left, out the back of the wagon. The rain was so thick, he couldn't see anything.

"I still can't believe it's raining," Feffer said.

"Yeah, so much for the fireworks. But at least now, we will have a good excuse to get inside and share a couple of my Momme's famous crown cakes."

"Mmm," Elwin agreed.

Feffer stared at him for a moment without saying anything.

"What?" Elwin asked.

"Do you ever think about your real ma?"

"Sometimes," Elwin admitted.

"Do you want to meet her?"

Elwin had actually thought about this at length. If there was anyone he wanted to talk with about this, it was Feffer.

"I think so," Elwin nodded. "But that doesn't change the fact that my real mother abandoned me. I grew up dreaming about being an elementalist and great adventures. But deep down, I always knew that I would live to be a farmer. Now that it isn't a dream. It turns out, I really just want to be a farmer. I would do anything to go back and save Biron. I killed a man, Feffer."

"I had forgotten about that," Feffer said.

They were silent for a time. Elwin was thinking of a way to bring up his upcoming trial, but Feffer interrupted his thoughts.

"What about her?" Feffer pointed to his pendant. "What do you think she was running from?"

Bain, Elwin wanted to say. *My father.*

"I don't know," Elwin said, instead. "And I am not sure I really care. Whatever happened, she left me, Feffer. But one thing that I do know is that family is more than blood. My parents, Poppe and Momme. And you are my family."

Feffer nodded, "Family is more than blood."

The wagon rolled to a stop.

"Finally." Feffer stood up, ducking not to hit his head. "Da will probably be at the ledgers in front of the shop. He rarely joins the festival until two past noon. Save a spot for me by the fire."

"I will," Elwin said, "and a crown cake."

His parents had stopped the wagon just in front of the inn. Feffer hopped from the back of the wagon and ran across the square toward his father's shop.

The rain lessened enough for Elwin to make out a tall, covered wagon on the other side of the square. Asalla? Of course, he came every year.

He stepped down from the wagon and moved toward it.

"I am going to need help with the pastries," his mother said. She stood at the front of the wagon. The hood of her cloak shielded her hair and face from the rain. His father was hitching the horses to a post.

"Can I see Asalla first?"

She raised a soft hand to his cheek and smiled. "Go. Your father and I can handle the pastries."

He hugged his mother. "I'll see you inside."

The wind increased, and the rain fell harder. Elwin ran across the empty square. Once he saw the book on the side of the wagon, he smiled. As Elwin got closer, he could see a leather awning covering the steps on the back of the wagon. A curtain of water flowed around it.

"Come in, Elwin."

Elwin paused at the first step. "How did you know it was me?"

"Lucky guess. Come in. Come in."

Elwin shook his head and entered. This was the first time he had ever actually been *inside* the wagon. The air was musky. Books lined the shelves on either side with parchments poking out at odd angles. Elwin felt very aware of how wet he was and feared moving. Asalla would likely not appreciate any moisture getting on his books.

Toward the front was a wooden desk with a chair pulled out in front of it. Asalla sat in the chair, facing Elwin.

"Hello Elwin," Asalla smiled. "Have you enjoyed the book I gave you last year?"

"I haven't read any of it. I have been training in Justice and accidentally left the book behind." Elwin studied the old man's face with great care. If he was surprised, Elwin couldn't tell.

Asalla's lips thinned into a smile. "There was a time when there were Words of Power. Words when spoken, commanded the Elements much in the way others command them without words. A time long gone, yet soon to come again."

"I've heard of them in my training," Elwin said. "How do you know they'll come again? The prophecies?"

A sudden hope rose in Elwin. Maybe Asalla would tell him what these prophecies really meant.

"I know a great many things, Elwin. The book I gave you speaks of these Words. They will help you on your quest."

"What quest?"

Asalla leaned closer to Elwin. "The time will come soon when you will leave this place. Your destiny has a greater purpose than even you can imagine. So long as your heart remains pure, there is hope."

Who in the abyss was this man? Elwin had seen him every year around the Summer Solstice since he was a boy, but he really didn't know him.

"I already left," Elwin said slowly. "I am living in the castle, in Justice. I'm an elementalist. Or … will be. Anyway, how do you know all of this? I thought you were a book merchant."

"Oh young Elwin, your desire for knowledge has always made you my favorite," Asalla said. "I am a librarian and scholar. I observe the world and chronicle its passing. In studying the past and the present, we may glean the future. As a rock thrown in the air must travel back to the earth, so too does a man follow his destiny. The observer watching the rock in its various stages, can see where the rock may land."

Elwin nodded, saying "I see," not really sure that he did.

Asalla stood. "The time has come, Elwin. Your future awaits you, and I must step aside and let the rock fall."

"Wait," Elwin said. "Do you have any more books for me? Maybe something on the prophecies."

Asalla smiled as if he told some great joke. "The prophecies were written by a rambling old man." Then in a more serious tone he said, "You would do better by reading the book I gave you."

Elwin tried not to let the disappointment show on his face. "I will."

"Life will be hard for one such as you," Asalla said, "but trust your heart and you will fare well. Now, I must be gone soon. This rain will soak an old man to his bones."

Elwin hugged him. "Thank you for everything. I can't help but feeling like this is a goodbye."

Asalla returned his hug. "So long as your heart remains pure, we will meet again."

"Farewell." Elwin walked down the steps and through the curtain of water.

He started to leave, but glanced back at the wagon one last time. It was gone.

"What in the abyss?" Elwin walked over to where it had been. There were no marks where the wagon had been.

He let the rain hit him for several minutes. "Who are you, Asalla?"

Maybe Jasmine would know. Certainly the book merchant had been to the capital.

There was no need to run. Elwin was already soaked to his core. He walked to the back of the inn to enter through the rear door. There was a wooden awning covering the back walkway. He shook out his hair like a dog and wrung water from his silk shirt and trousers, glad Harkin wouldn't see these. The green of the shirt looked much darker than it had, even after several minutes of wringing his clothes.

"Oh well," he said. "Nothing can be done about it now."

He wouldn't get too much water onto his Momme's wooden floors. That was a much more immediate danger than dealing with Harkin.

As he approached the door, he heard sounds of merriment rise above the spattering of rain. He stopped as his hand closed around the door handle. He hadn't stopped to think about how the townspeople would treat him.

Would they remember him for who he was, or would they remember what he had done? Would they see him as the boy they watched grow from a babe, or would they see him as the monster who had killed a man? There was only one way to know for certain.

He opened the door.

Warmth and light greeted him. Laughter and song filled the air. A female voice sang to a harp, and he could hear the pounding of dancing feet. The tune was lively and upbeat. Elwin walked down the hallway, listening to her sing.

"There once was a maiden so fair,
She could dazzle all men with a stare.
Her bodice was as full as her manner,
Making all the gro-o-wn men clamor.
She was never long without a suitor,
But no one had a temper to suit her.
Only one man could best them all,
Sending good knights away at a crawl ... "

Elwin stopped listening to the words as he left the hallway and entered the large common room. Faron leaned against the wall, tapping his leg and nodding his head to the beat.

"Elwin!" Faron said.

Taken aback at the delight in Faron's eyes, Elwin missed a step.

Faron caught him and hugged him with his massive arms. "It's so great to see you!"

"It's great to see you, too," Elwin said. "I thought you were in Justice?"

Faron released Elwin from the hug. "I asked the king for leave for the festival to come see my daughter. You are soaked to the bone."

"It's pouring outside," Elwin explained. "Kaylee didn't go with you to Justice?"

"I wanted to set a place up for her," Faron said. "Your Poppe let her stay in a room here and work as a serving wench until I had things ready for her. When I depart, she will come with me."

"How do you like working for the king?" Elwin asked.

"It's all I imagined it to be," Faron said, "and more. When I came here from Alcoa, all those years ago, I had dreamed that I may someday work for the king, but I had always known it was just a dream. The Lifebringer has truly blessed me. I have been chartered to make the thief-catcher blades. They are required to be balanced in pairs. It is quite a challenge to my skills, but it is an honor to serve our great king."

Elwin smiled. "After we return, I will try to look in on you. I had thought about trying to find you several times, but I wasn't sure that you wanted to see me after ... after last year."

"Elwin," Faron's smile tightened, and he took a quick breath. "Elwin, I know you didn't mean to kill that boy. Everyone knows. It was just a surprise to everyone. Forget about all this grim talk. This year, enjoy the festival. There are so many new people, a few lasses that might interest you, too. Go on, now. Enjoy the merriment."

Elwin smiled. "Thanks, Faron."

He turned from Faron to look for a place by the fire. His parents had not been exaggerating about the number of those displaced by the war. More strangers filled seats and danced with one another than those he knew. The inn was almost bursting with people.

Every barstool was taken, and all the tables had no vacancies, except one next to the stage, by the fire. A man sat there, alone. He had a crystal goblet in front of him with red grape wine in it. Momme only gave the crystal glasses to guests who purchased a bottle of wine. Otherwise, she would serve the wine from wineskins, poured into tin goblets.

The man had long, black hair that had a silky appearance. His face was smooth and pale with a narrow chin and high cheek bones. His black cloak and robes were not a type of cloth Elwin had ever seen. The dark folds in the cloak swallowed the light of the fire. He wore a silver chain with a silver pendant. The charm was two flat hands covering a black stone.

The man sat with his legs crossed, sipping his wine. When their eyes met, the man's lips smiled, but his eyes were wide. It was not surprise in his eyes. The look was more like a man who had worked all day in the fields without food, only to come home to a dinner of roasted mutton. The man licked his lips and gestured with his wine glass to an empty chair.

Elwin's feet moved before he was aware that he had made the decision to go over to the man.

"Are you in mourning, sir?" Elwin asked.

"Not anymore," the man said. His voice had a pleasant tone. "Please. Sit."

Elwin pulled out the chair across from the man and sat. He could feel the warmth of the fire. Elwin resisted the urge to pull off his boots and dry his feet.

"I am Elwin," he said.

"My name is Zeth," the man said. "My household name is Warwin. We are a minor house in the lands of Alcoa."

"Oh," Elwin said, "have you been displaced by the war?"

"One might say that," Zeth said. "I have traveled this world for fifteen years in search of something lost. Many times I had all but given up hope. Many times I had feared that I might fail in my quest. Then, I traveled across the Tranquil Sea to the Island Nations. I had known I was close, because the Father of Shadows had led me here."

"The Father of Shadows?" Elwin said. "Do you mean—"

"The Father has many names," Zeth said. "Some lands call him Father of Souls, others the Seeker. Some call him Lord of the Abyss, while others call him the Father of Death. He is all of these things and more. But teaching of His greatness is not my purpose, here. There is another, who is eager to meet you. My liege lord and king has sent me to sequester you."

Elwin felt his heart drum against his chest and echo in his ears. His breath caught, and he felt lightheaded. This man was sent from Bain. He was a dark savant, the type of man Feffer had told him about. Elwin was sure of it. The man's words had betrayed as much.

Was this the "quest" Asalla had spoken of? How could he have known?

"You are a dark savant," Elwin accused. He could think of not else to say. He dared not ask the man of Asalla.

"Black savant," Zeth said. "There is time for this later. On the morrow, you and I are returning to your father, King Bain Solsec. His grace has long awaited your return."

"No," Elwin was surprised at the anger in his voice. "My place is here. Bain is evil."

His raised voice drew the attention of the surrounding tables. He only recognized people at two of the tables. At one table was a man named Bram and a few of the men from his father's farm. At another table was Warne the apothecary, Jansen the brewer, and Bryne the carpenter. Danna the candle maker, at the same table was half standing from her chair with her empty wine goblet in hand. The rest of the tables were filled with strangers. Elwin avoided their gazes.

"You speak of matters beyond your comprehension," Zeth said in a gentle voice. "Your father is making the world ready for the Awakening. Without him, all would be destroyed."

"Drenen Escari is my father," Elwin said, then lowering his voice to say, "not Bain Solsec."

Zeth's eyes narrowed. His voice was just above a whisper and spoken through gritted teeth. "That mortal peasant is not your father."

Anger hit Elwin like a fist. "He *is* my father."

Zeth reached into the folds of his robe and pulled out a metallic chest, the size of a large hand and placed it on the table. Its dark sheen looked as if it had been tempered with coal.

"I will give you a choice," Zeth said. His voice was calm once more. "You can accompany me out of this inn and travel with me across the Tranquil Sea. I will deliver you to your father, and you will fulfill the destiny you were born to. Though you will not see these insipid people that you surround yourself with again, their pathetic way of life will continue as it has.

"Your father has commanded me to make an example of those who hid you away all these years. If you refuse me, I will make good on that command. If you refuse me, I will destroy all that you hold dear. Then I will take you to your father, anyway."

He paused for a moment. The corner of Zeth's mouth turned upward into a pleasant smile, his comeliness a stark contrast to his words.

Elwin opened his essence to Air, letting it fill him. His Poppe had taken the stage by the fire. Elwin hadn't noticed him until now. A beautiful woman with blond hair played the harp wordlessly behind him. Children surrounded the pair, listening to Poppe's tale. He could sense his Poppe's arms moving and feel the Air shifting from his motion. He could see every movement in the room with his mind's eye.

"I am not going anywhere with you."

Zeth rose slowly saying, "You have made your decision then?"

"I am not leaving," Elwin said, "and you cannot make me."

The whites of the man's eyes turned black, then he moved with surprising speed. Elwin felt something solid strike his stomach and face in rapid succession. For a moment, he thought he was falling, but darkness filled his vision, pushing his thoughts into oblivion.

Chapter 16

CONSEQUENCES

Feffer sat up on the bed, not sure how long he had been asleep.

Feffer's father had not been waiting in the front like he had anticipated, so Feffer had searched for him in the office on the second floor of the warehouse. He had not been there either. Instead of going straight to the festival, Feffer had visited his old room.

The small room was exactly as he had left it. Well, not exactly. His father had tidied his bed and cleaned his clothes, folding them neatly atop the bed. The window still had the same blue curtains, and the large chest still rested at the foot of his bed.

Feffer had sat on the bed and tried to remember the last time he had been alone.

"A year," he had said. "I have not been alone since we left."

He had laid back on the bed. The next thing he knew, he was waking up.

Feffer swung his feet over the side of the bed and stood, rubbing his eyes.

"The Lifebringer curse me for a fool. Why did I ever give up this bed for an old wooden bunk?"

A year ago, he had felt such excitement at the prospect of leaving for the capital. He was going to be a member of the White Hand of Justice. Wilton had called him a naïve fool. He hated to admit it, but Wilton had the right of it.

"I had been a fool," Feffer said. "But I have changed. I haven't seen war yet, but I know what war means now."

Wilton was not the only person he knew who had been sent to the northern islands to fight. He had heard word of ships being sunk by the Elements. Men he had trained with had been swallowed by water and flames. Others had been taken captive or killed outright.

War was not a thing of glory. The songs were not honest. Battles that bards sang of did not give the truth of it.

War meant death.

When he had last seen this room, he was a child. He had the innocence of a child. Wilton had tried to tell him, but he had not believed his brother. He stood from the bed, crossed the room, and looked out the window. He could see the Scented Rose Inn across the square. Hazy light fought to be seen through the rain and barely reached the streets.

He came to the sudden realization that he could have been asleep ten minutes or ten hours. It was still daylight, but the thick rain hid the sun. So, he had no notion of what the hour was.

"Curse me for a thumping fool again! I'm missing the cursed festival!"

As he turned to leave, his window shattered and something solid struck him in the shoulder, knocking him from his feet. Wind pushed billowing clouds of smoke into his room, as a wave of heat hit him in the face.

"What in the abyss?" he coughed.

Dropping to his hands and knees, he crawled out of the room. He stood and felt beneath his tunic where he had been struck. His shoulder would bruise, but his skin and bone were unbroken.

He ran across the upper platform, around the stairs to the ladder that led to the roof. The latch was not locked. His father had always said he kept the roof locked to keep out intruders, but Feffer had always known it was to keep him from climbing up there.

Feffer flung open the door and climbed onto the roof, then ran to the edge. Tendrils of smoke rose from the inn but no flames as far as he could see. The door and most of the right side of the inn were missing as if some giant's hand had knocked the building from the inside. He could see the common room clearly. Inside and out people were stretched out. Some were bent at odd angles, but some looked as if they were curled on their sides, sleeping.

At this distance he could not see if they were breathing.

"What in the abyss!" he said again.

A man walked through the smoke into the street, stepping on people. He wore black robes and a dark cloak. The rain did not land on him. It hit an invisible shield and rolled around him. In his right hand, he had a large sword that was jagged on one side. Over his left shoulder, he carried someone.

"Stop," he heard someone say.

Feffer searched the street for the source of the voice. The Escari's wagon had been knocked over from the force. The wagon had been led by four horses. One of them was trapped beneath the wagon. It laid very still. And the other horses were gone. If they had run off, it would take hours to round them up.

Behind the wagon was Drenen. "Please, stop!"

The man ignored Drenen and walked toward the stable to the left of the inn.

"Please!" Drenen cried. "He is my son."

The man stopped walking and turned toward Drenen. Feffer gasped when he saw Elwin's face. Feffer reached for his sword at his hip, but it wasn't there. He had left his sword at the farm.

"The Seeker take me for a fool," he cursed. Why had he left his sword?

The man eased Elwin to the ground and walked toward Drenen.

"What is your name, peasant?" the man asked.

"I am Drenen of house Escari."

"Come here," he said in a level voice.

Drenen took a step forward and hesitated.

"You wish to be near the boy?" the man asked. "There is only one way this can be. Come to me."

Drenen walked to the man.

"Kneel," he said as if commanding a dog.

"Why are you doing this? Please, give me my son."

The man's sword hand moved with a speed that made Feffer

blink, striking Drenen in his face with the hilt. Drenen stumbled backwards, then fell to his knees.

"Please." Drenen's voice was strained.

The man sheathed his sword and raised his hand in a claw-like grip, poised in front of Drenen's heart. His hand become black, outlined in a burning white glow. The front of Drenen's good tunic began to blacken and burn beneath the glowing hand.

Drenen cried out in fear and crawled backward from the man.

Feffer wanted to scream at Drenen to run, but he couldn't make himself move. His own instincts told him to hide or go for help.

Drenen did not back away very far before the dark man reached him. He grabbed Drenen's foot with the glowing hand and pulled him closer. A dark fog surrounded Drenen as the glowing hand thrust *into* his chest.

Feffer cried out before he could stop himself. "No!"

If Drenen or his attacker noticed, neither even glanced in his direction.

Drenen's mouth opened wide, but no sound escaped. The hand went beyond the limits possible of a mortal body as the man's arm was swallowed by Drenen's chest. Embers and bits of burning cloth rose from the hole in Drenen's shirt.

That's his festival tunic, Feffer thought. It was a stupid thought. Who cared about a tunic?

A stench wafted up to his nostrils. It was fowl like burning hair, but thick like ash and dust. Feffer covered his nose with the inside of his elbow and coughed into his sleeve. He stumbled backward and almost fell. He wanted to scream, cry out, do something. He felt helpless on the roof without his sword.

This wasn't real. He was still asleep. Maybe he had fallen and struck his head. None of this was possible.

When the hand left Drenen's chest, Feffer heard the faintest gasp echo in the air. It had not sounded like a man's voice, but like the wind itself. A brilliant light came into being, forcing Feffer to look away from the square. He shielded his eyes and watched through the cracks in his fingers. A glowing image the size of a man floated above the man's upraised hand.

Feffer dropped to his knees.

The light had the shape and appearance of Drenen. It wore his torn tunic and long breeches. Black fog lingered around the arm holding the light. For a moment, the man held the image between him and Drenen.

Drenen writhed on the ground, clutching at his chest. His mouth was open as if screaming, but no sound left his lungs. Feffer stood, both fists clenched. He judged the distance between himself and the man.

If he leapt …

The man reached into his robe and pulled out a metallic object about the size of a small foot. As he brought the image of Drenen near the box, the top opened.

Tendrils of black fog left from the opening and solidified in the form of chains, which elongated and sprouted shackles at their tips. When the shackles closed around the ankles, wrists, and neck of the image, Drenen arched his back until only his head and feet touched the ground.

The image shrank as it was pulled into the confines of the box. The light dwindled and disappeared, bathing the square in darkness once more. The lid slammed closed, making a heavy metal clink.

Drenen dropped into the dirt and laid very still. Where he had been breathing laboriously before, now his chest was unmoving.

Feffer held his breath, waiting for Drenen to move, breathe, do anything. Nothing happened. He wasn't moving. He would never move again.

Feffer looked at Drenen's ruined tunic and tears filled his eyes.

"He killed him?" he whispered. "The Lifebringer save me. He killed him."

After replacing the chest in the folds of his robes, the man walked back over to Elwin and knelt beside him, leaving Drenen in the square.

"He's a dark savant," Feffer realized. What would a sword have been against a man like this?

Feffer became aware that he was still standing and that his fists were clenched. He suddenly felt exposed. He dropped to his belly, crawled back toward the hatch, and climbed down the ladder.

Once he was on the landing, he began to pace.

"What is going on?"

He grabbed his head. "Think, think, think, think. I have to think."

This man could kill him without lifting a hand. How could he fight that? He couldn't.

"But I have to save Elwin. What is this man doing with Elwin?"

Then Feffer remembered something he had heard from Lord Zaak and Sir Gibbins discussing. The dark savants were seeking out all the elementalists coming into their power. This man was going to take Elwin and force him to wield the Death Element.

"The Lifebringer save me," Feffer said. "What am I going to do?"

Elwin awoke upon a hard surface that moved and swayed with the motion of a road. The morning was brighter than it had been the previous day, but there was still a misting rain hanging in the air. The water and the brightness blinded him.

His head ached. He had been unconscious, but he had not entered the shadow realm. Did he wake from a dream? No. He no longer dreamed. Zeth was real.

He sat up.

A cage surrounded him. It rose out of the long wooden board beneath him. There was no door. The misshapen bars were stained yellow and white. He touched one of them. It had a wet feel, like a mushroom after a rain but harder. Then he saw that one of the bars ended in boned hand.

"What in the abyss?" Elwin backed away from the bars. "Bone! These are made from bone!"

He had touched it. His stomach became ill, and he began to heave up his guts. When his stomach was empty, he continued to heave. After his stomach calmed, he struggled to breathe for several moments.

He needed to get a hold of himself. There had to be a way out of here. He looked at his cage, scanning for any weakness. Two horses pulled the cage, driven by a single man.

He could only see his driver's back. The man had short brown hair, soaked from the rain, and he wore a brown tunic with green stitching around the hem. The man's attire was much like what his father had worn to the festival.

"Please," he called to the man, "let me out of here!"

The man's pale face turned toward him. The center of his brown eyes swirled with a black fog, but there was no mistaking the face of his father.

"Father?" Elwin said. "Father, let me out of here! What is going on?"

His father opened his mouth to speak, but words didn't come out. Instead, his father trembled and the fog in his eyes swirled more violently.

"Father!" Elwin called.

"He was never your father," Zeth's voice said. The dark clad man rode alongside the wagon on a white horse.

"What did you do to him?" Elwin demanded.

"He is called a soulless one," Zeth said. "His mind is still his own, but his body is forever a slave to this."

Zeth pulled the dark chest from his robes. "This is called a soulkey. Whoever holds it commands the soulless one. His life is bound to this for all of time. These artifacts are rare, and the knowledge of how to craft them died with Abaddon. Holding a soul is but a fraction of its power."

"Release him," Elwin said. "I will go with you. Just release him."

Zeth's half smile belied the pity in his voice. "I am afraid it is too late. If I release the energy of his soul, his death will be absolute. Not even his soul would remain. Death now means complete destruction."

"No," Elwin said. "That isn't possible."

"You cannot fathom the powers of the Father," Zeth said. "You have been made weak by living a peasant's existence. Your mother is to blame. Had she not stolen you away, none of this would have come to pass. The war may not have reached these islands for many years.

"This peasant," Zeth gestured toward his father, "would have lived out a long peasant's life and never suffered at my hand. But we must all pay for our folly."

"What folly?" Elwin asked. "He was a farmer. He never hurt you or anyone."

"That is where you are wrong," Zeth said. "He kept a child who was not his to keep. He has paid the ultimate price for his crimes."

Elwin was at a loss for words. Zeth was a madman. There was nothing to say that would make the man see reason. Father's only crime was to love him. Elwin was orphaned, and Drenen raised him as his own.

"Where are you taking me?"

"As I told you. I am taking you to your father across the Tranquil Sea. Where you belong."

Elwin sat back on his feet. "I want nothing to do with him or you."

"Ah," Zeth said. "Another village lies ahead. I will need to make a few more skeletal warriors, there."

"Stop the wagon," he called. The cage slowed to a stop.

He had been about to ask Zeth what he had meant by *skeletal warriors*. Then, Elwin heard the shuffling of feet behind him. As he turned around, his stomach felt ill once more.

The question died on his lips.

Chapter 17

A LIGHT IN THE DARKNESS

Feffer rode Haven back toward the town with haste.

"I can't believe I left Elwin," Feffer said.

He had come back to the farm last night, hoping to find Melra or his father, Wilton or anyone. For the last year of his life he had learned to take orders. There was no one to give him orders now. But he had to do something.

As the town grew closer, Feffer slowed Haven to a trot. At a distance, he couldn't tell that anything had happened to the town. Rain sprinkled the redwood, making it a darker crimson. The buildings on the west side of the town had not been scathed.

The first building was Danna's. Normally, the strong smells of candles and odd aromas would greet him, but her windows remained closed.

He reigned Haven to a stop and tethered her to Danna's building. If the dark savant was still around, Feffer didn't want to be seen riding into town. Next to Danna's was Jansen's brewery. On the other side of the brewery was his Da's shop.

He crept behind the brewery, using all the stealth he had been taught. The wet grass made very little noise beneath his feet as he crept around the back of the building. When he reached the building's edge, he ran to his Da's shop and crept along the side toward the square. When there was no more wall left, he slowly peeked around the building.

Standing in the square, he saw Melra, Poppe, and Faron. The moment his eyes landed on them, he broke into a run.

"Mrs. Escari," he said. "What happened to Elwin?"

All three of them jumped at the sound of his voice. Melra placed a hand over her mouth and tears filled her eyes.

"Feffer," she cried, while pulling him into an embrace. "That man took him. And … "

Her voice broke into a sob, and she became heavy in his arms. He held her until her sobbing subsided.

"Melra," Poppe said at last. "We need to get inside. There is nothing we can do for Elwin out here."

Melra pulled away from him, and they started toward the broken inn.

"Wait," Feffer said. "Where is he?"

They stopped walking and regarded him as one. Melra's eyes were still filled with tears. And, Faron looked at Feffer like he was the same child who used to try to make off with his swords.

It was Poppe who answered him. "The man called Zeth took him. He arrived at my inn early yesterday and took a place by the fire. He was dressed in rich black robes, like none I had ever seen. He scoffed at our wineskins and ordered a bottle of wine. I had tried to make polite banter, but the man had not been interested. After tasting the wine, it was of Napri vintage, his manner was polite but curt. I took him for a lord. He had told me that he was waiting for someone and did not wish to be bothered. He said that if he wanted something he would call for me. I thought him some sort of nobility. Not … not this." It took great effort not to cut Poppe off before he finished the long-winded speech that really told him nothing.

"Where is Elwin?" Feffer knew his voice sounded impatient. "Which way did *Zeth* take him?"

"No one saw them leave," Faron said. "I am ashamed to say that I hid with Melra, Poppe, and the children in Poppe's wine cellar until this morning. I make a fine sword, but I wouldn't know the first thing about using one. But there are fresh tracks heading east. By the number of tracks, it looks like he took more people than Elwin with him. What would he want with all of them?"

"Right," Feffer said. "East it is then. Faron, you need to ride west. You know of the guard posting fifteen leagues to the west on the other side of Hillfast?"

"Yes, of course," Faron said. "But—"

"Great," Feffer cut in. "Make haste and tell them what happened here. Have them send word to Sir Gibbins, immediately."

He walked toward the shop, "I need supplies."

"Wait," Poppe said. "Feffer, there is something you need to know. It's your father."

Feffer stopped walking. He hadn't even thought to ask about his Da or Wilton. He had assumed they were alright. But, where were they?

"My Da?" Feffer asked.

"He was standing beside the door," Faron said, "when *it* happened."

"When what happened?" Feffer asked.

"I'm so sorry, Feffer," Poppe said. "He's gone."

"Gone where?" Feffer said.

Poppe placed a hand on his shoulder. "He's dead, child."

"Wilton?"

"No one has seen him," Faron said. "He might have been taken with the others."

"Who is still alive?" Feffer wanted to know.

"We can't know for sure," Faron said. The large man had tears in his eyes. "Everything happened so quickly. When the man pulled his jagged blade and began attacking people, most people ran."

Feffer didn't know what to say. He felt tears try to make their way to the surface, but he forced them away. There was no time for this.

Wiping his eyes, he walked to his Da's shop. The door was unlocked. He entered and walked past "the front," as his Da called it, and opened the double doors to the warehouse.

Feffer found a traveler's knapsack and began grabbing anything that might be useful and shoved it into the bag. Rope and tackle, artificer's tools and fishing line. He found a small tent that could tie to a saddle. Bandages and healing salts and salves could prove useful. Spy glass, tender twigs, lantern, sealed oil, dried bread and meat, wineskins for water.

He found a dark, leather saddle bag and filled it with more travel foods. In the middle of the loft was a leather tarp covering something. Feffer pulled it off.

Fireworks.

There were small, round ones, a couple of big round ones, and a large, oblong one with a wooden base. It was half the size of his leg.

He grabbed as many of them as would fit into the remainder of his pack. Then, he took a dagger and cut away enough of the tarp to wrap the fireworks and forced the bundle to fit into the bag.

His pack was heavier than it looked.

He left it where it was and walked across to the weapon rack on the far wall. He tested several swords, checking their weight and balance.

Feffer settled on a scimitar. These had come from the Alcoan nation, obviously crafted by a master. His father must have had too high of a price on it, or the blade would have sold. It was truly a beautiful blade. He left the sword Sir Gibbins had given him in its place and held the falchion in appraisal. It had an encircled raven engraved just above the hilt.

Only master crafted weapons carried such marks. Feffer grabbed the matching silver sheath with the encircled raven and fastened it to his belt.

When he was satisfied with his provisions, he went up the stairs to his father's room. There was a painting of his mother on the wall. He avoided looking into her green eyes as he plucked the painting off the wall and placed it gently on the floor.

An iron safe was fastened to the wall. He shifted the levers to the correct position and pulled the handle to open the safe. Taking the empty purse from the safe, he filled it with some silver scales and the heaviest gold crowns. After fastening it to his belt, he closed the safe and replaced the painting.

When he came down the stairs, the three of them were waiting for him.

"Feffer," Melra said gently. "Where do you think you are going?"

"I am going after Elwin," he said.

"You can't," Faron said. "You will be killed."

"I am not a fool," Feffer said. "I have no intentions of fighting a dark savant. I will sneak up when *Zeth* is sleeping and break Elwin free, then we can fly safely away. If possible, we can fly to the capital for reinforcements to come back for the others. If not, we can go north to Goldspire. "

He walked to his gear and began to lift it. "You have to trust me. I can be very stealthy when I put my mind to it."

"You are still a child," Melra said.

"I have been training for a year, and I am the best swordsman in my class." Feffer said. "I am not a child, anymore. "

"You are only fifteen years old," her voice sounded breathless.

"Sixteen," he said, annoyed that his defiance made him feel like a child. "Elwin is fifteen."

"Look," Feffer said. "I am all there is. Zeth is a dark savant. He is taking Elwin back to make him use the Death Element. I can't let that happen. Not to Elwin. I must go."

The whites of Melra's eyes were wide and tears fell down her cheeks. Poppe's mouth was open, but no words came out. He had them, he knew. They would not stop him.

"How do you know this?" Faron asked.

"I heard it from Lord Lifesong," Feffer said. "The dark savants are taking children with power to use them as weapons in their war."

"The only reason Zeth could be headed east is to reach Eastport," Faron said.

"Once he has Elwin on a vessel," Feffer said, "all will be lost. If I save Elwin, Zeth will not leave with the others. I can save them, but you have to trust me."

"Alright lad," Faron said. "I will ride west to send word to Sir Gibbins. I have made many weapons at his request. He will know my name and trust my word."

"Good," Feffer said. "Let us not waste more time."

Atop Haven, Feffer had a clear view of the countryside surrounding the dirt road. He had been traveling for half the morning, and the misting rain had provided little relief against the humid heat. The tracks left by the wagon and small contingent of footsteps never varied far from the road, making them easy to follow.

In the distance, he could see an occasional farm, but he dared not waste time to look for help. The dark savant had not ventured from the road, so neither had Feffer. It was unlikely that an untrained farmer or rancher could do much for Elwin anyway.

By noon, Feffer could see a city on the horizon. He had never traveled east, but Feffer knew Bentonville from one of his father's maps. Like Benedict, Bentonville was a small village with mostly of farmers.

Feffer could see smoke rising from chimneys. He spurred Haven from a trot to a gallop.

As he neared the village, Feffer realized that it was not the chimneys that were smoking. Several of the buildings were smoldering. One of the buildings had been caved in completely.

He reigned Haven to a walk. There were no people that he could see. Maybe they were hiding.

Feffer had not yet earned his red cloak, so they would not know he belonged to the king's guard. He was about to call out, but he stopped himself. What if Zeth was still here?

He pulled Haven to a halt. The only sound was the misting rain in his ears and the crackling of the smoldering buildings. He looked to the road. The tracks continued into the village.

Nudging Haven forward, Feffer watched for any movement.

Like Benedict, the buildings had been crafted from the redwoods of the Carotid to the north. Though the buildings here were farther apart, Feffer could not tell the difference between shops and homes. Most of them were of a size with one another. And much like Benedict, these people likely lived where they worked.

The largest building stood three stories high. The sign had a fool juggling red wooden balls painted on it. The paint had faded, and there was no script to name the inn on the sign. The door had been knocked inward hanging only on its lower hinge.

The tracks split off here.

Feffer stopped Haven at the hitching post in front of the inn and climbed down from his saddle. He wrapped her reins around the post.

No cobblestones made a village square here, but no grass grew at the large space in front of the inn. Feffer walked toward the east, looking at the tracks. Red darkened the mud, and there were impressions too large to have come from hooves or feet.

Bodies maybe?

He and Elwin had been on a few hunts with Wilton, Drenen, and his Da, but he was not as good at tracking as the others had been. Feffer had been better with a bow than Elwin, but his friend had picked up reading tracks much faster.

He could tell the wagon tracks continued east. Those at least were easy to follow. If the wagon had gone, so had Zeth.

Feffer yelled, "Hello! Is anyone here?"

He yelled a few times and received no answer. So he walked up to the inn to look inside. It was vacant.

"Hello!" he called again.

There was no one.

He walked to the building across from the inn. The door was cracked.

He pushed the door open, "Hello?"

The common room looked like a tornado had blown through. A small table was turned over close to the door. A feeble attempt at a barricade, perhaps. Wooden chairs and tables lay in pieces. The only sign of life was an active lantern still burning on the wall and burnt embers still releasing smoke in the fireplace.

After a few steps into the room, his boots contacted a sticky liquid. A thick puddle of red extended past the overturned table and splattered across the walls and destroyed furniture. He took a few more steps into the room and saw a hallway with two doorways on both sides. The beds in both rooms had been overturned. Red wool spilled out from mattresses.

Feffer stepped on something hard. He looked down to see a wooden soldier. It had a halberd in its right hand and a red cloak with a hand the palm facing outward, painted white. He picked it up. No blood stained the toy.

He felt tears creep into his vision. Gritting his teeth, he balled his fist and screamed a wordless cry.

How could anyone do this?

Feffer punched the wooden door. It banged into the wall. He kicked it and beat it with the flat of his fist, screaming all the while. He couldn't stop the flood of emotions.

Feffer slumped to the ground and sobbed into his hands. His father was dead. All of these people were dead. Why? Why would someone do this?

It didn't make any sense. None of these people were elementalists. Killing these people was an act of cruelty. There was no other reason.

When the tears subsided, Feffer saw he still had the little wooden soldier in his hand. It was a toy that all little boys had. When he had outgrown his own toy soldiers, he had given them to some of the younger boys in town.

The face of a little boy came to his mind. A little boy from Benedict. He had red hair and hazel eyes, like Feffer.

"Chadley," Feffer said, wondering if the little boy still lived.

Feffer forced his legs to stand and tucked the little wooden soldier into his belt pouch. The fire in the hearth had not been cold for long, and a candle still burned. The dark savant could not have been gone long.

He left the house and looked down the dirt road. It had stopped raining. All morning he had wished the rain would stop, but with all of these people dead, it didn't seem right. The sun was breaking through the remaining clouds, shining its light on Bentonville.

The red mud seemed brighter, when the thought struck him.

"How many people live between here and the sea?"

A sick feeling tried to work its way into his stomach, and he swallowed to keep the contents from emptying into the dirt. Feffer felt the wooden toy in his belt pouch.

"Not another child," Feffer said.

Feffer forced his feet to move. It was no longer about just saving

Elwin. As he climbed atop Haven, another thought occurred to him.

What in the abyss was Zeth doing with the bodies of the slain?

He pondered on it as he spurred Haven forward. There were no bodies in Bentonville. It was as if the town had been deserted, but there was blood everywhere. In that home, in the tavern of the inn, and in the streets.

He shook his head. Who could guess at the actions of a Death bound?

The daylight waned as he rode, and he tried to consider his options. Eventually, he would reach the contingent. He still had no idea as to what he would do when he did. If he attacked Zeth outright, Feffer knew he would lose.

He could try to attack him in his sleep, but Feffer knew about the shadow realm. Surely Zeth would watch over Elwin from the strange sleep state where Elwin went to at night. He played out scenarios in his mind as he rode, keeping a watchful eye on the horizon for Zeth.

After a day filled with no signs of movement in the distance, Feffer nearly jumped from his saddle when he realized there was something there.

There was an hour left until nightfall, just enough light to see the large wagon in the distance. He dug the spy glass from his saddlebag. It was made from wood and designed to collapse. Each wooden ring was smaller on the inside. He pulled on the outermost and innermost ring to expand the spyglass. There was a small lens of glass on the inner ring and a large lens on the outer ring.

He aimed the larger of the two rings toward the horizon and peered into the smaller lens. The encampment on the horizon leapt into view. To the left of the road, the Carotid Forest merged with the road and stretched northeast for many miles.

Horses and cattle were tied to the trees, and several people surrounded them, forming a circle. The animals jerked away from the people and fought one another to stay at the circle's center. He had never seen animals react that way to people. All of the people looked like commoners, not soldiers. But they did not appear to be tied or bound in anyway, so they must have been with Zeth. Perhaps he had met up with them in Bentonville. Maybe they had taken the village before even going to Benedict. That would explain the lack of bodies.

At the center of the road rested a small wagon. Feffer narrowed his eye, trying to get a better look at the occupant at the center of the cage. Bars surrounded a small figure with blond hair. He could not make out facial features, but he didn't need to.

"Elwin," he said. "It has to be."

He looked around for a man dressed in black, but Zeth was nowhere to be seen.

A single tent was erected several dozen paces to the right of the road. There were people scattered in the space between. They all stood very still.

He watched them for several moments. Like scarecrows, none of them swayed or moved. They did not pace or scratch a nose.

"Dragons take me," he breathed. "They are either heavily disciplined or made of wood."

He needed a closer look. If they were just scarecrows, this would be easier than he thought. Feffer turned Haven north and trotted toward the Carotid forest.

Elwin sat at the center of his cage watching the faces of the people around him. Men, women, and children, none had been spared. Some he knew. Others were strangers, but it pained him no less.

Willem's face was pale. Like the others, he stood without motion. He wore a green tunic and tanned trousers. The right side of his tunic had been burned. His exposed flesh was charred and flaking, but Willem did not seem bothered by the damage to his body. Elwin met Willem's eyes, but there was still no sign of life. There was no recognition in the swirling, black eyes looking back at him.

The man, Willem Madrowl, was no more. What stood in his place was called a skeletal warrior. Zeth had explained it to him, still Elwin did not want to believe it.

The dead could not walk. Souls could not be stolen. These things were not possible. The undead weren't real. They were children's stories, intended to frighten mischievous boys and girls into obedience.

Or so he had thought.

He could not deny what he saw. Mindless soldiers made from the bodies of the dead. Incapable of making decisions, they could only follow explicit commands, given with the Death Element. They did not eat. They did not sleep. They only followed orders.

Their scratch or bite was infections, or so Zeth had said. The Death Element was so great, the power of Death could cause the infection to spread to other victims.

He looked to his driver and whispered, "Father."

His father's brown eyes regarded him. The black fog had gone for the moment. "I am here, Elwin."

His father was different than the skeletal warriors.

Like the skeletal warriors, a soulless one was somewhere between life and death, but unlike the mindless soldiers, his father still retained his memories.

As Elwin had discovered, there were times when a *soulless one* still retained his will. So long as his father did not attempt to disobey Zeth's command, his father's will was his own. Currently, Drenen had the task of guarding him while Zeth slept.

"How many more villages are between here and the sea?"

"Seven," he said. "Try not to think on it."

After Bentonville had been attacked, it was difficult to think of anything else. How many more people would become mindless monsters?

"I will," he lied.

"Try to get some sleep," Father said. "I may no longer need it, but you still do."

Elwin laid on his back, not wanting to stretch out for fear that he might touch the bones of his cage. He did not want to think of who they might belong to.

Closing his eyes, he pushed all thoughts from his mind.

❧

He was almost surprised to be looking at his sleeping body. Zeth had not stopped the previous night, but Elwin hadn't even tried to sleep until now. He had not thought he would be able to find sleep in the cage of bones. He soared into the air, almost feeling free once more.

Soon, Zeth would sleep as well, then seek him out as he had promised. The black savant would give him his first lesson in the Death Element. Elwin wanted to run, flee, fly far away. But that would lead him straight to Abaddon.

There was nowhere he could go. Eventually, Zeth would find him. Still, Elwin had no intentions of making it easy for Zeth.

Elwin flew toward the forest. He could hide in the trees from him.

Motion from below pulled his gaze, and Elwin froze. Through the foggy haze of the shadow realm, he saw a red head poking through some brush.

"Feffer," he said.

His friend crept toward the edge of the treeline. He had a pack on his back and a curved sword at his hip. His friend moved with stealth. But, from the shadow realm, all the stealth in the world did not matter. Zeth would see him as surely as Elwin had.

Elwin had a brief moment of panic before he realized what he must do.

He willed himself into Zeth's tent. The man was lying down. Elwin watched his breathing begin to slow. He considered trying to form a lightning hurl, but a moment later Zeth's Spirit rose from his body.

He had expected Zeth's soul to be black, but it was a white glow, like Jasmine and Zarah.

"I am here," Elwin said.

Zeth did not respond. He looked past Elwin toward the cage.

"When the boy sleeps, I will take him to Abaddon." Zeth's voice was elated. "The Father will reward me with even greater power. Not Bain. Not Fasuri. Me."

Elwin was confused and frightened at the same time. He had no desire to meet Abaddon, but if Zeth caught Feffer, he would kill him. Or worse. He pushed his fears from his thoughts.

"I'm here," Elwin said. Zeth did not respond.

Elwin waved a hand in front of Zeth's face, saying "Hello. I'm here."

He stopped. "Why can't you see me?"

Zeth began to move toward the tent flap.

Elwin began to despair. He opened his essence to Air, attempting to distract Zeth. He let the power fill him. That was when he felt it. There was a pulsing. It was like a heart, releasing power with each beat. It was on his body's chest. Then, he remembered.

"My pendant!"

Jasmine had said it protected him from scrying. This must have been what she had meant. He probed the pendant with Air. It was an artifact. Jasmine had told him artifacts could be controlled. Why hadn't he spent more time working with the pendant?

He tamed Air into the stone, and willed himself to be seen by Zeth. But Zeth still hadn't seen him. It wasn't working. Taming more Air into the pendant, he continued to probe the artifact with his mind.

Then he felt it. He did not have to tame Air into the pendant. There was power stored in the stone. A river of power. Elwin reached for it, willing himself to be seen.

"I am here," he said.

Zeth stopped and half-turned to him. "I had expected you to flee. Instead you come of your own ...," His words trailed off, and Zeth gaped openly at Elwin. His eyes traveled up to Elwin's face, before he finished. "Accord."

He needed to keep him talking long enough for Feffer to ... do what? There was no door. What was Feffer going to do? There was no door on the cage!

That was when he heard Feffer's voice near his sleeping body. "Elwin. Wake up, Elwin."

"Every night I met with Jasmine in the shadow realm for training," Elwin said. Elwin could hear Feffer testing the bars, whispering his name.

The Lifebringer save him. Please let the bars break.

"The Life witch, Jasmine Lifesong, trained you herself?"

"She is no witch," Elwin said.

"I was told you had residence in the castle, but I had not been told of your training."

"Told?"

Zeth smiled. "Bain has agents everywhere. Now, I need to see what you are capable of. I felt Air in you earlier. What talents have you learned?"

Elwin could hear his father shaking on the driver's seat. He must have seen Feffer. His father had been ordered to guard Elwin. If he lost his will to the soulkey, Feffer would be captured. He wanted to return to his body, to rise, and to help Feffer, but he had to stay. If Elwin left, Zeth would leave and see Feffer.

"The Lifebringer save me," Feffer said breathlessly. "What in the abyss did he do to you Drenen? Help me get Elwin free."

"I ... can't ...," Father said. "Get ... away ... now. I can't ... can't fight it."

"I hoped I wouldn't have to use this," Feffer whispered. "Elwin wake up."

"I trained daily," Elwin said to Zeth. His father's shaking became more violent. "I have mastered flight and the wind thrust."

Elwin heard flint strike steel several times.

"Useless," Zeth spat. "A person with your power? And that is all you have mastered? Weakness. That will be corrected. You will come with me to the Father and accept his gift. Your retraining begins now."

Elwin heard the fire catch, then he heard a slow steady sizzle.

"Elwin," Feffer said with desperation clear in his voice. "Wake up and move back. Please."

He had heard that sound before. Poppe liked to light fireworks for his festivals whenever possible. Elwin and Feffer had filched some of the smaller ones one year. When placed in mud and lit, they would burst and send mud everywhere.

"Never," Elwin said. "You will have to catch me first."

He stopped the flow of power from the pendant and returned to his body.

Elwin saw the fireworks bundled together and tied to the edge of the cage with fishing line. There was one very large firework, cylindrical in shape, and several smaller round ones fastened together. The wicks were all wound into a single fuse. And they had been lit.

Feffer had moved several paces away and was watching the fuse. Feffer's wide eyes met Elwin's, then he motioned Elwin to back up.

Elwin tamed Air and flew to the furthest edge at the top of the cage. Behind him, his father still struggled with his command to guard Elwin from escape. He had fallen from the driver's seat and was convulsing on the ground. Black fog seemed to seep from his eyes.

"Fight it, Father. Just a little while longer."

As the fuse disappeared, Elwin closed his eyes, shielding his head with his arms. He heard a long, loud whistling sound, then felt more than heard the explosion.

His ears had a ringing sound, and Feffer's voice sounded like it was in a well. A strong burnt smell filled his nostrils. It was as if a thousand candles had been doused at once. Before he could make out Feffer's words, he heard the sound of animals stampeding behind him. He turned to see the horses and cattle running toward the tent, trampling it into the dust.

"The Lifebringer be praised," he said.

"Elwin, help me!"

He looked at the edge of the cage. Two of the bars were cracked but not broken. Feffer was pulling on them. Elwin flew to the bars and tried to squeeze through. It was no use. They were too close together.

Feffer unsheathed a long, curved sword. "Back up."

When Elwin moved back, Feffer took the sword with two hands and began to chop at the bone. His movements were precise and practiced, and the bone cracked with each swing. But it didn't break.

"What in the abyss," Feffer said. "It is too strong. What is this stuff made from?"

Feffer glanced toward the trampled tent. A figure was moving beneath the flattened folds.

"Hurry, Feffer," Elwin said. "If you can just get the one, I can squeeze through."

Feffer swung over and over, chipping at the thin bone with each strike. Zeth had emerged from his tent and started limping toward the cage.

Feffer's aim began to miss the mark, and his voice sounded desperate. "I am going to die."

"No you are not," Elwin said. He let the power of Air fill him, "Move back."

Zeth staggered toward the cage at a run. His legs elongated and blackened as he ran with increasing speed.

"Do something!" Feffer cried.

Elwin backed to the end of the cage, taming the power of Air into a wind thrust, centered behind him. Taming flight, he aimed at the weakened bone and pushed a good portion of his stored power into the wind thrust.

His left shoulder slammed into the weakened bone, and the bar shattered. His shoulder burned as if on fire, but he pushed the pain from his thoughts and grabbed hold of Feffer's waist.

Opening his essence wide to Air, he flew straight up. Elwin felt the flat of a sword hit his back, as Feffer's arms and legs squeezed around him.

As Zeth gained ground between them, he grew to an impossible height, towering over the cage. His body had transformed from head to toe into an animated shadow.

Feffer squeezed him more tightly. "The Lifebringer save us! Fly faster!"

Reaching the wagon, Zeth ran up the boned cage, like a person would a step, and leapt in their direction. Elwin felt more than saw Zeth moving through the air. The dark man soared through the expanse between them, gaining on them as Elwin flew higher.

"He's flying, Elwin, go faster!"

Elwin pulled at the Air and tamed it through his essence as hard as he could. He flew faster than he ever had.

"He's falling," Feffer yelled over the rush of wind.

Elwin slowed and looked down at the falling shadow.

"He can't fly," Elwin said. "He had used Fire and Earth at the inn. He doesn't have Air. He had only jumped."

Elwin felt relief and weariness all at once. He could feel his essence waning, and his shoulder began to pulse with pain. He hovered for a moment, not having the energy to do much more than hold Feffer. Beneath him the skeletons were still.

"Go northwest. We have to get Haven."

As he tamed more Air, it felt like nettles covered his body, but he forced the power to go through him. He flew, letting Feffer guide him northwest to Haven. Elwin set Feffer down beside the horse.

Shrieks echoed from the east.

Feffer looked at him, "What in the abyss is that?"

"I don't know," Elwin lied. If Feffer didn't know about the skeletal warriors, Elwin didn't want to tell him just now. "We should go."

Feffer sheathed the sword and slid into the saddle. "I couldn't agree more."

"I can't believe you held on to that," Elwin said, pointing to the blade.

"I wasn't letting go of anything," Feffer said. "Flying may feel natural to you, but I almost wet myself."

Elwin smiled, weakly. "You saved me, Feffer."

"Thank me, later," he said. "Did you see how fast he could move?"

"Right. We need to get back to Benedict. I need to find my mother, if … if she still lives and get her to safety. Zeth will go for her."

"Elwin, she's safe with Faron and Poppe. They know to hide, and we can't outrun him anyway. I want to get back as much as you, but it's not a good idea."

"Where then?"

His eyes met Feffer's. Light glinted off his cheeks in the moonlight.

"My father is gone, Elwin. He's gone." Feffer's voice cracked.

Elwin grabbed Feffer with his good arm and pulled him into an embrace.

Feffer held onto him with both arms and sobbed into Elwin's chest. Each sob sent barrages of pain down Elwin's arm, but he ignored it. This was all his fault. Had he gone with Zeth, none of this would have happened. "I'm so sorry, Feffer."

A few moments later the sobs subsided, and Feffer pulled away, his face a hard mask.

"Wilton is still out there, Elwin. I want to go home too, but we can't. We just can't. That thumping piece of dung will catch us if we try for the capital or west at all. I had half-expected something like this. We go north into the Carotid Forest. By the time we make it to Goldspire, Lord Zaak and Sir Gibbins will learn of the attacks. They will come for us."

Elwin nodded. Feffer was right. Without flying, they couldn't outrun Zeth. But without sleep, he wouldn't have the energy for long-distance flight, and he wasn't sure if he could carry Feffer on his back that far anyway. Plus, it would be easier to hide in the forest than along the roadway.

"North," he agreed.

Chapter 18

HUNTED

The nocturnal sounds of active insects were loud in the night air of the shadow realm. Elwin's eyes fell immediately to Feffer. His foggy form huddled next to his own sleeping body in the damp brush.

Elwin could still feel the pain in his shoulder. Moving over to his body, he inspected the wound. There was a small bone fragment sticking from his shoulder, and dark liquid dampened his silk shirt. In the dark of the shadow realm, it looked black. Harkin might just feint if Elwin ever made it back to the castle with that tunic. He shook his head. His shirt was the least of his worries at the moment.

Not for the first time, he was tempted to go back to his town to check on the survivors. Zeth may have gone to hurt them.

"We are more than twenty leagues from Benedict," he told Feffer's sleeping body. "It will take Zeth some time to get there. Besides, I can't do anything for them. I should try to find Jasmine."

She would likely be in the lecture hall with Zarah. Elwin imagined Zarah wouldn't get a reprieve from lectures just because he wasn't there.

Elwin closed his eyes and focused on his desk. He knew it was far from his body, but he would be careful. Jasmine needed to know what had happened. Forming the image of the chair in his mind, he willed himself back to the castle.

He could feel a disconnection from his body. It felt like he was being watched from every angle.

"Elwin!" Jasmine said. "What are you doing here?"

Jasmine was at the front of the room, and Zarah sat next to him.

The last days' events just poured out of him in a rush.

He forced every word of the tale from his lips, not slowing until he finished describing his escape with Feffer. When he finished the tale, Jasmine only stared at him.

"We traveled north for miles," Elwin said, after a moment. "We had to ride Haven, because I was too weary to fly."

Zarah's hand touched his arm. The sensation was unlike anything he had felt. The strength of her heart and the purity of her soul reverberated through him. He could feel the fabric of her existence. Her touch made him feel safe, as if the darkness around him could not harm him.

Her voice was a song. "Are you alright?"

The same time Jasmine said, "Where are you now?"

"I'm fine. Well I am fine under the circumstances. I scratched my shoulder, but it didn't seem to deep. We are sleeping in the Carotid Forest. But now I'm afraid Zeth will go back and hurt more of my friends and family."

"You did well to go north. You are safe for now." She released a quick breath. "This Zeth must be powerful, indeed, to make a soulless one. But at least there is no way he can follow you in the shadow realm. Your pendant will keep you safe from him, and it will be difficult for Zeth to follow you through the forest with an undead army."

"How come you never taught me about skeletal warriors?" Elwin asked.

"There is much history I have yet to tell you, Elwin. The abominations Zeth created are one of the many topics we need to discuss. Some undead creatures are created by those that surrender their souls to evil, while others are created from the Death Element. The power of each creature created depends on many things. The least of these is a skeleton warrior, and the most powerful is a Drakolich, an undead dragon. But, we do not have the time for this. You need to go back to the sanctity of your body."

"Alright," Elwin said.

"Wake at first light," Jasmine said. "And keep traveling on to Goldspire. I will meet you at the Hammer Forged Inn with any troops the king can spare."

"What about my family?"

Jasmine's tone sounded impatient. "We will send troops to Benedict as well. You need to go, but be wary. The Carotid Forest is full of animals but not many nefarious creatures. However, after making it through the forest, you will come to the Goldspire Mountains. It will be difficult to traverse, and there are mountain giants that reside there."

"Mountain giants?" Elwin said. "I thought those were just stories. But then again, I never thought undead were possible. Next you will tell me vampires are real, too."

"Aye," she nodded. "But they do not concern us now. It will take you several tendays to travel to Goldspire. Go now, I do not like you being this far removed from your body."

"Several tendays?" Elwin said. "What about my trial?"

"Let me worry over that," she said. "You do not need to be present for the trial to proceed. Now, go."

After a year of lecture, there was so much that she had not told him. It seemed like she had skipped over all of the important things, like giants and vampires. How big were 'giants' anyway?

Zarah pulled her hand from his arm. With the warmth of her touch removed, the feeling of separation that he had felt before returned. It was more intense than it had been.

He looked at her. "I'll see you soon."

"Farewell, Elwin."

He focused on his body and willed himself back to his sleeping form. The feeling of safety returned. Their campsite was the same, and Feffer had not stirred.

Elwin sat by Feffer and stared at the trees. Images of Zeth attacking the innocent people of Bentonville would not leave his thoughts. How long before Zeth reached Benedict? He had moved so fast. How long could Zeth run in that form? Was it like flying?

He stood. Elwin had to see his mother. The castle was much further than the farm was. He would be fast.

Elwin closed his eyes and thought of the swing on the porch. He opened his eyes, and he was sitting on it. The feeling of being watched was instant, but it was far less than before.

There was light coming from within.

"Mother?"

Motion from the edge of the field drew his attention. A figure in dark robes strolled across the field. Muscles bulged beneath the robes. The man's head was shaven, and his face carried a long scar that had just missed his eye.

The man approached the house, and Elwin did not like the look of the man. The black robes looked too much like Zeth's.

"Mother!"

Elwin thought of the common room of his home and transported there instantly.

Wilton Madrowl sat on the sofa, staring into the fireplace. Next to him laid a familiar basket and a letter from Elwin's real mother. Wilton picked up the iron prod and stirred the fire methodically.

What was he doing there? It didn't matter, the black savant was coming. What else could the man have been?

"Wilton, get out of here!" Elwin screamed.

Elwin ran to the window. He was almost here. What could he do? He turned around and looked for some way to warn Wilton. He could feel the power of Fire coming from the flames beside Wilton. He hadn't trained with Fire yet. Whatever he did could hurt them both.

Images of screaming people running from Zeth flashed in his mind.

Elwin focused on the warmth of the flames. He could see embers rise from the Fire and flow toward him in burnt-orange arcs. Wilton didn't seem to notice.

When the embers touched Elwin's hand, they merged into him. The warmth was different than Air. He felt, powerful. With a burst, he released all of his energy into the flames. The small fire flared, and Wilton fell backward over the sofa.

In that moment, the door slammed open, and Wilton jumped to his feet, drawing his twin blades. When his eyes met the bald man's face, Wilton sheathed his blades and knelt at his feet, placing a fist across his chest. "Savant Fasuri, I thought you were taking Elwin across the Tranquil Sea. I was expecting Savant Emmantis on the morrow."

"What?" Elwin looked at Wilton.

Fasuri moved several paces into Elwin's home, never looking in Elwin's direction.

"Elwin has escaped," Fasuri said. "We must alter our plans. Did you kill

Elwin's family, as I ordered?"

"Kill my family? What is this?"

Elwin backed away from Wilton. This wasn't possible. Elwin had known Wilton his entire life. How could he be with the black savants?

"I waited here," Wilton said, "but they never returned. Perhaps they are already dead? Either way. I found this letter."

Fasuri took the letter. After reading it he said, "You have done well. King Bain will want this."

Fasuri folded the letter into one of his robes.

Elwin gritted his teeth. "That's mine."

"The man Elwin called Father is now a soulless one." The man pulled a folded parchment from his robes. "On the morrow, the soulless one will return here. He is to be passed to Savant Emmantis."

"I don't understand," Wilton said.

"Take this."

Wilton took the parchment and stared at it as if he had been handed a snake.

"There are also a small contingent of skeletal warriors bound to the soulkey. These are to go to Emmantis as well. Without those papers, Zeth will not hand them over. Keep them dry and do not attempt to break the seal."

"Yes, my lord," Wilton said. But Elwin could see confusion on his face.

"There's a good lad." The praise sounded like a master petting his hound.

"What are my orders?" Wilton asked.

"You will march with Emmantis on this city, called Justice, and assist him in taking the castle."

"Take the castle my lord?"

"You swore your allegiance to the Father," Fasuri said. "I hope you have not lost your resolve. You would not want to fall under Mordeci's hand once more. Or would you?"

"I am faithful to the Father. I will do as you command." Wilton shook his head as he spoke. "I do not wish to disappoint King Bain."

"No, you do not," Fasuri's voice was an icy calm, "You have helped us find the Son of Bain. That will not be forgotten. Although, he did manage to escape. Zeth believes your brother is the one who rescued him. The one you asked me to spare? That will not look good for you."

"But my lord," Wilton said, "I told you King Bain could use my brother. He bested a full savant. Surely you can see his worth?"

Fasuri's smile was cold. "Zeth places the blame on the soulless one, but I see the truth of the matter. His incompetence allowed the son to slip away. We may yet be able to use this brother of yours. I have given the order to take him alive. So long as you do as commanded, those orders will not change."

Wilton's face sagged with relief. "Is there any more I can do? Perhaps, I can help you capture them. I have spent time in the Carotid, and I am a skilled tracker. I could—"

"Are you questioning my orders?"

Wilton looked away. "No, Savant Fasuri."

"I do not need your aid to catch children in the woods. We shall have them soon enough. If they go south or east, they will walk into our waiting armies, and if they travel west to the capital, my emissaries in the city will intercept them. Our trackers will push them north through the forest toward Goldspire. They have to go through the mountains whilst we go around."

"My lord, did you not say you can track people as a Spirit? Why not just go to Elwin directly?"

"I cannot track him through the shadow realm." Fasuri's voice tinged with irritation. "He has learned how to ward himself. If the Life witches have learned the skill, they have taught it to Elwin. That must be why we cannot see him. No matter, this island is ours, or will be soon enough. We will capture them. In the meantime, you have your orders. Do not fail."

"Yes, my lord," Wilton said. "I mean, I won't my lord."

Fasuri turned while Wilton stammered and left without a backward glance. Wilton stared at the man's back, his eyes burning with hatred and rage.

Elwin walked over to Wilton, "Why?"

Wilton stood, staring at the door.

Elwin dropped to the ground at Wilton's feet, "Why would you betray your brother, your father, me? My father is a soulless one because of you."

Wilton's face held no emotion. He returned to the fire and sat poking at it.

"I do what I must," he told the fire. "So much for not being someone's bait."

"What?" Elwin said. "You will answer for this, Wilton. Some day you will answer for what you have done."

"I'm sorry, Elwin," Wilton sighed. "Keep Feffer safe. Whatever you do, don't let Fasuri have him. Death would be better."

Elwin froze.

"Wilton?" Elwin moved between Wilton and the fire, avoiding the iron prod. "Can you see me?"

Wilton through Elwin, not seeing him.

"The Lifebringer save me," Wilton said. "Please keep Feffer safe."

The disconnected feeling became stronger. He wasn't sure if it was due to the distance from his body or the pain in his heart.

Elwin returned to his body, trying to find the words to tell Feffer that his brother had betrayed them all.

Chapter 19

COMPROMISES

Zarah leaned against the rail of her balcony overlooking the courtyard below. The morning's first light had just touched the courtyard.

A team of men and wagons were readying for departure, and a cohort of soldiers gathered beyond the gate. She shook her head. A single cohort to save the world. Her Vision was clear.

"Elwin needed help," she said.

Father moved along the side of the contingent and talked with servants and soldiers. It was his third time checking the supplies.

"You must trust your father," Mother said, placing a hand on her shoulder.

She glanced at her mother. Zarah had not heard her approach.

"My Vision," Zarah said. "It is happening. Elwin was in a bone cage."

"Feffer saved him," Mother said, more to herself than to Zarah. "It is possible that the worst of it is behind us."

"What if Zeth captures them again? Why is the king not sending more men. A hundred soldiers?"

"Zarah," Mother said, "you must understand. We have enemies on our shores. The Death Element is being used on our people. We cannot leave the castle undefended. Elwin is being chased by a single black savant. A single cohort shall suffice. Several of the men have touched weapons and know how to defend against elementalists."

"We should be with them," Zarah said.

"We have been over this," Mother said. "If we leave now, the Guardians will hunt Elwin. Let us not forget that I am as much on trial now as Elwin. I must give testimony on Elwin's behalf."

"Can *I* not go with Father?" Zarah asked.

"We can move faster flying than your father and the team of wagons on foot. We will catch him long before they reach Goldspire. After the trial."

"But Mother ...," Zarah began.

"That is final," Mother said. "If you argue with me further, you will stay here when I leave. Remember what your father said, you are to obey without question. Is that understood?"

Zarah felt her cheeks flush. She wasn't sure if it was from anger or embarrassment. Anger, she decided. She hated when her mother had that tone. She wasn't a child anymore. She tried not to grit her teeth when she said, "Yes Mother," but she did not succeed.

"Find me when your father departs," Mother said. "We need to continue working on your mask."

Her mother left her on the balcony.

She had always wanted to learn to mask her taming. Until this morning, Mother had said she was not ready. In truth, her mother had not thought she was mature enough, and she hated proving her right more than anything.

The memory of that morning was too fresh in her mind.

After Father informed the king of her Vision, he returned to his and Mother's bed chamber. They dismissed Zarah to discuss the king's word.

Zarah had strolled onto her balcony. If they had left the balcony doors open, she could not have been blamed for hearing them. But, of course they had closed the glass doors. She had not practiced Eavesdropping in some time, and it seemed as good a time as any.

It was several dozen paces, but she had Eavesdropped further than that distance before. She opened her essence to Air and focused on the balcony doors, feeling the vibrations bounce off the glass from inside. Taming Air, she felt the vibrations form words.

"... Not it," Father said. "She is too young."

Mother's voice was patient. "I was younger than her, when I went on my first adventure."

"And what happened on that adventure?"

"We found an artifact of power," Mother said.

"Not that," he said. "You *killed* people."

"They were Death bound," Mother said.

"But you *killed* people," he said. "Don't you remember what it felt like?"

"And I have killed more since, during the battles with Bain's army in Alcoa," Mother said. "I will likely kill again before the war is done."

"You didn't answer the question."

"I struggled with it," she said. "It is never easy to end the life of another, even one that has dedicated his soul to the Seeker."

"Do you want her to go through that?" he said.

"Yes," she said without hesitation. "Evil must be defeated. It is the life that He has chosen for her."

"But what if something happens to her?"

"You and I will be there, as well as Tharu and Hulen, and a small contingent of the White Hand," Mother said. "She is strong enough. There are few that could survive her lightning hurl. And her veil is improving. Only masters in Air can find her attempts at stealth. She has yet to learn how to mask *certain* abilities from other elementalists. In truth, I had avoided teaching her this trick, so that I could *always* know when she is eavesdropping."

Zarah's heart fluttered, and she stopped taming the Air, immediately releasing her unused power. Then, she ran into her room and jumped onto her bed. She forced her breathing to slow and played with her hair, as if she was bored.

The door to her room opened, *without* so much as a knock. Her parents entered the room and stood beside her bed. She continued to play with the ends of her hair, twisting it in her fingers.

"Well," her mother said, "I have been trying to convince your father that you are ready for this journey. Now, I am not so sure."

"I needed to know what was taking so long," Zarah said. "I am worried about Elwin. Well, I am not worried about *him*. I'm worried about the kingdom. We need to do something."

"That does not give you an excuse to eavesdrop on your father and me," she said. "Give me one good reason that I should let you come with us to Goldspire."

"I could have another Vision," Zarah said. "And I won't be able to tell you."

"Linadria is here," Mother said. "You could tell her of any Vision you have. She will be my voice in the council, while I am away. She is the *only* elementalist left to defend the castle. Perhaps, I should make you stay here so that our city is more secure. That is my first duty as High Counselor. "

"If Elwin dies, none of that will matter," Zarah said. "You know I can help."

Father's arms were crossed, and he stared down at her. Mother had a similar posture.

She saw her error. Brute force would not work on them today, but maybe it wasn't too late. Zarah bit her bottom lip and looked to her father. "I'm sorry. I'm just worried over my friend," Zarah said. "Please, let me help Elwin."

Her mother looked to her father. "The choice is yours, Zaak."

He gave Mother a look that Zarah could not read. His brow scrunched and his lips frowned. Then he looked to Zarah and said. "Once the trial is done, you can come. But you will obey your mother and me as if your were one of my new recruits. Is that clear?"

"After the trial?" she asked.

"Yes," he said, "*after* the trial. New recruits don't get to ask questions. Understand?"

She bit her lip. "Yes, Father."

Mother sat on the edge of her bed. "You and I still have matters to discuss."

"And I have final preparations to make," Father said. "The wagons wait my inspection below."

"Be safe, my love."

"You as well," he said. Then, he left, closing the door behind him.

"Now," Mother said. "We have a few things to discuss."

"Oh," Zarah said. "I need to prepare for the journey then."

"I have already had your travel clothes packed and placed on the wagon," she said. "When we depart, I want to carry as little as possible."

"What do you mean," Zarah said. "Father has only just said that I could go."

Her mother actually giggled. "I knew he would come around. Had you eavesdropped on us sooner, perhaps he would have come around even faster."

Zarah's jaw dropped. "You *wanted* me to eavesdrop?"

"One day you will understand," her mother said. "I wanted your father to feel that it was his decision for you to come. Men feel better when they feel like *they* are in control."

Zarah didn't know what to say.

"Don't look at me like that," Mother said. "He was never good at telling you no. And I believe you are ready for this. Well, almost. There are a few talents you still need. The time may soon come that you need to hide from other elementalists. I am going to show you how to mask your taming. If your flow is too great, the mask will not work. It is a subtle trick, and it does not work for every talent. Do as I do ..."

Mother had spent the hours until first light showing her how to mask her taming. When a servant came with a summons from the king, Mother had left her on the balcony to train on her own.

Instead of practicing, she had busied herself by watching the courtyard.

She continued to watch the wagons being checked and loaded. Hulen stood at the procession's lead, talking with Tharu.

Even at this distance, she could hear the dwarf's booming laughter. Hulen's whisper was a normal man's talking voice. His laugh could wake the dragons. The dwarf's torso was as thick as a redwood. His height was not a foot more than he was wide. His long red hair wove into his braided beard. The axe strapped to his back had a blade as wide as he and almost as tall. For longer than Zarah had lived, Hulen had been the emissary for Dargaitha, the dwarven city to the south.

Before the Shadow Wars, his people had called the Island Nations, Enthkarre, meaning many islands. After the Shadow Wars, dwarves fought the humans for control of the islands. The war had lasted just short of a century. Dwarven memories were longer than their life-spans, and their life-spans were much longer than a human's. Ten generations to a human was a single generation to a dwarf.

Forging a peace with the long-lived race had taken a special man. Brannon Mendlewar the Just was born into a nation at battle. He was a renowned as a tactician, winning every battle he had fought. He succeeded in pushing the dwarves back into the mountains.

Rather than pursuing them into their caves, Mendlewar had forged a peace with the dwarves. He had given the entire southern mountains to them as part of the Dargaitha nation and allowed an emissary to sit on the White Council to have a voice in the ruling of the lands. Any actions involving the dwarves required the voice of the emissary. After the Dwarven Treatise, Mendlewar was declared Brannon Justice, king of the Isles of Justice.

After the lords and ladies who had declared fealty to Mendlewar had died, the inheriting lords and ladies began to plot for power. The War of Houses only lasted four years. The entire northern isles had risen to defeat Justice and lost.

Although Mendlewar had won the war, he had given the northern isles to his loyal lords and ladies. The Kinging Ceremony had lasted a tenday. The traitors watched as Mendlewar dubbed his allies kings and queens of the northern islands. Then Mendlewar had executed the traitors with the knowledge that he would have given them their islands had they but asked.

Zarah sighed. Justice had not known war since the War of Houses.

Even though Justice had been at war for a year, Zarah had not felt the cost of the war until now. Before now, war had been a thing in history books.

All of those people in Benedict and Bentonville had died at the hands of a black savant. How many more would die?

"We need to reach Elwin."

She did not know how, but saving the country bumpkin would fix things. Her Visions never lied.

Zarah had always known Elwin was special. She could sense his purity and his power. He had a gift like none other she had seen. When Zarah was young, her mother had trained other elementalists with minor power. Since coming into her power, Zarah had surpassed all of them.

Three years she had trained her essence. Every year she could draw more of the Elements into her essence than the previous year. Mother had been training her own essence for more then two decades. Upon coming into his power, Elwin was more powerful than the two of them together.

And part of her hated him for it. Why him?

She could close her eyes and see his mystic, blue orbs smiling at her. They would make games out of training. Fly and seek was her favorite. Each would take turns, giving chase to the other. He was faster, and she knew he was holding back, but he would slow down to let her catch him. The idiot. His cheerful laughter would fill her ears as she caught him.

The memory sent a chill down her spine and made goose pimples rise on her arms. She rubbed at them furiously. What was wrong with her? She was no besotted fool.

Zarah looked up in time to see the last wagon of the procession clear the inner gates. She had been so lost in her thoughts, she had not noticed them depart.

Something like hope fluttered in her midsection.

"Help is on its way, Elwin," she said. "Help is on its way."

Elwin's left shoulder still throbbed, so he sat up slowly. Feffer had yet to rouse. How would he ever tell him Wilton had brought the black savants to Benedict? He shook his head. There would be time to figure it out while they traveled. They needed to be on their way.

Elwin placed a hand on his sleeping companion and gave him a gentle shake.

Feffer sat straight up. "Get away from me! Don't ... Oh. Sorry Elwin."

The motion made Elwin jostle his shoulder, and pain shot down his arm.

"What's wrong, Elwin?"

"There is a bone fragment in my arm," he said. "I need you to pull it out."

Feffer stood up and examined his shoulder. The piece sticking out was the size of a small, slender finger. Elwin shuddered and Feffer made a hissing sound with his teeth. "Ouch. Wait. Did you say bone?"

"The cage was made out of bone. It is kind of numb right now as long as I don't move a lot."

Feffer frowned at the bone fragment and started fumbling through his pack.

"What are you doing?" Elwin said.

"I brought some cloth bandages and healing salts," he said, as he pulled the supplies out of the bag.

Feffer stood and pointed at the bone fragment. "Are you ready?"

Elwin took a deep breath, "Yes."

As Feffer grabbed hold of the bone, Elwin felt numbness travel down his arm to his fingertips.

"I am going to count to three," Feffer said.

Elwin gritted his teeth and braced against Feffer. "Do it."

"One."

"Two."

If Feffer had said "three," Elwin had not heard it. Pain blinded his senses. He felt pressure on his shoulder as Feffer moved his arm. Elwin didn't remember lying down, but he realized that he was flat on his back when he saw the trees circling above him. It took a moment for his vision to settle and the trees to stop spinning. He must have lost consciousness for a moment, because when he sat up, there was a cloth bandage wrapped around his shoulder.

"Elwin?"

"I'm alright," Elwin said. "I will be alright. Help me."

The ache in his shoulder was different than it had been, but he could feel his fingers again. His arm was wet. He used his legs and right arm to scoot backward, and Feffer helped him to move against a large redwood.

"It bled a lot," Feffer said. "I don't know if you should move."

"We don't have a choice," Elwin said. "Help me up."

"At least eat something first."

"Alright." Elwin let the tree support him. "What do you have?"

Feffer grabbed the pack, pulled some dried bread out of it, and handed some to Elwin. It was dry, but Elwin ate every bite. He was surprised by his own hunger.

"Do you have more?"

"Yes," Feffer said, "but we will have to ration it out. I don't have a bow and arrow for hunting, so we'll have to make our food last. We have a month or more of travel."

"Did you bring enough to last that long?"

Feffer shook his head. "We will have to find nuts and berries along the way."

"Help me up," Elwin said.

"Drink some of this first." Feffer handed a wineskin to his good arm.

The water tasted like the leather, but Elwin drank a good amount and handed it back to Feffer and said, "We will have to find a stream to refill that, too."

"I have another one," Feffer said, "but a stream would be nice."

Elwin opened his essence to Air and tamed the power for flight. He lifted his body from the ground slightly, but his head spun from the motion. He had to use the tree to stable himself. He could tell that his essence was still weakened from pushing himself, but they couldn't afford to stay put. And he didn't think he had the energy to walk. After a moment, the dizziness subsided.

"I can't fly," Elwin said.

"You can ride Haven." There was concern in Feffer's voice. "She will need to be led through this brush, anyway."

Elwin nodded. Feffer being on foot would slow them down, but Feffer had the right of it. The large redwoods were not so close together, but there were thorns and brush that would need to be cut away for the horse to make it through.

Elwin grabbed the pommel of the saddle with his good arm and tried to pull himself up but slipped and bounced his shoulder into the horse. He felt his eyes spin into the top of his skull and his vision blurred.

When the trees stopped spinning, he found Feffer's arm bracing him.

"Maybe you should rest."

"Help me up," Elwin said. "We need to move."

"There's no way they followed us," Feffer complained, but he helped Elwin into the saddle as he spoke.

"But we can be sure they are looking."

"Yeah," he said as he took the reins, "I suppose we don't have much of a choice." Then he drew his sword with the other and began clearing a path. The brush and vines fell away like thread at the swords touch.

"It's really sharp," Elwin said.

"It wasn't sharp enough last night."

"The cage was crafted by the Death Element. Maybe that had something to do with it."

Feffer didn't respond. He led the horse forward, slicing as he moved. After a time he said, "Do you think the stories about giants in the Goldspire Mountains are real?"

"Last night I went into the shadow realm and spoke with Jasmine." Elwin said. "She said that the giants are real."

"I thought that was something my Da always told me to keep me from wandering around the Carotid. But of course they are real. Why wouldn't they be? Do you think they really eat people?"

"Well," Elwin said, "Jasmine suggested we should avoid them."

"We will certainly do that."

"There is something else, Feffer." He wanted to tell him about Wilton, but he couldn't make the words come out.

Feffer glanced over his shoulder. "What is it?"

He opened his mouth to tell the truth about Wilton, but his tongue betrayed him. "I saw Zeth talking to someone. He said that he has us cornered, and that he will wait for us in Goldspire."

Feffer stopped walking and faced Elwin. "Then why in the abyss are we going to Goldspire?"

"He doesn't know that I know his plans." Elwin said. "Jasmine is going there too. We can help *her* capture *him*."

Feffer opened his mouth to speak, then he closed it. He turned his back on Elwin.

"Feffer, you caught him by surprise once, we can do it again. He sleeps and eats, Feffer. He is human like you and me."

Feffer faced him. "Like you Elwin, not me. I am just human." Feffer felt at his belt pouch. "Believe me, I want to see him hang for what he's done. But, I don't know if I can do it. I'm not even a soldier yet."

"We won't be alone. Jasmine will be there."

Feffer studied him so long without saying anything that Elwin got uncomfortable. At last he said, "We need to move."

After a few moments of working his way through the trees, Feffer asked, "Who was Zeth talking to?"

"I ...," Elwin cleared his throat, "I couldn't see his face. Another black savant named Fasuri."

"Where did you see him?"

"Um ... they were in the shadow of the woods."

"It was foolhardy to spy on him, Elwin," he said. "Don't do that again."

"I won't, Feffer."

Both of them were quiet for a time. Feffer led Haven through the trees, finding the paths with the fewest brambles. When he could, Feffer would follow game trails, but most of the way had to be cleared.

The predominant trees in the area were the massive redwood trees. They had broad bases and thick bark. The trees were taller than the castle of Justice. The red hue made Elwin think of Benedict. Zeth would tear through it. Thinking about Bentonville made him want to tear at his eyes. He would if it could make him unsee the slaughter of all those people. Even the children. Maybe he could find Zeth in the shadow realm. Maybe he should surrender and bargain for his town. He could save the rest of them.

If Zeth caught up to them, what would happen to Feffer?

He closed his eyes making his best efforts push the images of the dying from his thoughts, but he was greeted with Bentonville once more.

"Maybe we should go back," Elwin said.

"What? Are you insane?"

"I could barter my life for theirs. I could promise to go with Zeth if he spares Wilton and the others."

"No," the venom in Feffer's voice made Elwin jump. "He will not have you. I know what he wants with you Elwin. And that is not happening. No. You are my family too Elwin. He can't have you. I don't want to hear such thoughts again. Is that clear?"

Elwin nodded. "Okay Feffer."

As the day pressed on, neither of them said much. The sun rose, and the humid air clung to his every movement. The shade from the forest provided little relief from the summer heat.

Elwin tried to think of things to say, but nothing really came to mind other than the lie he had told Feffer. They both had lost so much. Elwin lost his father because of Wilton's betrayal, but could he only blame Wilton? Elwin couldn't help but feel that all of this was his fault. Thinking on Feffer's anger, he couldn't help but wonder, did Feffer blame him, too?

Elwin pushed the thoughts from his mind and focused on avoiding thorns and brambles that Feffer missed with his sword. A few times he tested his essence, but he always had similar results to the morning. Lightheaded nausea.

He wasn't sure if it was physical exhaustion or that his essence was weakened from pushing it during the escape. But his essence felt restored, so he should have been able to tame flight. His back end felt sore from the saddle and his shoulder throbbed. Maybe that had something to do with it.

"Feffer," he said, "I need to take a break."

Feffer walked back to him and studied his face. Feffer's lips were tight when he said, "You're pale. You should eat something. Here, take my arm."

Elwin leaned on Feffer and let his friend ease him to the ground.

Feffer sat across from him, against another tree. "I could use a rest as well."

Feffer dug some dried bread from the pack and handed some to Elwin. They both ate in silence for a time. When Elwin finished his bread, he said, "Thank you, Feffer."

"For what?"

"You saved me. Our fathers are dead because of me, and you still saved me."

Feffer shook his head. "No, our fathers are dead because of Zeth. And besides, you would have done the same for me."

Elwin nodded. "I would."

Feffer held more bread up to Elwin. "Have another piece."

Elwin shook his head. "My stomach doesn't feel right."

"Your face is really pale," Feffer said. "I am afraid your shoulder is festering."

"It feels better," Elwin insisted. "I just need some water."

Feffer handed him the wineskin.

Elwin took a large gulp and handed the skin back to Feffer. "How far do you think we have traveled?"

Feffer took a deep breath, "Maybe a couple leagues or so. Honestly, how is your shoulder?"

"I feel better," Elwin said. "I promise. My stomach is a bit queasy, but I can move when you are ready."

"Alright," Feffer closed the pack and slung it over his shoulder. "Let me know when you need to stop."

He decided to try again. This would have been much easier if he could fly. Elwin felt for the Air, but opening his essence made his body twinge with pain. For a moment, a black fog seemed to fill his vision. He grabbed the tree for support, but Feffer was beside him before Elwin could blink.

"Okay. That's it. You are going to rest," Feffer said, as he eased him to the ground.

"Curse it all," Elwin leaned against the tree, "Maybe I just need to sleep for a bit, so I can regenerate my essence."

Feffer shook his head, "You are going to have to explain all that to me one of these days."

"I will, Feffer," Elwin said. "Just not today."

Elwin closed his eyes.

Chapter 20

TRIALS

Zarah sat in the front row, in the seat closest to the center aisle. The courtroom was not any less foreboding than it had been the first time she had been here. Again, she had been the first to arrive. Only she was alone this time. Mother had been meeting with the White Council all morning. In her younger years, Zarah had been known to eavesdrop, and now she knew how to mask it. That's why she had been sent from the castle. Not because she needed to stretch her legs before they left.

She hated being treated like a child.

Mother had been the one to teach her to mask the talent. How could she expect her not to practice? Apparently, it was *rude* to listen in on other people's conversations.

But she wanted to know what the council had to say about Elwin. It had been over a tenday, almost two, since she had seen him. He was lost in the forest, being hunted by a Death bound. Her Vision had him in a cage of bones, and the black savant had held him in a cage of bones.

Did that mean her Vision had already come true? Was Elwin safe now?

And now, his fate would be decided, despite his absence. The Guardians would be sure to know that Elwin was no longer in the city. Would they hold that against him?

That would not look good for him. Not that she was overly concerned for Elwin so much as that, well … he was innocent. And if he died, that whole end of the world thing.

"He is innocent," she told the empty chairs. "If you were not wasting our time with this farce, we could be moving north already."

Elwin was not Death bound. She knew he wasn't, because she had touched his essence. She had felt his Spirit with hers. It had only been a moment, but it told her much about him. Things she had already known, of course. But now she was sure.

He was too selfless for his own good and brave to the point of stupidity. Foolish boy probably charged Zeth the moment he realized the man was Death bound. That was how he got himself captured. A simple, country bumpkin, that's what he was. He had a profound sense of curiosity to his nature that would land him on a hotplate someday, but he was not Death bound. Unless, stupidity and obstinance were now crimes, Elwin was innocent.

From behind her, she heard the sound of feet shuffling on wood. Zarah turned her head to the side to look with her peripheral vision. The children had grown taller, but it was the same family as the year before.

The group walked to the front three rows. Despite being farmers, they were all clean. The mother wore a brown cotton dress. The father wore green trousers and a green tunic with brown trim. There was a boy a handful of years older than Zarah. She remembered him from last time.

He had dark hair and dark eyes, and his skin was tanned from years in the sun. He filled his pale shirt more than the previous year, and his trousers looked more snug as well. He carried a little boy, not more than two years old. The little boy had a touch of red mixed into his short hair. He played with a button on the older boy's shirt with one hand. His other hand held a small wooden soldier. The toy had a shield in one hand and a curved blade in the other.

The dark-haired boy sat next to the parents in the front row closest to the center aisle. He placed the child on his lap, facing the chairs. The little boy alternated between gnawing on the toy and bouncing it in his hand.

Zarah noticed the older boy's dark eyes on her, and she looked away. From her periphery, she could see that he continued to watch her. She had been sitting up straight with her hands folded in her lap, as was proper. But now she became aware of her posture, and had to make an effort not to fidget.

The boy looked away as criers started shouting in the square, outside of the temple.

"Come see the trial of Elwin Escari!"

"Is he guilty or innocent? Come and witness Elwin's fate."

At least they no longer called him a Death witch.

Guards entered much sooner this time. Their tunics had the symbol of the Guardians of Life, a red crescent moon with a golden sun centered between the moon's tips. They had twice as many guards as the year before.

Zarah's heart began beating faster. Why so many?

Other people began to enter as well.

A woman sat to Zarah's right. She had flowing, blond hair with a natural wave. Her sky-blue eyes reminded her of Elwin's. The dress she wore was made of a rich green silk, but her bodice was too small for such a large bosom. As more people began to fill Zarah's row, the woman squeezed in closer to her. She smelled of spiced incense and lavender.

Like the first trial, people filled every seat and lined the walls. The only unused space was down the center aisle. Being close to the sixteenth hour, she knew the heat of the day waned, but the number of bodies did not allow her to feel it.

"How do you think they will kill the witch?" A man's deep voice said from behind her.

"I don't know Gond," another man said. "They will probably burn him at the stake."

"I bet they behead him," Gond laughed. "Then they will burn him just to be safe."

The other man laughed.

Zarah felt her jaw tense.

Mother had told her about the pits in the Kalicodon nation. If a warrior was captured in battle, he had to either become a slave to his captor or prove his honor by battling in the pits. Either way, he would be a slave, but most preferred the pits. People would cheer as a man was killed by other combatants. Sometimes they would capture wild animals and force the warriors to battle the beasts with bare hands. Wagers would be made on the outcome.

It was barbaric.

These men seemed the type to enjoy such disgusting customs. The way these people talked about Elwin's fate made her stomach ill. She had been debating whether or not to give them a lecture, when she heard her mother's name on the lips of a woman across the aisle.

Mother wore white robes that announced her station. The crest at the center was a hand that balanced a multicolored flame on its palm. The flame was divided into five equal parts: red, brown, white, blue, and yellow. Platinum embroidered the hems, announcing that she was the highest elementalist of the White Council. All eyes were on her as she walked down the aisle and stood in front of the central chair.

Movement from behind the platform silenced the lingering whispers.

In pairs, the same inquisitors as the year before entered and filled the seats upon the dais, the last being the dwarf and the large Kalicodian. Then the bald man in white robes stepped from the doorway onto the platform and stood behind the center chair.

He was named Jorus Teblin, High Inquisitor. Mother had researched him. She had not ascertained as to why Jorus had been stationed in Justice, or even how long he had been here. She did know that Jorus was from Alcoa and had proceeded in many trials. In one hundred seventy-two trials, Jorus had only spared four of those accused of breaking the Laws of Life. Most of those tried had been children coming into their power.

Zarah took a deep breath and watched Jorus.

He had the same robe with the Guardian's crest and still held a thick shepherd's crook in his right hand. His face was not readable. Jorus raised the crook vertically for a moment, then he slammed the end against the floor three times. His voice held no emotion.

"Let us all, under the Lifebringer, bear witness to the proceedings. We call forth His righteous truth to guide our hands over the fate of one Elwin Escari, who under the powers of the Elements has prematurely ended the life of another, Biron Onderhill of Justice by way of the Elements. We, the Guardians of Life, Seekers of Truth, will judge him under the Lifebringer's wisdom. Let the proceedings continue."

Three more times he pounded the floor with the shepherd's crook in slow succession. Then, as one, the seven inquisitors took their seats.

Jorus cleared his throat. "Whom, if any, has come to serve as the defender of the accused?"

Who, not *whom*, Zarah wanted to say. She couldn't abide pedantic people.

Her mother's voice commanded attention. "I, Jasmine Lifesong, High Counselor of the White Council, right hand to his majesty, King Brannon Justice the twenty-sixth, have come once more to defend the accused."

"Please," he said, "what have you discovered from this annum by studying the accused?"

Zarah wanted to roll her eyes. More pedantry. Why annum when *year* would do? Besides, she was fairly certain per annum was a merchant's term.

"I am even further convinced of Elwin's innocence," Mother said in a confident voice.

"Please," he said, "elaborate. What action has he taken to convince you so?"

"A person's goodness is not measured by a *single* action," she said, "but by the sum of his actions. Elwin cares for others and wants not for himself. He humbly accepted all his gifts from the palace and has asked for nothing. Of all the elementalists that I have taught, he has the potential to be the greatest of them all.

"For a year, I have watched his remorse over Biron's death. For many months, every night, before bed, he would fly to the highest spire of the castle and weep for Biron's loss. I have heard Elwin pray to the Lifebringer and beg Him to take his powers in exchange for

Taming the Elements

Biron's life. Tell me, are there any Death bound that would act in this fashion?"

"Hmm," the man said. "Is it possible that the accused was aware of your presence?"

"No. I was under a veil, and I was taming Air to eavesdrop on him from quite a distance. There is none gifted that could have sensed my presence."

Zarah found herself wondering how many times Mother had watched *her* in such a fashion. She would bring it up later, and she would use *Mother's* lecture about rudeness.

"That is interesting," he said. "But, tell me, where is the accused now?"

"That is not your concern," Mother said. "By the edicts of the Laws of Life in accords to the Ninth Treaty, specific to the nation of Justice and the Guardians of Life, the nature of the training of an acolyte is to be determined by the appointed master. As I am the assigned master to the accused, he is in a location of which I am aware."

Zarah saw Jorus's jaw clench and eyes narrow for a brief moment. Despite her best efforts, Zarah could not keep the smile from her lips. She wagered the High Inquisitor was not accustomed to having his own rules told to him.

"This is true," he said. "So, the accused is in a location of *your* choosing?"

"I have given him a very specific task of which I am certain, he will perform," she said. "As I said, the details are not your concern."

Zarah almost smiled. Not one word was false.

"Is he in anyway connected to the events that have transpired in his home town of Benedict? This village was attacked by a Death bound, was it not?"

"As all here are aware," Mother said, "war has made its way to our shores, and Benedict has been attacked. Elwin was visiting his town for the Summer Solstice Festival when the attack took place. He, like many, barely escaped with his life. Elwin is as much a victim as anyone else there."

That is quite the understatement, Zarah thought.

"How can you be sure?" Jorus said.

"I have spoken to Elwin, and I have seen the evidence of the destruction myself. The damage was caused by taming Fire, and Elwin only knows talents in Air at this moment. I have begun his instruction on how to tame Water, but it will be some time before he learns any talents of destruction. He has a natural aversion to it. "

"Indeed," Jorus said in his monotone voice, "have you anything further to add?"

Mother was silent for a moment. "Not at this time. But, as master to the acolyte, I reserve my right under the Ninth Treaty to speak at a later time and to question any further witnesses."

"Yes. Yes. Of course. Are there any others here that would like to bear witness to events of the accused?"

"I would," the voice came from behind her. It sounded like the man named Gond.

"Jasmine Lifesong," the inquisitor said. "If it would please you, stand to the side?"

She took three steps to the side near Zarah and faced the center aisle. Her face was a mask of composure. Zarah was sure that her own face was not nearly so composed.

"Please," Jorus said, "come forward and bear witness."

He stepped into the aisle and walked up to where Mother had stood.

"I am Gond Forsithe," he said, "and I witnessed attacks made by Elwin Escari on innocents."

Several people gasped and began to whisper.

Jorus struck his crook three times. "There will be order."

After the crowd quieted, the inquisitor said, "Please sir. Continue."

"I have never feared more for my life," Gond said. "The boy with the blond hair, Elwin? I heard his friend call him Son of Bain."

Again, people began to whisper.

"Order I say." Jorus struck his crook. "We must have order."

Gond spoke over the lingering whispers. "The boy, Elwin, lights surrounded him and his eyes started glowing. The next thing I know, the front of the inn was on fire. The front door and half the wall was just ... gone. There was another man there, too. He walked through the fire like it was air, and out into the square.

"That was when I helped the old man, he called himself Poppe. I helped him and the blacksmith, I don't know his name, get the little ones locked into the wine cellar. Then I ran out the back. I left my horse for dead and ran west. I passed men at an outpost and told them what happened. Then I came here."

"Tell me," Mother said. "How much ale had you drank?"

"I'm sorry?"

The inquisitor's eyes widened as if Mother had cursed him, but she continued as if the room was her own. "Were you sober when the events took place?"

"I think I may have had two or three," Gond said. "But I sobered up in two shakes of a dragon's tail when the stabbing began. I know what I saw."

"You have not mentioned stabbing," Mother said. "Please, elaborate."

"It was all kind of a blur," Gond shivered. "The man in black robes stabbed people with this jagged sword. I hid behind the bar. There was an older woman there. But she had fainted. I just knew I was dead for sure."

"Tell me," Mother said, "this man was stabbing people before or after the front of the inn caught fire?"

"Uh," Gond scratched his chin, "it was before, I reckon."

"How did you see the accused's eyes glowing from behind the bar?"

"Well," Gond said. "His eyes... They glowed before then."

"Where then," Mother said, indignantly, "was the accused, during the massacre?"

"I ...," Gond said. "I don't know if I can say."

"Hmm. That is interesting. Perhaps we have the wrong person on trial here. We are fighting a war with Death bound after all."

Mother was silent for a moment and Jorus stared daggers into her. She returned his gaze with a quiet serenity.

Gond's feet began to shuffle, and he glanced over his shoulder toward the door several times before looking back up to Jorus.

"You heard this man in black call the accused, 'Son of Bain' ," Jorus said in a tight voice. "What happened before the murdering began? Start from when you arrived at the inn. Tell us about *that*."

Gond had a dirty kerchief out and wiped at his brow. "Well, I had arrived a little later than most. It was raining, so everyone was inside. There was only one table with spare seats. The man with the jagged sword was sitting at it. A man wearing black robes *and* cloak in the dead of summer? I should have known he was wrong from the start." Gond shook his head.

"I walked up, put a hand on a chair, and asked if he minded. He just looked at me with cold eyes. They was cold as the dead of winter, those eyes. Never said a word. He just tapped a finger on the hilt of that jagged sword. It was clear that the man didn't want conversation, so I decided I'd find a seat elsewhere.

"I made my way to the bar and got a few drinks. On the third or so, that's when I saw the dark man offer Elwin a seat at his table. I about dropped my drink. I know his name was Elwin Escari, because I asked the old bar maid if she knew who they were. She told me the boy's name and said that she had never seen the stranger before that morning. He had been there all day, waiting on someone. Old bar wench must have seen lots of strangers in her day. Even she sounded concerned."

He wiped his brow again. "I had to know what they was saying. I got closer. That's when I heard him say that Elwin was the Son of Bain. The music was loud, and people was talking everywhere. So, I didn't hear much else. I circled toward the fireplace to get a better look at Elwin's face. Then he stood up and his eyes began glowing. I felt a breeze, right there in the inn. That's when I *did* drop my drink."

Zarah almost cursed. She knew it. Fool boy attacked a trained elementalist. One who was Death bound to boot. Next time she saw him, she would slap some sense into him.

Gond unfolded his kerchief and wiped his entire face. "Everyone was screaming and running for the front door. I jumped over the bar and bumped into the old ...," Gond wiped his face again. "What I mean to say is that I jumped behind the bar. The bar maid had already fainted. She still had a heartbeat. I swear." He wiped his brow again.

"Well," Gond said, "I done told the rest."

"Indeed," Jorus said. "Would you like to say anything further?"

Gond shook his head, vigorously.

After a moment, Jorus said, "Are there anymore witnesses to come forth?"

Zarah's heart began to beat faster. She wanted to say something, anything that might help. But what would she say? She suddenly felt envious of her mother's poise.

The inquisitor looked to Mother. "Does the master of the accused have anything to add?"

Mother pursed her lips and said in a confident voice, "There is my testimony versus the words of a drunken fool, who is not even clear on what happened. I am sure there is nothing further to discuss."

"It is done, then."

As one, the seven white robed figures rose.

Jorus struck the crook's end three times. "Let us enter a day of prayer to ascertain the fate of the accused. We will reconvene at the sixteenth hour on the morrow."

A day? No! She was supposed to depart after the trial. Why did they need an entire day?

Zarah watched the seven inquisitors exit through the dark doorway. Jorus had sentenced so many to die. How much influence did the other six have? Did Jorus have the final say in the matter, or was he simply the orator?

Zarah felt angry tears begin to rise to the surface when Mother caught her eye. Her smile was warm. Her mother gave her the slightest of nods. It was an answer to the unspoken question.

Everything would be alright. Her mother would not let anything happen to Elwin.

Somehow, everything would be alright. It had to be.

༺ঙ༻

The afternoon sun burned bright in the sky, sending heat through the leaves of the trees above. Feffer wiped sweat from his brow and leaned back against the wide redwood. He hadn't wanted to stop, but his arm was numb from swinging at the brambles. Practicing the forms with each strike, he had grown almost as good with his left hand as he was with his right.

Elwin laid curled up next to him. He shivered as if cold, and his muscles jerked and spasmed. Mumbled words escaped from him, but few were audible.

Feffer removed the bandage to look at Elwin's shoulder once more.

Two tendays they had traveled. During the first tenday, Feffer had redressed Elwin's wound every hour or so. It wasn't until the third day he realized, Elwin's shoulder wasn't healing. By the end of the first tenday, Elwin started losing his strength. That was when Feffer noticed the dark puss coming from the puncture hole and blackened lines winding outward from the wound. The wound wasn't natural.

A normal wound would have begun to heal by now, but Elwin's shoulder was worse every time Feffer looked at it. He covered it with a fresh bandage. It had been days now since he had any healing salts. They hadn't done much for Elwin anyway. At least the bandages kept the dirt out. He needed to reach Jasmine, so she could heal him.

This morning, Elwin hadn't woken up at all. Feffer had even doused him with water, and Elwin hadn't budged. There was still a tenday until the mountains and a couple a tenday or more of hiking and climbing to make it to Goldspire.

He looked at his friend's pale face. Feffer had to find help before that. The Children of Nature were said to be in the Carotid. Maybe the Chai Tu Naruo would be able to help him. If he could find them. At this point, he would ask a mountain giant for help if it stepped out of the trees.

He walked over to Haven and patted her long neck. The mare nibbled on some dried grass.

"Elwin won't last that long," he told her. "I'll likely starve before then as well. At least you have plenty to eat."

Feffer had given most of their food to Elwin. Every time he had found a tree with berries or nuts, he would pick what he could. But the nuts were not easy to get open. What he wouldn't have given for a wooden nut cracker. He had been forced to use the base of his hilt to crack them open against rocks, and he had gotten his thumb as often as not. But now he was out of nuts and berries. And his remaining wineskin was only a quarter full.

"If you're up there," Feffer said to the sky, "I could use a little help here."

Feffer leaned against the tree, waiting to see if the Lifebringer had any immediate assistance. The sounds of the forest were many. Squirrels and other rodents were running in the trees. Gnats and blood flies were in abundance. Feffer hadn't seen any larger animals, but he had seen paw prints too large to belong to a fox or wolf.

Feffer sighed, deciding that no assistance was coming.

"I guess that just leaves me then."

He stood up and slung the pack over his shoulders. Then, he grabbed Elwin by the good arm and hoisted his friend across Haven's saddle.

Every swing of the sword was heavy, but Feffer forced himself to keep moving. When the way allowed, he took the path that would avoid brambles. It was easier to take more steps to avoid thorns than to try to slice at them.

The hours stretched on, but he tried not to count them. Every time he stopped for a rest, he wetted Elwin's lips with a few drops and did the same for himself.

He didn't allow himself to think about what would happen when he ran out of water. He kept moving north. Every step was a matter of will, not strength. Every thought was for the purpose of moving forward. The waning light cooled the air, but Feffer had long given up the attempt to keep sweat out of his face and eyes.

His arms and shoulders burned, and his legs felt like fire worked through his muscles. It was not quite night, but the sun was not providing enough light to travel safely.

Feffer eased Elwin from the saddle to a grassy knoll, then plopped down beside him. He had not passed a single nut or berry. And he had been looking. How much longer could he go without food? How much longer could Elwin?

Feffer leaned his head back against the tree. "I should have listened to Poppe and Momme. We are going to die out here. And it's my fault."

There was a rustling in the trees above him as something large jumped from tree to tree. It was probably just a monkey. This had happened many nights, but it hadn't bothered him before. He had known Elwin was watching over them from his shadow realm.

But there was no way to be sure that Elwin could see him now. Elwin had said that he could watch them when he was sleeping, but Feffer wasn't sure if the same was true in his current state. Even if Elwin did watch over them, how would he warn Feffer?

Feffer laid his sword across his lap.

Elwin sat up. "Wilton, how could you?" His eyes looked dark in the waning light.

Before Feffer could say anything, Elwin slumped back to the grass. Feffer realized that he was gripping his sword hilt and let his hand relax. Elwin was dreaming. Only, Elwin said that he didn't dream anymore.

That had been the first intelligible word from Elwin all day.

Feffer leaned back against the tree. What could Elwin be dreaming about? What could Wilton have done? It was probably just a fever dream. He was probably thinking about a time when they were younger. Wilton always tattled on them when he caught them setting up a prank. Where was Wilton? What he wouldn't give to see his brother right then.

Feffer hadn't realized he had dozed off until his eyes popped open. It took only a moment for his eyes to adjust to the dark. Something moved in the trees behind him. He gripped the hilt and shifted his position to see around the tree at his back. A fox darted off in the other direction.

He let out a sigh and leaned back against the redwood. He dozed more than slept through the remainder of the night. Several more times, he woke, grasping the hilt of his sword. But he never saw another target. His eyes were already open when the morning light came through the trees.

Ignoring the ache in his legs, arms, and back, Feffer stood. Each slow breath Elwin took held a wheeze. He shook Elwin, gently.

His eyes lulled open. "Feffer. Just a little bit longer."

Then, Elwin closed his eyes.

Feffer let Elwin rest for another hour before giving him another shake. Elwin did not rouse.

"You are going to be alright, Elwin," Feffer said. "Somehow, we are going to make it."

Once more, Feffer lifted Elwin into the saddle and continued north. He felt tears stinging his eyes.

Chapter 21

THE FATE OF THE ACCUSED

Zarah was more than a half hour early, but she was not the first to arrive. In the front row, in the place where she sat yesterday, was a woman. She wore a black dress with red trim. The fabric was a shiny silk. Her long, blond hair flowed about her shoulders.

It was the same woman as the day before.

As Zarah walked to the front, the woman's head turned toward her. Blue eyes regarded her with the casual dismissal one gave a servant. Zarah almost missed a step.

Zarah's silk dress had an embroidered hem. The design was a more modest cut across the bosom but was obviously not that of a servant. Not even one of the nobles' house heads would have dismissed her so. She walked in front of the woman and sat on the seat next to her, despite the ample seating choices. The woman's cool eyes regarded her once more. Her brow was raised and her lips were tightly pursed.

Who was this woman? She could have been of a noble family from the countryside. Perhaps she was from Paradine. The city was west of the River Serene. The Lord of Paradine sometimes forgot that he was the king's subordinate. Perhaps the nobles there were no different.

Zarah ignored the woman's stares.

Soon after, Biron's family entered and filled the first three rows. The same dark haired boy carried the toddler. Zarah was almost glad to have the woman as a shield between her and the boy's dark eyes. Zarah looked ahead, toward the empty doorway behind the chairs. That was where the inquisitors would come and tell her of Elwin's fate.

She had not seen much of Mother since the trial the previous day. After the conclusion, Mother had returned to meet with the White Council. Zarah had not gotten the chance to say more than a few words to her in the shadow realm that night either.

Mother had met with Linadria, the only other elementalist to remain in the city. Linadria was not as gifted in the Elements as Mother, but the older woman had trained Mother. Now, Linadria was always her mother's first choice for advice in all matters.

They were discussing Elwin, so Zarah had wanted to be present. But Mother had said *no*. Linadria and she needed to discuss matters that were *none of her concern*.

None of *her* concern? Even if he was a bumpkin, Elwin was her only real friend. Sure, there was Emmi and other nobles' daughters that she could talk to at socials, but Elwin was different than them. They could never understand her like he could. They would never know what it felt like to tame the Elements and the burden of wielding so much power.

Movement from the door pulled her attention. Soldiers lined the walls, bearing the crest of the Guardians of Life on their tunics. Soon, all the seats were filled, and people stood next to the soldiers. The soldiers scanned the crowds with their eyes but did not seem to move beyond that.

Again her mother entered and stood at the front of the room, adorned in her ceremonious robe. As if queued by Mother's stance, the other inquisitors entered the room, followed by Jorus. Behind their chairs, they stood above the crowd until all the whispers quieted down.

Three times the shepherd's crook struck the floor. This time, the robed figures remained standing.

"Let us all, under the Lifebringer, bear witness to this judgement. His righteous truth has been delivered to us, in regard to the fate of the accused.

"Based on testimony of Jasmine Lifesong, we have concluded; Elwin Escari, is found not guilty on the charge of *willfully* ending the life of Biron Onderhill of Justice by way of the Elements. We, the Guardians of Life, Seekers of Truth, pass judgement under the Lifebringer's wisdom."

Three times the crook struck.

Several people began to murmur, and Biron's family began to cry openly. The boy with the dark hair yelled, "No! This isn't right!" But his voice was muffled with the shouts of others. There were a few people arguing for Elwin and defending Mother. But most shouted protests.

"How could you betray us?"

"Kill the witch!"

"This isn't right."

"What about Biron's family?"

"We want justice!"

Zarah heard the woman, next to her say, "Fools."

She couldn't be sure to whom the woman was addressing, the crowd or the inquisitors.

The crook struck several more times before Zarah could hear Jorus speaking, "Order. I will have order."

The guards began hitting people with the butts of their halberds. She heard voices saying, "Silence," and, "Respect the High Inquisitor."

People covered their heads in defense or cradled wounded friends. But silence followed soon after.

"However," Jorus said, as if there was never an outburst. "We also must consider the testimony of Gond Forsithe. Elwin Escari has been seen consorting with a murderer, and he must stand to witness for the events of Benedict. He will be put to the question concerning his relations with the *dark man*, of which Gond Forsithe spoke."

"Jasmine Lifesong," Jorus said. "How long until you can return Elwin Escari from *training*?"

"I will be leaving on the morrow to retrieve him from his current location," Mother said. "But it is imperative that he finishes his current training. I will inform you upon our return."

"See that you do." Jorus said. "Until then, may the Lifebringer shelter you all in His loving hand."

Jorus struck the crook three more times. Then the inquisitors exited.

Although somewhat muffled, the arguments that had been raised before continued. The soldiers began to usher people out. Only a few used the butts of their halberd poles.

"Are you alright?" Mother said.

Zarah nodded. She was about to ask who the woman next to her was, but the woman was nowhere to be seen.

Where had she gone? A dress like that would have stood out in the crowd. The only other way out was through the dark hallway.

Mother ushered Zarah toward the exit. The evening sun was a few hours from the horizon, and only a few white clouds hung in the sky. Standing upon the steps of the temple, she noticed that the crowd in the square was facing them.

Zarah felt her mother tame Air next to her. An Air shield solidified in front of the two of them in time to deflect rotten cabbage and tomatoes.

"Let us go," Mother said. "Follow close to me."

Zarah let Air fill her and tamed her power of flight. She could feel her mother doing the same, while angling the Air shield to deflect the rotten projectiles.

When they were safely out of range, she felt the Air shield move in front to provide a buffer from the rush of wind.

"Why did you not call the guards?" she asked her mother.

"I could have," she said with anger in her voice. "But some of them might have been injured. The last thing we need is a riot."

"What's going to happen with Elwin?" Zarah said.

"I must meet with the king," Mother said. "Then, you and I have matters to discuss before we depart. Follow me."

Her mother tamed more Air and flew ahead of her.

Another delay. Zarah let out a sound of frustration that sounded too much like a shriek in her own ears. She tamed more Air and followed her mother.

The Fate of the Accused

Elwin felt himself being bounced up and down. Every bounce sent fire into his left shoulder. A foul odor filled his nostrils. It smelled of wet fur and old sweat. He opened his eyes but squinted at the brightness of the light.

His heart lurched as panic gripped him. Zeth. He had been captured. Wait. No. Feffer had saved him. The last thing he remembered was falling asleep in the forest. But why hadn't he entered the shadow realm? He forced his breathing to calm until his vision came into focus.

Elwin recognized Haven's coat. She needed a groom almost as much as he needed a bath. Before moving into the palace he only had a bath a couple of times a month, but he had grown accustomed to having one before bed every other day.

He craned his head to look around, and his head reeled as if all his blood had rushed to his head. For several moments, he held his head in an attempt to reorient himself. Once he thought he could move without losing consciousness, he raised up to look about.

Just overhead, the sun warmed his skin. He could see no sign of trees from this angle.

Haven moved at a slow but steady pace.

Elwin tried to ease himself from the saddle, and his ribs twinged with pain. Without invitation, a groan escaped his lips.

The horse stopped. A moment later, Elwin felt hands wrap around him and lower him to the ground. Tall green grass surrounded him.

Then, Feffer's face filled his vision. He had light sun freckles on his nose. Or was that dirt? His face had muddy finger smudges, wiped between unshaven hair buds.

His lips moved, but the words seemed foreign at first. After a moment, they made sense to him.

"Can you hear me?"

Elwin's mouth and throat were dry. "Yes," he whispered.

"Elwin, are you awake? Can you see me?"

"Feffer," he croaked, "where are we?"

Feffer disappeared from his vision but returned a moment later with a leather pouch. It was a wineskin. Feffer placed the opening of the wineskin to Elwin's mouth and squeezed the pouch. Several drops of water wet the inside of his mouth. The water was warm, and there was not enough to swallow. But it was good.

Elwin began to sit forward, but it was more difficult than it should have been. His shoulder screamed in protest, and the rest of his muscles didn't want to work right.

Feffer assisted him.

Once he was upright, the grass spun, as if someone had struck him with a club. His stomach heaved, but nothing came out. Elwin coughed for several moments.

"Are you alright?"

"I can't move my left arm," he told Feffer.

"Do you remember what happened?"

"Yes," Elwin said. "You saved me."

"The wound in your shoulder," Feffer said, "it isn't healing the way it should."

Elwin looked at his shoulder. It had a bandaged wrapped around it, but it felt *wrong*, somehow. And there was something else, he couldn't place. He felt a foreign power around him. It was everywhere. He could feel it in the grass and air, but that wasn't the source. Emanating a dozen paces away, he felt *something* pulsing with energy.

"What is that?"

"What is what?"

He tried to stand, but his legs refused him.

"Whoa," Feffer said. "You need to rest."

"No. It's not that. Help me up."

Feffer frowned, but he complied. He wrapped his good arm around Feffer's shoulder for support and pushed with his legs.

Across the field of grass were rows of tall trees all of an even height. Their bark shimmered in the sun light as if from a glossy sheen. The edges of the large leaves began to turn red and yellow, announcing the beginnings of autumn. The trees. The pulse came from the trees.

It was like …

"A heartbeat."

"What?" Feffer said. "Alright. You need to rest." He eased Elwin back to the ground. The soreness in his ribs protested the movement.

"Something's different with the trees. Can't you feel it?"

Feffer's frown deepened and his eyes glistened in the noonday sun.

"Did you not hear me before?" Feffer said. "Your wound. It's not right. The Death Element was used to make your cage. Maybe it is keeping your arm from healing. Or maybe it's doing something to you."

"I feel better now," Elwin said.

"You've been unconscious for days," Feffer's lips quivered. "I didn't think you would wake up again."

"Days?"

Feffer bit his bottom lip and nodded. Elwin knew that look. He had seen him make it when talking about his mother. She had died when he was young. Feffer was trying not to cry.

"I'm alright, Feffer," he said in the most cheerful voice he could summon. It might have sounded better if it hadn't come out a croak. "I feel better."

His lips felt cracked and his mouth was beyond dry. He was sure his ribs had been pummeled by pair of giants, and his stomach felt as if it had shriveled to a raisin. But he wasn't dizzy and his shoulder felt more numb than painful, so it wasn't a complete lie.

Feffer squatted next to him. "Some of the color has returned to your face."

"Where are we?" Elwin asked to change the subject.

Feffer watched him a moment before responding. "We have several days until we reach the mountains, then the Lifebringer knows how long to pass through them. Then we will be in wilderness. Once we exit the mountains, I won't know if we have traveled too far east."

Elwin nodded. "Maybe we can find a pass through the mountains instead of over?"

Feffer just stared at him for a moment. "How does your shoulder feel?"

He started to say he was fine, but he flexed it and pain stole his words. Flame traveled up his neck and down his arm, and he felt a moment of dizziness. He closed his eyes for a moment and calmed his mind in an attempt to alleviate the pain. That's when he felt a sense of *loss*.

He could feel the Air around him and sense its power. But there was something *wrong* with his essence. He tried to open his essence to let Air fill him, but he might as well have been trying to catch the fog with his hand. Focusing on it, he could feel it just above him, but he couldn't will it to move. That hadn't happened to him. Ever. Even before he had learned how to go through the forms, he could at least fumble around. His essence didn't respond.

"Elwin," Feffer's voice sounded near to panic. "Elwin!"

Elwin opened his eyes and looked at Feffer. He could see the fear in his friend's eyes, so he almost didn't tell him. But the words came out. "I can't tame the Elements."

"What does that mean?" Feffer said. "You still can't fly?"

Elwin shook his head. "No."

"Is it the wound?"

"Maybe. I don't know. I haven't been to the shadow realm for days. My essence must be depleted still. Maybe that's all it is. But, if that's the case, I shouldn't be conscious at all."

Elwin could still feel the pulse of energy from the trees. Did that have something to do with it?

"Do you think you can eat? I have a few rose berries and greenfoot nuts. Maybe once you get your strength back, you'll be fine."

The thought of food made Elwin's stomach churn. "I don't think I should do that yet."

"You haven't eaten for days. You need something. Here. Wash it down with this."

Feffer handed him the berries and wineskin. Elwin looked at them for a moment. The idea of eating made his stomach lurch. He held his breath for a moment, then popped the berries in his mouth, chewed, and swallowed before his gut was aware. He took several chugs of the water to keep the food down. Only then did he let himself breathe.

He handed the wineskin back to Feffer. He felt the bottom of it and grimaced, then he placed the cork in without taking a drink.

Elwin felt a stab of guilt. He hadn't even thought about conserving the water.

"How much is left?"

"Enough," Feffer said. His voice sounded confident, but the grimace never faltered. He glanced up at the sun. "Can you walk? We should try to get under those trees. Out of the sun."

"Help me up?"

Feffer helped him onto legs that wobbled. He had to lean on Feffer with most of his weight.

"Help me try a few steps," Elwin said.

Feffer wrapped his arm around Elwin's waist and assisted him with several steps. The ground didn't offer the support he remembered from the last time he walked on his own two feet. It was as if the earth pushed off of each footstep with different force.

It took several paces for the ground to feel right again, but he didn't let go of Feffer until he was a few paces away from the first tree. He had been too distracted to realize it, but as he grew closer to the trees, his legs felt stronger.

"Let go," Elwin said.

"Are you sure?"

As a reply, Elwin let go of Feffer's waist. When Feffer released him, Elwin stumbled the first few steps, but he was able to stay upright the remaining few steps to the first tree. The moment his hand touched the bark, he felt his essence give a start and move as if waking.

Air filled Elwin's lungs, and he felt strength return to his limbs. His pain even lessened, and some of the feeling returned to his shoulder.

"Elwin," Feffer said walking toward him. "You ... You glowed for a minute."

"These trees. I told you. They feel ...," Elwin searched for the word. "Alive."

Feffer stared at the trees for a moment. "They look planted. Look. They are all in perfect rows. And they go on for miles."

Elwin looked down a row. Each tree was spaced only a few paces apart and stretched as far as the eye could see in every direction.

"The Chai Tu Naruo," Elwin said. "This must be their grove. Maybe they can help us."

Elwin began walking into the grove.

"Wait, "Feffer said, "I need to get Haven."

Haven was only a half a dozen paces behind them, gnawing on the tall grass. Feffer took her bridle and led her to Elwin.

"Here, let me help you into the saddle."

"That's just it," Elwin said. "I feel fine. I might even be able to fly."

"No!" Feffer said quickly. "Don't push yourself. These trees are spaced enough for riding. You should get into the saddle. I just got you back." He cupped his hands for Elwin to step into. The look in his eyes held such concern, Elwin couldn't refuse him.

Once in the saddle, he tested his essence. He willed it through the stanzas of Air form without difficulty. He was certain he could fly.

"These trees," Elwin said. "I'm telling you. They must be from the Children of Nature. There is an energy. It is helping me some how."

Feffer frowned up at him. "I've seen Tharu, but I don't know much about them. Gurndol, my squad leader, said they are savages."

"Not at all," Elwin said. "Jasmine said the Chai Tu Naruo people have hidden cities in this forest. They believe their purpose in this life is to protect the balance of nature. If we can find them, they will help us. Death bound are an abomination to their ways."

"Pray we find them, then. But if not, we will be alright." His voice had a hopeful tone.

"We will," Elwin agreed. "Thanks to you."

"Naturally," Feffer said. "How many times will I have to pull your chestnuts off the fire? You really need to learn to take care of yourself."

"Nah," Elwin smiled. "I'll just keep *you* around. And what you can't handle, I have Harkin."

"Harkin?"

"I told you about my manservant."

"What?" Feffer's back became rigid. "You ... If you weren't crippled ..."

Elwin laughed.

"You know I'm going to make you pay for that, right?"

"Pay for what? Oh," Elwin said in a tone of feigned ignorance, "you mean a prank. I thought you had changed?"

"I did too," Feffer said. "But, there's something about blowing up a cage of bones and running for your life from a dark savant that makes you want to live a little. Gives you perspective. You know?"

"Black savant."

"Hmm?"

"They call themselves black savants."

"Dark, black ... whatever. Dragons take them all before I do."

Elwin flinched at the mention of dragons. Jasmine believed he would wake them. If she was right, what did that make him?

"Don't look upset, Elwin. I was just messing around. I didn't mean to curse. Gurndol's bad habits are rubbing off on me. That's all."

"No. It's not you. So much has happened this last year, and I want to do the right thing."

Feffer paused and looked at Elwin over his shoulder. "You always do, Elwin. I've been trying to make you do the wrong thing all your life. And you've never been good at it."

"I'm on trial, Feffer. For killing Biron."

"What? What do you mean, trial? The Inquisition? After a year?"

Hmm. Jasmine had been right. Feffer didn't remember.

"Yes," Elwin said. "A man named Jorus Teblin is the High Inquisitor. Last year, he placed me in the care of Jasmine. By now, the trial has already taken place. If they found me guilty, then they are going to seek me out for execution."

"Guilty of *what*? Murder? Everyone saw it was an accident."

"Guilty of being Death bound or of intentionally killing. Yes."

"That's absolutely ridiculous. I'll just have to set this Jorus straight."

Elwin smiled, despite himself. "You already did. Last year."

Feffer stopped walking. "What? I've never ... wait." He put a hand to his mouth and winced as if struck. "No. Don't tell me ... I?

I didn't?"

"You had a blood-soaked bandage wrapped around your head. Even in a state of delirium, you stood up for me."

"For the love of Life. And a right-fine job I did of it too, I'm sure. How come no one told me? Oh my ... that healer with the bosom. No *wonder* she stared daggers into me. How bad was it?"

"You accused the High Inquisitor of being Death bound."

Feffer covered his face with his free hand and groaned. "I can't believe it?! Tell me your joking. I would forgive you. I swear by my life."

"I'm afraid it's true."

"No wonder she didn't want anything to do with me."

"Who?"

"Oh, Elwin. You should see her. She had the most tender touch you could imagine and the bosom of Aridiati of legends. She nursed me back to health after I got my skull cracked open. I tried to go back to apologize for any of my ill-spoken words, but she wouldn't even see me after they released me. The Seeker take me for a fool. Now I know why. Curse it all!"

"I'm sorry, Feffer. I would have told you sooner, but I didn't see you for a year."

He waved a hand behind his head as if dismissing the notion. "I know. It would have been nice if someone would have told me, before I went back to ... I wrote her a letter, Elwin."

"You did?"

"Yeah. And unlike you, I'm not one with words. But, I said nice things, and she still refused me."

"Unlike me?" Elwin laughed. "I don't know what to say to women. Half the time I can't tell if Zarah hates me or just tolerates me. She loves me like a growth on her arm she can't get rid of."

Feffer laughed, but it sounded bitter. "At least you get to be on her arm."

"Well, until the inquisitor beheads me."

"That's not going to happen," Feffer touched his sword hilt. "I've gotten pretty good with this thing. Anyone wants to get to you, they come through me first."

"Thanks Feffer."

"You and Wilton are all I've got."

Wilton. How had he forgotten? He opened his mouth to tell Feffer the truth, but once again, he couldn't make the words come out. The silence stretched on as Feffer led Haven between the rows of trees. An hour passed, then another. None of the words he chose sounded right.

It wasn't as if he could come out and say, *"Hey Feffer, your brother brought Zeth and the Lifebringer knows how many other black savants to our home. He's the reason your father is dead, and mine is something worse. You really only have just me now, because when I see Wilton, I might just kill him myself."*

By the time the light beneath the trees turned pink, Elwin still hadn't thought of the words to tell Feffer about Wilton's betrayal.

Feffer reigned Haven to a stop and said, "Alright. I need to stop. These trees seem to go on forever. Here, take my hand."

Once his feet hit the ground, Elwin sat with his back to a tree, and a warm feeling washed over him. Feffer tethered Haven to a low hanging branch and joined him. Opening his pack, he pulled nuts and berries from a pouch and handed some to Elwin along with the wineskin.

"This is the last of our food and water. These worthless trees don't seem to produce anything edible, so pray we make it out of this forest soon."

"I'm still praying the Chai Tu Naruo find us."

Feffer nodded and began to munch on his meal.

The berries tasted tart, but they were wet. And the nut tasted bitter, but it was dry. Elwin ate them both together, which made it easier to swallow.

"Tell me more about these Children of Nature," Feffer said. "Do they all carry two swords?"

"I don't know," Elwin said. "Tharu is the only one I know of in Justice, and he's on the White Council. I've never spoken to him, so I only know the little Jasmine told me. He doesn't share much about his heritage. Apparently, they are secretive about most of their customs. He's served Zaak for more years than we've been alive. Something about his *honor quest*. Jasmine had a different word for it, but I don't remember it."

"They are a strange people," Feffer said. "But I'll take whatever help we can get. I haven't seen signs that anyone has followed us, but I have a feeling they are out there. Too many game trails for there not to be. If we find a village of people who can use swords like Tharu, we'd be fools to not ask for help."

Elwin nodded.

"Get some rest," Feffer said. "I'll take first watch."

Elwin opened his mouth to protest, but a yawn emerged instead. Elwin closed his eyes and laid back. "Wake me when you need to rest. Alright?"

If Feffer replied before sleep took him, Elwin hadn't heard.

Elwin opened his eyes and had to squint. Petals of light fell from the trees all around him. He knew he was in the shadow realm, because he could see his sleeping body. But, something was different.

He looked over to where Feffer sat and froze.

An image floated above his friend. It was a figure of pale green with features identical to Feffer. The eyes of the figure were closed as if sleeping. As Feffer moved, the image followed above like Elwin's essence followed him.

This didn't make any sense. Feffer had an essence? Did this mean he could tame the Elements? He tried to think back to Jasmine's lessons. He could almost hear her voice speak the words.

"Everyone has an essence, but only elementalists can sense it. Think of the essence as the mind's consciousness. The mind's eye of the gifted is awake. Those without the ability to tame cannot see through their mind's eye. It is as if their consciousness is sleeping."

Was that what he was seeing? Why was Feffer's green instead of white? And why had he never seen it before? He wanted to find Jasmine. She would know what it all meant. But she wasn't here.

Maybe there was a way to open his mind's eye.

Elwin went over and touched the arm of the sleeping image, and the real Feffer shivered. Elwin jerked his hand away. Then he sat and watched his friend. Had the eyes of the image fluttered open, or had that been Elwin's imagination?

Chapter 22

THE ENEMY

Bain walked down the dirt road toward the cobblestone square. He stopped in the middle of the square and looked at the inn.

The front of the building had been removed. Support beams of redwood held the front of the inn from collapsing. The reputation of the redwoods of Justice were not exaggerated, or so it would seem.

Still, Zeth's fireball had been foolhardy. Most other structures of the inn's size hit with a fireball would have been destroyed, along with the inhabitants. As it happened, his son had been in the inn when it was set aflame. Zeth would need to be reprimanded. The man had recovered his son, so the reprimand would be light.

Bain turned in a circle, glaring at the small village. If it could be called that. A dozen buildings or so had been erected on either side of the road. No training yards were there to maximize a child's potential. There were no mountains to teach him survival skills.

"This is where you left him," Bain said. "You left him with a stranger to keep him from me. You left him in a peasant's life to keep him from his destiny."

He could feel his heartbeat rise more than a thousand leagues away. Before the gift of the Father, he had not been able to travel more than a league from his body. He was beyond that now.

"Elwin would be beyond it as well," Bain said, "if you had not taken him from me."

Bain closed his eyes and forced his heartbeat to slow. He had tasks to accomplish. Allowing himself to anger would not be conducive to his goals.

"My liege," a female voice said.

Bain opened his eyes to see Lana standing in the middle of the square. Often her soul wore the attire she had adorned during the day. Her black dress had red trim and was crafted from hard cloth. Like all of her dresses, it was touched with the Elements. Her dress would protect her from extreme climates and deflect a sword thrust better than the heaviest armor.

She glided to him without moving her legs, "It is done."

"What did the inquisitors decide?"

"They have found Elwin not guilty, your grace," she answered. "However, they want to put him to the question for what Zeth did to this town."

"Being put to the question is no different than a death sentence," he said through his teeth. "They would kill my son, when he is innocent. They only condemn themselves further."

"It is as you say, my king."

"Have you spoken with your informant in the castle?" he asked.

"Aye, your grace," she said. "A woman named Linadria is the only elementalist remaining in the city. The main force of Justice's army is still garrisoned within the walls, but the Life witch and her daughter will be leaving on the morrow for Goldspire."

"Very good," Bain said. "I have a contingent of skeletal warriors and a lesser savant prepared to receive the cohort outside of Justice that is bound for Goldspire. Any survivors will not be enough to contend with Zeth, Fasuri, and the lessers that I have waiting for them."

"My liege," she said, "I must warn you. A few amongst their ranks have touched weapons and are trained to battle the Elements. Their commander, Zaak Lifesong, and two of his men, a dwarf and a Chai Tu Naruo are seasoned. They have battled with our number for Alcoa at the start of the war. They only returned to their home to prepare their own lands to receive us."

"I am aware of Zaak Lifesong," Bain assured her. "Fasuri met Lifesong in the battle for Brentwood and lost. He has been eager to regain his honor. Surprise is ours."

"What do you command of me?"

321

"You will return to my castle," he told her. "Elwin's retraining will require your tender hand."

"Your grace," she said, "will I not be better use in taking the castle?"

"There is a single elementalist," he said. "Mordeci and Emmantis have the soulless one and a score of skeletal warriors, as well as two dozen Lessers. Your skills will be better served at home."

"May I at least aid in Goldspire?" she said.

"That would be most unwise," Bain said. "Elwin might see you as his captor. I would have him see you as his ally. You have turned the ear of this other lord. Paradine? There is nothing more for you here. You will gather the Escari woman and sail on the morrow."

"Yes, my liege," she bowed, "I will do as you say."

After she was gone, Bain visited the farm where Elwin had been raised. He materialized in the fields.

It would seem the soulless one had been successful as a farmer. The evidence of the man's success would soon be no more. The livestock had been scattered and grazed freely. Soon, wolves would descend upon them or they would be recaptured by other farmers. Rows of tall stalks were flourishing, but it wouldn't be long before weeds and insects overtook them.

He looked upon the small farmhouse. The entirety of the wooden building could sit in a corner of his bed chamber. There was an iron tub to the right of the building.

His son had bathed outdoors like a savage beast.

He glided to the porch past the bench swing and through the door to the common room of the hovel. Small cushioned benches surrounded the heart where a fire blazed.

On the couch was Melra Escari with her stomach flat to the couch and her hands bound to her ankles. A leather strap connected the rope around her legs to a noose around her neck. If she squirmed an inch, she would choke herself. If she dozed off or slept, the weight of her legs would cut off her breath.

Emmantis stood next to a small table. He had been one of the first children taken all those years ago from Kalicodon. His soul was a reflection of his physical body, hard and practical. It was said the Kalicodians shared a common ancestry with the Chai Tu Naruo. Like the Chai Tu Naruo, his people wore loin cloths, but he adorned himself in trousers and a

322

sleeveless tunic. He had the shape of a warrior with long corded arms and the darkened skin of his Kalicodon nation. But he had the courage and pragmatic thoughts of a leader.

Emmantis knelt as he said, "My liege."

"I see you are giving the lady Escari all of the courtesies befitting a traitor. Very good. But make sure she still breaths when she reaches me."

"Yes, my liege."

"Are there any survivors in Benedict?"

"An old man and woman," he said, "and a dozen children. I spared them."

"The small ones don't make efficient skeletal warriors, and if they are ungifted, they have no worth to me. You did well to spare them."

"His grace is kind."

"On the morrow, command one of the lessers gifted with Air to carry the captive to Eastport. Lana will retrieve her within the tenday."

"Yes, my liege."

"Rise," Bain said. Emmantis obeyed.

"Where is Mordeci?" Bain asked.

"He is training the soulless one, my liege."

"Very good," Bain said. "Take me to him."

"As my liege commands," Emmantis said.

He felt the soul of Emmantis dissipate and materialize half a league away. Bain followed him.

The field had a score of skeletal warriors garbed in peasants' clothes. Some were wielding swords, axes or poleaxes, but many carried pitchforks or nothing at all. Their bites and scratches were an effective weapon as well.

The soulless one sat atop an undead horse. The Death mount was crafted from a living horse and bound by the same soulkey. They were as one mind, though the horse was subordinate to the man. With a thought, the soulless one could move his mount. Such a beast was the answer to a warrior's dream.

But the man with dark hair and brown eyes was no warrior. His strength was amplified and his speed increased, but he had no skill with the sword in his hand. Not as if it mattered.

A soulless one was beyond death. The most skilled swordsman could not kill the man. Hack a soulless one to pieces and his life would not be extinguished. There was but one way to destroy a soulless one.

The man Elwin had called Father moved through the sword routines at Mordeci's command. Bain studied him for a moment. There was a defiance in his eyes, befitting a warrior instead of a farmer. Bain smiled. A fitting punishment. Drenen Escari was a prisoner in his own body.

Part of a soulless one's will was his own. So long as he obeyed the commands, his own mind controlled the body. The struggle for control was the true punishment for the soulless one. Bain could order the man to kill his own wife, and he would. However he fought the command, in the end, a soulless one obeyed his master.

When next he saw Mordeci, Bain would commend him on the training.

Being in the waking world, Mordeci could not be aware of Bain's presence, even though he stood not more than a few paces away. Mordeci's asymmetric face and gaunt features belied the man's strengths. He was a precise tool. He found pleasure in the pain of others and knew how to incite fear like no other. But Mordeci had few uses beyond his cruelty.

"Perhaps the soulless one will be ready when the fighting begins."

"He will my liege."

The soulless one looked upon Bain. Their eyes met. Bain could see hatred burning in the eyes of the soulless one.

"Interesting," Bain said. "I was unaware the soulless one could see Spirits in the shadow realm. Can he hear one as well? There is still much to learn of the soulkey's power not spoken of in the book."

The man atop the horse began to tremble, and his eyes became a swirling fog. The Undead Stead began to rear, throwing the trembling man from its back.

"Poor farmer," Bain said. "He is too peasant-minded to know when he is defeated."

Bain turned to Emmantis, "I have seen enough here. You have your orders. There are other matters which require my attention."

"Yes, my liege."

Bain focused his mind on Goldspire.

Above Zarah, few dark clouds hid the starlit night. Chill wind flowed around her as she sustained her flight. She had never known the summer nights could be so cold. In truth, Zarah had never flown at night. Before now, she had always traveled in a wagon.

Though she would never admit it, flying several leagues at a time was more difficult than she had assumed. That first day had been the most taxing, only stopping for lunch before nightfall. She had collapsed before Mother had started the fire. The next several days had been marginally better.

The air surrounding Zarah gushed even colder for a moment. Beneath her wool dress, she felt goose pimples cover her flesh. She shivered and rubbed at her arms as she flew.

A hot bath, that was what she wanted. Maybe there would be a town or an inn waiting ahead. She wanted some spiced wine and a quiet place where she could brush the tangles from her hair.

She had pulled her hair into a tail for flight, but there was no time for a braid before departing every morning. The lack of a braid made her feel masculine. Zarah had seen several women with warrior tails, but they looked manly.

Mother had suggested she wear trousers instead of a dress. She opted for full leggings instead. They allowed her the modesty necessary without making her look like a boy. One would certainly mistake her for a boy if she had a warrior's tail *and* trousers. Though, the trousers would have been warmer.

Although Zarah could not see her mother ahead of her, she could feel her mother taming the flow of Air to sustain her flight. It was her beacon to follow.

Far below to the north was the small contingent. Men followed along the wagons, carrying torches or lanterns. Though she couldn't see their faces through the darkness at this distance, she knew her father would be on the horse in the lead. It had only been an hour since sunset, but it would be another hour until Father made camp.

It had taken Zarah and her mother less than a tenday to catch up to the procession. At this rate, it would take another tenday to make Goldspire.

Zarah felt her mother slow down ahead of her, and she caught up to her before she could slow her own flow of Air. It always grated her how Elwin could change directions much faster than she could.

"They were not supposed to stop," Mother said. "Wait here while I see what they are doing."

She felt Air stop flowing through her mother and watched her dive in the direction of the lights. The torches and lanterns moved back and forth in sporadic motions, and the procession of wagons had ceased.

There was a burst of power, and the rear wagon erupted into flames. It was *Fire*. Someone had *tamed* Fire.

"What in the Lifebringer's name?"

A surge of Air formed a lightning hurl. It originated just above the wagons and shot toward the rear wagon. She felt a flash of Earth erupt and the lightning dissipated.

A burst of Fire was flung at her mother, which was deflected with a Shield of water. Mother countered by throwing a lightning ball at her opponent. The glowing ball of white flew through the night and disappeared into a great explosion of crackling light. At the last a surge of Earth appeared.

Back and forth the battle went. Fire deflected by water, countered by Air deflected by Earth. Zarah felt useless, but she did not want to get in her mother's way. And she had her mother's orders to follow.

She opened her essence to more Air and tamed a veil. She felt the Air cling tightly around her body. Anyone that looked upon her would see the empty space being reflected from the other side of her.

Having just learned the trick of masking a talent, she did not have much confidence in her ability. The trick was to pull in just a little more power than necessary to tame the talent and to release at the same time to balance the natural flow of Air. This would mask the taming of her veil. But, flying as she was, it wouldn't matter much. Flying took quite a bit of power, but eavesdropping and veils did not. Masking only worked for talents that did not require much power, but she did as her mother had bidden her.

If any fighting occurred, she was to veil herself and wait for direct orders from her mother. Of course, how could she hear her mother's orders way up here?

Zarah flew lower.

People surrounded the wagons in all directions. There had to be more than a hundred of them. As she moved closer, she realized something was not right about the attacking soldiers.

Black fog leaked from their eyes, and torn faces and flesh didn't bleed. One man had a broken arm exposed to the bone, and he still clawed at a soldier as if not phased. Men, women, *and* children fought with pitchforks or hands and teeth.

Then she felt it. Like dropping offal in a clean pool, the stink of the Death Element rocked against her essence. She had never felt it before, but there was no mistaking the taint. It was the force that opposed Life.

A feeling of helplessness seized her, and she watched the battle with rigid horror.

The *creatures* outnumbered the soldiers ten to one. When one of the creatures fell, another one took its place, clawing and biting their victims.

One of the soldiers fell. Before Zarah could think to act, a dozen of the creatures surrounded him. They thrashed and ripped at his flesh. His screams rose above the sounds of battle, then cut off.

This wasn't happening. How could this be happening?

A sword of pure light came into being at the front of the wagons, swinging in intricate patterns. She moved closer to the figure. It was her father.

He was surrounded, but the creatures were not faring well against him.

Zarah had never seen her father use his sword outside of practice. He wielded it with both hands. The blade moved through the air with speed and precision. Each swing cleaved through a figure or deflected an attack. It was one continuous motion.

Several paces away, she saw Tharu and Hulen fighting together. Hulen had an axe as large as he, swinging with both hands. Every attack fell one of the creatures, but there were dozens of them.

As Hulen swung his axe, it would expose his backside. As the creatures tried to fill the gap, Tharu would dance in with his twin blades, slicing through the enemy ranks. When Hulen's axe severed a arm at the shoulder, Zarah's stomach lurched.

These *things* were no longer human, but they *looked* human. She had to close her eyes and grit her teeth to keep from becoming sick.

Beyond the wagons, she felt surges of the Elements. Flows of Water, Air, and Life wrapped around tamings of Fire, Earth, and Death. She needed to do something.

Zarah took a deep breath and opened her eyes.

Three soldiers had been backed onto the top of a wagon by a dozen enemies on each side. Back to back, they fought. Each swing was a desperate attempt to keep the creatures from overtaking the wagon. Zarah could see no sign of any other soldier.

She increased her flow of Air, letting it fill her. While positioning herself above the remaining soldiers, Zarah tamed a lightning hurl. One of the *things* was atop the wagon. She took aim as she gathered the power in her hand. The air solidified and felt like a solid rod in her hand.

Zarah threw the lightning hurl toward the creature. As the bolt left her hand it crackled and gained speed. A sulfurous odor filled the air as the lightning hurl struck the creature in its chest.

Its upper torso burst, and its left arm flew free. The sight made her stomach churn, but she gritted her teeth against the feeling.

Another one of them was climbing up the other side. However the soldiers sliced the creatures, nothing deterred them. One had lost its arm, another had a gash in its neck that would have killed a normal human.

She tamed another lightning hurl and threw it at another creature. That one was smaller than the first one had been. Zarah did not let herself think about it. As fast as she could, she continued throwing lightning at each target, trying not to watch as the rod of light struck home. Even in her periphery, each one that fell made the pit of her stomach ill as pieces of it flew aside.

Seconds felt like hours, and she felt her essence being taxed. Each rod of lightning became heavier in her hands and more difficult to produce. Even sustaining her flight became a chore. Sweat stung her eyes, and her breathing became heavy.

There were so many of the creatures. Where had they all come from?

A wind thrust originated beside her and crashed into a tide of creatures, flinging them from the wagon in every direction. Without pause, a rod of lightning hit a different target below. Then a second. And a third.

"Mother."

Alternating her throws with either hand, Mother threw lightning hurls in rapid succession. One by one the enemies around the wagon fell. Father, Tharu, and Hulen attacked the creatures from the rear. They cleaved through the crowd until only a dozen remained.

Even after the things were outnumbered, they did not attempt to retreat. Within seconds the remaining few were dispatched.

As her father's sword took the head of the last one, Zarah eased to the ground. Her muscles were weak. She felt as if something was swimming in her stomach. She bent over in time to throw up without getting any on her shoes.

She hadn't seen her mother's approach, but Zarah felt her gentle touch across her forehead. Her mother held her hair back as she emptied the contents of her stomach. After there was nothing left to come up, Zarah continued coughing and heaving for a few moments.

Zarah wiped her mouth off with the palm of her hand and straightened.

Her mother tapped Zarah's chin to make her look up at her. "I am proud of you, Zarah. Without you, those men would have likely perished."

"What were those *creatures*?" Zarah said.

"They are skeletal warriors," Mother said. "They were made with the Death Element. Just like Elwin had said. They first came into being during the Shadow Wars. They are—"

"Jasmine!" It was her father's voice.

"Here," she called.

"I need you, here!"

"Come, Zarah" she said.

Zarah followed her mother to the other side of the wagons.

Father and Tharu were huddled next to an injured soldier. Kyler, her father had called him. Hulen and the remaining three soldiers stood nearby, watching the darkness beyond them.

"Kyler is the only one fallen that still lives. He is hurt," her father said. "Can you help him?"

Kyler had scratches on his arm that could have been made from razors. Teeth marks had gone through his chain shirt and into his side. There was so much blood.

Zarah felt the power of Life emanating from her mother. Unlike the other Elements, the power of Life came from within. It was more taxing on a person's essence than taming the other Elements.

The power of Life flowed from her mother. Zarah's skin tingled as the purity of creation filled the air. The cuts on Kyler's arm and side mended as if they never were.

"I healed his physical wound," Jasmine said. "But I can feel the taint of the Death Element coursing through him. It is the same power that animated these bones. These skeletal warriors. It might take some time for me to reason out how to heal the Death Element from him. I have never seen anything like this before."

"I have," Zaak said. "Tharu?"

Tharu knelt next to the soldier, "I can ask the Lady Nature for assistance. My people have dealt with this before. Not for centuries before Bain, but we never lose any knowledge that will preserve life."

"Thank you, Tharu," Mother said. "I know what it means for you."

"Zaak. Hulen," Tharu said. "Could you hold him down?"

Father grabbed Kyler's arms and shoulders.

Hulen moved toward Kyler's feet, grumbling with his thick accent. "Why do I get stuck with the kickin' end?"

Tharu placed both hands on Kyler's side. Zarah felt a foreign power emanate *from* Tharu. It didn't start in the Air, Earth, or the other Elements. The power came from Tharu. It felt similar to how the power of Life had come from her mother moments before. Tharu wasn't an elementalist.

How was he doing this?

His hands began to glow the color of grass. The light streamed from Tharu's hands into Kyler's side where the wound had been.

Kyler began to thrash against her father and Hulen. He arched his back, and his mouth twisted in agony. Dark fog seeped from Kyler's eyes, and he let out a screech too loud and high pitched to be natural.

Tharu drew his blades and stood watching Kyler.

Several moments passed before the screeching stopped. When it did, Kyler became still.

"Is he …," Zarah said.

"He will live," Tharu said, sheathing his blades. "The Darkness of Spirit is no longer in him."

"What would have happened to him," Zarah said, "had you not healed him?"

"I did not heal him," Tharu said. "I forced his soul to battle for his body."

"What?" Zarah said. "What do you mean?"

"The Darkness of Spirit had poisoned his body," Tharu said. "His wound was great, so the longer it was allowed to spread, the less of a chance he had to win. The longer it had to spread through his body, the more difficult that battle would have been. I forced the good in him to fight against Death. Fortunately, there was much good in him."

"What would have happened," her mother said, "had he lost?"

"His soul would have been lost," Tharu said. "Body and soul would have belonged to the Seeker of Souls."

"Do you mean Death bound?"

Tharu nodded.

Her mother stood up. "Was anyone else scratched or bitten?"

The three remaining soldiers looked at one another as if the others might grow a tail or a beak.

"I wanted to be much farther," Father said. "But we will camp here for the night. We need to bury our dead."

"We lost our entire cohort," Mother said. "We cannot bury a hundred bodies and still reach Goldspire in time."

"I will not leave my men to become a feast for crows."

"I am sorry, my love," Mother said, "we do not have a choice."

"Mistress," Tharu said, his eyes downcast, "we need to dismember the heads of the bodies, or the corpses will become like the creatures we just defeated. With no one to lead them, they will roam the countryside attacking any living being."

"I can pray over their bodies," her mother said. "The power of Life will allow them to rest in peace."

Tharu nodded and spoke without lifting his eyes. "My Patwah is to Zaak Lifesong, and he already knew of this knowledge. But, as soon as we have rescued this child, I must seek penance for the knowledge I have given to the rest of you. It was given to preserve life, but I must speak with the elders of my transgressions."

Father clasped Tharu's shoulder and nodded. "The elders will not likely fault you for sharing such knowledge, but do as you must."

Then he turned to the remaining three soldiers.

"Bensen, Bender, you two start gathering the bodies. Separate ours from the enemy," Father said. "Adler, you start going through the supplies. We need to move everything into three wagons. First light will come quickly and we still need to get some rest before we travel."

"Jasmine, Zarah," Father said, "I need to speak with you."

Zarah followed her father's torch away from the others. She was not sure how to respond to being included, so she obeyed without response.

"I know you two want to pray over the bodies," he said. "But you have the right of it, there are too many men. And you are already drained. We can purify the men by fire."

Zarah saw her mother's jaw clench, and she looked away. Zarah hadn't noticed it, but Mother's eyes were sunken. Mother had fought the other elementalist *and* the skeletal warriors.

"I know you are right, Zaak," Jasmine said, "but, it does not feel right."

"No," he said. "It doesn't. But what if more of them are out there. There is a guard post not far north of here. How could so many of these things move across the countryside without notice? We have not had a runner."

Her mother nodded. "Either the guard post has been taken, or someone has been careful to avoid them."

"Someone?" Zarah said. "These things were being led?"

"The black savant," Mother said. "She was leading them with the Death Element."

"Yes. I guess I felt it."

"Where is she now?" Father said.

"Her body is over here."

"Take me to her."

Her mother led them to the rear wagon. A dark robed figure was lying on its backside. Half of the stomach was missing. The smell of burned flesh filled the area. Zarah had to hold her breath not to wretch again. The torch light danced off her face. Blond hair spilled out of a black hood, and wide blue eyes stared at them. Her father's words echoed her thoughts.

"This girl is two years or more younger than Zarah."

"And she was well trained," Mother said. "Several times, she almost bested me. There is no question in my mind. She was trained for this purpose."

Father shook his head. "How could someone do this to a child?"

"She had to have been trained to kill since the day she came into her power," Mother said. "Bain truly is evil. We must not let Elwin fall into his hands."

Father's jaw was tight. He knelt down and picked up the girl's body as if she was a sleeping child. His eyes faced forward.

"We need to burn this body as well."

"Let us be done with this," Mother said.

Chapter 23

THE STONES OF SEEKING

Elwin watched Feffer sleep like he had for the last two nights. The pale green image was still there, but the eyes had not fluttered open again. The image felt solid to the touch, and he even shook it once. Feffer shivered, but the image didn't budge.

That wasn't the only thing. There was something different about the shadow realm. If he walked more than a dozen steps from his body, it felt as if there were eyes on him. It was the same feeling he got when traveling far from his body.

Jasmine had said that with time, the distance he could travel would increase, but he lost several inches every day.

"It has something to do with this wound."

Elwin studied his shoulder. His arm was shadowy but solid. The dark lines in his shoulder were devoid of light. They grew longer, as well. It had a strange odor while in the shadow realm. During the day it felt wrong.

"Jasmine will know what to do," Elwin said. "We just need to reach Goldspire."

Elwin looked into the night. Something appeared to move beyond the sanctity of his body. He shook his head. It was probably just his imaginings.

Then, to the side he saw a large shadow move through the trees. When he looked, there was nothing there. But he could have sworn that two glowing eyes had been looking at him for the fraction of a second.

It wasn't his imaginings. The darkness beckoned him.

⟋⟍⟍

Feffer followed Elwin. He was glad that his friend was gaining strength, but he still worried over the wound in Elwin's shoulder. The dark lines grew beyond the bandage and up his neck.

This would be their third day with no water. They had resorted to licking the morning dew off of the grass. But that did not quench their thirst during the heat of the day. For that matter, it didn't do much to quench his thirst in the morning either.

"Nothing will matter if we don't find water," Feffer mumbled.

"What was that?" Elwin said.

"We need water," Feffer said. "My tongue is dry enough to catch fire in this heat."

"I have the energy to fly," Elwin said. "I could go above the trees to see if I can see a stream or a lake."

"Only if you are sure that you're up for it," Feffer said in a resigned voice. He was tired of having this argument. Besides, Elwin wanted to fly, and Feffer didn't want to die of thirst.

"I can," Elwin said. "I have regained most of my essence over the past two nights."

Elwin had tried explaining the Elements to him. Feffer wasn't sure he understood it. He had tried to compare his soul to a cup. Somehow, he could fill that cup with air?

It just didn't make any sense. Cups always had air. How could anyone fill a cup with AIR?

"If you say so," Feffer said. "I think I'll just sit here until you come back."

Feffer felt the air stir as Elwin lifted off the ground, and he felt shivers go up his spine.

"I'll be right back," he said.

"Hey," Feffer said. "How are you going to find me again? All of the trees look the same."

"Hmm. I hadn't thought of that," Elwin said. "I know. Let me borrow your sword."

"Okay," Feffer said hesitantly.

Feffer unsheathed the sword and handed it to Elwin, hilt first.

Elwin took it and flew above the treeline. Feffer couldn't see Elwin, but he saw limbs and leaves falling. Several moments later, Elwin came back down, smiling.

"Now they aren't the same," Elwin said, handing Feffer his sword.

Feffer sheathed his sword. "I guess that works."

"I'll be   right back," Elwin said.

Feffer sat down and watched Elwin disappear through the leaves once more. Haven began to gnaw on the grass. The horse was even tempered, so he let her graze freely. Though Feffer had noticed, Haven was becoming uneasy around Elwin. His friend may have his strength back, but those black lines were not good.

Feffer leaned his head against the small tree and closed his eyes. He awakened to a hand shaking his shoulder. "Feffer."

Feffer opened his eyes. Elwin had his hand out for him to take. Feffer hesitated to let Elwin help him up. Elwin claimed that it hurt less than it had, but just days before, his friend couldn't walk. A day before that, he had been comatose. Feffer grabbed Elwin's hand as if letting him help, but he used his own legs to stand.

"Feffer," Elwin said, "I have never seen anything like this. It's not far." Elwin's eyes changed to white, and wisps of light followed him as he flew a few paces above the ground. "Follow me."

"What is it?"

Elwin flew ahead. Feffer put a foot into Haven's stirrup and swung into the saddle. He had to spur Haven to a gallop to keep up with Elwin.

Several moments later, he was no longer under the cover of trees. After days of traveling under the shade, the noonday sun was bright. Feffer reigned Haven to a stop and shaded his eyes with his hands, squinting against light as much as the heat.

There were several hundred paces of short grass, the greenest grass he had ever seen. The clearing formed a circle around a raised, circular mound. Atop the mound were spherical boulders the size of small houses made of black glass.

Feffer licked his lips. Surrounding the mound was a trench of water. Elwin came to hover beside him.

"Do you think it's safe to drink?" Elwin asked.

Feffer spurred Haven to a gallop and called over his shoulder. "There's only one way to find out."

The pool was wider than it had looked. It was at least ten paces wide.

As Feffer got closer to the structure, he noticed a strange pattern etched into the boulders. He did not let that stop him. He slowed Haven to a stop a few paces from the pool and dropped from the saddle. He led the horse to the pool and Haven began to drink the water.

Reaching into the water, he found it cool to the touch. His hand shook as he brought the water up to touch his tongue.

It was crisp and cool. Fresh.

Feffer began to lap water into his mouth and felt the cold of the liquid spread into his stomach. It was painful at first, so he had to stop. But once the pain subsided, Feffer buried his head in the water and drank until his belly sloshed. Then, he splashed water on his face and tunic.

After wiping water from his eyes, he looked around for Elwin. He was a few paces to his right. Elwin's face and hair were soaked as well.

Their eyes met, and they both laughed. Feffer splashed water at Elwin. His friend laughed and splashed water back.

Feffer turned his head aside and continued splashing water. For several moments, he felt small splashes hitting his side. Then, a wave of water hit him and knocked him into the pool head first. It was deep enough that he could not touch his feet to the ground.

The water felt good, but he hadn't had time to catch his breath. He swam to the surface with all his might. The wall to the pool was slick, but he grabbed hold of the grass and was able to pull himself out of the water.

"Not fair, Elwin."

Feffer looked up. Elwin was on his knees, and he had both hands raised to his head, gritting his teeth, as if in pain. His eyes were wide. For a moment, his pupils appeared to swirl like fog.

"What in the abyss?" Feffer said. "Elwin, what's wrong?"

Elwin's head turned toward Feffer. And his friend's eyes regarded him as if he had never seen him. Elwin's hands trembled and his body began to spasm.

Then, Elwin stopped shaking, and his eyes returned to normal. Elwin blinked a few times with a dumbfound look on his face.

"Did I fall asleep?"

"No." Feffer did not remember grasping the hilt of his sword, but he released it. "Your eyes were like the skeletons that Zeth made. I thought ..." Feffer wasn't sure what he had thought.

"I was dreaming," Elwin said. "I saw shadows. It was like my first time to the shadow realm. There was a dancing fog. It doesn't make any sense."

"You mean," Feffer said, "it was like the night you met *Abaddon*? The night before you killed Biron?"

Elwin winced. "Yes. It was like that."

"I'm sorry, Elwin. I didn't mean it like that. You scared me."

"It's alright," Elwin said. "I didn't meant to scare you."

Feffer glanced at the water. "Why do you think it happened?"

"I don't think it was the water," Elwin said. "You drank it too. Nothing happened to you."

"But, I am not like you. I don't have your *gifts*."

Elwin nodded. "It could have something to do with taming the Elements."

"Maybe you should avoid using them then," Feffer said, "until you talk to Jasmine."

"What do you think these stones are?" Elwin said.

Feffer gritted his teeth and tried not to curse. He hated it when Elwin avoided a topic by changing the subject.

"Elwin," he said. "You'll avoid them?"

"Sure," Elwin shrugged. "Let's take a closer look at these."

Feffer followed Elwin into the water. They swam to the other side, but now that they were there, he could see that the mound was over three paces high. The glassy wall was slick.

"How are we going to get up there?" Feffer said.

"I could fly us," Elwin said.

"You said you would avoid using your powers."

"I don't see any other way up it," Elwin said.

"One last time, then."

"Grab a hold of me."

Feffer swam to Elwin and clasped his arms around his waist. He felt his body raise out of the water and tensed, not relaxing until the black stone was beneath him. Atop the platform, the autumn breeze felt cool. He shivered.

"How do you feel?" Feffer said.

"I am alright," Elwin said. "This is amazing."

Feffer looked at the spherical boulders.

The round stones were larger than they had appeared, and there was nothing to support the boulders from rolling. Each sphere was three times the size of a man and spaced the same distance apart. Except there was one, much larger than the rest at the platform's center.

"What do you think they are made of?" Feffer said.

"It is obsidian," Elwin said. "They come from volcanos. These marks are called eloiglyphs"

"How could you possibly know that?"

"I have a book that talks about exotic stones and where to find them. It talks about rubies, diamonds, and emeralds, also. And Jasmine is teaching me to read eloiglyphs, though ... I don't know any of these. Oh wait! This one means travel."

"Eloi-what? I have to start reading more," Feffer said as he walked up to a boulder. "What do you think they do?"

Feffer froze when a sing-song voice spoke.

"Do not touch the Stones of Seeking, lest you know that which you seek."

Feffer placed his palm on his hilt. "Who is there?"

"In your language I am 'He Who Rides With Wind.' To my people I am Da kairuo wut Whudin. But you may call me Daki."

The voice had come from behind the central boulder. Feffer turned his head as slowly as he could to glance at the figure through his peripheral.

The man's hands were held up in a passive manner as he approached them. There was confidence in his gait. His height was not much more than Elwin, but his grace was comparable to a large cat. Feffer wanted to draw his blade just to test his skill against him.

The green in his eyes was as vibrant as the grass below, and his long, black hair flowed freely past his shoulders. He had a clean face with olive skin. Feffer would guess Daki to be of an age with him. Like Tharu, he wore nothing, save the white skins of some animal stitched together, which only covered the necessary parts. The leather strapping protecting his feet were made from the same beast's skin. Two curved blades like the ones Wilton carried were strapped at either hip.

"I uh … I am Elwin Escari and my companion is Feffer Madrowl." Elwin gestured toward Feffer.

"I am honored to know you both." Daki's bow was deep but awkward.

"As we are you," Elwin said.

Despite his desires to find help, Feffer did not remove his hand from his hilt.

Daki nodded toward Elwin. "You are of my visions. I have been waiting 'in the place where stones bend truth' to save 'he who is chased by the dead.' Your enemy is now my enemy."

He knelt to the ground before Elwin.

Feffer shared a look with Elwin, before walking over to stand between his friend and Daki.

"Chased by the dead?" Feffer asked, "Zeth? How do you know that? More importantly, how do we know we can trust you?"

Daki cocked his head to the side and raised an eyebrow. "If I wished you harm I would not have revealed myself but instead would have slashed you down without warning." His tone suggested that he was explaining something as obvious as, "one must breathe air to live."

And his tone was so genuine, Feffer felt a bit foolish. Still, he didn't remove his hand from his hilt. "How did you get up here? Did you fly?"

Daki regarded them with unblinking eyes. His forehead creased.

"He is Chai Tu Naruo," Elwin said. "Remember, I told you they cherish their secrets."

"I am as you say," Daki said. "Knowledge is a burden to carry. It is a gift, which always has a price, paid by he who bears the knowledge. The penance is his."

Feffer felt a profound amount of annoyance. After days of wanting to find help, this was what he had to deal with. A thumping riddle. "Can you at least tell us what this place is?"

"It is the Stones of Seeking," Daki said.

"You already mentioned that," Feffer said through his teeth. "What is its purpose?"

"That knowledge need not be yours to bear," Daki said. "It will not aid you in your quest."

"What do you know of our quest?" Feffer asked.

"Only that the Darkness of Spirit pursues you, and you will need my aid to survive."

"We are grateful for your help, Daki," Elwin said. "We are making our way to Goldspire. If you know it, you can lead our way."

Feffer grabbed Elwin by the arm and pulled him closer, whispering, "Why are you telling him where we are going? He could be working with Zeth."

"He is Chai Tu Naruo," Elwin said just above a whisper. "We were just saying how it would be nice to find help. I don't believe he means us harm. I can't explain it, but I feel a *connection* with him. Besides, we need the help."

He had been ready to argue, but his heart wasn't in it. As much as Feffer hated to admit it, Elwin was right. Without help, they might never reach Goldspire.

"I can take you to Goldspire in a tenday's time," Daki said.

"A tenday?" Feffer said. That was half the time he had figured. Maybe Daki would be a help to them after all. Still, he kept his hand near his sword hilt.

"Is there food near?" Elwin asked. "We have not eaten in days. We need to find nuts or berries."

"There are not any within the Grove," Daki said. "But if we move swiftly, we can find food in two days."

"Two days!" Feffer said. "Another two days without food?"

"The body is a slave to the mind," Daki said. "Do not allow your needs to master you."

"Well," Feffer said. "My mind is a slave to my stomach. And my stomach is in rebellion."

Daki's eyes caught hold of Elwin's neck and tensed. "The Darkness of Spirit is on you, but it has not defeated you."

Daki looked away and his brow furrowed.

"That is why I need to reach Goldspire," Elwin said. "There is someone waiting there for me that will heal me. She is a master of the Elements of Air and Water, and she is Life bound."

"This," Daki said. "This cannot be healed by the Elements." Daki turned his eyes away. "The wound is no longer physical."

"Of course, it's physical. I can *see* the wound," Feffer said. "What do you mean?"

"I cannot speak more," Daki said.

"Curse it all," Feffer said. "Fine. Help us reach Goldspire then. We are wasting time here."

Daki nodded. "This way," he said and led them to the edge.

"It is deep enough that you will not strike bottom," he said. Then he leapt into the water.

Feffer jumped in, and he felt Elwin hit the water right behind him. Once he was on the shore, his stomach growled at him. The talk of food had made him more aware of his hunger. He stuck his face in the water and drank all that he could, attempting to appease his empty stomach. Then he returned to his pack, retrieved his wineskins, and filled them with water.

When he finished, the other two were both were for him by Haven. Daki eyed Elwin's shoulder warily, his muscles tense.

"Curse it all," Feffer said beneath his breath. Then louder, "Lead the way, Daki."

Elwin sat next to his own sleeping body, watching Daki settle next to Feffer who had already fallen to sleep. His friend's image rose almost the moment Feffer leaned against the tree. He had pushed himself to near collapse to find them some help, and now that he had, Feffer looked at Daki as if he had a tail. After the events of recent tendays, Elwin couldn't blame Feffer's hesitations to trust someone they had just met. But Elwin knew he could. The moment he had met Daki, Elwin had felt some unexplainable connection with him.

Elwin looked at his shoulder. It didn't ache. In truth, he could no longer feel any pain from the wound, but the black lines had climbed up to his face and across his chest over the course of the day. He no longer questioned why the sanctuary around his body had grown smaller and smaller.

He couldn't walk more than a pace away without feeling the eyes upon him. It seemed he couldn't escape it in the waking world either. Black fog kept appearing in his vision that caused him to go into a stupor.

In the stupor, he could almost hear a whisper of a voice. He had the feeling it wanted him to do something, but he couldn't even guess as to what. If he could figure that out, maybe he could stop his sanctuary from shrinking. If not, he didn't want to find out what happened when his sanctuary vanished completely. Was that even possible? He needed to reach Jasmine.

He looked out toward the dark of night. The eyes were waiting for him out there. How long until his body did not protect him from Abaddon? What would happen then?

Daki's breathing slowed, and Elwin flinched when a pale green figure rose from Daki's body. When the eyes opened to regard him, Elwin jumped out of the radius of his sanctuary. The feeling of being watched was instant.

He moved closer to his body, gaping at Daki. The image stood a foot taller than the body it had come from, but it was still far shorter than Elwin was in the shadow realm. Daki too gaped at Elwin, craning his head to meet Elwin's eyes. "You're an elementalist?" Elwin said.

Daki shook his head. "No. I have been blessed by the Lady Nature's Embrace. It is not the same as your gifts from the Father."

Elwin waited for him to continue, but Daki only stared at him. Then Daki turned to look at Feffer, and he flinched as if struck by a hammer. He looked at Feffer for many moments before turning back to face Elwin.

"What is it? Elwin said. "Is there something wrong with Feffer?"

"I have never heard of one outside my people receiving Her Embrace."

"I'm not sure what you're speaking of, but I am pretty sure his mind's eye is closed. I thought that once he opened it, he could tame the Elements like me."

Daki looked back to Feffer and didn't speak for several long moments. "I may tell you things that I cannot tell others. But there are some truths I cannot share with you either. I will tell you that he is not an elementalist. Of this I am sure."

Again, Elwin waited for more, but Daki only stared at him.

"How can you be sure?" Elwin pressed.

Daki's gaze weighed Elwin for a full minute before he said, "The Grove. This is where the Lady Nature's Realm touches the Realm of Shadows. Both realms are encouraged to coalesce here because of the Grove. That is why you can see me. This must be why she wanted me to meet you here. To ensure you would know of Her Embrace."

"Her?"

"The Lady Nature," Daki said reluctantly. "She has come to me in my dreams and given me her true name. She is the one who led me to you."

Elwin didn't wait to see if more was coming. He felt certain Daki would be content to stare at Elwin until morning if he did not press the conversation forward. "Why? To what end?"

"I do not know," Daki said. "But when I do know, I will be ready."

"Ready for what?"

"What comes next."

That wasn't going anywhere, so he decided to change his line of questioning. "What can you do with the Lady's Embrace?"

Daki glanced at Elwin's shoulder. "If you survive the Darkness of Spirit, you will see."

"Can you tell me anymore about this ... Darkness?"

"Only that when it happens, you must remain pure."

"Great," Elwin said, trying not to sound too annoyed. "That helps a lot."

Judging by Daki's smile, he didn't quite grasp sarcasm.

Elwin looked out to the darkness. He began to seeing movements in his periphery, but when he turned to look, nothing was there. Desperately wanting it to be his imagination, he tried his best to ignore it until morning.

Chapter 24

NEW FRIENDS

Elwin's breath caught when Haven carried him into the clearing beyond the grove. The light of the sun felt like a tidal wave of heat, and his limbs felt heavy. For the first time in days, his shoulder began to throb and his stomach felt ill.

Daki took hold of Haven's reins. "The Grove no longer protects you. It will come soon."

"It?" Feffer said with his hand on the hilt of his sword, looking around for an attack.

"How soon?" Elwin asked.

"I cannot know," Daki said with a shrug. "Hours. Minutes. Soon."

"What is he talking about?" Feffer half drew his sword.

"Your sword will be no use," Daki said. "Neither will mine. It is a battle he must fight alone."

"Curse it all," Feffer glared at Daki. "I wish you wouldn't speak in thumping riddles."

"We should move," Daki said.

"Are those the mountains?" Feffer asked, pointing north.

Fighting the urge to wretch, Elwin looked up. A field of tall grass stood before him. On the horizon he could see a forest. Beyond that, trees rose higher and higher into the sky.

"That is what your people call the Goldspire Mountains," Daki said. "We will make shelter shortly after nightfall. A friend awaits for me nearby."

"Does this friend have food?" Feffer said.

After having only water for a few days, the idea of food still made Elwin's stomach churn. Without a stream, they would be out of water soon as well.

Daki looked at them both for a moment, then nodded as if coming to a decision. "Aye. He will have food, but let us rest here for a moment. Gather wood for a fire. I see game tracks."

Without another word, Daki ran into the high grass, and he disappeared without a sound.

Feffer leaned on his knees and squatted as if he wanted to sit. "That man is part horse."

"Lucky we found him," Elwin said, climbing from the saddle.

Feffer shook his head. "I don't like the way he looks at you, Elwin. How do we know we can trust him? And what did he mean by *it* is coming soon? What is *it*?"

"The Darkness of Spirit. It is coming for me. I don't know what will happen, but it doesn't sound good."

"What in the abyss are you talking about?"

Elwin struggled to keep his voice calm. "My shoulder Feffer. The bone fragment was tainted with the Death Element. It has done something to me. I think," Elwin swallowed. "I think, I will have to face Abaddon."

"Dragons take me!" Feffer said. "What in the thumping abyss does that even mean?"

Elwin took a deep breath. "I don't know, Feffer. But, there is something else you need to know."

"What?" Feffer said.

The Death Element did something inside Elwin. He could die or worse. He could become like Drenen. Worse, he could become like Zeth. What would happen to Feffer if that was the case? Elwin met his friend's hazel eyes and saw strength. And trust. Feffer had to know, and Elwin owed his friend the truth about his own brother.

"I have wanted to tell you this, but I didn't know how. And I didn't want to hurt you."

"Hurt me? Elwin, what is it? You can tell me anything."

Just out with it then. There was no easy way to say it.

"Wilton," Elwin said. "He betrayed us. Wilton was the one meeting with the black savant in the shadow realm the night I learned Zeth was going to Goldspire."

Feffer's face became blank, and he stared at Elwin for a full minute without saying anything.

"Say something," Elwin said.

"You lied to me?"

"I'm sorry," Elwin said. "I didn't want to hurt you."

"But you *lied*. To *me*."

"I know. I'm sorry. I wanted to tell you the truth, but ... you only have me and Wilton left. I didn't want to take that from you."

"Why now?"

Elwin looked at his shoulder and followed the black lines down to his hand. "This could kill me, Feffer. And you deserve the truth."

Feffer's eyes lingered on the lines before returning to Elwin's face. "It's not possible. Not Wilton. He would never do that to me. It was a trick. They fooled you somehow."

"No," Elwin shook his head. "He is the one who betrayed us, Feffer. He called the black savant by name, and the man knew Wilton. Think about it. Wilton is a thief-catcher. He could have helped us. But where is he?"

Tears filled Feffer's eyes, and he looked away. He stumbled a couple of steps and sat in the grass. Elwin sat next to Feffer, and placed an arm around him. "I am so sorry, Feffer."

"It doesn't make sense," Feffer said between sobs. "How could he do that to me? To our father. Our father is dead now. How could he work with a dark savant?"

"I don't know, Feffer," Elwin said. "I saw it, and I still can't make sense of it."

Feffer sat up and his tears cut off. "What if Zeth or this Fasuri *made* Wilton betray us, somehow? What if he did that soulless power on Wilton?"

"I don't know," Elwin said. "I don't know what they can do with the Death Element. I don't know what all I can do with my *own* abilities."

"We have to hope that we can save Wilton somehow," Feffer said. "I just can't believe that he would *willingly* cause us harm. It was Zeth. I *know* it was. We will save him, Elwin."

Elwin nodded. The hope in Feffer's voice left little room for argument.

"But promise me something?"

"Anything, Feffer."

"Never lie to me again." His voice took on a wry tone. "Even if my Ma comes back from the grave and starts stealing babies, I want to know."

Elwin gave him a weak laugh and said, "I promise." And he meant it. Elwin *could* trust Feffer with anything. And Feffer was strong enough to handle anything Elwin told him. He nodded to himself. There was something else Feffer needed to know. The Awakening. Elwin wasn't sure if he even believed it, but Jasmine and many others did.

Elwin sat up straighter upon coming to a realization. Others *did* believe. Zeth and Bain believed Elwin would be the one to Awaken the dragonkin. That's why they wanted him. *That* was what they thought he was destined to. Why? Why would they want to loose that on the world?

It didn't matter. Feffer needed to know. Elwin opened his mouth to tell him, but Feffer jumped to his feet and drew his sword. By the time Elwin stood to join him, Feffer had already lowered his weapon.

Only then did Elwin see Daki, but his heart raced and legs wobbled. He leaned on his knees for support.

"Curse it all," Feffer said, sheathing his blade. "You shouldn't sneak up behind people."

Daki gave Feffer a nod of approval, quickly followed by a look of disappointment. "Where is the firewood?"

Daki carried a medium sized rabbit. It was gutted, skinned, and drained. And it had been tied to a wooden stick with strands of bamboo. Daki jammed the end of the stick into the ground.

"That was fast," Elwin said. "You tracked it, killed it, *and* cleaned it, while we sat here?"

"There were two, but one eluded me," Daki said. He smiled, "I thought you would have already burnt through your wood by now waiting on me."

"We can gather wood," Elwin said, standing up straight. "We will meet you back here."

"Not you," Daki said at the same time Feffer said, "You can barely stand."

Daki and Feffer exchanged a look. This time, Feffer gave the other man a nod of approval. They got on either side of him and began to ease him to the ground.

"You should sit," Daki said as if Elwin had any say in the matter.

"Fine. Fine. I'll sit. You two get wood."

"We should gather twigs in the Grove," Daki said. "They burn very well as kindling."

"We'll be right back, Elwin. Food will make you feel better." He turned to Daki. "After you."

Feffer's legs gave a slight wobble as he followed Daki toward the trees of the grove a few paces away. Elwin shook his head. Feffer needed food and rest as much if not more than Elwin.

Elwin could still hear their voices as they gathered wood.

"Why do you call it a Grove?" Feffer asked.

"Because that is what it is," Daki said. "I do not understand your question."

"Yeah," Feffer said. "But *you* say Grove like *we* say Lifebringer."

"I am sorry," Daki said with confusion in his voice. "I cannot say I understand your meaning."

"What I mean to say," Feffer explained, "is you say 'Grove' with reverence."

"Should I not revere the Life-giving Grove?" Daki said. "Without the trees, we would not have Life."

"But they don't *create* Life," Feffer said. "They are not the Lifebringer."

"But don't they?" Daki asked. He continued collecting fallen branches and kindling twigs. "Do you not *feel* them exhale? Without their air we would not have breath."

"What are you talking about? They are just tree," Feffer said, emphasizing with the stick. "This is what they are good for, firewood and woodworking."

Daki stopped and placed his hand on a tree. He closed his eyes, letting out a slow breath before speaking. "This tree for instance. She has a Spirit within her that lives, breaths, speaks, and feels. Her Spirit has wisdom to those who can hear her voice."

"Can you really talk to animals and travel miles through the trees like the stories say?"

Daki chuckled. "Anyone can speak to an animal. It is listening that requires patience."

"Bah," Feffer said. "You're impossible to talk to. This should be enough to get a fire going. If you find a larger log, I will begin to work with this kindling."

Feffer stomped back with a scowl on his face. He dropped the wood and marched over to the saddle bags, mumbling curses as he fumbled through them.

Daki had no expression as he placed the wood atop Feffer's, and he said nothing before turning toward the trees and disappearing into the forest.

"We need to clear this grass and make a fire hole."

Feffer dropped to his knees beside Elwin and pulled the grass up from the roots. Elwin helped him. When the ground was exposed, they began to dig at the dirt with fingers.

"The hole needs to be wide enough to breathe," Feffer said.

"When did you learn how to build a fire?" Elwin asked.

"While you were playing with books in the castle and ordering about your *manservant*, I was in the woods and fields, learning useful skills."

Elwin laughed, "Like hunting?"

Feffer looked at him for a second. "I can hunt, but I need more than a sword. Hand me those larger pieces."

Elwin helped Feffer arrange the wood and kindling. Then Feffer placed some of the pulled grass between the wood. He rummaged through a pocket, and he pulled out a metal flask, along with flint and steel.

"I also brought lamp oil."

Feffer removed the top of the flask and sprinkled some of the oil onto the dried grass. It only took one strike of the flint and steel to catch fire.

Daki returned with two pieces of wood that made a Y-shape and a small log. He placed the log on top of the kindling and arranged each Y on either side of the fire pit, then he placed the skewered rabbit atop the pit. As the rabbit roasted, Elwin's stomach began to feel stabs of pain that made him feel queasy.

"I could eat the rabbit whole and two more, besides," Feffer said.

"I am pleased that you are pleased," Daki smiled. "A little while longer."

For several moments, the only sound was that of the crackle of the fire and scraping wood as Daki turned the skewer.

"I have to ask you something," Feffer said. "You look to be our age. Why are you in the woods all on your own?"

"These woods are a part of my Plauo Tu Patwah, path of proving. A boy must become one with his Patwah. Once he finds his path and masters it, he may return to his people a man. For some, the path is long, for others the path is short. If one does not master his path, then it masters him. Either his disgrace will be his end, or he will wander the world alone, forgotten by his people."

"But you're *our* age," Feffer said, again. "And your psarents abandoned you to fend for yourself in the wild?"

Daki smiled. "I do not expect one from the soft lands to understand the ways of my people. Nature is not nearly so wild as that of the men of cities. Are there not men amongst you that kill each other simply to take what he wants or for pleasure?"

An image of Zeth came to Elwin's mind. And of the burning village that had once been Bentonville. "There are those type of people amongst us."

"Ah. You see. Animals kill out of necessity for sustenance, or in defense, trying not to become food for another. My people are closer to Nature. Our ways are not yours. My parents did not abandon me here. I chose this for my Patwah. More accurately, it has chosen me."

Daki's gaze settled on Elwin. "Can you not feel that we are one? Our destinies are connected despite our choosing. Despite your … taint."

Elwin nodded his agreement. There *was* something. He could feel it in the same way he felt his essence. He still wasn't sure what it meant.

"I do," Elwin admitted. "I've felt it since the Stones of Seeking."

Feffer scowled at Daki.

Daki stood and turned the rabbit. "It won't be long now."

"What would you have done," Feffer said, "if we hadn't let you come with us?"

"That was not our fate. I was fated to travel with you."

"Do you ever give a straight answer?" Feffer said as if not expecting any answer at all.

"I gave you truth," Daki said. "What other answer should I have given?"

"I will take that as a *no*, then."

"I like you Feffer," Daki said. "You seem to always hear the answer that you need. You are wise."

Feffer's scowl only deepened.

Daki pulled a piece of the meat off the top of the rabbit and tasted it. Some of the juices dripped from it into the fire, causing the flames to sizzle and pop.

"It is good," Daki said. "We can eat the outer layers."

Feffer didn't hesitate. He reached for the rabbit and began to peel off pieces, but he juggled the meat back and forth before shoving it in his mouth. "Mmm. Good."

"Elwin," Daki said. "You should try to eat."

His stomach lurched at the thought, but Elwin began to take strips off of the rabbit. Although the heat stung his fingers, the meat peeled off with ease. He shoved the first bite into his mouth and moved it around to keep from burning his tongue. As the juices touched his tongue, he felt a chill move up his spine. His queasiness vanished, and he began to chew the meat. He felt a moment of pain as the bite went down and filled his empty stomach.

Feffer's look suggested, he felt much the same. He drank on the waterskin and passed it to Elwin. "This will help."

Elwin took a sparing gulp. And the water did ease the pain. Then, as if he had never taken a bite, hunger took hold of him. He peeled off another bite and took a sip to cool the meat. After taking his turn to peel off meat, Feffer reached for the waterskin and Elwin handed to him. After taking a drink, Feffer handed the water to Daki. This rhythm continued until the rabbit was almost gone. Each bite tasted as good as the last. In moments, the rabbit became mostly bone.

Feffer pulled the skewer from one of the ends and held it up.

"We can't get past the bone until it cools."

Daki stood and kicked dirt onto the fire.

"We have many hours until we meet my friend," Daki said, "and it appears as though the Darkness will not come for you just yet. Let us be off. My friend will have more food for us."

"Then you two don't mind if I have the rest of this?" Feffer held up the rest of the rabbit.

"I can't eat any more," Elwin said. "My stomach doesn't seem to hold as much as it did a few days ago."

"Can you eat it while we travel?" Daki said.

"After you," Feffer smiled. "Can you help Elwin into his saddle?"

His legs still wobbled as he stood, so Elwin took Daki's help into the saddle. The other man took the reins and guided Haven north. Feffer blew on his skewer as he trailed behind, gnawing to get to pieces of meat.

Plains of grass gave way to copses of trees in thick patches. If cleared, these lands were flat enough to yield crops. Elwin envisioned a farmhouse between the collection of trees. Instead of a porch swing, he could tie a hammock between those two small redwoods, both good for climbing.

How long had it been since he climbed a tree? Part of him wanted to drop from the saddle and run to the tree. He would have to jump to reach that lowest branch, but it wasn't too high. Though it would have been a challenge the year before.

His fantasy shattered, and he had the sudden feeling of being watched. He looked over his shoulder, but the field behind him was empty. Shaking off the feeling, he looked back to the tree. Zarah would call him a country bumpkin just for thinking about climbing trees. He had no need to climb trees, when he could fly to the top.

Feffer threw the remnants of his rabbit bones aside and frowned. "How much farther?"

Daki never slowed his trek. "After this large thicket, we will reach a round clearing. It is not more than two leagues beyond this. We will be there by nightfall, if not before. "

Feffer groaned a complaint, but his face became resigned to the task. He walked on the other side of Haven and patted the mare's side. Feffer reached to take the reins from Daki but stopped midway, using the same hand to wipe at his mouth. Elwin could almost see the thoughts passing on Feffer's face, as he studied the Chai Tu Naruo. Daki had given him a meal, so he couldn't be all that bad. Elwin almost laughed. Apparently, the way to Feffer's heart was through his stomach.

Daki continued to lead the horse, and Feffer fell into step on the other side, scanning the countryside as they walked. As promised, they stepped into the clearing where white peaks loomed on the horizon. In the distance, Elwin could make out the beginnings of a forest that stretched as far as the eye could see in both directions.

"Just a little farther," Daki said.

Elwin glanced up. The sun had little more than an hour left before it disappeared in the western sky. The feeling of being watched returned, even stronger than before. He looked around trying to find the source, but it seemed everywhere just like ...

Elwin held his breath. Just like when he left his sanctuary in the shadow realm.

"Good," Feffer said, "I am not sure how much farther my legs can carry me."

Daki began to angle them east but still veered mostly north. By the time they reached the forest on the other side of the clearing, the sun had touched the edge of the horizon. As the light began to wane, the feeling of being watched became more intense.

Night would be upon them soon.

Elwin felt a giggle coming to his throat, but he stifled it. What had gotten into him? He shook off the feeling and ignored the unseen eyes. He tried to focus his thoughts on his surroundings, but his vision kept blurring. Even with his eyes closed, Elwin knew the moment when dusk became night, because the unseen gaze seemed tangible.

A thin fog appeared in the trees, but he could see the waning moonlight begin to trickle through the trees to guide their path. Shadows moved through the trees.

Haven must have sensed something as well, because she began to fidget and dance.

"Alright," Feffer grabbed the reins and pulled Haven to a stop. The horse stamped and moved as if wanting to run. "We need to make camp. You said we didn't have much farther, and I can't see where I am going any longer. I can barely see Elwin and Haven right in front of me. I have lamp oil, but we should stop. I don't want Haven to step into a hole and break a leg."

"We are here," Daki said.

"Where?" Feffer said, "I don't see any shelter."

"That is a good thing, don't you think? Our shelter is well hidden. Look through that copse there." Daki pointed ahead, just a few paces in front of them.

"I can't see anything," Feffer said. "It's just more trees."

Through the growing fog, Elwin could see the grouping of trees. The copse rustled as a large, dark shadow emerged making a deep groan. Haven reared, and Elwin clung to the saddle to keep from being thrown clear. He grabbed a hold of her rein in time to keep her from bolting. His shoulder throbbed from the effort and his vision began to blur.

Feffer unsheathed his sword and stepped in front of the dancing horse.

"Wait! This is my friend!" Daki moved in front of Feffer and raised both arms as if in surrender.

The large figure lumbered forward on all fours and stepped into strands of moonlight. Its brown fur was clean and tasseled around the neck with rope made from bark. It moved up to Daki, sniffing his hair. The massive bear plopped down onto its rear and opened its mouth into a massive yawn.

Daki scratched with both hands in between the bear's shoulder blades. "This is my friend, Taego. Taego, this is Elwin, Feffer, and Haven."

Feffer sheathed his sword with a little too much force. "You could have told us your friend is a thumping BEAR." He moved to take Haven's reins and whispered soothing words in her ear.

The fog began to thicken, and his shoulder throbbed from exertion.

Daki shrugged. "Well, we are here. Come. He has fish. Tomorrow we must begin our journey through the mountains. We are near the Jojindun tribe of mountain giants. They are aggressive. I can lead us past most of the dangers, but we must work as one if we are to survive."

"Thumping great, Elwin did you hear …"

Elwin tried to focus on Feffer's face, but the black fog filled his vision.

"I need to rest," Elwin heard himself say.

Then, he leaned from the saddle to climb down. But, the fire in his shoulder spread to his other muscles, and he could no longer feel his grasp on the pommel of the saddle. Before he could fall, he felt strong hands around him. He fought to remain conscious for as long as possible.

Daki's voice sounded strange. "Let us get him inside."

Chapter 25

THE DARKNESS AWAITS

Upon entering the shadow realm, Elwin did not move away from his body. But he opened his eyes and looked around.

The foggy moonlit haze of the shadow realm lit up the small cave. Feffer and Daki stood over him.

Somewhere in the distance, he heard echoes of a deep-throated laugh.

"What is happening?" Feffer demanded.

"It is happening," Daki said.

"What? This Darkness of Spirit? What do we do?"

"There is nothing we can do. It is up to him now."

The echoes of laughter grew closer.

"Dragons take your thumping soul. What is up to him?"

Unperturbed by Feffer's curse, Daki sat next to Elwin. "Everything."

Cursing, Feffer sat on the other side of Elwin, fingering the hilt of his sword.

Next to his ear, Elwin heard a low growl.

Without turning to see what it was, he flew straight up through the cave's ceiling.

Bain sat on the shore in front of his castle. He knew it wasn't possible, but he could hear her singing. Though he couldn't make out the words, he

remembered the tune. *She had sung the song to Elwin.*

The Father had not spoken to him in days, but he felt an energy in the air. It was the same as when the Father spoke to him but somehow different. It was pure like She was.

Was he going mad?

She had died. He watched her be consumed. He had felt her life force snuff out like the fire of a candle being pinched from existence. Why was he hearing her voice?

"*Elwin will be mine once more my love,*" *he said to the singing voice.* "*There is nothing you can do to stop me this time. He will Awaken them, and the world will be mine.*"

❧

The laughter followed Elwin out of the cave.

He flew high into the sky. In the shadow realm, he didn't have to tame Air to fly. Similar to dreaming, one could just move in any direction.

Elwin thought he could hear a woman's voice. She was singing a wordless lullaby. It made him think of Zarah. The voice was south and east. He followed it.

Below him, he could see shadows moving in the trees. Hundreds of shadows. That's when he saw that the shadows had eyes. Hundreds of pairs of eyes like fire looked up at him from the tops of the trees. The shadows began to fly toward him.

He could feel his body several miles away. His shoulder pulsed with pain and his heart was beating faster. His breath became labored, and he could feel sweat rolling down his cheeks.

That's when a thought occurred to him.

"I need to wake up."

He returned to his body. Then he laid down atop his sleeping form, like he had always done in an attempt to step back into the waking world. But nothing happened. For several moments, he remained inside his body willing himself awake.

But he did not wake up.

❧

Zarah sat across from her mother. She could hear her mother's voice, but she did not hear her words. There was a fire between their sleeping bodies. They had camped just off the road where the three remaining wagons were parked. The men slept atop bedrolls on the other side of the road.

In a few more nights the moon would no longer wane. It would be dark, then begin waxing. Perhaps this was a good sign. New things to come.

That thought could not take hold.

The image of the guard post plagued her thoughts. There was blood everywhere but no bodies. All of the soldiers would have had chain shirts and the royal crest. The skeletal warriors they had killed all had peasants clothes. That meant there were more of them out there.

Their home was under attack.

To their east was the Carotid Forest. It spanned most of the northeastern part of the island, from Justice all the way to the Goldspire Mountains, stretching to the east coast.

"Zarah," Mother said, "repeat what I just said."

"I am sorry, Mother," she said. "I cannot stop thinking about the guard post. It is difficult to listen to lectures on undead."

"Zarah," she said. "This information will likely save your life. You need to understand how each type of the undead can be killed."

"I know, Mother. But, what if we do not find Elwin? What if Zeth has captured Elwin since we last spoke to him? I cannot just pretend that all is well and listen to lectures. How many people have died? Our country is it war. How many people will die?"

Mother watched her for a moment. Then, she said, "You are becoming the woman I always knew you would become. I am proud of you Zarah. You will be a great advisor to this kingdom after I am gone."

Zarah felt her cheeks flush at the compliment. "I am worried. What if we lose?"

"I am worried, too, Zarah. But, we must have hope. We have not heard word of attack from any of our major cities. All of them have elementalists in them patrolling the streets for these black savants. Whether we have him or they have him, we must still have hope."

Zarah nodded. "I do have hope."

"Good," she said. "Now, tell me how to kill a vampire."

❧

Elwin flew through the clouds toward the singing voice. The shadowy forms were moments behind him. He knew that he could not return to the cave again. They would be waiting for him there.

He closed his eyes, thought of his farm, and willed himself to it.

The deep laughter became distant once more, but it would find him again. Elwin went inside the house. The fireplace was cold. A stool by the fire was overturned, and the fire poker had been left on one of the sofas.

His mother had not returned. She would never have left the house without everything in its place.

Elwin looked out the window toward the Carotid Forest. Shadows emerged from the trees and moved toward him with increasing speed.

He took one last look at his parents' house and came to a realization.

"I can never come back here."

Elwin jumped into the air, passing through the roof, and he flew toward the woman's singing voice.

❧

"The Element of Life is the best weapon against all undead," Zarah said. "But the other Elements work very well if used properly. For instance, the lightning hurl is effective against skeletal warriors."

"How does Life work as a weapon against undead?"

Zarah sighed. "Undead are abominations to Life. They were created by Death. Healing them with the Element of Life is harmful to them. I still do not see how that would work, but if you say it is true, then I believe you."

"I admit," Mother said, "I have not tried it myself. I have not faced many undead. But I have read much lore that speaks of this. The healing power of Life unmakes them. I should have tried it on the skeletal warriors, but I will still have my chance, I fear."

"We do not have long before first light," Zarah said. "Can we take a break?"

"One more time," Mother said. "What is the best way to kill a vampire?"

A flash of light appeared before her, and Zarah jumped backward.

Rather, she willed herself backward at a rapid pace. She stopped when she recognized the face in front of her.

"Elwin," she breathed.

He took hold of each of her arms. There was something different in his touch. His purity was still there, but there was a taint. It emanated from his shoulder. He was wounded. Dark lines covered his face and spread thinly over the rest of his body.

She heard a low voice laughing in the distance.

"Elwin," Mother said. "What are you doing here? Wait... What is that? You are tainted."

"I have nowhere left!" he said. "Nowhere is safe! He is going to take me!"

"Elwin!" Zarah said. "What is going on? What is wrong with your shoulder?"

"When I escaped," Elwin said, "some bone fragment from the cage pierced my shoulder. It didn't heal properly. My body is not safe. I no longer have a sanctuary, and Abaddon can get to me there."

Elwin looked over his shoulder, toward the tree line. "They are coming."

"I don't see anyone," Zarah said. "Who is coming?"

"Elwin," Mother said. "Where are you right now? Where is your body?"

"We have just arrived to the mountains. Daki said that we could arrive in Goldspire within half a tenday or so. Do you hear the woman singing?"

"Daki," Zarah said. "Who is Daki? What woman?"

"They are here," Elwin said, and he flew straight up.

Zarah could only see an empty field and the trees beyond the clearing. "Elwin, wait!"

He was less than a dozen paces above the ground and darkness enveloped him.

"ELWIN!" Zarah screamed. "Mother do something!"

Zarah started to fly after him, but stopped as the darkness vanished, taking Elwin with it.

Floating above her body, Zarah stared into the empty night trying to make sense of what she had seen. Gone. Elwin was just ... gone. The sun began to shine its first rays of light on the edge of the horizon.

A new day was coming.

Chapter 26

THE BATTLE FOR A SOUL

Zarah kicked out of her bedroll. Her mother had already risen.

"Mother," she said. "What happened to him?"

"I cannot be sure, Zarah. He said that the bone from his cage pierced him. That must be how the Death Element tainted him. The taint felt like Kyler's had. That has to be it."

"What does that mean?" Zarah asked, though she knew what her mother would say.

"I believe Elwin is battling for his soul."

"We have to help him," Zarah said.

"Listen to me." Her mother stepped toward her. "There is nothing we can do for him from here. We need to break camp and keep moving. The battle will be his to fight. He has a good soul. You and I both know this. If he wins, he will need us to meet him in Goldspire. When we find him, we will help him. Alright?"

Zarah nodded. Then she bent to her bedroll and started re-rolling it. The leather strap was sewn in. She tied the roll closed.

Father came around the wagons, and Mother greeted him. She could not hear her words, but she knew what she would say.

Mother had not spoken about what would happen if Elwin lost the battle. But she understood the implications. If Elwin lost his soul, then he would be lost to Abaddon's will. That would make him Death bound. There was only one penalty for becoming Death bound.

"This is not right," she walked over to her parents. "Can the Seeker force Elwin to become Death bound?"

"I have never heard of it," Mother said. "But I had not heard of being able to force a person to battle for his soul until Tharu showed us the truth of it."

"I have to speak to Kyler," Zarah said.

"There is a reason that he is lying in the back of a wagon instead of steering a wagon," Mother said. "Kyler is injured and needs his rest. He has already told us what he knows."

"But he did not tell us anything useful."

"Zarah," she said, "you are to let him rest. Is that understood?"

"Yes, Mother."

"Good," she said. "Now, load your travel gear. The men are already packed for travel."

The morning spilled in from the opening of the cave, and Feffer's eyes jerked open. He had not meant to fall asleep, but Elwin had not moved upon falling from the saddle. To Feffer's *ungifted* eyes, this so-called *Darkness of Spirit* looked a lot like sleeping. Maybe Daki was a prankster.

Feffer sat up.

Daki sat next to Elwin without moving as he had the night before. Not a prankster then. Maybe, the Chai Tu Naruo was simply wrong. Or maybe this *Darkness* was like this *connected-ness* they had spoken of.

Elwin's eyes popped open. Swirling black fog filled his eyes, and Elwin's mouth twisted, as if he was pained.

A high-pitched squeal escaped his lips.

Daki was standing over Elwin with both blades in his hands, faster than Feffer thought was possible. Taego rose almost as quickly and hunched toward Elwin, baring his teeth.

Feffer pulled the sword from its sheath and stood over Elwin. "What are you doing?"

Recognition entered Daki's eyes, and he lowered his blades. Taego did not back down. The bear growled. The sound was loud in the small cavern.

Feffer's heart raced, and he fought the urge to drop his sword and run from the cave. Thumping bear. How could someone become *friends* with a thumping *bear*?

"Taego," Daki placed a hand on the back of the bear. "It will be alright."

The bear closed his maw, and he leaned back against the cave wall.

"How did you do that?" Feffer said, though he did not lower his sword. He tried to watch the bear and Elwin. "Never mind. I don't care. What is happening to Elwin? Tell me! I know that you know."

There was sadness in Daki's eyes. "His battle has begun for true. There is nothing we can do but sit and wait."

"Battle?" Feffer said. "What are you talking about? Wait for what?"

Daki looked away from him.

"Tell me!" Feffer yelled. "Thumping tell me what is happening to him!"

"The Darkness of Spirit battles for his soul," Daki said. "We must wait to see who wins."

"His soul?" Feffer said. "How will we know who wins?"

Daki met his eyes. "If Elwin does not win, he will try to kill us."

Feffer lowered his blade. Elwin's teeth were clenched and all his muscles tensed. More importantly, the dark fog seemed thicker than before.

He was running in a field of wildflowers. They were yellow. The sun was low in the eastern sky.

Why am I running? he thought.

He stopped running.

"Where am I?"

He looked around. There was a forest to the east and hills to the west. North, he could see a road winding east toward the horizon. Shouldn't he be following a road?

Behind him to the south, mountains loomed.

"Hello," he called. "Can anyone hear me?"

It seemed like he should be running. But he wasn't sure why. "Is someone there?"

There was a low hum. He tried to listen to it. The voice was strained, but it sounded like a woman's humming. It came from the east, away from the road.

But roads led to places.

He started running again. Reaching the road seemed important. As it neared, he could see a wagon. It was a tall wooden wagon, and it was parked in the middle of the road. Two horses stood in front of the wagon. The carriage was slightly tipped in the front, leaning toward the other side.

He walked around to see the wheel to the wagon had broken off, and a man in black robes was trapped beneath it to his waist. He had pale skin and long, black hair. The man's dark eyes regarded him. He thought he knew the man, but the man was *wrong*, somehow.

All of his instincts screamed for him to run, but he couldn't leave. This man needed help.

"Please," the man said. "Help me."

He moved closer to the man and saw the side door to the wagon stood open. Jewels, gold, and platinum spilled onto the ground. Littered beneath the coins were books. The books were all leather bound tomes, their pages yellow with age. The books seemed to be more important to him than the jewels or coins. Rain would ruin them.

The thought tugged at a memory, but he couldn't bring it to the surface.

Leaning up against the rear wheel was a large jagged sword without a sheath. Beside that was a spare wheel.

He heard a voice whisper in his ear, "Kill him. This wealth can be yours. You can be the king of all. Just kill him and take what is yours by right."

"No," he told the voice. "I have to help him."

He ran to the wagon and tried to lift it, but it was too heavy.

"Help me push," he said to the man. But the man had lost consciousness.

The humming became louder. He could almost make out the tune of a lullaby.

The man's neck twisted toward him, and his eyes opened. In place of his eyes were a void, blacker than night. The man's voice was deeper than he thought possible. "You belong to me, now."

He backed away from the man but tripped on a book.

Dark shadows appeared all around him. They had the shape of small humanlike creatures. There were hundreds of them running toward him from all directions. He had no where to run. If only he could fly.

The image of a girl entered his thoughts. She had a smooth face, long auburn hair, and dark eyes. She had a name. Why could he not remember it?

Just as the darkness enclosed him in its grasp, her name graced his memory. "Zarah."

Elwin Escari's blond hair bounced about his shoulders, as he swung down from the lowest branch of the large, redwood tree. The short sleeve of his green tunic snagged as he dropped onto the dirt road beside the tree. He stopped to inspect the tear.

"Phew," he told the empty road, "it's not that bad. Mother will probably never notice."

The anticipation of climbing that particular tree was the reason for wearing the brown trousers. Dirt was harder to see on brown. After they were wiped to his satisfaction, he checked the coin purse at his belt loop that his father had given him. It still dangled on his belt. Satisfied that he was presentable, he walked up the dirt road in the direction of the town.

The sun hit its zenith by the time Elwin reached the first building at the edge of town. He could see Danna placing new candles in the window of her small shop. It, like the rest of the buildings in Benedict, had been constructed of the strong redwoods from the Carotid Forest to the north, which Elwin could see at the edge of the horizon.

The summer's cool, northern breeze brought the apple-scented candles to Elwin.

Danna's dark hair was pulled back and tied up. A smudge of red wax had dried to each cheek, just below her eyes. Elwin noticed that her apron was covered in waxes of various colors, but her linen dress remained spotless. Danna smiled and waved as he passed.

He waved back and continued into town.

The rich smells from Warne's Apothecary on Elwin's right and pungent odors from Jansen's Brewery on his left provided a stark contrast to the sweet-scented candles just moments before.

Several more paces brought him to the town square in front of his Poppe's Inn. Across the square was the Madrowl dry good shop. Didn't he need to do something there? He walked toward the step, but stopped.

A woman's voice was humming a lullaby in the west.

To the east, a man walked toward him. He wore black robes and had long, black hair. Elwin thought he knew him, but that wasn't possible. His mother and father did not like him to talk to travelers.

His stomach felt unsettled. The closer the man came to him, the stronger it felt. Elwin felt the need to run, but he could not make his legs move. He felt angry at the man, but he could not say why.

The man's dark eyes regarded Elwin with recognition. "Hello, Son of Bain."

Why did that sound familiar?

"You are mistaken, sir," Elwin said. "My father's name is Drenen."

The man's hand blurred toward Elwin's face, then he found himself on the ground. He looked up at the man, feeling the sting across his face as an afterthought.

"You ... you struck me."

"You are pathetic," the man said. "Living on a farm has made you weak."

Elwin heard the door to the inn open.

His Poppe exited, carrying a large broadsword. "You get away from him!"

The man smiled. "I will make you an offer, Son of Bain. If you leave with me now, I will let the peasant live. If you resist me, I will destroy all that you hold dear."

His Poppe had slayed trolls and evil wizards, surely he could defend Elwin against one man. A thought in the back of his mind nagged at him, but nothing coherent came to the surface.

"I am not going anywhere with you," Elwin said.

Poppe took a step toward them. "I said back away from the boy."

The man held his hand in front of him, palm facing upward. Red embers appeared and disappeared around him and a small ball of flame appeared above his palm.

Elwin blinked. How had he …? The question vanished in the next moment.

The man threw the ball of flame toward his Poppe. Time seemed to slow. He could see the ball of fire expanding as it flew toward his grandpa. The sword fell from his Poppe's hand and moved toward the ground as if through water. Both Poppe and the man moved the same speed as the falling sword.

Elwin could see a smile in the man's eyes as he watched the flame move toward Poppe. His grandfather covered his face with his arm and turned away from the growing ball of fire.

When the flame hit Poppe's side, it made a loud noise, then burst.

The intensity of the blast hit Elwin in the face, and he closed his eyes against the heat. He felt his body moving through air, until a solid surface slammed into him. It took him a moment to realize he was laying on the ground.

He pushed himself to his feet and looked all around, but Poppe was no where to be seen. The front of the inn was missing and the roof was on fire. Where his grandfather had been standing was the broadsword. The man stood between Elwin and the blade.

Dark eyes followed Elwin's gaze to the sword.

The man smiled. "Go on, then. Take the sword, farmer."

Elwin did not hesitate. He walked wide of the man and grabbed hold of the sword. It was lighter than it had looked, but it did not feel awkward. He was sure that he had held it before. But that did not make sense. His Poppe rarely let him in the private dining room where he had kept the sword. And he would never have let him hold it.

As the man in the black robes walked toward him, Elwin held the sword in both hands and broadened his stance. This, too, had a familiar feel.

"You are too weak to strike me down, farmer." The man dropped to his knees and threw his head back, exposing his throat. "Let me make it easier for you." The man closed his eyes.

Elwin looked at the man's pale neck, where his life vein pulsed. Elwin could hear his own heart beating. He gripped the hilt in both hands and held the sword high.

He could hear a woman singing somewhere in the distance. Her voice was louder now. Elwin could hear her words lulling him.

> Sleep my weary child,
> Rest your eyes for a while.
> My love shall always endure.
> So, your heart must stay pure,
> There is nothing you need fear,
> Mother will always be near.
>
> Sleep my weary child,
> Rest your eyes for a while...

Elwin dropped the sword.

"No!" The man's eyes opened, but the whites were gone. He turned his head toward the singing and shouted, "This is my realm! How are you here?"

The man's face contorted into a look of rage, and the void of night looked into Elwin's eyes. "You *will* be mine Son of Bain."

The sun vanished from the sky, and his surroundings faded away. But worst of all, he could no longer hear the woman singing.

Elwin held his baby girl in his arms, while Zarah napped on the bed. There was a wooden bassinet next to the bed. The white bedding with pink trim matched the blanket he had wrapped around his sleeping baby.

Both of his ladies slept soundly. The thought gave him a feeling of peace.

He needed to put Asa down, but he didn't want to wake her. Asa needed her midday nap. Soon, he wouldn't have a choice. Within the hour, there would be a White Council meeting. An emissary from Alcoa had arrived and wished to discuss the terms of the alliance with Justice, under the new ruler.

Bain Solsec was his name.

The name seemed familiar to Elwin, but he couldn't quite place it. King Alcoa had died without producing an heir. Some mystery surrounded Alcoa's death, but the emissary was to shed light on this as well. For the first time since the founding of the great nation, a man not of the Alcoan bloodline ruled Alcoa.

Elwin had never met King Alcoa, but for some reason this saddened him. Maybe, it was because he realized the importance of family now that he had one of his own.

He watched his wife from the balcony. Now that Asa was here, she couldn't get enough rest. Her face was as smooth as the day he had met her, five years prior. They had to get permission from the king to marry, since he was not of noble birth.

If not for his ability to tame the Elements, he would have likely never received permission. But then, he would have likely never met Zarah. Or if he had, it would have been as a soldier. Like Feffer, he would have been recruited all of those years ago.

But unlike Feffer, Elwin doubted he would have become a thief-catcher. With Wilton's disappearance, Elwin had been surprised Feffer had wanted to become one.

Elwin often wondered what had become of Wilton. For Feffer's sake, he had inquired about Wilton. His squad had been sent to a northern island that had been raided by an unknown enemy. They were never heard from again. A few months later, without explanation, the enemy left the Island Nations altogether. Later there had been a search for bodies. None were ever found.

When Wilton and his entire squad had disappeared, Elwin hadn't wanted Feffer to follow in his older brother's footsteps. Nothing Elwin had said could deter Feffer. But the streets were safer now with Feffer patrolling them.

Elwin pushed those thoughts from his mind and looked down at Asa. He almost wished she would open her brown eyes, just so he could see them. Her hair was too short to determine what color it would be, but the little she had was light colored like his. She had her mother's nose and his high cheek bones.

Asa Escari was beautiful.

Elwin walked around the bed and eased her into the bassinet. She stretched when he released her, opened her eyes for just a moment, then fell back to sleep. Her lips curled into a brief smile.

He walked over to the balcony and leapt off, taming Air before he fell and flew above the castle. His destination was a spire facing the River Serene on the other side of the castle. He reached the balcony he needed within moments. The doors were open to provide a pleasant view for the emissary.

Elwin landed just inside the room next to the redwood table, long enough for a few dozen people. Even though the light of the sun gave the room ample light, several dozen candles burned in the crystal chandelier that hung above the table's center. The lacquered chair at the head of the table was larger than the rest. A small crown had been carved from the wood atop the chair. White tapestries lined the walls with the symbol of Justice embroidered in red, a sword with the hilt replaced by balanced scales.

He had been the first to arrive. Elwin did not think that he was that early. Jasmine had always beaten him to meetings. Perhaps she was indisposed with greeting the emissary.

As the balcony doors slammed closed, he felt a trickle of power. It was Air. A veil had been concealing several black robed figures in a circle around the room. All but one had their faces hidden behind hoods, a man standing next to the table.

He had pale skin and long dark hair. At first, Elwin thought his eyes were black, but they were a deep blue color. The man looked familiar, but he could not place his face.

"What is the meaning of this?" Elwin said.

"I have been searching for you for some time," the man said. "I am Zeth."

The name had a familiar tone. "Do I know you?"

"Resist him," whispered a woman's voice in his ear. He looked to the black robed figures behind him, but they were too far away. Where had the voice come from?

"You do not know me," he said. "But I know you, Son of Bain."

Elwin heard a ringing in his ears, and he remembered the image of a burning inn. It looked like the Scented Rose. But that wasn't possible. He had just seen his Poppe's inn at the Summer Solstice Festival last month.

"Why did you call me that?"

"Your bloodline has a greater purpose, Son of Bain," Zeth said, "which means, she has a greater purpose as well."

Another veil was released. Next to Zeth, a black robed figure appeared, holding Asa. She was still wrapped in her white blanket with pink trim. Her eyes were closed.

How had she not woken up?

Zeth pulled a knife from beneath the folds of his robes and touched it to the top of the blanket, near Asa's throat, "The blood of his blood shall Awaken them, and the dragonkin shall rule the land once more. Are you familiar with this line?"

Elwin felt his muscles tense.

He could hear a voice singing. Zarah always sang the tune to Asa, but it wasn't his wife's voice.

Sleep my weary child,
Rest your eyes for a while ...

It sounded as if the woman was in the room. None of this made any sense. Was he dreaming?

He pushed the words of the song from his mind. "Give her to me, now, or I will destroy every one of you."

Even as he said the words, they sounded *wrong*. Not that he was making an idle threat. He had only trained for five years, but he knew that he *could* destroy them all. But he only wanted Asa back, safe in his arms.

"Come now," Zeth said. "That is no way to speak to an emissary. We are here to speak of a truce. Do you wish to insult an allied kingdom?"

Elwin took a few steps toward Zeth.

"Stop, right there." Zeth brought the steel of the knife to touch the skin of Asa's neck.

Elwin stopped walking, but his heart became like thunder in his chest. He could feel the Air surrounding every figure in the room. He could feel Water from the moisture of last night's rain around him. The stones beneath their feet held the power of Earth, which he could tame to crush them all. The heat of the sun lingering in the air could be tamed to engulf them all in flames.

Asa's eyes lulled open. For some reason he couldn't rationalize, he did not want her to see the knife.

Elwin opened his essence to Air, Earth, Fire, and Water, allowing them all to flood into his essence. He began to tame Air to hold the knife in place. As he did, the light in the room became brighter, far beyond the incandescence of the chandelier's capabilities. He had to squint to see.

"No!" Zeth's voice became deeper than was possible, "He is mine. I almost have him."

The woman's voice spoke, "He will never be yours."

The intensity of the light became too great for Elwin to see anything. He covered his eyes for fear of being blinded.

"Asa!" he cried. "Give me my child! What is happening?"

Then, a blanket of warmth covered him, and a feeling of calm washed over him. He could no longer feel any power in his essence. Arms surrounded him and picked him up, like he was a child. It felt as if strong arms carried him, and he couldn't remember what had been so important just a moment before.

The sun was warm in the blue sky, but the breeze was cool.

Elwin sat on a green field speckled with white flowers. He picked one. Rounded at the base, it narrowed toward the top, then flowered outward making lips all around. He wasn't sure what it was called.

A woman stood before him. He had not noticed her a moment ago.

She wore a simple white gown with long sleeves. Her long blond hair hid her face as she bent over to pluck a flower. She flipped her hair over her shoulder and sniffed the petals. Her smile made the day seem brighter. Her eyes were crystal blue, like his, and she had smooth cheeks.

He would place her age at not more than twenty years.

"These are tulips," she said. "They were always my favorite flower."

"Your voice," Elwin said. "I know your voice."

"As you should," she smiled.

"Who are you?"

"My name is Athina."

Elwin remembered his dreams. Zeth had been in all three of them. Then he realized, "Asa wasn't real."

"None of it was," she said. "Yet, it was more real than you know. But that is over now."

"You were the one singing," Elwin realized. "What is happening?"

"Abaddon, the Seeker of Souls, has been battling for *your* soul," she said. "And he lost."

He remembered falling asleep in the cave and being chased through the shadow realm. His dreams that followed had seemed as real as ... *this*.

"I am still dreaming."

"Yes, in a way," she said. "And you will wake soon."

"I don't understand," Elwin said. "How were my dreams a battle? How did I win?"

"Abbadon is the greatest deceiver the world has known," Athina said. "He was trying to poison your soul with greed, malice, and hate. But he was blinded by his own vices, and you could not be corrupted."

Elwin looked away from her.

"What is the matter?"

"I remember how angry I was," Elwin said. "I was ready to kill Zeth. If I had stayed for much longer, then I think I would have. What does that mean?"

"There are those in this life who are born to oppose the evils of this world," she said. "Destroying evil does not make you corrupt. Finding joy in your heart in *causing* destruction is what makes one evil. Did you find any joy in the moment you decided to kill him?"

"No," Elwin said. "It felt wrong. I never want to kill anyone ever again. I only wanted to save Asa. I would have done anything to save her. I would have killed everyone in that room to protect her from them."

"That was Abaddon's error," Athina said. "Your actions were born from a place of love, not hate or malice. That is why Abaddon could not gain power over you. He *is* malice, hate, and deceit. Every time you denied him, he lost power over you."

Elwin stood up. "Your voice. You sang to me in every one of the dreams. I heard you my first night in the shadow realm. Who are you really?"

"You are my heart, Elwin," she touched his face. It made him feel at peace. "I am with you everywhere you go."

Her skin began to fade, as if she was an apparition.

"Wait," he said. "What happens now?"

"You must wake," she said. "And always remember … The good that is within you is greater than the evil that is in the world."

Then she was gone.

Elwin's eyes began to lull. He sat down. The ground was soft like a feathered bed. He laid on his side. Perhaps he would rest for just a moment.

Elwin blinked several times. His eyes were dry.

Light filled the cave, but his surroundings were slow to focus. Feffer and Daki stood over him, holding their weapons. Taego watched him with unblinking eyes.

"They're blue." Feffer's voice held a tone of disbelief. He lowered his sword and looked at Daki. "His eyes are blue."

"What else would they be?" Elwin said.

Daki smiled, "The Darkness of Spirit is no longer in you." He sheathed both of his blades with a single motion.

Elwin tried to sit up, but his muscles were slow to respond. Both Feffer and Daki rushed to help him into a sitting position and leaned him against the cavern wall.

"I feel like I have been running for days without sleep," Elwin said.

"What happened?" Feffer said.

Elwin thought about his dreams for a moment. They felt like memories of events that had happened rather than dreams. He could remember the feel of holding Asa. In that dream, he had memories of being married to Zarah. He felt his cheeks flush. Those memories would be difficult to forget.

"I was dreaming," Elwin said, "but I wasn't. It is difficult to explain. I don't think that I understand it myself."

"But," Feffer said, "you are fine, now?"

"I think so," Elwin said. "I just feel really weak."

"Perhaps, we should rest here for one more day," Daki said.

"No," Elwin shook his head. "I need to get to Goldspire. I need to get to Zarah as fast as possible. And Jasmine. Give me a few moments. I think I can sit a saddle."

"Elwin," Feffer said. "We will only be delayed by one more day. It has been several tendays."

"I found them last night," Elwin said. "Before I was *taken*. I need for her ... uh ... them to know that I am alright."

"Can't you find them, tonight?" Feffer asked.

"I am going to try," Elwin said. "But I am not sure how I even did it. I just remember that I had nowhere else to run. Then, I closed my eyes, preparing to be ... I thought I was going to die. But, when I opened them, there she was. Then, I was taken."

"Taken by what?" Feffer asked.

"Abaddon," Elwin said. "The Seeker of Souls."

Feffer stared at him with a blank expression. Daki looked toward the exit.

"Help me up," Elwin said.

Feffer and Daki both offered him a hand. He let them do most of the pulling and used the cavern wall to steady his legs. They felt weaker than he wanted to admit.

"I can ride," Elwin said. "You will have to help me into the saddle."

Daki crossed his arms over his chest. "I will take us to the pass. But I will not take us farther, until you have rested."

Feffer was nodding, and his mouth made a slight frown.

"Alright," Elwin said. "Where is this pass?"

"We will travel west along the mountain's base," Daki said. "Then we will come to a crevice that will pass us through the mountain, rather than over it. It will save a day or more of travel. On the other side of the pass will be the Mystic Valley. This is giant territory, so we need all our strength."

"I am fine," Elwin said. "By then, I will be as good as new."

Elwin ducked to walk out of the cave opening, and Feffer followed close behind. His legs wobbled with each step, but he forced them to comply with his will to leave the cave. Elwin had to move bushes and limbs aside to pass through the copse. He was careful not to let them fling back at Feffer.

On the other side, the trees were not as thick but still thick enough to hide the opening to the cave. The rock face behind the thicket went straight up. Even craning his head, he could not see the top of it.

"A whole mountain," Feffer said. "And I never even saw it."

"It was dark," Elwin said. "I didn't see it either."

Elwin realized he had been moving his shoulder around without the lingering soreness. He pushed his shirt aside. The black lines were no longer there. There was a round, pink scar about the size of the tip of his small finger. "The lines are gone," he told them.

Feffer let out a long sigh. "I would be lying if I said that I was never worried."

"Maybe we will survive this after all," Elwin said.

Feffer raised an eyebrow. "Did you not hear, Daki? We have to pass giants."

"I just fought the Seeker over my soul and won." Elwin shrugged.

"I think I can handle a few giants. Besides, I don't think giants can fly. Have you heard that they can?"

"No," Feffer said, "But neither can I. And don't be pompous." He shivered. "Let's not talk about that other thing. You're fine now. Let's just get out of these woods."

"We have to wait for Daki."

Feffer slapped at a bite-me on his neck. "Where in the abyss is he?"

As if summoned, Daki exited the copse, the bushes did not so much as rustle. A small pouch of white leather hung from a cord around his shoulder. A moment later, the copse rattled as if shaken by a giant's hand, and Taego emerged.

"Finally," Feffer said swatting at a fly. "Can we get out of this giant and bite-me filled abyss already?"

"If fate smiles upon us," Daki said, "we will not see any giants. I can do little about the insects."

"Well," Feffer said. "Pardon me, if I don't trust *fate*. Fate has not been to kind to me over the last couple of tendays."

"Don't mind him," Elwin said. "He is always grumpy until he has eaten."

"We are not far from sucrais."

"Sucrais?" Feffer asked.

"Bushes that hold red berries the size of a fist."

"Lead the way," Feffer smiled.

Chapter 27

HUNTING GROUNDS

Elwin looked up. A tower of grey cliffs stretched up for leagues on either side of him, just wide enough for light to squeeze through. In a few places, both sides would come together, making a bridge across the narrow passageway. They had to coax Haven to climb over or crawl under the joining boulders. But for the most part, they could just walk, sometimes two abreast.

Elwin followed behind Daki. Ahead of the Chai Tu Naruo, Taego lumbered forward as far from the horse as possible. Feffer trailed them at a distance to keep Haven under control. Despite two days of traveling with the bear, the horse remained skittish. Not that he could blame her. Traveling with a bear wasn't exactly an everyday occurrence.

He had to admit, the bear seemed more docile than even Haven. Elwin no longer worried whether the bear would grow hungry and decide to eat anyone. In fact, the bear seemed to prefer berries and nuts to anything else. He snubbed rabbit but loved fish. But Haven didn't seem convinced the bear was harmless. Maybe she would with time.

Elwin liked riding her, but it felt good to be using his own legs again. He felt stronger than he had since before leaving Justice. It had taken half a day to reach the pass, then they had camped the remainder of that day to rest. That night he had entered the shadow realm to find the protective sanctuary around his body in tact. He had tried to find Zarah, but he could not figure out how to do so. Focusing on a location, he could *will* himself to *be* there, but no matter how he had focused on Zarah, nothing had worked. He felt like a coward, but it had actually been a relief. Elwin may have *defeated* Abaddon, but he still feared him. He did not want to feel those unseen eyes on him ever again. Now, he knew what lurked beyond sight. He felt a chill and shivered.

At first light, they had entered the crack in the mountain. A full day of travel had taken them most of the way through the pass. Before long they would emerge into what Daki had called the Mystic Valley. And it couldn't come soon enough. The Elements felt different here.

He could feel the power of Air, but the power of Earth overpowered almost everything. If pressed, he could probably tame enough energy to fly, but it took effort to even pull Air into his essence. He had tried to open himself to the power, but he had to actively focus to draw any in. And it was too exhausting to be productive. He could sense the power of Water even less, though Fire was still in abundance. Heat still emanated in the rocks and air around them.

Still, even Fire paled in comparison to the overwhelming power of Earth. Many times, he found himself opening his essence to Earth without thinking about it. The last time he had tamed power without knowledge, he had killed someone. Fortunately, releasing the power was the same as it was with Air; otherwise, the experience could have ended in disaster. Being that there was a mountain on all sides of him and all.

"We are almost there," Daki said.

Without seeing the sun, he couldn't track the hours. But when they had stopped for lunch a few hours past, Daki had said it was noon. If Elwin had to guess, he would say it was the sixteenth hour.

Long before seeing the path widen, Elwin felt the power of Air rush toward him. He almost opened his essence to it just to feel the power fill him, but he refrained. His essence felt no lasting effects of the battle for his soul, but he wanted to conserve his strength for what may lay ahead.

A few more paces, and Elwin could see the bright of day. Judging by the sun in the western sky, he had been correct on his estimation of the hour.

Taego stopped at the opening and Daki knelt down. He placed a hand on the bear's back and peered into the valley.

Elwin looked over Daki's shoulder. Extending from the opening, countless large boulders, stacked atop one another, sloped downward into a natural stair-like formation. To his right, the rocks of the mountain rose to great heights and stretched far to the north. Below and above, trees had grown as far as the eye could see. Beyond the trees at the edge of the horizon, he could see white peaks rising into the sky.

"Wow," Feffer said in Elwin's ear.

"Welcome to the Mystic Valley," Daki said. "My people use this for a training ground."

"Training?" Feffer said. "Aren't there giants?"

"Of course. How else could we train to hunt giants?"

"You *hunt* giants? Why would you do that?"

"If we don't hunt them, they will hunt us. And when their populace grows, they venture into the soft lands. We have an agreement with your king to keep this from happening."

"Wait," Elwin said. "Your people have an alliance with Justice?"

"Of course. We are neighbors."

Feffer leaned over Elwin's shoulder and looked into the valley. "Well. I am not interested in hunting giants. In fact, I would like to never meet one. So, how can we make that happen?"

"Once we reach the valley floor, we will travel north alongside the mountain. This is where the forest is not so thick with trees, but the pass is narrow. So the giants avoid it. Once we reach the river, we will travel north and west."

"What river?" Feffer said. "There is no river on my map."

"He has taken us this far," Elwin said. "If he says there is a river, then I believe him."

"I know," Feffer said. "I believe him. I just don't understand how a cartographer missed an *entire* river."

"The river comes from snow melting in the mountains," Daki

said. "It then empties into the mountain and travels to the Depths. The men of cities have no use for it. That is probably why it is not drawn on your maps."

"Why are we still standing here?" Feffer said.

"I must warn you," Daki said. "The giants will sometimes come here for game, and they are rarely alone. We must travel with caution. If you see one, there will be more."

"Wait," Feffer said. "You just said they avoid it here."

"They do. Mostly, they visit the river. But sometimes they chase their game here."

Feffer took in a deep breath. "Maybe giants aren't as bad as the stories say."

Daki laughed as if Feffer had told a great joke. "I don't know the stories you have been told, but the Jojindun tribe will kill you simply to enjoy watching you die."

"Do they really eat people?" Feffer asked.

"Yes. But, they will make sport of your death first."

"Sport? What do you mean?"

Daki shook his head. "If we come across any Jojindun, you will see what I mean. We should move quietly."

"How is the *bear* going to move quietly?" Feffer asked. "And what do we do with Haven?"

"Taego can move with stealth when he needs to," Daki said. "And I will speak with Haven."

"You'll speak with Haven?" Feffer said doubtfully.

Daki nodded but gave no reply. He moved to the horse, stroked her side and murmured in her ear. She nuzzled him when he was finished.

"What did she say," Feffer said with mockery in his voice.

"She will move quietly," Daki said in a serious tone.

"Are you sure it won't be better to go over the mountain?" Elwin said.

"There is less cover for us," Daki said. "And it will take us a tenday or more to circle the valley by climbing the mountain. We have at most three days through the path I know."

"Through the mountain then," Elwin said.

"Lead the way," Feffer said. "Lead the thumping way."

Daki nodded and turned from the crevice. He leapt, more than stepped from rock to rock, and he bounded far ahead of them toward the valley. If Daki's steps made any sound, Elwin could not hear it.

Taego took precise steps, no louder than Daki's. In the same fashion as Daki, even Feffer sprung from rock to rock without a sound.

Haven moved to follow Feffer without being guided. Elwin reached for her reins out of reflex but missed. She moved with more precision than Taego had, and even the horse made little sound. He took a breath and moved to follow.

However he tried to avoid them, every twig and bramble on the boulders seemed to jump beneath his feet as he stepped. Every step made a crunch, even when it appeared there was nothing to crunch.

Daki stopped ahead.

When Elwin caught up to him, Daki turned and whispered, "Do you think that you have the energy to fly?"

"Yeah," Feffer said. "*Maybe* you can make less noise by flying."

Elwin felt his cheeks flush. "I can fly, but shouldn't I preserve my strength?"

Daki shook his head. "We will attract attention unless we move with stealth."

"I could move slower. Maybe I could miss more twigs?"

"You already move too slowly, and we do not wish to camp in the open. We must reach our destination before nightfall."

"Maybe I could just follow you and Feffer more closely."

"It is not our path that makes our movements quiet. It is training."

Feffer's voice was a harsh whisper. "What he's trying not to say is that you move louder than a deer in rut. You need to thumping fly. And try not to make any noise doing it for Life's sake."

Elwin felt a twinge of anger but bit his tongue. He took a quick breath and said, "Fine. I'll fly."

He had no reason to avoid taming, and he had tested his essence many times since waking from the *dream*. He felt normal. Still, Elwin hesitated before opening his essence to Air. In truth, he *wanted* to fly. He missed the rush of wind around him. So, why did he fight so hard to avoid it?

As he opened his essence to Air, memories of his dreams became vivid in his mind, and he realized why he had been avoiding taming. There was a moment in that dream when he had *known* how to tame all of the Elements. And he had been ready to kill with them. It *had* been just a dream, but Elwin thought he remembered how to tame the Elements to kill. Above all else, *that* made him afraid. Anything that had come from Abaddon, even knowledge, could not be good.

He took a deep breath and tamed flight. A slight breeze stirred, making the leaves on the ground rustle, and knocked a small pebble fall off the closest boulder. It skipped down the mountainside. Reverberations from stone striking against stone echoed into the valley.

Feffer turned his head and stared at Elwin with wide eyes. He shook his head and breathed, "Dragons take me. After all we've been through, we're still going to die."

Elwin felt his cheeks flush as he rose a few feet off the ground. He began to pull Air from above, rather than all around. The leaves below settled.

Daki breathed a sigh of relief and said, "Come." Then, he continued leaping down the mountain, and Feffer followed after him.

Taming Air, Elwin became more aware of his companions movements. He did not have to look behind him to know Haven followed, because he could feel movements in the Air as she stepped. What had Daki said to her to make her step so softly? It didn't matter. Whatever it had been, it worked. Though the horse was the loudest of their group, he could only make out a faint clopping with her steps.

Daki led them along the mountainside, and Elwin followed, trying to watch everywhere at once. He did not see how an *entire* race could be inherently evil, but he did not want to find out why they were infamous first hand either. But, none of the trees rustled or shook. Surely, they would have heard a giant coming a league away.

The boulders leveled out and gave way to grass as the mountain met the valley floor. Daki moved from boulder to boulder, keeping the forest and trees to his left. They traveled with few words beyond discussing the best path. Feffer's eyes watched the trees as intently as Elwin. Even Daki's eyes were wide and alert.

By the time the sun fell beyond the mountains, Elwin felt exhausted. Not from the exertion of taming Air for an extended period, but from staring at the unmoving trees. When Daki stopped, Elwin almost flew into him.

"We will rest in this cave," Daki whispered.

Elwin looked to the mountainside to his right. He could not see any caves. A boulder the size of a farmhouse nestled up against the mountain.

"What cave?" Feffer said quietly.

"Come."

Daki walked around the massive boulder. At the boulder's base, there was a small crack. It was just large enough to squeeze into. Beyond the hole was darkness.

Elwin eased to the ground and emptied his essence.

Feffer said what Elwin had thought. "I don't think Taego and Haven can fit in there."

"It is much larger on the inside," Daki said. "Taego and I have slept here before, but you will have to tether Haven to a tree."

Feffer tied Haven off on a nearby tree, then returned to the small opening.

"So," Feffer said, "do we have anymore of those berries?"

"No," Daki smiled, "but we passed over game tracks. If you will gather some wood for a fire, I will find us a meal. Gather enough to last the night. After the sun leaves the sky the cave will become dark."

"I'll have a fire built before you return," Feffer said. "I am glad we met you, Daki."

Daki's smile was as wide as his face. "I am glad our fates intertwined as well." In the next moment his face was serious once more. "If you see any giants, come back to the cave. Even they would have trouble moving this boulder."

Feffer's smile faded as well. He regarded the massive boulder. "They can move the boulder?"

Daki looked at it. "Well, it would take several of them."

Feffer started picking up wood, mumbling beneath his breath. Elwin would wager a farm to a sheep that he was cursing, but he found himself staring at the boulder.

He shook his head. "I am pretty sure that I don't want to meet anything that can move *that*."

"They are poor fighters," Daki whispered. "But one strike from a giant's fist can crush your skull. They are strong but clumsy."

"You have really fought a giant?"

Daki nodded, "I have crossed paths with a giant."

"What happened?"

"He tried to kill me," Daki said. "But I killed him instead."

"Do they really send you to hunt them so young?"

"Aye," Daki said. "Now, we can speak more later. I must find the game before the trail is cold."

Elwin watched his new companion disappear into the forest. It took him a moment to realize he was alone with Haven. Feffer had gone for wood, but how did the bear slip away unnoticed?

He looked at the boulder again. Giants. Something else that had only existed in stories before now. How many creatures and beasts would he find that were no longer just a story?

He took a deep breath and began to gather kindling.

Feffer moved over the brush, clenching his teeth at every soft scuff or rustle that he or his companions made. His heart pounded in his chest like a hammer on a forge as he crept along the line of the ridge, careful to keep his head below the dirt and rocks. His hands and knees shook from the effort. And, despite his best efforts to avoid them, he felt like all the dried twigs of the forest littered his path.

In front of him, Daki led Haven by the reins. The horse had her head low as she took each slow step forward. What had Daki said to Haven to make her move so quietly? Feffer had never even heard of a stable master capable of controlling a horse like Daki could. He would wring secrets out of the Chai Tu Naruo, if he had to do it with his fingers around the stubborn boy's neck.

He glanced over his shoulder at Elwin. Just above the foliage, Elwin floated parallel to the ground. The twigs and leaves rustled as he moved over them. Feffer wanted to curse. He couldn't even *fly* quietly, but thank the Lifebringer, Elwin *could* fly. If they had to rely on Elwin's stealth, they would have been dead, long since.

Even Elwin wasn't as loud as Taego. Behind Elwin, the bear shuffled on his large belly. In the forest and on the rocks, the bear had made little noise, but Taego was too big to lumber below the ridge line on all fours.

Together, the noises from his companions seemed like a cacophony of voices screaming, *"Come eat me Mr. Giant."*

On the other side of the ridge a mirthful laugh, too loud to have come from normal size lungs, rose above the sound of the distant waterfall. The laughter, if it had not been so *big*, sounded as if it could have come from a young boy.

The Lifebringer save him. Before this moment, Feffer had been beginning to believe he might actually live through all of this. He could have taken his adventures back to his squad, and maybe someday long from now, he could tell the same stories to children around a fire. Like Poppe.

The closer he got to Goldspire, the more he thought about them, but who was he kidding? Gurndol was never going to believe this tale. None of his squad would, not even Fandar. And the giant would be the least of it all. But, it would be good to see them all again. Maybe Sir Gibbins wouldn't make him do extra drills for taking too long of a furlough.

He would never admit it aloud, but if he lived, it would be thanks to Daki. He and Elwin would have never even made it this far without him. And Taego. It was good to have a bear on their side. Though he wasn't sure what a bear could do against a giant.

Once more, Feffer peeked over the ridge.

To the east, water fell from the mountain's bend into the mouth of the river and pushed the water west alongside the mountain. If he tuned out the sound of breaking twigs and freakish laughter, Feffer could hear the soft splatter of the falling water.

Their ridge sloped twenty paces to a sandy embankment that ran alongside the river not more than ten paces wide. Beyond the riverbank on the other side, a cliff stretched into the sky. Feffer could see a small crevice in the side of the cliff face that a normal-sized human could fit into. Maybe even a horse and bear.

His eyes found the source of the eerie laugh, and his knees began to shake again.

By the embankment on this side of the river, a LARGE humanoid sat with its back to the ridge. Its arms moved as if the giant played with something in front of it. The giant let out another deep cackle and stood up.

It looked like an overgrown child. Dark hair encased a boyish face. If it had been a normal size, Feffer would guess that he was not more than ten or eleven years of age. It wore brown trousers and a white jerkin. Its legs were as thick as the Redwood trees, and its arms weren't much smaller.

Elwin whispered from behind him, "Keep moving."

It took Feffer a moment to force his legs into motion. He continued to peek over the ridge as he crawled.

Even at this distance, the child giant was as tall as the Scented Rose Inn. Feffer would have been surprised if he could reach up and touch its knees. Its knees! And it was a *child*? Feffer didn't want to see an adult one of these.

The giant gave a slight kick to the thing in front of it. When the giant's toy bounced to a stop, Feffer recognized the bloody mass as an injured doe. The deer's hind legs had been twisted backwards. It tried to crawl away with its front legs, but when it got too far from the giant, he grabbed its injured leg and pull it back, laughing.

With a sudden jerk, the giant picked up the deer by one of its front legs and dangled it for several moments. Then, the giant snapped the leg with his thumb and forefinger. He laughed with the hysteria of a madman as the deer snorted and wheezed. The poor thing squirmed against the giant's grasp.

The giant laughed even harder and dropped the deer. Using its head and one working leg, the deer crawled toward the river. The giant picked up a tree that had been ripped up from the roots. It looked like a club in the giant's hand. It used the club to push the deer toward the water. Then, he stepped on the back legs, while pushing the deer's face into the water.

Feffer felt his fear of the giant dissipate, and he grabbed the hilt of his sword. The Lifebringer hadn't made such evil creatures. This thing came straight from the abyss.

Snap.

Feffer froze, as he felt the loud crunch beneath his knee. Daki stopped moving in front of him.

Feffer peeked back over the ridge. The giant was looking in their direction. Without thinking about it, he moved his head under cover, as fast as possible.

He held his breath, hoping that it hadn't seen him.

Boom. Boom. Boom. Boom. The ground shook beneath him.

Haven whinnied and reared. Feffer tried to grab her reins, but she bucked him. Feffer reached for the saddle, but he only got a hold of the backpack as Haven began to gallop in the opposite direction. The backpack came loose, knocking Feffer into the dirt. Standing as if the abyss had come for him, Feffer shoved his arms through the straps and slung the pack onto his back.

Daki stood and unsheathed his swords, holding them in a reverse grip. They curved around the length of his forearm just past his elbow. "Elwin, you and Feffer take cover."

"The Lifebringer curse me!" Feffer said, drawing his sword.

Elwin's eyes widened, and he did not respond.

The child giant covered several normal-sized paces in one stride. Five strides at most and it would be on top of him. Feffer's anger vanished, but he did not allow himself to panic. A quick look around, and he determined the best chance for survival would be to use the trees for cover. Maybe, they could tire the thing out and get away.

He opened his mouth to suggest as much but stopped and gaped at the Chai Tu Naruo. Daki dove over the ridge and leapt from his forward somersault into a run, *toward* the giant.

"He's gone mad!" Feffer said. "What is he doing?"

Taego roared behind him, and Feffer jumped three feet high.

"Thumping bear!"

Feffer grabbed Elwin's shoulder, but Elwin just stared at the giant, still not moving. Feffer shook him. "Snap out of it! We need to move!" He tugged on Elwin's arm.

Elwin's face snapped to Feffer, as if surprised to see him there. He opened his mouth to say something, but no words came out.

"Come on," Feffer said. He turned to run, looking over his shoulder to make sure Elwin followed. He flew behind Feffer as if in a daze. Feffer ran next to the ridge line, and he could see Daki and the giant clearly.

It still carried the tree and raised it like a club over its head as it ran toward Daki. A look of pure glee filled its eyes, and its mouth twisted into a smile.

"Human smash!" Its booming words were slurred and unpronounced. It laughed as it ran.

The tree swung down, making a loud crash into the ground where Daki had been.

Daki dove through its legs, slicing wide with both of his blades just below each knee. The giant howled in pain and staggered forward a step before falling face first into the ground. Still howling, the giant rolled over swinging wildly with its club. Taego charged its throat and bit down with a sickening crunch on the giant's windpipe. Its howl became a gurgle, but it continued to thrash about. A wild swing struck Taego. The bear flew free, making blood and flesh spray into the air. Massive amounts of red gushed from the giant's neck.

Feffer's legs stopped running, and his stomach lurched at the sight. He held his breath to keep from becoming ill.

The bear flew several feet and smashed into a tree, then he fell to the ground laying very still.

Daki ran up the giant's midsection and stabbed both swords into its heart. Blood gurgled from his neck and mouth as it breathed its last few moments of breath. Within moments, its giant eyes glazed over and stared at nothing.

"It's ... It's dead," Feffer said. "He killed it? He killed it."

It took Feffer a moment to realize Elwin had flown over to the fallen giant. Feffer ran after him.

Without glancing at them, Daki ran over to Taego and knelt beside him. The bear moaned as if laboring to breath.

"He has broken ribs," Daki said. "Four, maybe five."

"Is he going to be alright?" Feffer asked.

Daki closed his eyes and placed his hands on Taego. His hands began glowing green for several heartbeats. When Daki's hands stopped glowing, Taego rolled from his side to his feet, and Daki slumped forward, taking several deep breaths.

"How did you do that?" Feffer said.

"You killed it." Elwin's voice held a dangerous tone. "How could you do that? It was just a child."

Without looking at Elwin, Daki retrieved his blades from the giant's chest and wiped them on the giant's jerkin. He sheathed his blades and turned to face Elwin. "Did you see what this *child* did to the deer?"

"I did," Elwin nodded. "But it was a child."

Feffer blinked at the ferocity in Elwin's voice and decided to stay out of the argument. But, that thing was more than *just a child*.

"If given the chance this *child* would have killed you in the same manner as the deer," Daki said. "Only, he would have taken longer. The death I gave it was a clean one. More than a Jojindun deserved."

"It still feels wrong," Elwin said, "killing."

Daki pointed a sword at the deer. Its head was buried in the water. Daki's voice was calm. "The giant does not share your views. Better to kill him now, than to let him grow up to kill my people. Or yours."

The ground began to vibrate ever so slightly.

"Do you two feel that?" Feffer asked, trying to look everywhere at once.

It vibrated harder, and then began to shake.

"Um ...," Feffer said, "I think he was not alone."

Boom, boom, boom. It was faint at first but increased in intensity. Boom, boom, boom, boom.

"No Jojindun is far from his tribe," Daki said in a calm voice. "We need to run."

"There," Feffer pointed to the crevice he had seen before. "On the other side of the river is a cave. Can we reach it?"

"I see it. Run," Daki said and ran toward the opening with Taego close behind. Elwin flew past them, faster than even the giant had run. Then, it donned on Feffer. He was last. He didn't want to be last.

"Wait for me, Elwin!"

He glanced over his shoulder. Five thick heads towered above the forest. Trees jerked to the side and bounced as the giants tore through them, snapping trees aside like twigs. Each one carried a boulder as if weighing no more than a pebble.

Feffer found an inner strength he didn't know he had, and he made his legs run faster.

A sound like thunder crashed beside him, causing the earth to quake beneath him. The boulder bounced and broke a part, showering him with pieces of rock. He saw a large sliver as it clipped his shoulder and shoved him toward the ground. Feffer dove into the fall. As his hands hit the ground, he arched his back and flipped back onto his feet. The backpack bounced into the back of his head as he landed, but he didn't let it slow him. His legs pumped with all the strength he could find as he ran toward the river.

Reaching the edge of the bank, Feffer jumped with all of his might and dove as far into the flowing stream as he could. Just before he hit the water, he saw Daki and Taego ahead of him in the river, already halfway to the other side.

His dive plunged him well beneath the surface, and the current carried him slightly down river. He could see the riverbed. Kicking with all his might, he dove toward the bottom and pulled on the rocks to propel him forward. The pack dragged, but the moment he considered stopping to lose it, the water shook above him, and a tree smashed into the rock bed next to him.

The water continued to splash and rock around him, but he didn't slow. Pulling on the rocks and kicking with his legs, Feffer swam for the other bank. He rose to the surface and felt a moment of panic as small hands took hold of him. When he saw Elwin's face, Feffer let out his breath.

"Come on!" Elwin shouted. "It's right here!"

He could see the thin crack in the side of the mountain, not more than ten paces away. Daki pushed on Taego's flanks to help squeeze the bear into the cave. Once inside, Daki slipped in without hesitation.

Feffer took Elwin's hand to get to his feet and ran after him toward the opening. An explosion of rock and dust slammed into the side of the crevice, just missing Elwin as he ran inside the cave.

The last several paces felt like a mile. Feffer glanced over his shoulder, and some part of his mind registered every detail as he calculated his remaining distance to the safety of the cave.

The giants had reached the ridge. Four of them paused around the body of the giant child, but the fifth one never slowed.

For a fraction of a second, Feffer's eyes flickered to the giants kneeling over the child. Two of them had the curves of women. Feffer had almost expected horns or fangs, but the grown-up giants looked like people. Like the child giant, their faces and auburn hair could have been from Benedict.

Motion from the fifth giant pulled his focus. An arm thicker than a horse cart arched into a throwing position, and Feffer could see an intense focus in the giant's dark eyes. The arm blurred as it swung forward. Feffer saw a flash of grey leave the giant's hand before he turned his gaze back to the opening less than a pace away.

Feffer saw Elwin several paces beyond the narrow opening. His blue eyes looked behind Feffer and widened with terror.

As his first foot cleared the opening, the sound of thunder rang in his ears and pain erupted from his back. Dust and rock filled his senses. Then nothing.

Filled with Elemental power, Elwin could see, hear, and feel more clearly. Behind him, the narrow crevice went deep into the mountain, and the power of Earth surrounding him dampened the flow of Air into his essence. The power became difficult to hold, and taming Air felt all but impossible.

In front of him, Elwin watched Feffer run, and he could feel the ripples in the Air as his friend came closer with each step. He felt it long before he saw it. Like a tidal wave moving through the ocean, ripples in the Air crashed toward the crevice.

Behind Feffer, Elwin saw the grey stone streaking forward and reached his hand to Feffer. But it was too late. The impact rang in his ears as dust and debris shot into the entrance. He flinched away from the blast but lost his feet as something slammed him to the ground.

Streams of light trickled into the dust-filled air, and Elwin could see Feffer's limp body atop him. The ground began to shake, and Elwin could feel the earth outside vibrate with the impact. Large feet ran toward the crevice.

"Elwin," Daki said from somewhere behind him. "Get him inside."

Elwin pushed Feffer to the side as gently as possible and climbed to his feet. He grabbed below both arms and began pulling Feffer deeper into the crevice. Feffer's head hung to the side, and a small trickle of blood leaked from his nose. Elwin's heart leapt into his throat, and he began to pull faster.

The vibrations outside came to a sudden stop, and an eye the size of a plate peered into the opening. Elwin's muscles froze, and he gaped at the size of the thing. The pupil dilated in the shade of the crevice and the dark eye focused on Elwin. A moment later, large fingers reached into the cave, each one as thick as a human leg.

Elwin panicked into motion, when a forefinger touched the edge of Feffer's boot, and he pulled Feffer deeper into the cave. Outside, the giant let out a bestial growl that echoed into the cave. The farther Elwin moved away from the opening, the more the giant howled.

Thank the Lifebringer! The mountain around the crevice was too thick for the giant to break. Still, Elwin didn't stop moving.

More than two dozen paces later, the crack opened into a cavern. The front of the opening began to shake as cow-sized fists beat against the mountainside. Debris began to fall into the entrance as the large hand tried to punch and reach deeper into the opening.

Elwin eased Feffer to the ground and placed his head on his knees. Shadows moved across his face as the giant's hand blocked the light at the cave's entrance. Feffer took shallow breaths that came out like a wheeze. Cuts and scratches covered Feffer's arms and neck. Elwin pulled a sliver of rock from a cut in his cheek.

He had to shout to hear himself over the pounding. "Can you help him? Like you did with Taego?"

Daki knelt to Feffer and placed a hand on his chest. "His back ribs are broken and his lung is punctured and filling with fluid. I can help him, but when I do, it will make me weak. Hold him still."

For the second time today, Elwin felt the foreign power radiate off of Daki. The Air did not stir, nor did the Earth. No Water or Fire entered into him. Something else went happened around Daki and coalesced into his hand. After a moment, the energy spread into Feffer's chest and back.

Feffer began to squirm, and a gasp escaped his lips. Elwin held his arms to keep Feffer from moving. A moment later, the energy stopped flowing into Feffer and the remnants dissipated. Feffer's breathing had lost the rasp and sounded more like that of sleep. Dried blood covered his arms and neck, but the cuts had vanished.

"It is done," Daki staggered backward and sat hard. Taego lumbered over to Daki and sat next to him.

"Are you alright?"

His lips were tight, and he gave Elwin a terse nod. "I only need rest. Much of the energy came from him as well. He should sleep through the night."

"You will need to regenerate your powers in the Lady's Realm?"

Daki only looked at him. For several moments, the only sounds were the crashes on the front of the cavern. Then, it stopped.

Elwin looked to the entrance. Dust still hung all around, but the giant shadows had disappeared.

"They have given up," Elwin said "How long do you think, until we can get out of here?"

"They haven't given up. Though their speech suggests they have little intelligence, this is untrue. Our common tongue is not their first language. More likely, they have sent others for tools to tear the crevice open. They will wait for us out there. I would wager they will camp several nights. If they capture us alive, you will envy that deer by the river."

"Well," Elwin said feeling a surge of anger. "Perhaps if you hadn't killed their child, they would have left us alone."

Daki shook his head. "We are food to them. Had we never harmed them, they would still try to dig us out."

"You still didn't have to kill him."

Daki was silent for a long moment, then he met Elwin's gaze. "Why did you not fly Feffer into the cave? Had you flown him, you both might have reached the opening in time. Why did you run instead?"

"Too much Earth," Elwin said in an impatient tone. "I can't fly in here. This isn't about me."

"Ah," Daki said. "But it is. You could not fly inside the cave, but you could have flown to reach the cave."

"Yeah. So?"

"It could have saved you the precious seconds needed for both of you to reach safety. Now, Feffer is lying there unconscious."

"I know you saved him, Daki. And I am grateful. But this doesn't have anything to do with you killing that child."

"But it does," he said in a patient tone. "Why did you run instead of fly?"

A feeling of frustration welled up inside Elwin. "I didn't think about it. I just ran."

"You acted in accord with your instincts. Someday they will tell you to fly, but today your instincts told you to run. You did not think; you reacted."

Elwin stared at Daki. "What are you even talking about? Are you saying your instincts told you to kill the child?"

"No. My instincts told me to kill the Jojindun. I did not kill a child. I killed a threat to my people. And yours. In the same way, my instincts told me to save Feffer. Today is a good day. I have killed a threat and preserved a life worth living. This is balance. This is my purpose. One day, balance will require my own life. And I will gladly give it."

Elwin stared at Daki. His face and tone held no touch of mockery, and his voice was calm. Giants were outside waiting to *torture* and *eat* them, and Daki could have been sitting in a field of roses or waiting on his turn for the cakewalk at festival.

"What are we going to do?" Elwin asked.

Daki glanced over his shoulder into the dark of the cavern. "It goes deep. We will have to see if there is another way out. Though, we must be even more careful than before. The depths are filled with delvers. They are to be more feared than the giants."

Elwin sighed. "What in the abyss are delvers?"

"These histories come from your libraries in Justice," Daki said. "Many years ago, Dargaitha, the city of dwarves, had a civil war. King Darfth had two sons, Brinionth and Hurvith. When he died Brinionth—the eldest—was heir. The war that your people call the War of Shadows began. Brinionth did not want to join sides. Hurvith deceived his brother and joined the side of Abaddon, taking a legion of dwarven warriors with him. This was before the Great Fall."

"The Great Fall?" Elwin asked.

"I thought you would have known of this, being an elementalist."

"I am not an elementalist yet, Daki. I am still in training."

"Well," Daki said, "the Great Fall is what your people call the discovery of the Darkness of Spirit. When Abaddon rose to power, he twisted and warped those following him. These dwarves became the first of the delvers, just as the elementalists following him became the first of the vampires and Death seekers."

Elwin pinched the bridge of his nose and massaged his eyes. Why did everyone want to give him lectures of history? He tried to keep the irritation from his voice and failed. "Why should we fear the delvers?"

"When they fell, like the vampires, they were no longer able to feel the sun's light. It will destroy them. They have all the strength of their dwarven predecessors, but they disdain the goodly peoples that live above ground. If we are captured, they will eat our flesh while we are still living. They will keep us alive as long as possible so that they may find joy in our suffering."

"Didn't you say the same of the giants?"

"The giants will torture us over a day or so," Daki said. "Delvers will make it last for months, possibly even years."

A chill went down his spine, and Elwin shivered.

"You are right," Elwin said. "I would rather face a giant. How could the king allow giants and delvers and such to remain in his lands?"

"The delvers rarely come above ground," Daki said, "and no wise king would venture into the depths where they reside. As for the giants, most of the tribes do not have a taste for humans. We are at the edge of the Jojindun territory, and they are the smallest of the tribes. The mountains are vast, and the other tribes war with each other over territory. Their battles rarely make it this far west. The Jojindun live as close to humans as we allow them."

Elwin shook his head. "Okay. I've heard enough. We need to get out of here."

He removed the pack from Feffer's back and eased his friend to the cavern floor. A realization came to him. Had the pack not been there to soften the blow, Feffer might not have survived. No. He didn't want to think about that. Feffer was alive. Taego and Daki were alive. Now, they needed to find a way out.

Elwin shifted the pack into one of the shafts of light and dug through the contents. He pulled the cloak at the top out and placed it under Feffer's head. Pieces of glass crumbled to the cavern floor as he examined the broken wood that had been the spyglass. The small lens was intact, but the large lens had shattered. He rummaged through the remaining supplies and gave Daki a report.

"The spy glass is broken, and both of the wineskins are busted. But, by the Lifebringer, the lantern is still in tact. The oil flask was in a side pouch or would likely be ruined as well. And the rope is soggy, but it is still usable."

"That is good. We will need the light to explore the depths." Daki turned to look into the darkness behind them, and Elwin followed his gaze.

The rays of light pierced the dark for several paces and vanished. No matter how hard he tried, his eye could not penetrate beyond the edge of the light. It could have gone on forever.

"We don't even know if this leads out," Elwin said. "What if it only leads down?"

"That is a good observation. I do not know, Elwin."

"Do you at least know how far we are from Goldspire?" Elwin felt a stab of guilt at his tone. Daki would not be in this predicament if he had not offered to help. This wasn't Daki's fault.

Daki answered as if he had not taken offense. "If we can find a path that leads up and out of here, then we can make it within a day. Two at most, but first, we must find a path."

They didn't have enough oil for a search, so once they moved away from the entrance, they may have a few hours before the oil ran dry. Elwin sighed.

He saw little other choice. Elwin would have to search a path from the shadow realm. And, he would have to face the unseen eyes to do it. Then, a thought occurred to him.

"Daki, do you know how the shadow realm works?"

He nodded. "It is where you replenish your essence."

"You have to go somewhere to replenish your ... Do you call yours an essence as well?"

Daki looked away, his face looked tired.

"Anyway. My thought is that we can both search out a path while we sleep. It will allow—"

"Her realm does not work like the Realm of Shadows," he said in a tight voice. "I cannot do what you ask."

"But I saw you in the grove. How is it not the same?"

Daki grimaced.

Again, Elwin felt anger rise up, and the words poured out of him. "What is it with you? We need to get out of here. If we don't, we won't survive. If I am your Pat-whatever, will it honor you if I die?"

For the first time since meeting the Chai Tu Naruo, Daki flinched.

The guilt was immediate. "I'm sorry. I'm just so ... frustrated. I can find a path. I just need some sleep."

"The Grove is where Her realm merges with this world and the Realm of Shadows. When I sleep, I do enter her Realm, but I must guard the Grove. I cannot help in your search."

Guard the Grove from what? he wanted to ask. Instead, he nodded and said, "Okay. Thank you for explaining."

Daki turned away from him.

Elwin arranged the pack to serve as a pillow and laid against it.

Falling asleep had become a simple mental exercise. He made his breath calm and cleared his mind. Sleep soon took him.

❧

Elwin opened his eyes and welcomed the familiar light of the shadow realm. He stood from his body and took a good look at the cavern.

He and his companions rested at the mouth of a wide cave.

Feffer slept soundly a few paces from Daki and Taego. Daki leaned against the bear with his eyes closed. His own body stretched out closest to the entrance. If the giants found a way through, they would reach him first. That thought brought him to his first order of business.

Elwin willed himself just outside the crevice. Rocks and boulders had fallen around the entrance, and the surface had large cracks running up the side of the mountain.

As a boy, he had thought of Faron as a giant. Even he would have looked like an infant in the arms of a real giant. Not more than a dozen paces away, one of the giants stood poised over the entrance.

It looked almost like a man with the common garb of a merchant or well-off farmer. How many sheep had it taken to make such a large shirt? Or did they have giant sheep? Elwin couldn't discount the notion. At this point, anything felt possible.

Elwin willed himself into the air and looked around for other giants, but they were nowhere to be seen. Maybe Daki had been right. Perhaps, the other giants went to get tools. He turned around to inspect the cracks in the entrance. Bare fists had fissured the rock. What could the giants do with a giant-sized shovel?

No time to think about that. Elwin returned to the cave and looked into the depths.

Several paces behind his companions, the cave widened and dropped off. Below was a large pool of water that dripped into another pool somewhere deeper into the cave. But he didn't want to go down. Maybe there was a way to use Earth to burrow a hole above.

He looked up and felt a moment of hope.

Above the pool, an opening led upward. If it led out, the others could reach the opening by climbing up the eastern wall. He could leave no room for chance. Following it up, he could see some spots would be tight for Taego, but not impassable.

As he ascended, Elwin felt the sanctuary of his body grow more distant, but he continued to follow the tunnel. He could not be sure how much time passed, but he knew the moment the eyes were upon him.

He stopped and watched for the slightest movement. If a shadow appeared or if the fog turned dark or even twitched, he would return to his body the same instant. Being still made him more aware of the rise and fall of his chest a thousand paces below. His heart beat out a steady rhythm. He counted to five hundred and nothing happened.

Slowly, he began to rise, looking for any reason to return to his sanctuary. It was difficult to look in every direction at once, but Elwin did his best to do just that. He spun in slow circles and glanced up and down as he made his way up the tunnel.

After a moment he saw the waning crescent nestled in a sea of bright stars. Elwin emerged from the crevice and surveyed the mountain. Few trees grew from the wide plateau, but some of the red sucrais berries grew not far from the entrance.

"The Lifebringer be praised," Elwin said.

"Hello, young one," a man's voice said below him. "Do not be alarmed. I only wish to talk."

Elwin stopped his ascent and looked below to see a man in fine, blue silks leaning against a boulder below. Even his shoes were silk. Elwin recognized the face from his first venture into the shadow realm.

"Abaddon," Elwin breathed.

Elwin almost fled to his body the instant he recognized the man, but something made him hesitate. The man did not seem as ominous as before. In fact, he looked ... not old exactly. Weary?

"You do not need fear me, child." His voice had a calming tone.

"I do not fear you," Elwin lied. Of course he feared him. Even fools and halfwits feared him. He was the thumping Seeker. In fact, what was he doing? He should be back at his body.

"That is good." His smile was warm. "Do you like the mountains? I find them peaceful at night this time of year. I used to come here when I was a boy. My first time, I was not much younger than you."

Did he like the thumping mountains? No. He didn't. Cursed giants trying to eat him and delvers waiting to torture him for years. The mountains could go to the abyss. But that was beside the point. Why was Abaddon asking him about the thumping mountains?

"I prefer the view on my farm," Elwin said. "The one you took from me."

He made a face as if pained. "I did not take that from you. She did, when she tried to steal you from your destiny."

The words erupted from Elwin before he could think to stop them. "Prophecies and Destinies. To the abyss with you all. Have you ever considered what I want? I don't want any of this."

Abaddon's eyes widened as if offended, and his voice held not even a hint of mockery. "Such language. Let us speak civilly."

Elwin's anger faded to incredulity. The Seeker of Souls, creator of the Death Element, and bringer of destruction had chastised him on his foul tongue? Despite himself, Elwin laughed. The sound was more bitter than mirthful.

Almost quicker than he could follow, Abaddon's eyes flickered to Elwin's chest. Elwin looked down. The green stone radiated with a pale light.

"Interesting artifact," Abaddon said with a smile. "It is the only one of its kind. I know. I made it."

Elwin felt a moment of horror as he looked at the pendant. He knew the inscription on the back without looking.

Stay safe, my darling Elwin.

It had been a gift from his mother. His birth mother.

"You're lying."

"There was a time when all could travel the Realm of Shadows. Only, it wasn't called that in my time. We called it the Realm of Spirits, and anyone could meander where they chose. When I declared war on the Rose House, I needed to be able to hide from the others. It took me a month to make the pendant."

"I know you're lying. It was a gift from my mother."

"True. She did give it to you to prevent others from tracking you to Justice. The artifact even shields you from me. Or it did for a time." *Abaddon smiled.*

Elwin swallowed. Rather, his body far beneath his feet swallowed. He prepared himself to flee, to will himself back to his sanctuary, but Abaddon spoke before he manifested his will to be away.

"But I digress. When I Transcended, I had no need of it. All of my wondrous artifacts remained behind, untouched for centuries. She found the pendant in my castle, your father's home."

"He is NOT my father."

Bain smirked, but his eyes narrowed. "Your defiance will become your greatest strength in the end. The Old Man is not the only one to gaze into the future, and I see a world made in my image. With or without you, they will Awaken. With your help, fewer deaths will be necessary. Without …," he shrugged. "Who knows?"

Elwin blinked. Old Man? The Lifebringer? Elwin shook his head. Jasmine had called Abaddon the father of all falsehoods. He should have been gone long before now. Lies had kept him here.

"Before you go," Abaddon said as if reading Elwin's thoughts. "Let me make you an offer."

"I don't want anything from you." As he willed himself back to his body, Abaddon's final words echoed in his thoughts.

"Not yet. But someday you will ask for my gift. I have seen it."

The cave came into existence around him as if he had only taken a step. His companions appeared as if none had stirred a hair's width in his absence.

Elwin stared at them a moment, trying to process his conversation. Abaddon was lying. He had to be. Nothing could make him take Abaddon's "gift." He shook his head and pushed it from his thoughts, then went out the crevice to check on the giants.

He jumped back as a massive hammerhead slammed into the opening. The sound of breaking stone echoed into the cavern and rung in his ears. A large chunk fell away from the opening.

He all but jumped back into his body.

Chapter 28

THE HUNGER OF GIANTS

Elwin awoke with his ears still ringing from the first blast. Another thunderclap cracked into the opening and sent his head spinning. He sat up to wake the others, but Daki was already on his feet. Feffer's eyes opened, and he looked around groggily.

The next crash made him sit up straight grabbing at his ears. "What in the abyss? Where are we? I can't see! Why can't I see?"

"Have you found our path?" Daki said in a calm voice.

"Yes. But I need to light this lantern."

"Elwin? Is that you? Why can't I see?"

"I'm working on it."

Elwin had slept with it next to him along with the flint and steel just in case the giants returned in the night. Between the hammer blows sending vibrations into his arms and his trembling hands, it took him three tries with the flint and steel to get the lantern to light.

He stood as another crash rocked the cave. The quake sent him tumbling into Daki, who did not appear to be phased at all by the quaking earth or the giants trying to get into their cave.

Feffer bounded to his feet and looked to the crevice. Elwin followed his gaze. The same massive eye as the day before peered in at them. It was at least half-a-dozen paces closer. Elwin could see the grin in its eye, and the light reflected off a few large teeth. The eye vanished, and the pounding resumed.

"This way!" Elwin shouted, and he ran toward the back of the cave.

He didn't have to look to know the others followed, but he did. Despite himself, Elwin smiled. A part of him was overjoyed to see Feffer on his feet. Instead of fear, Feffer had a look of undeterred determination on his face.

The quakes lessened as they moved away from the entrance. When he reached the drop, Elwin held up a hand for the others to stop.

"Down there?" Feffer said, looking over Elwin's shoulder.

"There," Elwin pointed to the opening above.

"Me first," Feffer said and pushed past the bear to the eastern wall. The layered rocks made the climbing look easy, but Feffer grunted with effort.

"Now you," Elwin said to Daki.

"Then you," he answered. "Taego is a clumsy climber. He will knock rocks on your head."

Taego turned his muzzle to the side and arched an eyebrow. The human mannerism made Elwin blink.

"Fine," Elwin said. "Go."

As Daki lumbered up after Feffer, Elwin felt for the Air around him. He was surprised to find enough to fill his essence. As he tamed flight and rose toward the hole, a gush of wind moved through the cavern, knocking up dust and debris.

"Sorry."

Feffer coughed and cursed as he reached the tunnel, but he seemed to have little trouble pulling himself up. The space was narrow enough that Feffer did not have to stretch his arms to full length to reach both walls. As Feffer disappeared into the hole, Daki was right behind him in reaching the opening, and Taego had already started his climb.

Elwin spared the front of the cavern a glance before flying into the crevice above.

The tip of the hammerhead had broken through. It came free as if yanked from the other side. A moment later the giant's hand came into the opening. Its massive forearm caught in the opening, but its fingers still probed around in the dark. Only a few paces of empty space stood between him and those thick fingers.

Elwin flew into the chute, and the flow of Air became impossible to tame when the wall of Earth smothered it. He almost dropped his lantern as he scrambled for a hand hold, and he panted for breath in the confines of the tunnel. Why hadn't Jasmine warned him of this? Then he laughed. As if she could have anticipated he would be hunted by giants through a cavern.

"Elwin?" It was Daki's voice. "Are you well?"

"Perfect," he said as he scrambled higher to make room for Taego behind him. "Never been better."

"Hand me the lantern," Daki said in a low voice, "you will need both hands."

Elwin handed it upward, glad to get a better hand hold.

"How far to the peak?" he asked.

"Maybe two thousand paces. It flattens out a bit and angles north."

"Six thousand feet?" Feffer called from above him.

"Shhh," Daki whispered. "Go higher."

Feffer mumbled curses, but he climbed higher. After about ten minutes of climbing, light vibrations began to move through the mountain, but after a moment, Elwin realized he sensed this through his essence, not his body.

"They are still digging," Elwin said.

"Good," Daki said. "They will continue to do so until they can hollow out the entrance. If fate favors us, it will take them half the day or so to find the chute. Then they will attempt to track us above. But, if the Lady smiles upon us, they may dig out the way to the depths to see if we are hiding in a dead end."

"How long do you think it will take us to reach the top?"

Daki was silent for a moment before responding. "Taego and I could make the climb in five to six hours, but we have been on many climbs. I do not know how long for you and Feffer, but I would guess most of the day."

Feffer's voice echoed from above. "How long will it take the giants to scale the mountain?"

"It will take them a third that time."

Feffer's curses became more audible, but the scrapes of his boots on stone increased. Daki picked his pace up as well, and Elwin followed, letting the bouncing light be his guide.

After a time, the climbing became routine, but Elwin had to work hard to keep up. He had trained with swords once a tenday and taming all day wore on him, but his muscles had never been conditioned for this. He tried not to think about the burning in his thighs and arms, even though he had to focus on moving his thighs and arms.

He glanced down to see Taego catch him again.

It had taken an hour of climbing for Elwin to realize the bear would catch up to him and take a break to give Elwin time to get ahead. Often, Elwin would look down to see the bear an arms length away. Other times when he looked down, he couldn't even see the top of his head.

It was smart of the bear. At first, Elwin had knocked several pebbles and mountains of dust into the bear's face, causing him to snort and sneeze.

Though Taego never groaned or growled, Elwin could almost see the bear's impatience when he reached him again. He would have to make it up to Taego by catching him some fish.

Elwin almost slipped when his hand reached a flat surface. Daki caught his arm and helped him climb onto the level surface. Elwin moved aside to make room for Taego and looked around. After a few paces the tunnel angled upward, where Feffer leaned on his knees, breathing heavily.

Daki held the lantern up for Elwin to see it. A thin line of oil filled the bottom of the lantern. If they were lucky, it would last the hour.

"When this runs out," Daki said, "we must climb in the dark. But the path will be easier if it slopes like this the rest of the way."

"It does," Elwin said, "but it will get tight for Taego in a few spots."

"Let us make haste. We will keep the same order?"

Elwin nodded.

Daki moved toward Feffer, but he didn't move.

"Feffer?" he said.

"Yeah, yeah. I'm going." He pushed up with a grunt and turned up the slope.

Going up the angle did seem faster, but instead of climbing, he had to stoop not to bump his head, which he did on several occasions. In some places, the stones became smooth, and he could crawl or scoot on hands and knees. But most of the way, he was forced to avoid rigid and sharp rocks. Still, walking up the angle became as routine as climbing up the chute had been. Only, on top of the pain in his arms, legs, and neck, his back began to ache from being hunched over.

The entire time he moved, he expected the lantern to quit, but he was still not prepared when he was plunged into complete darkness. Memories of the shadows enveloping him rushed into his mind, and he felt a yell escape his lips. His heart thundered in his chest like the giant's hammer. This was just a dream. It wasn't real.

"Elwin," Feffer called at the same time Daki said, "What is it?"

Their voices unfroze his thoughts, and his mind remembered where he was. Just in a cave. Around him, the power of Earth called to him even louder than before. He opened his essence to let some trickle into him. Immediately, he felt strength return to his muscles, and the aches in his legs and back seemed to dull. He could feel the vibrations of his companions moving around him, and his heartbeat began to slow.

"I'm here," Elwin said. "The light went out. Just keep moving."

Even though he only held it in his essence, he could feel the power in him draining. He had to open his essence wider to let more in just to keep Earth from seeping out. As more flooded into him, he could feel further up and down the slope, and he felt *aware*. Even though he couldn't see them, he could point to the rocks around, and he *knew* they were there in the same way he could touch his nose without having to think about how to find it. As his companions began to move in front of him, Elwin followed.

After a few moments, his heartbeat and breathing slowed slightly, but it did not return to normal. His essence began to feel labored as he did when flying. But that didn't make sense. As far as he could tell, he wasn't doing anything with the power. The Earth in his essence continued to be *used,* but it didn't feel like it did to tame Air.

If not taming, what else could it have been?

Taming a wind thrust and flying required his will. Even with the power in his essence, he had to make a mental effort to tame the talent. But, the Earth just *burned away* as he pulled more in.

But, he was *willing* it to do *something.* How else could he see in complete darkness? Like, for example, he knew this jagged rock was above his head. But, he didn't *will* to see it. Did he?

Elwin stopped focusing on his surroundings. It felt like closing his eyes. Once more panic overwhelmed him. But part of his mind realized the Earth stopped being *burned* from his essence. He reached out for his surroundings again.

Once more, he could feel the vibrations of Feffer and Daki ahead of him. Behind him, Taego sniffed and snorted at Elwin's boot.

He laughed. "I discovered a new talent! I can see everything. Well not *see* exactly, but I can *feel* every rock as if … Oh. Feffer. Look out for—"

"Ack! Curse it all! Thumping, Life-cursed, thumping rock!"

"Sorry," Elwin said. "It gets a bit tight right there, but we are almost to the top."

Feffer's curses became less audible, but Elwin could feel him drop and scoot forward beneath the low tunnel. Daki's body pressed against the ground earlier than necessary, and he scrambled after Feffer.

"This will be tight Taego, but I think you will fit. Follow me."

Taego snorted but complied with Elwin's commands to guide him under the low-hanging rocks to the other side.

"There's light!" Feffer called. "You were right. We are almost there."

Elwin helped Taego the last few feet by pulling on his massive shoulder. Once the bear was free they both scrambled after Feffer and Daki. Less than a hundred paces, Elwin could see the light at the end of the tunnel. Ahead of him, two dark silhouettes ran on hands and knees. He stopped taming Earth and ran after them. The last of his power burnt out as he reached the exit.

Climbing out, he had to squint against the light of the sun, low in the western sky. Daki and Feffer both offered a hand. He clasped wrists with the pair and let them pull him to the mountain peak. Elwin sat with a thud and took several deep breaths.

The air was clean and crisp compared to the musky air of the tunnel. He leaned back against a boulder and let his legs and back rest. A moment later, Taego scrambled out of the hole and plopped next to Elwin. The bear had small pebbles and dust matted into his fur. Elwin began to pick at the easier to reach rocks.

"Lucky this was here," Feffer said looking at the crack in the mountain.

"It was formed over many years," Daki said. "In the winter, water freezes. But in the spring, it melts and must find a path. Before we ever knew of its existence, the Lady Nature has provided us a way."

Feffer clasped Daki on the shoulder. "However it's here, we are *alive*. And look! There are those red berries. The Lifebringer be praised!"

He picked a berry and stuck it in his mouth, then proceeded to find every berry and shove them into the pack. Elwin blinked. He had forgotten about the pack. Good thing one of them had the presence of mind to grab it. Though the cloth had rips and scrapes, it was better than nothing.

Elwin rose to join him and began helping Feffer pick the berries. He shoved one in his mouth. The sweet juice wet his dry tongue and throat as he chewed it. Even Daki ate without regard for the juices running down his chin.

He stopped when his eyes fell on the boulder next to Taego, where Elwin had been sitting a moment before. It was the same boulder Abaddon had used the night before. He shook his head. The Seeker had looked and acted so normal. No. He wouldn't think about him. He wouldn't think about the lies Abaddon had told him.

"What is it?" Feffer asked.

"Nothing. I just want to go home."

"We should go," Daki said. "It doesn't look like the giants have been here, but they may still realize we climbed up the tunnel and try to track us. They will not come too close to Goldspire. We need to move."

"You won't hear me argue," Fefffer said. "Go go go."

Daki nodded and began to walk west atop the ridge, and Feffer followed. Elwin let Taego go next. The bear had followed him for long enough.

As he turned to go, Elwin spared a backward glance at the boulder. Abaddon's words seemed to echo in his thoughts.

"Not yet. But someday you will ask for my gift. I have seen it."

A cool wind rose, and Elwin shivered. He ran to catch up with the others.

Chapter 29

GOLDSPIRE

With the sun overhead, Elwin's shadow ran along the rocks and trees as he flew just above the ridge. Every time he passed a tree or tall rock, the oblong shape of his shadow stretched in disproportions with the flat ridge. He flew high enough to avoid the few trees speckling the mountaintop, but avoided going higher. The height of the mountain peak provided a clear enough view of the countryside, and going much higher made his head feel light.

From his vantage above the mountain, the rocky peak looked like a sinewy line cutting through an ocean of green. Either side of the peak dropped off at odd angles and gave way to lush green valleys far below. The trees swayed in the wind that swept through the mountain.

With so much of it around him, he felt a part of the Air. Though he did not travel at a swift pace, he had flown all morning, and taming for so long had not even begun to fatigue him. The breeze seemed to carry him over the mountain, and he was not the only one riding the wind. On both sides of him, he could make out flocks of birds in the distance.

For the first time in a long time, he felt free. A part of him wished the feeling would never end. But it would. Others had plans for him. Prophecies and fates and the Lifebringer knew what else. Once he reached Goldspire, his freedom would end.

Jasmine would be waiting for him to take him back to Justice to finish his training. Or would she? What had become of the trial? Maybe there had been an order for his execution. Would the warders be waiting to behead him?

Suddenly, he felt heavier. That could be a best-case scenario. Jasmine would not be the only one waiting for him in Goldspire.

Zeth and his other black savants would be there, too. Should they try to find them? Zeth was just a man. He could be killed. The memory of the child giant entered his thoughts. There had been so much blood. It had felt *wrong*. No matter what Daki said, the loss of any life felt like a tragedy to be avoided at all costs. Even Zeth?

Elwin shook his head. Even if Zeth didn't belong to Abaddon, he was a murderer. Zeth's death would be a justice to those who died by his hand. To Feffer's father and Elwin's. Whatever had happened to Wilton, that too could be laid at the black savant's feet.

But could Elwin kill him? The dream that was not a dream had taught Elwin he was capable of such a thing. But that had been different. Asa was his little girl. Rather, she had been his little girl in the dream. Strange. The feeling to protect her still had not diminished. Part of him wanted to find her and keep her safe, no matter the cost. Not just her.

Zarah needed him. So did Feffer and Daki. His mother would need him before this war was through, and by the Lifebringer, he would find a way to save his father. His *real* father. There had to be a way to free Drenen's soul from the soulkey. Somehow, Elwin would find a way to save him. He would save them all. To the abyss with prophecies and fates. He would save his family. If it killed him, he would find a way to protect them all.

In the distance, he saw smoke streaming into the sky, and he stopped. Lost in his thoughts, he had missed it.

Buildings like wooden toys of various sizes nestled against the base of the mountain. Smoke rose from hundreds of red chimneys. Though more spread out than Justice, the city was a fraction the size, and Elwin could just make out small specks moving between the structures.

"Goldspire," he said. "We actually made it."

Studying the rocks below, he mapped out the best course to the valley below. Then, he turned back toward the east and put a hand over his eyes as a shield from the sun. Far to the north, he could see white peaks and ridges even higher than this one. Squinting, he surveyed the sinewy ridge for his companions.

Elwin had flown at his slowest pace, but the others had lagged far behind. He saw Taego first, lumbering over a tall rock. In front of the bear, he could see the other two. Taming more Air, he flew toward them.

Sweat streaked through the dirt on Feffer's face, and his eyes looked as if they had been blackened. Daki also had the sunken eyes of little sleep. Sweat soaked his brow and streamed down his face. Elwin found himself wondering if he looked as rough. They had gotten little sleep the night before, not stopping to make camp until well into dark. And Feffer had been healed in a way. He should have been in a bed, not on a mountain. They could have spared some time to rest.

There had been no sign of pursuit, and Elwin had scouted out for the giants in the shadow realm to be sure. He had not found them, but Daki had insisted that the group should rise before first light to put as much distance between them and the Mystic Valley as possible.

"How much farther?" Feffer called.

Elwin lowered to their level, so he wouldn't have to shout. "Not far. Maybe fifty paces. This way."

Elwin led them to the place he had scouted.

Daki smiled. "The giants helped us to find a shorter path than the one we knew. My way would have taken us another day."

"How will we get down?" Feffer leaned over the edge to look down.

"You will need your rope," Elwin said.

Feffer pulled the rope from the tattered pack and looked at it doubtfully. "This won't be long enough."

"Tie it here," Daki said. "Elwin can untie it when we reach that cliff and then we can tie it again and lower to the next."

Feffer began to tie the rope to the peak of a boulder with Daki's help. Just to be sure, Elwin held the rope in place as Daki and Feffer climbed down. Taego dangled his hind legs behind him and used his sharp claws to descend. When his companions reached the ledge below, Elwin untied the rope and joined them.

"I never thought we would make it," Feffer said, staring at the city. He turned to Daki and placed a hand on his shoulder. "It is thanks to you. Without you, we could have never survived that valley. I owe you a debt."

To Elwin's surprise, Daki's cheeks reddened. "It is I who owe you. My path is yours."

"I mean it," Feffer said. "I will find a way to make this up to you. And Taego. I promise."

Elwin wanted to give Daki the same promise but decided against it. At Feffer's words, Daki's face became a deeper crimson, and he looked away.

"Feffer," Elwin said. "Help me tie this rope."

They tied the rope and lowered to the next cliff, then the next. Seven more times took them to haphazard stacks of boulders that sloped into the valley that housed Goldspire. Far to the east, Elwin could see people with picks going in and out of entrances to the mountain that were supported by wooden columns in the mountain's base.

The trees became thicker as they moved down the slope. And, as the land flattened out, Elwin eased down next to his companions. He could see the first building through the trees.

"I have never actually been into the walls of men," Daki said in an anxious voice. "I have always looked at the city from afar."

"Don't worry, my friend," Feffer said. "It is not all murder and mayhem. Can you smell the crowncakes and mutton?"

Elwin took a deep breath. It smelled like spiced fruit. "I can."

"What was the name of the place Jasmine told you to find?" Feffer asked.

"The Hammer Forged Inn."

"I need an ale," Feffer said. "I'm going to have a pint. Maybe I can trade this well-used rope and lantern for some coin."

"I have never had an ale from your lands."

"You haven't?" The incredulity was thick in Feffer's voice. "It is the most amazing drink ever. At first it is bitter, but after the third or fourth drink, you don't care. It makes you feel really good. I could feel really good right about now. A bed will be nice, too."

"Yeah," Elwin said, "a bed would be nice. I could use an ale, as well."

"I must try your ale," Daki said. "Do you think Taego can come?"

Feffer's smile showed all his teeth. He always gave that smile when considering a mischievous act. "I am willing to wager that no one will try to stop us."

"I am sure it will be fine," Elwin said. "The buildings are spread out. Besides, Zeth may be in here, and we might need him."

"The black savant is here?" Daki asked.

"Could be," Feffer said. "Hopefully, Jasmine is here too with Lord Zaak and a legion of the White Hand. Come on. That ale is waiting."

Feffer took the lead, but Daki followed close behind. Both of them had hands on the hilts of their blades and tried to look everywhere at once.

The trees thinned into a clearing that stretched to the city. Elwin could hear the familiar sound of a hammer smashing down on an anvil. A feeling like butterflies began to move through his stomach and spread through his chest as images of Faron working his forge came to his mind. He followed the sound to the first building on the edge of town. A large man with brown hair slammed a hammer down on a piece of metal. Sparks flew from the red-hot metal with each strike.

It wasn't Faron. But Faron was alive. He had made it out with Poppe and his mother. Elwin would see them again.

Feffer walked toward the smithy with a bounce in his step.

The smith looked up, and his eyes widened. "The Lifebringer save me! It's a bear!"

He had the hammer raised as if to defend himself and backed away from them. He bumped into the door behind him and tried to work the handle without taking his eyes off Taego.

"He is a friend," Elwin said in a calm voice. "He won't harm you." He held out his arms to make a calming gesture and saw his sleeves.

Then he saw the dirt and dried blood smeared into the silks. He hadn't noticed it before. It must have come from Feffer.

He glanced over at his friends. Feffer's jerkin had spots of blood as well, and he gripped his sword as if he was ready to use it. Daki appeared to have no red stains on him, but his hands rested comfortably on the hilts of his blades.

The hammer shook in the smith's hands. "Wha... What do you want from me?"

Feffer's voice held no compassion. "Tell us how to get to the Hammer Forged Inn. Is that a pie I smell?"

Elwin sighed.

It was just past noon when Zarah saw Goldspire in the distance. The red-tiled roofs matched the redwood boards that constructed the buildings. Only a few of the buildings stood taller than the others. One was the Miner's Guild and two others were inns. The mining community had a few small shops but not much else here. Most of the gold and metals the miners pulled from the earth went to the king, but the supply gave the small city a bit of wealth as well.

Her mother flew next to her. Below her were the three remaining wagons traveling along the cobblestone road. She wished she could *will* the wagons to move faster.

Over the last tenday of travel they had seen no more signs of skeletal warriors, but she had not stopped worrying over Elwin. When she had *finally* been allowed to talk to Kyler, the man had not been able to tell her any more. He had dreams he couldn't quite remember.

If Elwin had gotten himself killed, she would kill him. What if he had become Death bound? It was not possible. He had to have won.

Again she glanced at the wagons below. It appeared as if they had not moved an inch, but they had. She knew they moved several paces, in fact. It was the height that made them look as if they were parked on the road.

She tried to battle down the frustration. Impatience was beneath her station.

But now she could see the city. He could be here. But instead of flying ahead, she watched the slow wagons inch their way up the road.

"We should join the others," her mother said above the rush of wind in her ear.

Zarah stopped the flow of Air and fell toward the ground. The rush of the wind surrounded her as she plummeted toward the earth. She angled her body to move to her father's horse at the front of the caravan. Hulen sat atop his horse next to her father, and there was no sign of Tharu.

A few paces from the ground, she tamed enough power to slow to a stop. Similarly, her mother landed next to her. Father's horse came to a halt in front of them. The procession stopped as well. Zarah suppressed a sigh.

"We arrive within the hour," Mother said. "I do not know if Elwin has arrived before us. But, more importantly, we do not know how far Zeth is behind him. The black savant could already be here. He could have already taken Elwin. We must be prepared for anything."

"Tharu has not seen any more tracks that suggest an army," Father said. "But Zeth could have come with few others. Or even alone. He attacked Benedict without aid."

"You are right, my love," Mother said. "If Zeth only desires to capture Elwin, then he would likely have left his army behind. It is not easy to hide an army."

Tharu appeared next to her. She knew Tharu couldn't tame a veil, but she would love to know how the Chai Tu Naruo could disappear into thin air and reappear *without* taming the Elements.

"As far as I can tell, the city has not seen any attack." Tharu turned to face the city. "The miners still go in and out of the mine, and people walk the streets without fear."

Father nodded. "Perhaps, we have arrived first."

"Mother and I can fly ahead," Zarah said. "We will be able to sense any Death bound."

"No," Mother said. "We will move together."

"We could go under a veil just to scout out, then return to tell Father."

"No," Father said. "You will not go another step without permission. Understood?"

She nodded.

"And do not pout," Mother said.

Zarah opened her mouth to protest. She had not been pouting. She had been annoyed. It was time they stopped treating her like a child.

"Flowers bloom in ways that are not of our choosing," Tharu said. "We have but one choice. Allow the flower to grow of its own volition, or pluck it and watch its beauty fade."

Hulen laughed, "Ye shouldn't talk vulgar, there's a child here."

Father and Tharu shared a perplexed look. Zarah wasn't quite sure what Tharu had meant, but she had seen nothing vulgar about his words.

The dwarf stopped laughing. "It wasn't supposed to be vulgar?"

"No," Tharu said. "It is a saying amongst my people. Zarah is becoming a woman before our eyes. Soon, Zaak and Jasmine must allow her to make her own mistakes."

"But not yet," Mother said. "Zarah, you and I will travel with the others as your father said. Climb up. If Zeth is here, I do not want our taming to warn him of our presence."

Zarah climbed atop the first wagon and sat next to her mother. She sat up straight and proper, but she did not meet her mother's gaze. She was *not* pouting.

When Father nudged his horse forward, Bender snapped the reins to urge the coach into motion. A *very* slow motion.

The road into the town of Goldspire was surrounded by forests coming down from the mountains. Fewer redwoods dotted the forest than in the south, but she could see several rising above the smaller evergreens.

It became a chore not to fidget as the city grew closer, but Zarah managed to retain her posture as the coach crawled toward Goldspire. The main road led past the Hammer Forged Inn. They had stayed there on the recruitment expedition the previous year, so she knew the way. If she tamed Air and flew, she could have reached the inn in minutes.

She busied her thoughts by watching the city and their people.

The populace was a fraction the size of Justice, but the homes were larger than most of those from the capital city. And each building had wide spaces between them. The red-tiled homes lined the road, leading in from the west. Each garden had a variety of vegetables, and most of them had a fruit tree, mostly pearnut or appletwig trees. In a way, their lifestyles could be envied.

In the capital city, all of the homes and structures were almost on top of one another. Except, of course, those in the Nobles Quarter.

Children played in the cobblestone streets without fear of being run over by merchant's carts or rushing horses. Well-groomed dogs ran along with them. Young boys had long slender sticks and played at swords, while young girls had dolls and wooden tea sets. Several of them stopped to watch the procession with wide eyes. She smiled and waved to the children, and they giggled, waving back. As their wagons passed, the children turned back to their play.

Their wagons approached the largest building in the center of the town, and her father stopped in front, halting the procession.

"The Hammer Forged Inn," Zarah read the sign. "We are finally here."

Her mother began to dismount. "We will get rooms and consider our options. If we do not ...," She stopped mid-step and began to stare at the inn as if a snake had appeared.

"What is it, Mother?"

"Zarah stay back!" She raised her arm as if to protect her.

Then Zarah could feel it. Her essence began to quiver in a way she had never felt. Her stomach became ill. It was as if she had inhaled open refuse or had tar dumped on her. She focused on her essence to find where the *stench* had come from. The power of Spirit radiated from within the inn, but it had been twisted and deformed somehow. Her breath caught when the realization hit her.

Death bound. At least a dozen of them. They were here.

Chapter 30

THE CAPTURE

"We are almost there," Elwin said. "The blacksmith said the next street would lead us to the inn."

Feffer reached the broad cobblestone street ahead of Elwin, and then he stopped. His knuckles gripped his sword hilt. Elwin followed Feffer's gaze down the broad road, and he froze. Rising above several smaller buildings, the inn stood a dozen stories high.

In front of the inn was chaos. No other word could describe it.

Several black-robed figures poured out of the inn and began to surround three wagons. Steel glinted as swords left the scabbards of the men on horses and atop the wagons. Women screamed as they grabbed children playing with sticks and ran into alleys and buildings.

Elwin's eyes found the tall figure standing atop an upward balcony. He had long, dark hair and pale skin. Even at this distance, Elwin recognized Zeth. His heart began to beat faster. It felt like his dream that was not a dream. Only, he knew this time was real.

Elwin felt a burst of heat coming from Zeth as he tamed Fire. A flame appeared from his hand, forming the shape of a sword as he leapt from the balcony. Then, the foreign power emanated from Zeth. It felt like taming, but was different somehow. It was the same that he had used in Bentonville.

As Zeth moved, his arms and legs darkened, and his body

morphed into *something* not human. Light fled from him, and his arms elongated like the night he and Feffer escaped.

A figure in a white dress rose from the ground to meet the shadowy form. It was Jasmine. Wisps of light surrounded her, and javelins of crackling energy formed in both hands.

As the shadowy form fell toward her, Jasmine threw both javelins upward. They streaked through the air toward Zeth, and struck his chest with a thunderous sound. But, his path never wavered. His fiery sword swung toward her.

A burst of Air and Water made the space in front of her shimmer into a dome. The sword dissipated in a puff of smoke when it struck. Jasmine continued to rise, catching Zeth in the dome. A different power pulsed in her, and Zeth was flung in the opposite direction. He fell behind the inn, and Jasmine pursued him, disappearing from Elwin's view.

"Elwin," Feffer said beside him. "What should we do?"

The entire exchange happened within two heartbeats.

They needed to do something, *anything* to help. Before he could decide what that should be, another black-clad figure flew out the balcony. His bald head shimmered in the afternoon sun. It only took Elwin a moment to recognize Fasuri. This had been the man Wilton had spoken to. The one who had ordered Wilton to murder *his* friends and family.

Javelins of lightning appeared in Fasuri's hands, and he threw them toward the wagons. Wood splintered with the crash of thunder as horses and soldiers were flung in odd directions.

Several other men and women, wearing black robes, rushed out the front door of the inn. Elwin knew he should be afraid, but the fear was somewhere outside of him.

Another figure in white flew between Fasuri and the wagons.

He felt a torrent of Air and Water surge through her, and a shimmering dome appeared in front of her. It had the same shape as Jasmine's had, but it was much thinner. Javelins flew from Fasuri's hands and battered into the shield. The thunder clap was muted, but the impact knocked Zarah backward and sent her tumbling backward.

An image of Asa came to Elwin. A man in black held the innocent babe with a knife point to her throat. With that image came the memory of the power that could save her.

Thoughts ceased.

Elwin opened his essence wide to the power around him. First came Air like a storm entering into him. Ripples of dust rose through the cobblestones and vanished as it merged with his essence. He pulled heat from the ground at his feet and from the warmth around him. As the power of Fire filled him, red embers appeared and disappeared. Moisture accumulated around him and vanished into blue wisps as it fell toward him, giving him the power of Water.

All four Elements fused with his essence to the point of aching, and Elwin felt a clarity, a focus, like never before. The men moving in front of the inn seemed to slow, and he could feel the vibrations stomping onto the cobblestones.

He could almost *see* the ripples of wind between Fasuri and Zarah. He could count the droplets of sweat on her face and feel the heat of her breath. For that moment, they seemed frozen in the expanse above the buildings.

He flew toward them and felt the wind push against his body until he could move no faster. His body ached against the force slamming into him, but he did not slow. Taming Air, his mind formed a buffer around his face and body, and the pain vanished.

Elwin caught up to Zarah and the bald man in an instant and cut between the two as a javelin of light soared past. He aimed a wind thrust at an angle and tamed a trickle of Air to send the javelin wide of Zarah. A thick odor like spoiled candles burning hung in the space where the lightning had been.

His heart raced in his chest, but Zarah and Fasuri moved oddly as if in thick water. He saw the same was true of those below. Zaak was there with Tharu and Hulen. They moved through black-robed figures and swung blades as if moving through a pool of thick molasses.

A part of his brain wanted to stop and puzzle through how any of this was possible, but his gaze settled on the man before him. The scar beside Fasuri's eye traveled up his skull and twisted as his dark eyes stretched wide.

The Elements burned inside Elwin faster than he could refill his essence. Earth seemed to vanish the fastest of all. He pushed the thought from his mind, and focused on the man before him. The man who had ordered the deaths of his loved ones. The man who had tried to kill Zarah.

Then it occurred to Elwin. The power of Air moved just above Fasuri and merged into the other man's essence. He could feel the power of Air sustaining the man's flight.

Elwin opened his mind's eye to see with his essence. If he could grapple the other man's essence, Elwin could steal his flow of Air. Moving into the aggressive stance of fire form, Elwin approached Fasuri's essence and prepared to grapple.

The other man resisted Elwin's hold, but Fasuri's response was too slow. He grasped the other man's essence on his first try. When he had touched Zarah's essence, Elwin had felt a softness like a thousand roses with the strength of a lioness. Grappling Fasuri's essence felt like touching the scales of a snake that had slithered through pond scum. This man would kill anyone to further his own ambitions.

Reaching with his mind, Elwin ripped the flow of Air from Fasuri's grasp. The surprise in his eyes came as slowly as his other responses.

As he fell toward a tiled roof, Fasuri yelled in a slurred voice. "Yoouu'rrre hiiiiiim. Sssonnn ooofff Baaaiiin."

Fasuri's essence moved, somehow breaking Elwin's grapple. Air began to fill the man again.

A lightning hurl. He had to strike before Fasuri did.

Taming Air and Fire, Elwin gathered power in his hand like Jasmine had told him. A different memory replaced Jasmine's instructions. He didn't stop to think of where the thought had come from. Instead of the solid shaft of a spear forming, a ball of burning white began to grow above his hand. He threw it toward Fasuri and pushed all the Air and Fire he had left into the taming. Power flowed through his arm. White heat leapt from his hand, leaving blue streaks as the bar of light struck into the man's chest. Fasuri crashed through the tiled roof of a small building below.

Elwin's heart slowed down and everything around him sped up.

His *awareness* of his surrounded vanished as if closing his eyes. His vision blurred and his body became wracked with pain. His head throbbed and his lips felt dry.

Fighting to remain alert, he reached for more Air to sustain his flight, but he felt as if he was trying to get water from an empty cup. The world spun closer to him, and distant houses grew larger and larger.

At least Asa is safe.

The thought was distant, as if someone else had placed it in his mind. For a moment, the brief smell of lavender and lilac filled his senses.

⌒〰⌒

Feffer tried to call out, but Elwin had flown ahead toward the large inn. The thunder his leaving made still echoed in his ear. Feffer had never seen Elwin fly at that speed. He had never seen *anyone* move that fast.

Elwin crossed the space between here and the inn within the blink of an eye. Then he had thrown a beam of *light* at the man in black, all before Feffer could take three steps. His heart lurched when Elwin began to fall, but Zarah caught him before he struck the ground. With Elwin in her arms, she flew toward the tall ridge to the south.

Feffer continued to run toward the inn with all the speed his legs could produce. Sparing a glance over his shoulder, he could see Daki hadn't moved. He stared at the sky as if torn between what to do.

"Come on," Feffer yelled. "We can't help him."

He turned his attention back to the inn, not waiting to see if Daki and Taego followed.

Feffer didn't remember drawing his sword, but he tried to hold his sword steady as he ran. This was what he had trained for. He took deep breaths and tried to ignore the thunderstorm in his chest where his heart should be.

The battle was still fifty paces away. The front of the Hammer Forged Inn had double doors, which were wide open. Several people in hooded black robes were running out the front door. A dozen maybe? All of them wore hoods.

Zeth and Jasmine had disappeared between the buildings, and the hooded figures rushed toward the remaining soldiers.

Two of the soldiers had chain shirts under red tunics, bearing the white hand. They wore swords at their hips, but both soldiers wielded halberds against their attackers. Fiery swords appeared in the hands of the three black robed figures facing them. The soldiers used the reach of their weapons and coordinated their strikes to back the two figures toward a building.

One of the soldiers swung his halberd too low, and the sword of Fire sliced through the wooden shaft. Without pause the soldier drew his sword. Feffer was surprised when the metal deflected the fiery blade. Both soldiers moved through complementing forms. One used earth stance, while the other used the stance of air. When one switched to water, the other switched to fire. Together, the two soldiers pushed black-robed figures into a retreat, and the soldiers gave chase.

In front of the inn on the road, there were two of the White Hand, lying still, near charred horses and a damaged wagon. On the other side, in the middle of the road Lord Zaak Lifesong raised his sword in the stance of earth. Of all the forms, earth provided the strongest defense against so many opponents. Four dark savants approached him.

Feffer tried to run faster, but his legs still ached from days of climbing and running from giants. The inn was still too far away.

Two of the enemy facing Zaak held swords of crackling light. One of the dark savants jabbed with the sword, while the other jumped back with a spear of light appearing in his hand. He threw it at Zaak, and the large man dodged with a quick side-step. Zaak's sword became a beacon of yellow light as it blurred through his hands, deflecting bolts of lightning and sword thrusts. The other two dark savants circled around to Zaak's rear.

Dust rose around one savant and earth-toned blades thrust through the cobblestone road toward Zaak. He rolled to the side avoiding the blades, but a spear of light struck his armor and knocked him from his feet. He rolled with the blow and bounced back into earth form before Feffer could open his mouth to cry out.

A blue glow emerged around the fourth savant, and mist began to accumulate around Zaak's legs. Steam rose from his legs as the mist turned the color of ice. Zaak jumped backwards and struck at the blocks. The ice shattered into steam at the touch of Zaak's glowing sword, but his lowered blade gave his opponents an opening. Zaak flung himself to his back to avoid the crackling blade, then flipped backward to his feet.

Beyond the wagons, Feffer could hear more sounds of battle. A large axe rose above the wagons in tune with a deep-throated yell. A short, thick man rolled into view, swinging his axe at the head of a dark savant without even attempting to dodge a spear of lightning. A bolt hit him in the chest and sizzled, as fire would on water. The axe sunk into the neck of the black robe with a loud crunch. Then the short man charged other figures behind the wagon, leaving Zaak alone with the four.

Two of the savants had their backs to Feffer, and the other two were fixed on Zaak. By the Lifebringer, they didn't see him. Feffer charged the one surrounded in mist, but as he got closer, the figure turned to face him. A blue sword materialized to deflect Feffer's downward strike.

Steam rose off the other blade like ice melting in the sun, but it looked sharp. Feffer moved into water form and pushed his attack. Though he knew them all, this was the form he had practiced the most. The icy blade deflected each of his attacks but never countered. He pressed his opponent away from Zaak.

After a moment, his feet began to grow cold. He glanced down to see mist forming around his boots. He tried to jump backward, but the mist followed him. His feet became heavy, but he still moved through the forms. The icy sword came faster forcing him to retreat.

A downward strike from his opponent gave Feffer a glimpse into the hood, and he almost dropped his sword. The pretty face of a young girl had fixed into a sneer of determination. He continued to retreat, just deflecting her blade.

A girl? She was just a girl.

Her gaze wandered past Feffer for a second, and her advance stopped. A moment later, brown fur streaked by him. Her sword moved to intercept the rushing bear, and Fefffer blocked it. Taego never slowed. He leapt onto her and sunk his teeth into her throat.

As Taego took her to the ground and ripped at her neck, the hood fell away to reveal the girl's face. She had fair skin and a few freckles beneath her blue eyes. Her empty stare looked up at him. Feffer backed away from her, almost losing the grip on his hilt.

"She's my age." He shook his head. "Younger."

Daki ran past and struck at one of the two remaining on Zaak.

On the other side of the battle, Feffer could see another dark mound at Zaak's feet. The cowl had fallen away from the savant's face. A young boy looked up without blinking. His lifeblood leaked from the neat slice running across his upper torso.

The sword tumbled from his hand. He didn't want to watch, but he couldn't look away.

"Wait," he said to others. "Children. They are just children."

If Zaak or Daki heard Feffer's pleas, neither spared him a glance. They struck at their opponents, who retreated into defensive forms. Taego began to circle around and squatted as if getting ready for another charge.

The savant in the rear still threw spears of lightning, but they were angled to make Zaak and Daki dodge rather than direct throws of one pressing an attack. Each spear struck the ground with a flash of thunder, forcing Zaak or Daki to jump backward.

The savant in front held a blade of crackling light but used it to deflect blows from Daki or Zaak, while trying to gain ground between them. As the savant jumped back, Feffer winced as Zaak's blade missed her head by a hair.

The cowl fell away to reveal a tanned face framed in short black hair. She couldn't have been a year older than him. Her eyes darted back and forth between Zaak and Daki as she fought off their blows. Now that he was looking, the black robe curved around feminine curves.

He took a step toward her but stopped. There was nothing he could do. She was a dark savant. Why did he even care? He needed to grab his sword and help his companions. His Lord. But he couldn't make himself move. All he could do was watch.

"Now," she called out.

The other savant threw two spears at once, and at the same time, the girl threw her sword at Zaak's face. The blade dissolved before it reached him, but Zaak and Daki both jumped back from the attack.

Both savants sprung backward and flew into the air. As they moved higher, each formed a spear of lightning. Both bolts flew toward Zaak. He dodged one and swung his sword at the other. The light soaked into the blade. Without pausing Zaak aimed the tip of the sword at the girl, and the bolt exploded from the blade and flew back toward the girl.

Feffer held his breath as she dodged. The bolt missed, but it came close enough to singe the bottom of her robe. He only let his breath out when the bolt vanished in the distance.

The girl's eyes brushed his for a moment, then light shimmered around the two floating figures, and they vanished.

Zaak held his sword high and watched everywhere at once. Daki mirrored the stance. No enemies were in sight, but the sounds of clacking steel echoed in the side street beyond the inn.

Feffer's eyes settled on the girl at his feet. He couldn't tear his eyes away from her ruined throat. Her wide stare seemed to accuse him. His stomach became ill, and he fought not to wretch.

What had they done? What had *he* done?

Feffer began to step backwards. It all felt wrong. It was wrong to kill children. It was wrong to send children to fight.

Who could do this?

The memory of Bentonville came to his mind, and he reached to feel the toy soldier in his belt pouch. Feffer clenched his jaw and looked around for the shadowy figure. *Zeth* was responsible for this. *Zeth* had caused these children to die. He looked once more into the dead girl's eyes and reached for his sword on the road.

Two hands emerged from the cobblestone and grabbed at his ankles. He tried to jump away from them, but the hands latched on before he could take a step. And he tripped.

"Feffer!" Daki ran toward him.

As he reached for Daki's hand, something wrapped around his middle and pulled him *into* the ground. Darkness filled his vision as rock and dirt pummeled his face. He took deep breaths that tasted like dirt and metal.

Feffer could remember a time when he was younger. He was outside playing with Wilton. They were throwing rocks at a target painted on a tree behind his Da's shop. Feffer got really excited and walked in front of Wilton's throw. The rock had bounced off the side of his head, and he had awakened several hours later.

He could never forget the concern in his Da's eyes as he held Feffer's face. The image was the last he saw as something smashed into his nose.

Pain filled his thoughts, and then there was nothing.

Chapter 31

DEFEAT

Zarah eased Elwin onto a flat boulder overlooking Goldspire. His green tunic had been stained beyond repair, and he smelled as if he hadn't bathed in months.

She placed a hand on his chest and tamed the power of Life to feel for Elwin's life force. His heartbeat was strong. A sigh of relief escaped her lips, and she delved further to find his ailments. It only took her moments to realize Elwin's pain was not physical. His essence had been depleted. She had never met another elementalist with so much power. How had he moved so fast? It just was not possible.

She felt a shiver go up her spine. Was this fulfillment of the first prophecy? Was this lost knowledge made new?

He had tamed all four Elements. Mother would be angry when she learned of it. Burning his essence like he had, the fool bumpkin. He could have culled his essence or worse. He could have untethered his essence and died.

There would be time for chastisement later, now she needed him to be conscious.

She opened her mind's eye to look for his essence and gasped when she found it. It floated limply behind him, and his eyes were closed. An elementalist never had her eyes closed, unless she completely burned through her essence. Biting a curse, Zarah moved her essence to join his and placed all of her focus on their joining.

Zarah had only practiced this talent a dozen times, but lending was so similar to linking, she had no trouble with the taming. She took a deep breath and began feeding some of her essence into his. Just enough for him to become conscious.

Zarah felt her essence become smaller by the moment. After flying all day and her short-lived fight, she felt the effects of her shrinking essence rather quickly.

She began to fear she would not have enough to wake him when the eyes of his essence fluttered open. He regarded her with a confused expression.

"Where are we?"

It was more difficult to talk through her essence when her consciousness resided in her body. She knew her speech sounded slow, but she forced the words out. *"You need to wake."*

His essence merged with his body. A moment later, his crystalline eyes looked up at her. His cheeks were tanner than when last she had seen him, but he was still as handsome as she remembered. For a country bumpkin.

He lifted his head as if to rise, but laid his head back down. "What happened to me?"

"Do not try to tame the Elements," she instructed. "You must spend a good amount of time in the shadow realm before you can do much. Your essence is drained. What you did was more than foolish. All four Elements? Where you trying to cull yourself? "

"We need to get back," he said.

"No!" She placed a hand on his shoulder when he tried to get up. It didn't take much effort to hold him down.

"Feffer and Daki are down there!"

"There is nothing we can do for them," she said, "and I have my orders. You and I are clear of the fight. We need to wait here. If the city is lost, we will need to report to the king."

She tried not think about what would have to happen to her parents for the town to be lost.

Elwin laid on his back, breathing hard for several moments with his eyes closed. Finally, he spoke.

"I wasn't in the shadow realm just then. This isn't the first time. When I fell unconscious in the woods, it was like that too."

She had been preparing further chastisement to give him, but discarded it when he didn't press going back to Goldspire. Still, her tone held the reprimand he deserved.

"You *were* in the shadow realm," Zarah said. "Your essence was so depleted that your consciousness could not manifest. Because you acted like a foolish, country bumpkin." In case he missed her tone, she had decided to add the chastisement after all.

His eyes narrowed. "If I recall, I saved your life. Fasuri would have killed you had I done nothing."

"I had him handled," Zarah said. "What you did was dangerous. Did you not listen to Mother's lessons on culling?"

"Um." His forehead scrunched like it did when he was deep in thought. She rolled her eyes at him. His tone suggested he was guessing. "It has something to do with hurting my essence?"

Zarah used the best imitation of her mother's *lecture* tone that she could muster. "This is why you should not daydream during lecture. Part of our training is learning our limits. The limits will change as we grow in our power, but we will always have limits. If you push those limits too fast or too hard you can cull your ability completely. In bumpkin, that means you will never be able to tame the Elements again. Ever. That is if you don't just die."

He winced, and his face took on the proper amount of chagrin. A moment later he lost it by giving her a boyish grin. "Well, at least I have finally learned the lightning hurl. Well … kinda."

"That was *not* the lightning hurl. I am not sure what that was, but it felt like you tamed Fire and Air together. It came from your hand. The lightning hurl is more like tossing a rod. Mother will be *livid* when she finds you have been experimenting."

He forced himself into a sitting position. "I didn't experiment. I just …knew how to do it and threw everything I had at him. If I hadn't burned all the Earth or thought to use Water, I'd have tamed that too. What? Don't look at me like that."

Zarah felt her scowl slip for a moment, but forced her eyes to narrow and stared him without blinking.

"Look," he said. "I'm sorry. I only wanted to help."

"I do not want your excuses. You can tell them to Mother."

"But I—"

"No buts. We follow her rules for a reason. And I ...," The smell of burning wood filled the air. It was faint at first but was increasing in intensity. "Do you smell that?"

"Smoke," Elwin pointed.

In the city, two buildings had caught on fire.

"We have to get back down there," he said.

"Have you been listening to me?"

"This isn't the time for a lecture," he said with irritation in his voice. "We need to get down there."

Zarah sniffed. She disagreed. Elwin *did* need a lecture. Maybe two. But, that could wait. He needed to learn what it meant to follow orders.

"We wait here."

He stood on shaky legs and looked down. Zarah followed his gaze down the mountainside. After a short drop, the land sloped toward the city.

"You can stay here if you want, but I'm going."

She stepped up to him. It irritated her that she had to look up to meet his gaze.

"No. You. Are. Not."

"I can feel that my essence is too weak to fly, but my legs will still support me. I am climbing off this ridge with or without your help."

She crossed her arms beneath her breasts and flinched when his gaze dropped to her chest. She almost slapped him. How dare he? He actually had audacity to glance at her ... her bosom.

He met her gaze and said, "Fine. Without it is."

Turning from the ledge, he began to look for a path into the city. In the distance, smoke continued to rise. The fire was somewhere behind the inn, and she could no longer see any signs of battle. She could feel that the tamings had stopped and no clangs of steel rung in the air.

"Wait," she said. "I will take you. But I will speak with Mother about your insubordination."

He turned back to face her and stretched his arms out in exasperation. "Fine. Whatever. Tell her. Just get me down there."

She sniffed and decided to give him one more lecture.

"When our powers grow, we will be able to lift others with Air. Mother has begun my training on lifting objects. It is always better to practice with chairs and tables, rather than people. Though, when flying with people, we call it carrying. In the meantime, I will pick you up like a useless log and tote you."

Elwin gave her a flat stare but said nothing.

She let a few moments pass for him to brood. After his eyes narrowed to a satisfactory low, she said in a chipper voice, "Are you ready?"

He gave her a terse nod and stepped closer.

For some reason, her heartbeat became faster when she embraced him. Her nose and lips touched his shoulder. It was probably the smell that caused her stomach to flutter. She had grown used to the smell, but now it filled her nostrils again. As his body pressed to hers, she feared he would feel her increased heartbeat and get the wrong idea. She almost took a step back to slap him. He had no right to gape at her bosom like he had.

Instead, she focused on the task at hand and opened her essence to Air. As it filled her, she tamed flight. Elwin tightened his grip on her as they ascended, but his body still slid down hers. She felt her cheeks flush as his chin settled on her shoulder, and she squeezed him tighter. To keep him from falling, of course.

She flew low to avoid breathing in the smoke and to hide amongst the buildings.

"I can't hear anyone still fighting," he said in her ear.

She couldn't either. More importantly, she still could not feel anyone taming the Elements.

As she neared the inn, she could see her father and the others in front of the burning buildings two streets to the north. Had this been Justice, such a fire would have been difficult to control. The distance between the homes had saved Goldspire from complete destruction.

On the road by Tharu, there was another young Chai Tu Naruo

and a bear. A bear! She had never seen a bear up close. Even sitting on his haunches, he was larger than her books described.

She had read that many of the Chai Tu Naruo walked with animal companions, but she could not get Tharu to explain the unnatural bond. When Zarah was young, Tharu had walked with a large black cat. One day, the animal was not with him. He would not speak of it.

Several people bustled in the streets with buckets of water, running toward the burning buildings. Several threw water onto the flames, while others ran up with more filled buckets.

She landed in the middle of the cobblestone street and dropped Elwin on his backside with a satisfactory thud. Look at *her* bosom did he?

Releasing Air, she focused on the Water in the buckets. She had not trained much with Water, but this was one of the few talents her mother had insisted upon.

Blue wisps of light rose from the buckets and some from the air and joined with her essence. She focused her thoughts on the fire, and she tamed the Water to smother the heat and began the dousing. She could feel the heat resist the flow of Water as she fought the flames. Sweat began to bead on her forehead and back, and she felt her weakened essence draining. After a few minutes, billowing clouds of smoke filled the air as the last of the Water poured out of her.

She sagged to her knees, breathing hard from the effort. But at last, the fire was out. The townspeople began dropping their buckets, calling cheers and bowing to her.

"Thank you, mistress."

"The Lifebringer be praised!"

Zarah felt her cheeks flush at the praise, and had to force a smile. The smile faded when she heard Elwin's voice several paces away. "Where is Feffer?"

Zarah looked up to see him running down the road toward a wrecked building. It suddenly occurred to her that her mother was nowhere to be seen either. Why had *she* not doused these flames?

She would have flown to move clear of the crowd, but her essence was all but depleted. She would have been a poor example to Elwin, if she did not heed her own advice. Offering polite courtesies, she gently pushed her way free of the crowd to hurry after Elwin.

Down the street, Father stood with Hulen staring at a wrecked house. The side of it had been knocked inward and char marks surrounded the hole. When Elwin reached them, Father handed a parchment to him.

Zarah ran to catch up. As she grew closer, she could see Kyler and Bender in the alley, moving bodies clear of the wreckage with the help of the other Chai Tu Naruo boy. She grimaced when they placed a body far too small to be an adult next to an elderly couple.

"What happened here?" she asked when she reached them. "Where is Mother?"

"It's all my fault," Elwin said, lowering the parchment. Tears filled his eyes. "I did this."

"What are you talking about? What is your fault?"

He shoved the letter at her and ran toward the inn.

"Stop," Father called as he ran after Elwin. The Chai Tu Naruo boy followed after them at a run as well. She turned her attention to the parchment.

After reading it twice, Zarah stared at the letter for a moment in disbelief. It had been written in a hasty hand and the red ink began to drip down the page. No. Not ink, she realized.

"Blood. It was written in blood."

She looked at the body of the child again, and her stomach lurched before she could stop it. She dropped to her knees and wretched. She felt thick fingers brush back her hair. When her stomach emptied she fell backward, sitting hard on the cobblestone. Tears began to blur her vision, and she had no willpower left to keep them from falling.

Hulen knelt down beside her. His thick thumbs began to wipe at her cheeks. The compassion in his dark eyes made her cry even harder.

"We've lost," she said. "We can't do it without her."

"All is not lost yet," Hulen said. "We still have the boy."

"So what? What does it even matter anymore? This is all his fault. Had he just … He could have…"

"No child," he said in a soft voice. "You do not mean that. You are upset. All is not lost. We must have hope that the Forger is still in control."

Hope? She looked down at the parchment, crumbled in her fist. Without Mother, there was no hope. The black savants had won.

∾

Son of Bain,

Again, you elude my grasp. I must say, this time you have even impressed me. You almost managed to kill a trained black savant on your own. Instead, you have more corpses of the innocent to be lain at your feet.

I have acquired the Madrowl boy and the Life witch, called Jasmine Lifesong. I will deliver them to King Bain in your stead.

Must they too perish before you rise to your destiny?

Cross the Tranquil Sea to the nation of Alcoa, and go to a city named Turney Fay. There you will seek out a man named Tavier at the Fighting Chance Tavern. Come alone. Anyone you bring with you will be destroyed. Their blood will be on your hands as well.

You have spat on my generous offer to see you safely to your father without bloodshed, and you have seen the consequences of your defiance. I am not without mercy, but do not test me further.

We will await your arrival. But do not tarry. We will not wait for too long.

Zeth Lifesbain

Chapter 32

HOPE

Elwin looked at the sword lying on the cobblestone street. The curved blade broadened toward the tip and had a heron just above the hilt. He had never asked Feffer what the blade was called. Feffer would know. He knew more about being a soldier than Elwin ever would.

Now Feffer was gone.

Why had he ever left Feffer? Zarah was better trained than Elwin. She didn't even want his help. She had admitted as much. Why hadn't he let her handle Fasuri? If he had, Feffer wouldn't have been taken.

He kicked a loose cobblestone, and the rock flew past Feffer's sword and fell into the small crater. It sunk a pace into the road and spanned two paces across. This must have been where they had captured him. Feffer never would have left his sword if he had been able to fight back.

Elwin bent over to pick up the blade by the hilt, then turned to look at the wreckage along the wide street in front of the Hammer Forged Inn. Amongst the rubble of splintered wagons were the scorched corpses of two soldiers and several horses. Black-robed figures laid on the street as if sleeping, but young faces stared upward with unblinking eyes.

His gaze settled on a girl with blue eyes. Her golden hair spilled out of her cowl, and she had small freckles on her pale cheeks. Dried splatters of blood stained her chin above a ruined throat.

Beneath him, the cobblestones began to spin, and the sword felt heavy in his hand. He dropped to his knees beside the girl and let the sword clamor to the road next to him.

How many had died because of him?

"Elwin," a gentle voice said in front of him.

He looked up to see Zaak standing in the alley beside the inn. His face looked hard, but his eyes held a hint of moisture. "We have much to discuss."

Elwin's voice broke on the first word, and he didn't try to stop his tears. "All these … children. Feffer and Jasmine. This is all my fault."

He hid his face and felt tears wet his hands. The sobs came in uncontrollable fits that stole his breath. Something squeezed his shoulder, and he flinched to see Zaak kneeling over him.

"Elwin," Zaak said. "What happened here is not your fault. This was Bain. I have seen him do far worse during my time in Alcoa. You cannot blame yourself. Alright?"

"If I would have gone with Zeth, he—"

"He would have still killed as many of our people as he could. Bain's undead army is already moving across our lands, Elwin. Had we not ventured north to find you, we would not have known of the skeletal warriors in our midst."

Elwin wiped his tears. "What do you mean?"

"We were attacked on our way here, and our northern post has been destroyed. King Justice has called the majority of our elementalists back and prepared the defense of our gates to receive an attack. Had we not come to find you, we might not have learned of this until it was too late. Now, we have hope."

"Hope?" Elwin said in disbelief. "How can we have hope? Jasmine and Feffer were taken. If I don't go to Bain, he will kill them. I know he will. My home … Bentonville. You don't know what he's capable of. I—," his voice broke, and he swallowed. "I have to go to Bain. *Alone.*"

"That is my call to make, child." Zaak's eyes hardened.

"No one else can die because of me."

Zaak studied Elwin for several minutes. By the time the large man spoke, Elwin felt as if he had been weighed and measured for auction. "Jasmine believes in you, and I trust her judgement. More importantly, I made her a promise. I cannot surrender you to Bain. Too much depends upon you for it to ever come to that."

"No," Elwin stood and backed away, crossing his arms over his chest. "Nothing depends on me. I'm a farmer's son. Ask Zarah. I'm just a country bumpkin. She'll tell you."

Zaak stood and pointed to the hilt of his sword. "Jasmine has told you about touched weapons?"

Elwin's eyes settled on the massive blade. It had eloiglyphs etched into the hilt sticking above Zaaks shoulder and more running along the scabbard. So did his armor. Elwin had learned a few, but these were all foreign to him. Though, some of them matched the markings at the Stones of Seeking.

"Yes," he said.

"This sword is not just touched. It is an artifact of power. It offers me advantages beyond even a touched weapon. With this in my hands, I can wield the Elements in a way. But, I can also sense them being tamed around me." He paused and leveled his gaze on Elwin for several moments. "I felt your tamings this afternoon, and I still cannot make sense of what you did. Jasmine told me of your abilities, but I did not quite believe it until that moment. You have already begun to fulfill the prophecies. I would wager, the dragonkin are already beginning to become restless in their slumber."

Elwin looked away from him. "I didn't want any of this."

"Look at me."

Zaak's eyes had hardened once more, and his jaw was tight.

"Much has been placed on your shoulders, but you do not have time to sulk like a child. I will not be able to train you in the Elements, but you must be ready. But we will have time, I think. Turney Fay lies far to the east where Alcoa meets Kalicodon. We have many months of travel before we reach the City of Two Nations. I will continue your sword training on our way to Alcoa."

Zeth had said to come alone, but Elwin felt a spark of hope. No. Elwin shook his head. He would not see anyone else die because of him. Once his essence regenerated, he would leave. That would be best for everyone.

"We are coming, too," Daki stepped out of the shadows of an alley with Taego trailing him.

Zaak half turned to him and raised an eyebrow. "Daki is it? I suspected you would."

"I will be coming too, Father," Zarah said, coming out of the alley. "Someone will need to see to Elwin's training in the Elements. He has yet to learn the lift or dousing, and his lightning hurl needs a lot of work." She crossed her arms beneath her breasts and set her jaw as if to argue.

"You will come," Zaak said.

"I ...," she said as if to protest and stopped with her jaw hanging open. "I will?"

"I do not have the soldiers to send you back to the castle, and I will not send you back without escort. When we reach Alcoa, I will leave you in the king's care while the rest of us venture to Turney Fay. As soon as I find a moment, I will begin to draft letters to announce our intentions in his lands. Alcoa will wish to know there are black savants hiding in one of his cities."

She opened her mouth as if to argue but paused for some reason. When she spoke, her voice was calm. "I have thought on this, Father. Lower Turney is ruled by Kalicodon. What if they are aiding Bain? Is it possible the tribes have betrayed Alcoa?"

Tharu appeared at a light run and stopped to whisper into Zaak's ear. Both of their gazes went to a house with a collapsed roof. It was the same building Fasuri had crashed into.

He rubbed a hand through his beard and shook his head. "That is a matter for another time. The sun will set soon, and we still have dead to bury. You go inside and wash up. I need to speak with Elwin for a moment."

"But Father, I—"

"Go."

His voice never rose, but Zarah flinched at the word and closed her mouth. She stuck her chin into the air and turned toward the inn, walking as if it had been her intention all along.

Zaak watched her open the door to the inn without expression. When the door closed, he turned to Elwin and said, "Come."

Elwin turned to follow him and Daki did as well. Zaak spared the Chai Tu Naruo and Taego a momentary glance but said nothing. Elwin didn't look at the bodies as the walked passed the wreckage from the battle. Zaak stopped in front of a building with a small garden. The peach tree had started to bloom.

The door to the house stood open, and a lantern lit the common room. Hulen was inside, speaking his native tongue. By his tone, Elwin would have guessed every word to be a curse. When Zaak stepped into the home, Hulen's mouth snapped shut, but his eyes threw daggers in every direction. Then he stomped out of the house. Elwin had to move aside to keep from being knocked out of the dwarf's way.

"Come inside, Elwin. I want you to see this."

The boards creaked when Elwin stepped inside, and the air smelled like rotted meat left in the sun. A hole in the ceiling brought a breeze into the small space, but it did little to abate the stench. He moved a few paces in and stopped when his eyes found the source of the smell.

Just inside the room beside a broken chair, a thin man was curled on his side. The skin around his face was stretched so thin, Elwin could make out the shape of his skull. The hands protruding from his sleeves were gaunt and mostly bone. His eyes bulged and protruded from his sockets.

Elwin had no warning before his stomach wretched. He didn't open his mouth in time, and some of the it came out his nose. His eyes and nose began to water from the burn. Elwin's legs were moving into the street before he had made up his mind to leave.

He sucked in the fresh air and almost wretched at the acid taste in his mouth. His breath wreaked of the spoiled remnants of the sweet, red fruit he had eaten earlier.

Daki stood in the street with Taego wearing a deep frown.

"Did you see that?" Elwin asked.

Daki nodded.

Zaak came out of the house and handed Elwin a flask. "Water."

Elwin snatched it from his hand and took several gulps. He wiped his mouth with the back of his hand and didn't bother to mask his anger. "Why would you want me to see that?"

"This is what we are fighting," Zaak's voice was hard. "The man you knocked in here, the black savant, he drained the Life out of this man to heal the wounds you dealt him. I've seen it before. This is why we can't afford to lose. Bain cannot win. If he does," Zaak gestured to the desiccated corpse through the door, "this is the type of ruler we will have over us. You cannot surrender to him."

Elwin stared at the corpse through the doorway for a moment before he tore his eyes away. He didn't want to go to Bain. But, he had no choice. "If I don't go, he will kill Feffer. And Jasmine."

Zaak shook his head. "You will go. But you will not go alone. It is time you started to believe in something beyond yourself. I am placing my hope in you, Elwin. As are we all."

"What if I can't do it? What if more people die because of me?"

"More people *will* die, Elwin. We are at war. Do not let those lives be given in vain. All that we do, we do for a purpose. We cannot lose hope."

He looked back at the corpse and shuddered. Zaak was right. He could not trust Zeth at his word. The black savants could have already killed Feffer and Jasmine. Even if they were alive, Bain could kill them just to teach Elwin some sick lesson.

"Alright," Elwin said at last. "I won't surrender. But what will we do?"

Zaak's eyes narrowed, and he gritted his teeth. "For starters, I intend to get my wife back. "

❦

Feffer awoke to the sound of men talking. Their tones were short and snappish as if arguing, but his mind would not quite make sense of the words. He didn't remember drinking, but his head hurt beyond reason, much worse than the day after having drunk himself into a stupor with Gurndol and his squad. A metallic taste had dried to his tongue.

He tried to open his eyes, but the left eye would not respond and the other slow to focus. The sun stung his eye through thin trees above him. The ground beneath him felt solid, like a boulder, and he could hear the sounds of water crashing against rocks.

Closing his eye, he tried not to move for a moment, focusing all of his thoughts on listening. Birds cawed not far away, and the voices began to blend into words.

"I was trying to catch his whelp," a deep voice said.

"You were trying to kill his whelp," replied another man. "Had you helped the lessers defeat Lifesong, the man would be dead. Were you frightened by him?"

The other man did not answer. After a moment the melodic voice continued. "If you were frightened, it would be understandable. He has defeated you before. Perhaps that ugly scar goes deeper than your flesh?"

"I was not frightened," the deep voice said through gritted teeth. "Zaak Lifesong cannot fly, but his whelp was getting away. How could I have known the son would intervene? You told me his gifts were not developed. He moved like King Bain and struck me with a firestorm that knocked me through a building. Had I not drained the peasant inside the hovel of his life force, I would have died from my wounds."

"Yes," the other voice said, "it seems the son has learned much from his time in the woods. Or perhaps he simply needed the proper motivation. Is it possible he feels something for Lifesong's daughter?"

His wits returned to him, and he realized where he was. He had been taken. Feffer opened his eye and craned his head, attempting to see the source of the talking men. The sun was still too bright through the trees, and his eye refused to fully focus.

"He's awake," the deep voice said.

"So he is," replied the other man.

Feffer tried to sit up but felt a heavy weight begin to press on his chest. When his eye finally focused, he saw a black boot on his chest. The boot was attached to a leg covered in dark robes. He could tell the body beneath the robes was heavily muscled.

The man's head was shaven, and his face carried a scar extending from the back of his skull to his dark eyes. Whatever had made the scar had missed the eye by a hair's width. The man's smile showed too many teeth. Feffer wasn't sure if the smile was intended to frighten him or to be reassuring.

The other face came into view. Zeth's dark eyes looked down at him.

"Fortunately for you," Zeth said with a casual tone, "King Bain wants you alive. Otherwise I would destroy you piece by piece."

Feffer could hear footsteps approach.

"Savant Lifesbain," a young female voice said, "the ship is ready for sail."

"Fasuri," Zeth said, "please take your foot off the prisoner."

The larger man complied.

"On your feet," Zeth commanded.

Feffer did not move. He knew he should have been frightened, but Zeth had already said Bain wanted Feffer alive. Besides, his muscles were too sore to move. His head pounded like gongs ringing in his skull, and his face and left eye felt like a giant had struck him. He touched his face and forehead gently. His forehead had a knot the size of a plum. When his finger found his left eye, he winced away at the touch. It was swollen shut.

A boot kicked Feffer's leg, but he couldn't feel any pain over the fireworks sounding in his head.

"I said on your feet," Zeth said through his teeth.

"Go thump yourself," Feffer said. "I wasn't finished napping."

"Get him up," Zeth said.

Fasuri's rough hands lifted Feffer to a standing position. Feffer was forced to either stand or allow himself to fall. He chose to stand. A fall wouldn't do his head any good.

The large man held Feffer's arms from behind. And, as much as he hated a dark savant touching him, he wasn't sure he could stay upright without the support.

Now that he was standing, Feffer had a better view of his

surroundings. They were on a cliff. A few small, pearnut trees provided the bluff with shade. Beyond the cliff face, there was a long drop, where waves crashed against the rocks below. The waters looked deep, but a swimmer would be forced to take caution or be smashed between the waves and the cliffside.

He blinked. The sea?

He must have been unconscious for days. If he remembered his map, the Tranquil Sea was a tendays' ride north of Goldspire.

Jasmine Lifesong laid face down a few paces beside him. She wore a plain white dress, which had a few drops of blood on the neck. Her hands and feet were bound behind her back with a rope tied around her neck that joined to her feet. Her auburn hair was disheveled and her face had a long red welt. But, Elwin wasn't there. The Lifebringer be praised, Elwin wasn't there.

A girl stood behind Zeth. Her black hair rested a hand above her shoulder, which was much shorter than most women he had seen. He could make out the shapely curves of her body beneath the black robes. Her skin tone was tanned, darker than any natural tan Feffer had seen. Her high cheek bones rounded her face in such a way to highlight emerald eyes. Her smile made her eyes dance in the morning light. It was her, he realized. The one who had fought Zaak.

"Look at me," Zeth said in a calm voice.

Feffer tore his eyes away from the girl to look at Zeth. The man's glare could have set wet leaves on fire.

"You will speak to me with respect."

He felt a giggle try to rise in his throat, and he made himself cough to disguise it. What had gotten into him? A man with the power to take his soul stood in front of him, demanding respect. Still, his gaze wanted to return to the girl's green eyes. The giggle escaped and became barks of laughter.

The motion made his ribs hurt and head spin, but he couldn't stop laughing.

Zeth took a step closer to him. "Care to share your musings?"

The irritation in Zeth's voice made Feffer laugh harder. Why was he laughing? There was nothing to laugh about. He had been betrayed by his brother. All the people he loved were dead. His father was dead. He had saved Elwin from Zeth to become lost in the woods. He had been chased by giants and lost Haven.

She was *his* horse. He had paid for the mare with the coin he had earned. For all he knew, the Life-cursed giants ate *his* thumping horse. After escaping the wilderness and reaching Goldspire, he had been taken captive. He was prisoner to the man who killed his father.

Anger built up in him like a well during a storm. He balled up his fists, ignoring the pain in his swollen fingers.

"You do not deserve my respect!" Feffer spat at him. The spittle scattered and rained Zeth's face. "You killed my father and stole my brother's will. The Lifebringer as my witness, I will kill you. Somehow, I will kill you."

Feffer's heart raced. What was he saying? He couldn't kill a dark savant. He didn't have a sword, and he could barely stand. Feffer wanted to cry, scream, and shout at the same time. What had gotten into him? His arms started to tremble. He clenched his jaw to keep his teeth from clattering.

Zeth calmly wiped his face with the sleeve of his robes.

"This one has potential," Fasuri's breath was hot on the back of Feffer's neck, like sludge running down his spine. He could smell spiced wine.

"Silence," Zeth said and stepped closer to Feffer. "Wilton chose to sacrifice you and your village to save himself. He has seen the power of the Father and chooses to serve rather than be slaughtered. Soon enough, you will see the right of your brother's choice."

Feffer clenched his fists even tighter. One solid swing to the man's throat. The Lifebringer help him, but that's all he asked for.

"The Awakening is upon us," Zeth continued. "Elwin will serve his purpose. Now that we have you, he will come to us. When he has accepted the Father's gift, you will serve at his side."

Feffer's hands stopped trembling, and he began to breath more easily. This man wasn't going to use him. Elwin would remain free.

Feffer looked into Zeth's eyes and announced each word with care. "Go. Thump. Yourself."

Zeth swung a backhand at Feffer's face, but Feffer had anticipated the strike. Dodging Zeth's hand, he threw his head backwards into Fasuri's face and felt a satisfying crunch. The impact on the back of his skull was dizzying, but he felt the grip on his arms loosen.

Pushing off of Fasuri, Feffer leapt from the cliff. His shaky legs had not carried him as far as he had hoped, but he cleared the rocks. The deep, blue sea rushed up at him and struck like a boulder thrown by a giant. The water struck his feet and enveloped him like a grasping hand. The force of the water's grip closed around him, and he sank beneath the waves.

Chapter 33

TRAITOR

Wilton touched the wall above, feeling for the next groove. He was careful to place each foot before moving his hands up farther. The waxing moon did not shed enough light to betray his position, but his night vision could not see the grooves of the stone ladder.

Still, he preferred the darkness. It was better not to be seen. Thief-catchers were denied few places in the city, but he would have been hard-pressed to provide an explanation as to why he needed to access the outer wall this time of night.

The soldiers walking the streets below announced the battle to come.

He had arrived to Justice the previous day, and the city had long since received word of the approaching army. The gates had been closed, and the portcullis had barred access to the city. The villages surrounding the castle walls had been abandoned, and the villagers had taken to the city commons or fled west toward Paradine.

Wilton had not known the men at the gate. Had they not recognized his raqii dath at his hips, they would have denied him entry. Being perceived as a thief-catcher still had its uses. At least, it would for one more night.

The larger part of him wanted to betray Bain. He could have gone to Sir Gibbins to warn him of the dangers outside the walls. But, they had Feffer. Zeth had promised Feffer's safety. He only had to do this one last thing for them, then he and Feffer would be free of this war.

Besides, what use was it to warn the grains on a beach of an oncoming tsunami? The beach could do nothing to avoid the powerful waves. Soft shores would be destroyed or formed into something new. The knowledge of their doom would do nothing to stop their demise.

Reaching the top of wall, he peeked over. Every four paces were sconces for torches, but only every other one had been lit to reduce visibility from the fields below.

There would be patrols atop the wall, but most of the archers were under the protection of the watch towers, evenly spread every thirty paces. Two to a patrol marched back and forth between each pair of towers.

A dozen paces to his left, the door to the closest watch tower was closed. If his source had been trustworthy, there would be three archers inside watching the eastern fields.

He knew what the archers would see.

Black fog filling empty eyes. Like twenty thousand scarecrows propped in a field, the skeletal warriors stood facing the walls of Justice without flinching or swaying. Grouped in rows of one hundred, each line had a black savant commanding the charge. Behind the savants, dozens of catapults were loaded with spheres of rock that had been ripped from the soil by the power of the Elements.

It wouldn't be long now.

Wilton saw the dark armored figures atop the wall walking toward him. Their chain shirts clanked as they moved. He pressed his body closer to the wall as they passed by him. Both were looking away from him, over the parapets.

They stopped outside the tower and watched the fields.

Wilton could not see their faces, but he could see their weapons. Both carried halberds and wore swords at their hips.

"Abominations," one spat. His voice shook with the word, betraying his fears.

"The Lifebringer save us," the other said. "You think it's the

Awakening?"

"Life, I hope not."

The first man began to walk in the direction they had come, and the other man followed.

"Priest Braist was out last Lifeday, and Inquisitor Teblin gave a special sermon on. I never thought I'd live to see it. But, he warned us."

Once they were well past him, Wilton climbed atop the wall and followed them. Neither moved with real purpose. They walked their patrols, staring out at the undead army.

He could kill them both and no one would be the wiser, but he wouldn't. His actions made him a traitor, but he only killed when he must kill.

"It can't be the Awakening," the other said. "There ain't no thumping dragons."

Wilton stalked the one in the rear and unsheathed his raqii dath and slammed the butt of his hilt on the back of the man's head. Wilton caught him as he crumpled.

The other man turned, his mouth opened as if to say something. His eyes widened just as the flat of Wilton's blades struck the sides of his temples in rapid succession.

The man's head knocked into the parapet as he fell, his halberd clanking against the ground. Wilton froze for several moments, waiting to hear a sound of alarm. When none came, he sheathed his twin blades and moved toward wooden rungs that controlled the portcullis.

He would need to remove the bars from the gate in order for the gate to be battered down. The walls of the city and bars of the portcullis had been crafted by the Elements to resist destruction. They would withstand a giant's hammer without a dent and could absorb Elemental blasts.

The gates, however, were made of redwood. They were strong, but the black savants had the power to rip through them in moments.

There were over two hundred black savants readying to take the city. They had an army of skeletal warriors. And they had the soulless one. The soulless one, Wilton feared most of all.

Drenen Escari would spend an eternity in servitude because of Wilton. He was no longer a man, but his mind was still intact. Every time Wilton looked into Drenen's eyes, hatred burned in those dark eyes. If Drenen's will was ever his own, Wilton would die by his hand. He had no doubt.

Wilton reached the wooden rungs. It looked like the wheel of a ship.

He grabbed a torch from its sconce and began to wave it back and forth. He watched over the wall. Wilton could not hear the command, but he could see the skeletal warriors become animated. Each foot fell in unison, making the sounds of marching echo into the stillness of the night.

It had begun.

Wilton would have to move quickly. The portcullis was on the outside of the gates, but moving the ancient metal would make noise. The skeletal warriors would distract the watch, but they would soon realize the portcullis had been compromised.

He replaced the torch and moved to the wheel, turning the rung. Forty paces below, he could hear the metal portcullis lift. It was heavy and slow to move. Wilton put all his weight into each turn, glancing back and forth to watch each tower for motion.

Neither of them stirred, but it was only a matter of time until someone realized what was happening.

"Alarm!" he heard a voice cry. To his surprise, it had come from one of the guards he had knocked unconscious. Heavy boots stomped in his direction.

Sweat began to cover his brow. He continued to turn the wheel until he heard a heavy thunk, the sound of the metal safety bar falling into place. He kicked and stomped on the bar until it bent around the rung. He kept kicking to bend the spokes of the wheel. It would take several hours to fix. By then, it would be too late.

"Alarm! Alarm!" The voice was closer.

Wilton drew his raqii dath.

He did not want to kill the guard, but he might not have a choice. Perhaps death by the sword would be a more merciful fate than the one that awaited many this night.

The man came into view. Wilton raised one blade in front of him, one high and one low with his legs in fire stance. The guard had reach with his halberd and the offensive stance was more practical on the walkway.

"Yo-yo-you're a thief-catcher!"

"I do not wish to kill you," Wilton said. "I have not held these blades very long, but I know how to use them."

"TRAITOR!" the man yelled. He held his halberd defensively in front of him. "OVER HERE! DEFEND THE PORTCULLIS!"

Wilton saw a large, spherical shape fly overhead and crash into the city below.

A loud crash echoed in the city, followed quickly by another. Then another. Cries of pain erupted in the streets below as soldiers were overrun by flying boulders. The boulders continued coming without any discernible pattern. He gritted his teeth and tried to ignore the screams from the city.

Wilton spared a glance over the parapet toward the eastern field. Below, the skeletal warriors reached the gates. Even at this distance, he could see the discoloration of rotted flesh holding swords at the ready. Rigid bodies ran without hesitation as the soldiers of the White Hand clashed into the front of their ranks.

The scuff of a boot warned him, and Wilton jumped back in time to avoid a downward strike. The blade of the halberd sparked against the parapet where Wilton's head had been.

"Last chance," Wilton said, keeping his voice calm. "Please don't make me kill you."

"OVER HEAR! TRA—"

Wilton feinted toward his right. When the soldier dipped his halberd toward him, he spun to the man's middle, slicing through his throat just above the chain gorget. The soldier dropped the halberd and clutched his throat, stumbling to his knees.

Wilton continued forward not wanting to watch the man die. He sheathed his blades without bothering to wipe the blood from them. His raqii dath would see more blood before the night was done.

He made his way back toward the ladder. The door to the watch tower was still closed. Wilton heard bowstrings snapping from within. The archers inside were too busy to answer the other man's call.

He looked over the parapet. Arrows were loosing into the darkness. Even if the archers hit their targets, it didn't matter. They could not kill men who were already dead.

For a moment, he considered telling the men inside they were wasting their lives. He wanted to tell them to run and hide.

"You are defeated," he whispered. "There is nothing you can do. The world belongs to Bain. And Bain belongs to Abaddon."

A whisper. That was all he could give them.

Wilton moved down the ladder and slipped into the darkness, watching the fall of Justice from the shadows. The world would fall to Bain, and Wilton would watch from the shadows. That was the only way he and Feffer could survive. Whatever the cost, he would keep that promise to his father.

Bain sat on a large rock by the shore watching the ocean's morning tide. His usual spot on the sandy shore was overrun by the high waves. But from his perch atop the rock, he had a better view of the southern horizon.

Dark clouds merged with the ocean's distant tides. The gathering storm had an energy that didn't feel natural. Storms could be crafted from the Elements, but they were not easily controlled. Without an artifact of power, a storm wrought from the Elements could become a hurricane over the sea or a tornado by land. However, that could have been the purpose.

The question was, why would someone want to cause such a storm?

The dark tides would bring his son home to him. Elwin sailed on a ship called the Dancing Lady, and storms were ever a hazard of the sea. A mishap while traversing the deep waters would not be amiss. Few would suspect a storm as a weapon of murder.

Betrayal.

The word plagued his thoughts. Few could be trusted, and even those few had agendas not of Bain's choosing. Of his savants, only Lana gave him loyalty. Zeth, Fasuri, and the others craved power above all.

But, who would want to sink Elwin's ship? Alcoa?

Thirod Alcoa was likely to have informers in the Lands of Justice. Alcoa had an old relationship with Justice. Bain had informers in their lands, so it would be foolish to think otherwise of Alcoa.

Thirod would wish Bain harm, but would he murder his son? The man had the resources. Thirteen elementalists taming Water and Air could make a storm. Though most of them were not of great power, there were elementalists in abundance in Alcoa. In truth, Aloca had more gifted than even Bain had collected.

However, the majority of the guild elementalists in Alcoa were only gifted with a single Element. But, an assembly of thirteen could create enough energy for a storm, regardless of the individual strength of each in the assembly.

That wasn't likely. Thirteen elementalists had thirteen mouths. Bain had enough ears in Alcoa, and such an assembly would have drawn note.

Jhona?

"No," Bain dismissed the thought aloud. Jhona would not betray him again.

His brother had betrayed Bain to steal the boy, but he had thought his actions to be in Elwin's best interests. Jhona had thought he was *saving* the boy. He would never raise a hand to destroy the very life he had saved.

Besides, after banishment his brother had settled on the western coast of Alcoa, and this storm felt as if it originated in the south. Then the obvious choice came to him.

Donavin. His older son had no limitations. Betrayal was one of many tools in Donavin's chest.

Bain's eldest son was on the southern slopes of Alcoa in a coastal city called Dalton. It was the first city Bain had taken from Alcoa and was the main stronghold for his garrison in Alcoa. He had given his eldest son the honor of being Savant of the southern region.

Donavin had the most to lose if Elwin were to join Bain's army.

His eldest son had a thirst for battle that was insatiable, but Donavin wore deceit and trickery like other men wore armor and shield. It was not in his nature to share. After his own failure all those years ago, Donavin would carry a hatred for Elwin for his destiny. Where his oldest son failed, Elwin would succeed.

"Donavin," he decided.

He could not reprimand Donavin without proof. But Bain would not allow the petulance of his oldest son to destroy all he had worked for. The Father had allowed Bain to see what was to come. Elwin would Awaken the dragonkin, then Bain would become king of them all.

"King of dragons," Bain said.

That was what the world would call him as they knelt to his rule. He stood upon the rock to get a better look at the dark clouds on the horizon. Lightning rumbled through them as they began to shift north and west toward the coast of Alcoa. It would continue to gather energy as it spun its way up the Alcoan coast.

"Come home to me, son," Bain said. "Come home."

For the first time in a long time, Bain allowed himself to feel hope.

Epilogue

Dearest Melra,

Time passes poetically, standing still only in the depths of our minds. The events of one passing life can have the power to alter the lives of all who cross his path. The remaining touch can be as tender as an artist's brush or as bold as a warrior's sword. It is a rarity that one life can alter all the world with his passing.

We were not wrong to have shaped his youth. Your heart is in him, and for this reason, I still have hope.

Just as one small stone can cause a tremendous avalanche, so too can this one small life mold the world for good or evil. Is this final twist left to chance or fate? There are those who believe fate is left to chance. And there are those who believe that chance is an illusion created by fate. Are both correct? There are two sides to every coin, but it takes both sides to make the coin whole.

As for me, I am a twig floating down the rapid rivers of life. When the river forks, it is the rapid which chooses my way. Can one call this fate? Well, if it is so, there is one truth that I may learn from fate. When the coin is flipped deciding my destiny, it always lands heads down.

I exist for the few moments my mind is allowed to be my own, and I cling to my humanity with every ounce of my being. I am not sure if seeing you here helps me to hold onto my sanity, or if your beautiful face pushes me beyond redemption. But, I do know that it is because of you I can fight the darkness. And it is for our son that I do not give up.

Forever
yours,
Drenen Escari
Soulless One

❦

Feffer opened his eyes. Wood was beneath his face and the floor rocked gently, back and forth.

Natural light came in from somewhere outside the bars of his wooden cell. More entered through a small, round window in the wall. If he laid on his back and stretched, he could touch both sides of his cell.

He sat up.

The aches in his head were gone, and he realized he could see out of both eyes. How long had he been unconscious this time? And what in the abyss had possessed him to jump of a cliff?

Feffer felt as if he had slept all night in his bed, but his clothes were still damp from jumping in the sea. He felt a chill go up his spine as he realized the implications. They must have healed him somehow. That meant they had used the Elements on him. What if it was the Death Element?

He shivered.

Feffer stood and looked out the round window. He could see the waters of the ocean lapping against the side of the ship. In the distance, he could see cliffs moving farther away.

Feffer pried at the portico for a few moments, but it would not budge.

"Curse it all!" he whispered.

Then he remembered the hidden pocket in his belt. His fingers felt beneath the wooden buckle. The compartment opened, and he dug the lockpick out. Feffer moved to the door of his cell and inspected the lock. It was a simple lock, like the one Wilton had trained him on.

Feffer smiled.

The Awakened,

Born as one there shall be two,
Whom Wield the Elements True.
Ashes give birth to Light,
Only if the True will fight.
So long as one remains two,
Hope shall be born anew,
If one yields to the other's call,
Then all of Arinth shall fall.

Seeking souls sharpens His tool,
His Spirit shall rise when his cup is full.
The earth will grovel at the feet,
Of He whose power is complete.
Or all shall know a time of peace,
Except for the war never to cease.

For a Wayward World in this day,
Has Lost its Life and how to pray.
The bane of Life will have a Son,
Wielding power that will stun,
Upon a choice he lays his head,
To disturb those fallen from dead.
Or rescue Nature's loving Wife,
And Restore her fallen back to Life.

The future of all depends upon this,
The simple touch of Love's First kiss.
Forsake this, and all is for naught,
Meaning is found, 'tis never caught.
Before these things may come to pass,

An Age long gone will come at last.
Power forgotten will reappear,
Warning that the end is near.
The child of hope is never small,
His valor may lend salvation to all.
Forged from fire in a foreign land,
Ripped from childhood to become a man.
Returned to the mountain a world away,
And Master himself from His own clay.

Death from Life and Life from Death,
Shatter the pieces of Love's new Breath.
He shall live where others have died,
With Nature's friend at his side.
Power turns True, and an Age will pass,
When a child that's True has come at Last.

The blood of His blood will bid them call,
The Dragon shall rise to rule them all.
Death shall rise and all is Forsaken,
Before, the Drakonkin shall Awaken.

Translation of the first prophecy from Ancient Arinth
to New Common by the hand of Aristotis Platus,
Chronicler Magus of the Guild of New Tanier.

The End
of the first volume of

THE ELWIN ESCARI CHRONICLES

Look for the next book
in the Elwin Escari Chronicles.

Mastering the Elements

THE ELWIN ESCARI CHRONICLES
Volume II

BY DAVID EKRUT

ABOUT THE AUTHOR

David Ekrut was raised in a small community in Arkansas, where the abundance of nature fostered his imagination. Whether lost in a book, table-top gaming, or roaming the countryside from coast to coast, expanding his mind inevitably led him to the craft of writing. Only in the infinite workspace of heartfelt creativity has he ever felt any sense of freedom. Ekrut holds degrees in Liberal Arts-Theatre from Arkansas State University, both a Bachelor's and Master's of Science in Applied Mathematics from the University of Central Arkansas, and a Master's in Biomedical Mathematics from Florida State University with a Ph.D. in Biomedical Mathematics pending defense of his dissertation. His scientific expertise aided in creating physically believable fiction with rules and structure to bring his universe to life.